UP POPS THE DEVIL

Also by Angela Benson

The Amen Sisters
Abiding Hope
Awakening Mercy

UP POPS THE DEVIL

ANGELA BENSON

An *Imprint of* HarperCollins*Publishers*

This book is a work of fiction. The characters, incidents, and dialogue are drawn from the author's imagination and are not to be construed as real. Any resemblance to actual events or persons, living or dead, is entirely coincidental.

HarperCollins books may be purchased for educational, business, or sales promotional use. For information please write: Special Markets Department, HarperCollins Publishers, 10 East 53rd Street, New York, NY 10022.

FIRST EDITION

Designed by Diahann Sturge

Library of Congress Cataloging-in-Publication Data
Benson, Angela.
Up pops the devil / Angela Benson.—1st ed.
p. cm.
ISBN 978-0-06-146850-6
I. Title.
PS3552.E5476585U6 2008
813'.54—dc22 2007049177

08 09 10 11 12 OV/RRD 10 9 8 7 6 5 4 3 2 1

Mary, Mike, and George—this one is for the three of you. Your loving support and not-so-gentle prodding were exactly what I needed.

For our struggle is not against flesh and blood, but
against the rulers, against the authorities, against
the powers of this dark world and against the
spiritual forces of evil in the heavenly realms.

—Ephesians 6:12 (NIV)

PROLOGUE

Sean Jones paced outside the Boss's door. He was in trouble and he knew it. He paused in front of the plate-glass windows comprising the left wall of the reception area and stared at his reflection. He might have the look of a successful 3Sixes executive, with his tailored suit and designer shoes, but the summons from the Boss told a different story.

Sean had joined 3Sixes a couple of years ago, working his way up the ranks from rookie tempter to his present position as closer. Once a soul was deemed a strong candidate for 3Sixes, it was Sean's job to close the deal and reel him in. His normal caseload was about a thousand souls, more than any of his peers. Sean took great pride in his work and his 80 percent close rate indicated he was good at it, though this summons from the Boss did make him wonder.

Sean cast a quick glance at the receptionist, who had done nothing more than acknowledge his presence with a slight incline of her head. Evidently, pacing executives were nothing new to her. He didn't know if that made him feel better or worse. He began pacing again.

"Jones!" a loud voice bellowed. "Get in here, now!"

Feeling like a chastised little boy, Sean cast a baleful glance at the receptionist. He was grateful this time for her indifference. She didn't even look up.

"Pull yourself together," he muttered to himself as he turned the knob on the Boss's office door.

"Are you an idiot, Jones?" the Boss began before Sean could even close the door fully. "How did you lose one of our best men? All you had to do was keep him busy doing our work and you couldn't even do that." The Boss paused in his tirade and let his eyes travel from the top of Sean's balding head down to his Gucci shoes. "Tell me why I shouldn't demote you on the spot? There's a seat in Third Hades with your name on it."

The mention of Third Hades sent shivers of fear up Sean's spine. That's where the Boss sent employees who were no longer useful to him. He moved closer to the Boss's desk. "Give me another chance. I know I can win him back."

The Boss raised a brow. "Jones, you lost the man while he was in prison. You gave him time to become a Christian, instead of influencing some of his prison mates to kill him, the way I told you to do." He slammed his fist down on the desk. "You had the perfect opportunity to have him killed, and then he would have been ours for all eternity."

"I'm sorry, sir."

"That's the understatement of the millennium," the Boss said with a sigh. "So you think you can win Preacher back, huh? How do you plan on accomplishing that great feat when you couldn't even do the small task I gave you?"

Sean fought back his fear. Preacher wasn't the first soul under his watch to have almost escaped and then been snatched back. He could handle this situation. "You know those jailhouse conversions rarely last," he said, forcing a confidence into his voice he didn't really feel. "We can win Preacher back."

The Boss flopped down in his chair and then peered up at Sean. "You really are an idiot, aren't you? You still can't tell the difference between a true conversion and a fake one. What were you doing in those training classes—sleeping?"

Sean shook his head furiously. The Boss was deliberately misinterpreting what he said. "No, sir," he said. "I paid close attention."

The Boss leaned forward. "You could have fooled me. What did you learn? Your handling of the Preacher situation makes me doubt you learned anything."

Sean searched his memory for some tidbit from his early training. "I accept full responsibility for losing Preacher," he finally said, remembering his trainer's advice for dealing with the Boss. "I thought we had him lock, stock, and barrel. Given the experience his sister had at the hands of the Holy Rollers, I didn't think he could be converted. I thought he liked the lifestyle we provided him too much."

"I don't pay you to think about what they like," the Boss said. "I pay you to plant thoughts and lies in their minds about what they *should* like. You fell asleep on the job, Jones. You thought you had him and you stopped being diligent. You stopped planting our thoughts and allowed the thoughts of our enemy to take hold. That's a rookie mistake. You have to remember that the game isn't over until they're dead. We can't count them fully on our side until they take their last breath. You got too confident and we lost him."

"But I can win him back," Sean proclaimed. "I know I can." He resisted the temptation to list other occasions like this when he'd won souls back. His trainer had advised against bragging.

"And how are you going to do that?"

Sean considered the question and searched his brain for the answer he thought the Boss wanted. "I'm going to do what I learned to do in training class," he said. "I'm going to find out what he values most and then use that against him."

The Boss eyed him. "Any fool can parrot back what he's heard in a training class. How are you going to implement what you were taught?"

Sean was feeling better now that he'd gotten into the rhythm of the game the Boss was playing. "I'm going to watch and listen. Preacher will tell me what I need to know, and then I'll use it against him."

The Boss nodded. "Good. Good. Don't go around guessing what any of them want. Watch them; listen to them; and they'll tell you without even meaning to." He eyed Sean closely. "How are you going to use what you learn against him?"

"Preacher's been talking a lot about family these days, so I'll start with them. I already have the ear of a couple, and I'm steadily planting negative thoughts and lies in their minds. I'm sure I can use Preacher's feelings for them to draw him back to us."

The Boss nodded. "That's a good beginning, but don't forget that you need to stir up some negativity among this new church family of his, too. Sometimes we forget how easy it is to get to some of those folks. We may not be able to win them over, but we can plant enough negative thoughts and lies with them to create havoc in Preacher's life."

Sean bobbed his head in agreement. "Yes, sir. I haven't forgotten. Most of those church people don't read their Bibles, so they can't tell our voice from our enemy's voice. Then you have some of them feeling so guilty for stuff they've done in the past that they're confused about everything. Both of those groups are usually good candidates for me. I drop a thought here and a lie there, and off they go to stir up trouble. It's funny to watch them sometimes."

The Boss laughed, a strong belly laugh. "Like sheep for the slaughter, Jones. Sheep for the slaughter."

Sean began to feel encouraged. He'd get his second chance. That was all he wanted. He'd show the Boss what he could do and keep himself out of Third Hades.

"You sure you're ready for this job?" the Boss asked, his piercing eyes searching Sean's.

Sean swallowed hard and then he nodded. "I won't fail you again."

The Boss leaned back in his chair. "See that you don't. And to make this interesting, I want you to get Preacher back and I want a couple others along with him." He gave a guttural laugh. "Collateral damage, Jones. That's what I want. Lots of collateral damage."

"Yes, sir." *What else could he say?*

The Boss steepled his fingers across his nose and gave Sean an icy glare. "And I want frequent reports. I want to know what you're doing at all times. Third Hades will be waiting for you if you fail again."

CHAPTER 1

Three months later

Loretta Winters propped her hands on her hips and stared down at the woman sitting under the dryer at Tanya's Curl and Weave in Atlanta's Buckhead suburb. She tapped on the dryer head. "I can't believe you're sitting here getting your hair done when you're supposed to be down at the prison picking up Preacher," she said when Tanya peered up at her.

Tanya Miles looked from her recently manicured nails to Loretta's angry face. "It's not like he's going anywhere," she said, adding in a grin she knew would make Loretta even angrier.

"Look, Tanya," Loretta said between clenched teeth. "Don't get smart with me. You must have forgotten who's footing the bill for this shop and the one across town as well as these beauty treatments you're always getting. You're not exactly the second coming of Madam C. J. Walker. Your name might be on the door, but the last time I looked, my name was on the checks deposited into your bank account each month, so you'd better get a grip."

Tanya smirked. "You're too uptight, Loretta. Have you thought about a massage?" She rolled her shoulders forward. "I had one this morning, get them every week, in fact. So I can guarantee you'll feel better if you get one."

"I'm not playing with you, Tanya," Loretta said. "We have a deal and you'd better uphold your end of it or—"

"I know, I know, or you're going to cut off my funds." Tanya stood and rubbed her hands down the tight-fitting sheath that covered her slim body and accentuated every inch of her five-foot-ten-inch frame. Looking down at the much shorter and less curvaceous Loretta, she experienced a feeling of superiority. "You know," Tanya said, "something tells me that I don't need to depend on you for money. I'm sure some man out there, some rich man, that is, would consider it an honor to spend his money on me."

Loretta grinned. "He might want to spend it on you and those greenish brown eyes you're so proud of, but I'm not too sure how he'd feel about those two little rascals of yours. They're my nephews and I love them, but not many men want a woman with kids—not when there are so many other women without the strings. Face it, Tanya, you need me as much, if not more, than I need you. And what I need for you to do is get your behind down to that prison and pick up Preacher."

"I'm going already," Tanya said, tossing her long dark-brown mane of white-girl hair over her shoulder. "You know how Preacher likes his women to look." She cast a catty grin at Loretta.

Loretta so wanted to wipe that smug grin off Tanya's face, and she would one day, just not today. No, today she needed Tanya. Since Preacher had been sent off to prison and found religion, he'd changed on her. He wasn't interested in her or the business they shared. All he could talk about was the family God had given him and how he wanted to make that family right. Loretta thought he was crazy to think he could have a family with Tanya, but there was no telling Preacher anything these days.

Before he found religion, he'd seen Tanya for what she was—a high-maintenance wannabe looking for a man, any man, to take care of her. She knew Preacher had never wanted kids, certainly not with Tanya, but Tanya's pregnancy, which should have ended her relationship with Preacher—and there were many women who could attest to that fact—had instead served to bind him to her forever. Loretta would never have thought Preacher was the settling-down type, yet that's exactly what he said he was now. Loretta thought he was going through a period of temporary insanity.

Preacher had always been religious, carrying Big Momma's Bible around and everything, but now he'd gone too far. All she needed to do was get him away from those Bible-thumpers and life would return to normal. She wanted the brother she knew back, not some Jesus-spouting imitation.

Though she hated to admit it, she needed him. Not as a business partner, though. No, she'd kept their narcotics distribution business perking right along while he was away, even expanded on it in ways that surprised her and should have made him proud, but all he'd given her was some lame line about how that part of his life was over. She couldn't accept that, she wouldn't. She loved Preacher and she needed him. From the day she'd entered foster care, she'd learned that needing others was a bad thing, so she'd trained herself to need only herself. That had worked until she'd been reunited with her brother years later. She'd learned that everybody needs somebody—deserves somebody—they can trust. For her, that somebody was Preacher. The blood bond they shared was eternal. It was deeper than the bond he'd shared with any woman, including Tanya. It was only rivaled by the bond he shared with his boys, a bond she didn't resent or find threatening. No, she wanted Preacher to have his boys. They were his family, hers too. She understood their bond and its value, and Preacher used to understand it. Now she just needed him to remember it. And for that she needed Tanya.

"If you don't leave within the next couple of hours, he's going to have to stay in there an extra day. You'd better not let that happen."

"I hear you, Loretta. I hear you."

"You'd better. And you'd better have that apartment over your garage fixed up for him, too."

Tanya rolled her eyes. "Your contractors finished the work yesterday, as I'm sure you're well aware. The furniture was delivered this morning, so everything's ready for your dear Preacher."

"You're living with the man, Tanya. He's the father of your two children. Don't you have any feelings, any compassion, for him?"

Tanya pouted like a little girl. "I didn't bargain for this, Loretta. Preacher was supposed to give me the good life. Instead I get a jailbird husband-to-be and two kids that I didn't even want. I'm too young for this."

"You're not that young," Loretta said under her breath.

"And how's Preacher going to support us? He's said he's not going back into the drug business, so how's he supposed to support a family?" She tossed her hair back again. "I'm not the type of woman who lives hand-to-mouth. Been there, done that, won't do it again. Not even for your precious Preacher."

Loretta almost felt sorry for the selfish twit. Loretta was more familiar with poverty than Tanya was, so she knew the fear of being hungry that could drive a person to do things most people would never do. "You take care of Preacher and I'll take care of the money."

Tanya stared at Loretta for a long moment.

"What?" Loretta asked.

"Why do you even care, Loretta?" she asked. "Preacher has made it clear that he wants nothing more to do with the drugs, or you as long as you're in the business, so why are you doing all this for him?"

Preacher had explained his decisions to Loretta, but she wasn't about to share those details with Tanya. The woman was so self-absorbed she would never understand the brother-sister bond she and Preacher shared. "I ask the questions, Tanya. What's between me and Preacher is none of your concern. You do what I tell you and you'll be okay. You don't and you'll pay."

"So now we're back to threats, huh?"

"Not threats, promises. And I always keep my promises. Now get off your behind and get down to that prison. And make sure you take those two kids with you. You know Preacher's gonna want to see them."

Tanya stomped her foot like a little girl about to embark on a major tantrum. "*Aww,* Loretta, I'm not taking those kids down there. I can't put up with their yakking for two whole hours. You can't expect me to do that."

Loretta folded her arms across her chest. "If nothing else gets Preacher off that God kick he's on, you will."

"What do you mean by that?"

"Please, girl. How can anyone think a loving God would be so cruel as to make you a mother? The Man can't exist and you're the only proof Preacher needs. Let him hang around you for a while and he'll be back to his old self in no time. Now enough talking. It's time for you to get up and hit the road. You're done here."

Serena Jenkins pounded around the track at the local women's gym and spa that she co-owned with her sister-in-law, trying unsuccessfully to pound the unwelcome thoughts of Preacher Winters's letter from her mind. Why had he bothered to write to her? Why couldn't he have pretended the past never happened? Using the white towel around her neck, she wiped the sweat from her face, forcing her almost numb legs to make it around one more time.

She should have told Barnard about her past with Preacher a long time ago. He may have understood then. After all, at some level, the only thing between her and Preacher was a youthful indiscretion. Yes, Barnard may have understood then, but she wasn't sure he would understand now. Why had she waited so long to tell him? A part of her knew the reason: guilt and shame. Guilt at what she had done almost fifteen years ago and shame that she'd turned her back on her faith for the so-called love of a no-good man. She knew the Lord had forgiven her, the Bible told her that clearly, but she couldn't seem to forgive herself.

"Hey, girl," a familiar voice called to her.

Serena turned in the direction of her sister-in-law, business partner, and closest friend, Natalie Jenkins. Forcing her thoughts to the back of her mind, she trotted over to her friend. "Hey, yourself. I didn't know you were here."

"I know you didn't. You've been running around this track so long and so hard you're making me tired. You're working out like you're trying to catch a man, but I know that can't be the case because you dragged my brother to the altar five years ago." She patted the space on the bench next to her. "Sit down here and tell me what's up."

Serena used the towel to wipe her face again. "I'm fine, girl," she told Natalie. "Just needed a workout before I closed up and headed home."

Natalie leaned into Serena's shoulder. "This is your sister-in-law and prayer partner talking to you, Rena. You may be able to sell that story to someone who doesn't know you as well as I do, but I'm not buying it. What's on your mind, Sis? I only want to help."

Serena's guilt grew anew as she suffered Natalie's scrutiny. The two women had met seven years ago at a local gym and become fast friends. Soon, Natalie began to sing her brother's praises to Serena, capping it off with a proclamation that Serena and Barnard were perfect for each other. Her friend had been right. Natalie had proven then and many times since how well she knew Serena. She wondered what her friend would think if she knew Serena's troubles. Now was not the time to find out. "No, really I'm fine," she said. "Just have a lot on my mind these days."

Natalie nodded. "Adoption?"

"That, too," Serena said, referring to the ongoing disagreement she and Barnard had about whether to adopt a child. He wanted to but she wasn't sure. It was causing a strain between them, which was another reason she didn't want to drop the news about Preacher on him. "But I don't want to discuss it now. It seems to be all Barnard and I talk about, and I need a break. Why don't you tell me what's up with you and this new guy you've been seeing?"

Natalie's eyes gleamed with excitement. While Serena was happy to see joy again in her sister-in-law's eyes, she worried about the cause. Natalie had suffered a deep scar and public embarrassment when she'd learned Benjamin, her fiancé of two years, had fathered a child with another woman during the course of their engagement. When she'd learned the news, Natalie had broken off the engagement and ended the relationship. At one point, Serena had worried that Natalie might not fully recover from the pain of it all. For one thing, Natalie had stopped going to church activities as regularly as she had when she and Benjamin had been dating. She still went to Sunday service and she volunteered at the Children's Center during the week, but that was about it. No more Singles group, no more Missions group, no more anything. Serena understood that it was difficult for Natalie to attend the church where everybody knew the sordid details of her history with Benjamin. It had to be doubly hard now that Benjamin, his son, and his baby's momma regularly attended the church and rumor had it that a marriage was in the works.

Barnard didn't seem to worry about Natalie as much as Serena did, but then Barnard never worried much. He was much better able to take his cares to the Lord and leave them there. He accepted what Natalie was going through as normal, given what had happened to her, and he knew that her faith and her love for God would eventually heal the hurt in her heart.

"You're sure you don't have something you want to talk about?" Natalie asked, practically bubbling over with the obvious need to share her news.

Serena smiled, trying to take on some of Barnard's optimism. "I'm sure. Now tell me about this relationship."

"Oh, Serena," Natalie began. "He's wonderful. He's so different from any man I've ever met. He's kind, he's courteous, he's generous." She looked away shyly. "Listen to me," she said, "thirty-five years old and going on like some teenager. If anybody should know better than to pin all her hopes on a man, I should."

Serena tucked her hand under her friend's chin and turned her face to her. "You're happy. There's nothing wrong with that. Have you been praying about this guy?"

"I've been praying a lot," Natalie said. "You know, I really didn't expect this, Serena, not after Benjamin. I wasn't even sure I could ever trust a man again. I went into that dealership to buy a new car, not to fall in love with one of the owners. Finding a man was the last thing on my mind. God really does have his own timing."

"So you believe God brought you and this man together."

"Dante," Natalie said. "His name's Dante."

"Okay, so you believe God brought you and Dante together."

Natalie nodded. "I know it. I can already see how the Lord has used me in Dante's life and Dante's definitely enriched mine. You don't think so?"

Serena shrugged her shoulders. "I just want you to be careful. You've been seeing this guy for a while now and neither Barnard nor I have met him. That's not like you at all." Natalie looked away instead of giving an explanation. "Is he a Christian, Natalie?" she asked.

"He believes in God."

Oh no, Serena thought, she sounds the way I did when I first started seeing the Bible-toting Preacher. "Believes in God? What does that mean? Does he go to church?"

"Going to church doesn't make you a Christian, Serena," Natalie said. "Please. You know that."

Serena didn't bother to respond; she gave her friend a stern glance.

"Okay," Natalie admitted. "Dante was struggling with some issues about walking with the Lord, but he's changing, Serena. I see it in him. I see the desire for God."

"Are you sure you see it or do you just *want* to see it?"

"What do you mean? Just come out and say it."

Serena rested her hand on Natalie's arm and spoke from her own experience. "I want you to be careful. I know how emotions can make you see situations and people the way you want to see them. I want you to be sure you're hearing God's voice and not your own voice telling you what you want to hear."

"I don't think I am," Natalie said. "Dante is good to me and I believe he's good for me. I know he's a better man than Benjamin was. Benjamin had all the outside trappings of a Christian but when it came down to it, he didn't behave in a very Christian way. A man can say a lot of things, but it's what he does and how he treats you that counts. Dante treats me better than Benjamin ever did and I know he won't hurt me or lie to me the way Benjamin did."

Serena forced herself not to flinch at the bitterness in Natalie's voice when she mentioned Benjamin's lying. Maybe Natalie and Barnard could have forgiven Benjamin for cheating if he'd come clean about the baby as soon as he found out, but keeping it a secret from Natalie for two years was too much for brother or sister to understand. They'd both cut Benjamin off completely. Serena couldn't help but wonder if they'd do the same to her if they knew her secret. "But is he the man you prayed for?" she asked Natalie, forcing her thoughts back to the subject at hand. She didn't want Natalie in a dead-end relationship with a guy who wasn't a Christian. She'd been there and she wanted better for her sister-in-law. "Does he have the attributes that you asked the Lord for in a mate?"

"Well—"

"You don't have to tell me," Serena said. "Just think about it. You told me that you wanted a man you could trust to be the head of your household, a man you could follow in all areas, including your faith."

"Maybe what I was asking for was unrealistic. Maybe that's

what the whole mess with Benjamin was supposed to teach me. You know what Sister Reynolds said in the last Singles meeting I attended?" Not waiting for an answer, Natalie continued. "She said that in her family, and in most families she knew, the woman was the spiritual leader. She said if she didn't call for family Bible study, there wouldn't be any at her house."

"Is that what you want?"

"Everybody can't have what you have with Barnard. There aren't a lot of men like my brother, Serena. Believe me, I know and I have the scars to prove it. Those like him are already taken. Besides, I'm not talking about marrying Dante tomorrow. We both have a lot of growing and getting to know each other to do before we can even start talking about marriage."

"But you have been thinking about Dante in marriage terms, haven't you?"

"Let's just say that I can imagine him in my future. Don't get too worried though, because I'm not going to do anything stupid. I'm going to enjoy where we are and listen to the Lord for where the relationship should go. How's that?"

"It's great," Serena said, knowing it was the best she could hope for at this point. She'd have to pray the Lord opened Natalie's eyes to what she was doing. "Barnard and I still want to meet him."

"I've asked him about signing up with the prison ministry jobs program. He's thinking about it."

"Great!" Serena said. "But I want to meet him, too. Why don't you invite him to church on Sunday and we'll have you both over for dinner after?"

"I'll ask him," Natalie said, but Serena wasn't too encouraged by her sister-in-law's lukewarm response.

"You know I love you, don't you, Nat? You're the sister I never had but always wanted."

Natalie leaned over and hugged her. "I love you, too, and you *are* my sister."

Serena smiled as she moved out of Natalie's embrace, but her heart was heavy. She didn't want Natalie to end up the way she had after her involvement with Preacher. "Now we'd better hit the showers because one of us is a bit smelly."

Natalie laughed. "Gotta be you 'cos I exercise like a girl while you exercise like a machine."

Tanya had better not be leaving me sitting here in this jail, Preacher Winters thought as he turned his six foot eleven, two-hundred-sixty-pound athletic frame from the prison library's barred windows. He knew his girlfriend, soon-to-be-wife, had issues with him being incarcerated and all, but she didn't have the nerve to leave him here. Or did she?

"Are you sure she's coming, man?" Barnard Jenkins, the director of Faith Community Church's Prison Outreach Program and Preacher's mentor and friend, asked from his seat at the metal table in the middle of the sparsely furnished room. He pumped his brawny arms in mini bicep curls while he sat, a habit of his. "I can give you a ride home."

Preacher sat in a metal chair across the table from Barnard and stretched out his long legs. "No way will she stand me up. She may be angry but the woman's not crazy." *At least, I hope not.*

"Things have changed, Preacher," Barnard said.

"I know," Preacher said. "I'm now a jailbird."

Barnard stopped pumping his arms and caught Preacher's eye. "No, you're now a child of God."

"I know that, man," Preacher said. "My faith in God is what's kept me sane for the two years I've been in here. I'd never have made it otherwise."

"It's more than that."

"I know, man," Preacher said. "Things are gonna be different on the outside because I'm different."

"And not everybody in your old life is going to like you being different."

Preacher knew that, too. He was already feeling the pain. Tanya was acting like his newfound faith was something akin to leprosy. But he firmly believed that God would change Tanya's heart. He'd get out of here, go back home, and they'd get married; provide a real family for their two boys. God had saved him for a reason and he knew a part of that reason was for him to get his family together. Even though Tanya was acting crazy right now, he had faith in God to make things right. Preacher knew He would. "It's gonna work out, man," he told Barnard. "I'm believing God that it will."

Barnard shook his head. "Preacher, you've got to face facts. Neither your sister nor Tanya is very happy with your decision to follow Christ."

"Loretta's my blood, my sister. Tanya's the mother of my two boys. They're family. God didn't save me so I'd lose my family. I don't believe that." At least, Preacher didn't believe it about Tanya. Loretta was another matter altogether. His younger sister held "church folks," as she called them, in disdain because of the abuse she'd suffered as a child at the hands of one of her churchgoing, Bible-thumping foster mothers. "Every day I've spent with Him, my hunger for my family has grown," Preacher added.

"Just because you become a Christian, Preacher, doesn't mean that everything works out for you. God only promises that He'll be with you through the hard times. He never promised there wouldn't be hard times."

Preacher waved his friend off. He stood and walked to the window again, looking out but not really seeing. He knew Barnard had the best of intentions, but sometimes the brother needed to know when to leave well enough alone. "I know that scripture," Preacher told him. "And I also know the one that says God will give you the desires of your heart. And I believe He gave me this desire for a family."

Barnard sighed deeply.

Preacher knew his friend wanted to say more, but was glad when he didn't. He walked over and clapped Barnard on the back. "It's going to be all right. Wait and see. I'm going to be testifying about how far God brought my family within the next year. I believe it."

Barnard leaned his chair back on its two rear legs, and Preacher waited, as he often did, for the chair to buckle under his friend's weight. Barnard had to be about thirty pounds heavier than Preacher, even though he was a good three inches shorter. "I want you to be prepared for what you're going to face when you get out of here," Barnard said.

Preacher patted the leather Bible that was the last remnant he had of the elderly grandmother who represented the only stable family life he'd ever had. She'd died when he was twelve and Loretta was nine, leaving them to the non-care of the foster care system. Her Bible had been the lifeline he'd held on to as he made his way through the system after her death. In fact, his ever-close Bible had led to his Preacher moniker. It was a name he liked, much better than the Wilford on his birth certificate, so he kept it. As he thought about the road that had led him to this day, he thought the name was fitting.

Since being in prison, he'd gone from leaning on his grandmother via the Book to leaning on the man behind the Book. Maybe one day the Lord would lead him to preach, but for now he was happy to be saved. He knew his grandmother would be proud that he'd found Jesus while under the jurisdiction of the Georgia Department of Corrections. Well, she'd probably be more proud without that Department of Corrections tag, but she'd be proud nonetheless. "I'm prepared, man," he told Barnard. "You've got a new career lined up for me. I've got a place to live. And I've got two sons, a sister, and a fiancée waiting for me. I'm blessed."

Barnard rested his chair back down on all fours. "I still think you'll be better off staying with your sister instead of in the house with Tanya and the kids. No need to set yourself up for temptation."

Preacher shrugged off his friend's concern. "Don't worry about it, man. I've got it covered. Nothing's happening between Tanya and me until we get married."

"Get real, Preacher," Barnard said. "You and Tanya have two children. You've been living together and sleeping together for more than six years. Not sleeping with her when you're used to doing so is going to be more than hard. Don't fool yourself."

"I'm not going to be living with her," Preacher reminded his friend. When Barnard lifted a brow, he added, "I'm living in the apartment above the garage."

"Right. Like that makes a difference. I still say you're better off staying with your sister."

"I'll be fine," Preacher said. "Besides, I don't want to be away from my kids." Even as he said the words, Preacher knew an equally compelling reason for not staying with his sister was that she still ran their narcotics distribution enterprise. Though they kept it quiet—he hadn't even told Barnard—he and Loretta were partners. She was his right hand, his backup, and he was hers. Or had been. Now that he was an ex-con, there was no way he could live with her without causing the police to track her as much as they were going to track him. He wanted his sister out of the business, but he didn't want her to end up in jail because of her association with him. No, he didn't want her to hit rock bottom before she figured out the path she traveled was a dead-end one. He wanted better for her. He'd have to find a way to convince her to leave the life before she landed in prison like he had, or worse, ended up dead. "I'm fine," Preacher said again, "and I'll be fine living in the apartment above the garage."

Barnard sighed. "Okay, man," he said. "You've got it all figured out. I'll just wait with you until Tanya gets here."

Preacher shook his head at the skepticism he heard in his friend's voice. "Have a little faith, man. You can head home. Tanya's coming."

"Serena's not expecting me until much later," Barnard said. "She knows you're getting out today."

Preacher tensed at the mention of Barnard's wife. He had history with Serena, history he was sure Barnard didn't know about. There were many times Preacher had wanted to tell his friend the full story, but he owed it to Serena to give her the chance to tell her husband first. He'd prayed that she would have by now, and had let her know his wishes in a letter sent to her through Loretta, but he knew she hadn't and that saddened him. Barnard had been a good friend to him, more than a friend. They'd met through Barnard's work with his church's prison ministry. Barnard had handed him a lifeline when Preacher was at the end of his rope. He owed the brother for that and he didn't like keeping secrets from him.

"What you thinking about, man?" Barnard asked. "You looked like you were miles away."

"Just thinking about life outside these bars. I know I've only been in here two years but it feels longer."

Barnard merely nodded. One of the things that Preacher liked best about his friend was that he didn't offer empty platitudes. Barnard had no experience with life on the inside and he didn't try to pretend he did. What Barnard did have was a genuine compassion for men behind bars—the innocent and the guilty. That compassion was rooted in his heritage—his father had died in prison. So Barnard's leadership of the prison ministry was truly a labor of love. Under his leadership, Faith Community Church shared the Gospel with inmates, through words and deeds. They held weekly Bible studies and worship services, and they provided reentry counseling and skill-development training to prepare prisoners for their return to life on the outside. It was to the ministry's credit that partaking of the reentry services did not require participation in the religious services.

"The only downside I see before me is the two years of probation I have left on my sentence," Preacher said. "I wish that when I walked out of here I'd be free of the criminal justice system altogether. Don't get me wrong; I'm glad to be getting out. I know I could have gotten a straight four-year prison sentence. It's just that I don't look forward to the Department of Probations looking over my shoulder for a full two years. I'll make it through though. With God's help."

"You're right about that. You bet you will. I know we didn't have Bible study today, but why don't we take some time to pray while we wait for Tanya?"

"Sounds like a plan to me," Preacher said.

The two big men dropped to their knees and bowed their heads in prayer. The library door opened a short while later as they were saying their amens.

"Sorry to interrupt," G-Money said, stepping into the room and closing the door behind him.

"No problem," Preacher said to the young man he'd come to

look on as a little brother. G-Money was a small time gangsta-wannabe doing his second prison stint. Preacher feared for his future, but the brother wasn't yet ready for salvation.

G-Money looked from Preacher to Barnard and back again. He moved closer to Preacher. "I wanna talk to you 'bout sum'thin'." He cast another glance at Barnard and added, "Private like."

Preacher looked at Barnard and both men smiled. G-Money didn't like Barnard. Preacher thought he might be afraid of the big man and what he represented. "Go on home, man," Preacher said to Barnard. "G-Money'll keep me company until Tanya gets here."

Barnard clapped Preacher on the back and then left him and G-Money alone. As soon as the door closed behind him, G-Money said, "You were set up, man, and I know who did it."

CHAPTER 2

Unlike Loretta, Tanya knew there was a God and she sincerely believed he had a warped sense of humor. How else could she explain having to deal with her mother and Loretta on the same day? Heaven knew the only reason she was visiting her mother was Loretta's command that she take the boys with her when she went to pick up Preacher at the prison.

Getting out of the Acura in her mother's driveway—she didn't dare show up at the prison later in either the Porsche or the Benz and have Preacher throw a hissy fit—she pulled back her shoulders in preparation for dealing with Momma Maylene. As she walked up the concrete walkway from the drive, she couldn't help but reflect on how far both she and her mother had come. From Perry "ain't you never seen a ghetto" Homes in southwest Atlanta to Wyndham "mecca of middle-class working blacks" Park in southwest DeKalb County, Maylene and her daughter-with-an-attitude had made the leap that few of their ilk made. Tanya didn't want to dwell on how long the trip had taken or the sacrifices it had required.

She rang the bell—she'd long ago given back her key—and waited. Maylene's laughter beat her to the door, but her smile faded when she saw Tanya. "What do you want?"

Tanya frowned to mask the hurt. "Nice to see you, too, Momma," she said, brushing past her mother and coming into the house.

Maylene closed the door and followed her. "Don't get smart with me, missy," she told her daughter who had plopped down on the blue leather couch in the family room. "All I'm saying is I didn't expect you."

Tanya cut a glance up at her momma. Looking at her hurt, because Tanya knew she was seeing herself in twenty years. Maylene was still a good-looking woman, no doubt, but she'd lost the battle to keep away those twenty extra pounds that seemed so determined to become a permanent resident on her body. The extra weight she saw on her mother didn't cause Tanya the pain, however. No, the pain came from the hardness in her mother's face, a hardness that came from living a hard life and being defeated by too many dreams gone wrong. Tanya didn't want that for herself, but every time she looked at her mother, she knew she was looking at her destiny. "I've come to get the boys," she said, deciding not to play games with her mother.

"You just brought them here yesterday. I thought you were going to pick up Wilford."

Tanya smiled at her mother's use of Preacher's real name. "I know that, Momma, but I've changed my mind. Preacher's going to throw a fit if they're not with me and I'm not up for the fight."

Maylene bobbed her head from side to side. "I don't believe you, Tanya. How can you take those boys around that criminal?"

Here we go again. "He's their father, Momma, in case you've forgotten."

"I haven't forgotten," Maylene said with a huff. "You don't forget when your daughter is fool enough to get pregnant by a drug dealer. How could you do it, Tanya?" She brushed her hand down her daughter's long dark brown hair. "You could have had any man you wanted. Why him?"

Tanya leaned slightly into her mother's touch. It was so rare for Maylene to show affection. "It's too late to look back now, Momma. What's done is done. Don't you love your grandkids?"

Maylene dropped her hand. "Of course, I love those boys. More than anything in the world. That's why I want more for them and you than a drug-dealing ex-convict. You're a beautiful woman, Tanya. You can find another man, a better man than that drug dealer."

"Stop calling him a drug dealer," Tanya said. "One day you're going to say that in front of the wrong person."

"Please," Maylene said. "Everybody knows now. There's no use trying to keep it a secret. That prison record will brand him for the rest of his days. And you, too, if you stick with him. I don't even want to think what that stigma is going to do to my grandbabies."

Feeling a headache coming on, Tanya rubbed her forehead. Between her mother and Loretta, she knew she was going to have a zinger of one pretty soon. "I don't want to argue about this with you, Momma. I just want to pick up the boys."

"Aren't you listening to me, Tanya? Sometimes I wonder if you aren't a bit slow in the head. Didn't you learn anything from the way things worked out between me and your daddy?"

Tanya jumped up from the couch. She didn't want this lecture again. "Where are the boys?"

Maylene stood, too, and since they were the same height, the two women faced eye to eye. "You have to use them before they use you, Tanya. You've got a bad habit of hanging around too long. You did with that broken-down basketball player, T.J., and now you're doing it with Wilford. You need to get out of this relationship now, while you're still young and you've got your looks. There are other men out there who can give you the kind of life you deserve, a life with money and status. You've only had money with Wilford and that may be gone now. Get out before it's too late."

Tanya wished she hadn't come over here. While her mother's tirade was nothing new, the words stuck with Tanya because there was always some truth to what she said. The biggest truth for Tanya was that Preacher wasn't going to have anywhere near the kind of money going forward as he had in the past. Loretta was picking up the slack now, but Tanya didn't expect that to continue forever. Momma Maylene didn't have to worry about Tanya sticking with a man who couldn't support her at the level to which she'd become accustomed. She'd come too far up to even think about going one step down. She looked at her watch. "I hear you, Momma. Now tell me where the boys are. We're going to be late if I don't get a move on."

Maylene sighed but she gave Tanya the information she wanted.

"Amen," Barnard whispered when he entered his home later that evening. He'd spent the two-hour drive from Jackson State Correctional Institute in Jackson, Georgia, praying for Preacher. The brother had a heart for God but he was ignorant to the challenges he was going to face as he began to live his new life around people who knew the old Preacher, especially his sister and his girlfriend, the people closest to him. Barnard had no idea what the women were going to do, but from what little Preacher had told him about them, Barnard didn't think they were going to fall easily into Preacher's plans for a godly marriage and family. He prayed the Lord would prepare Preacher's heart for the worst even as he prayed for the best.

"I'm home," Barnard called as he followed his nose toward the smells of the kitchen.

His wife's "I'm in the kitchen" made Barnard smile. Try as she might, Serena was not a very good cook. He prayed for spaghetti because she did a pretty good job with that dish.

"I smell you," he called. Her answering laughter made his smile widen. "Hi, you," he said when he entered the kitchen.

She smiled back. She walked toward him and lifted her mouth for his kiss. "Hi, yourself."

He leaned down, way down—his wife was a petite five foot three—and kissed her. "Missed you," he said when he lifted his head.

She folded her arms around his waist and pressed another soft kiss against his lips. "Missed you, too."

Holding her in his arms, he said, "You make a man want to come home."

"I certainly hope so."

Barnard read the uncertainty in her eyes and her voice, and his heart ached. "I love you," he said. "I'll always love you." That was true. Barnard had loved Serena since the day his sister had introduced him to her. A bit of a thing, especially when compared to his hulking body, Serena had fit him perfectly in all areas that mattered. Well, almost all. They'd both been raised in strong Christian families, he and Natalie with their mother and stepfather; Serena with her preacher father and housewife mother. Thus, they both shared the same basic Christian values. They both loved the Lord and wanted to serve Him and His people. Marriage had been a foregone conclusion long before he'd found the courage to propose. But their marriage had not been perfect.

"I love you, too," she said. "You know that, don't you?"

Sometimes I wonder. "I know," he said, rubbing his hand across her back in a gesture of comfort. He knew she was apologizing for their latest argument and everything else that was wrong between them, but he didn't want words now; he too wanted comfort. He pulled her close again and kissed her more deeply. After a refreshing drink from her mouth, he lifted his lips from hers and began to press soft kisses along her neck. Oh, how he desired this woman he loved! "Let's go to bed," he whispered between kisses. At his suggestion, he felt her stiffen in his arms, an act that almost brought him to tears.

"What about dinner?" she asked, her voice a feeble plea to be left alone.

He pushed back the disappointment he felt. "I'm only hungry for you," he whispered. "It's been so long, Serena, too long." He pressed his lips against hers again trying hard to sustain his passion. When he felt his wife's less than enthusiastic response, he lost the battle and his passion died as quickly as it had flared. He lifted his lips from hers and pressed her face into his chest. He couldn't bear to look at the tears that he knew filled her eyes.

"I love you," she said again after a few moments.

Barnard shut his eyes in pain. "I know," he said.

She leaned back and waited until his eyes were open. "Is love enough?" Her eyes pleaded with him to answer in the affirmative.

"I love you, too," he said, "so it has to be."

He knew he'd given the wrong answer when she stepped out of his embrace with a wobbly smile. "I guess," she said, returning to the stove. "Did you eat anything?"

So they weren't going to talk about the elephant in the room. He guessed he could table it for now, since it would surely come up again and soon. "No, I didn't eat. I stayed at the prison longer than I expected, since Tanya was late coming to get Preacher. So late that I thought she wasn't coming. Preacher never gave up on her though. I have to give the brother credit for using his faith."

"You sound worried," Serena said, as she mixed salad greens in a big wooden bowl. "Something wrong with Preacher?"

"Not Preacher," he said. "Tanya."

"Say no more," Serena said. She placed a small salad bowl on the table before him and one at her place setting. "From what you've told me, I don't think she's going to be much support to Preacher in his walk with the Lord."

"No, I don't think she will. I just don't want her to be a hindrance. Preacher's pinning a lot of his hopes on building a family with this woman. They have the kids already and he plans to make it legal in hopes that one day he'll have the godly family he so desperately wants."

Serena didn't say anything. The elephant had reared its head. "You like him a lot, don't you?" she asked.

Barnard nodded. "Yeah, I do. We're alike in a lot of ways. A couple of different decisions in my life and I could be in prison. A couple of different decisions in his life and he could be the one directing the prison ministry."

"But for the grace of God . . ."

"Yes," he said, "but for the grace of God. You know, we haven't talked a lot about this but I'd like for us to be as much support to Preacher as we can. Do you think you can reach out to Tanya?"

Anything but that, Serena screamed inside. Just talking about Preacher was hard enough. "I don't know, Barnard. Do you really think it's a good idea for us to go crowding around them?"

"I'm not talking about taking the whole church over there. Maybe we could start by inviting them to dinner. We're two young couples. We're bound to have some common interests. I'm going to ask Natalie to try and befriend his sister. They're two young single women; they're bound to have something in common."

Serena brought their plates of spaghetti to the table and took a seat next to her husband. "We'll see," she said. "But not this Sunday. I've invited Natalie and the new guy she's seeing to dinner after church on Sunday. That is, if he comes with her to church."

"New guy? I didn't know Natalie was seeing anybody."

"Exactly. That's why I'm inviting them over. She's being secretive about this guy and it makes me nervous. She did say, though, that she'd asked him about participating in the prison jobs program. He owns the dealership where Natalie bought her car."

"Good," Barnard said, with an idle nod that told Serena he didn't share her concern about Natalie's new relationship. "I'll make a point to follow up with her about the jobs program contact. If he joins, that'll tell us a little about his character."

Serena nodded her agreement, deciding not to push the issue, and then Barnard blessed the food and they began to eat.

"I think it's a good idea," Barnard said a while later. When she looked up at him with a question in her gaze, he said, "Inviting Preacher and his girlfriend to dinner, I mean. It's nonthreatening. We'd get a chance to know them as a couple."

Since Serena couldn't think of a legitimate objection, she nodded her assent. They ate quietly for a few minutes before Barnard spoke again. "You know they have two boys—four and six, I think. We should probably include them in the invitation. I don't think Preacher's going to want to spend too much time away from his kids."

Serena knew Barnard was talking about himself as much as he was talking about Preacher. "Okay," she said.

"It'll be good to have the voices of children in this big house."

Serena put down her fork and stared at her husband. "If you have something to say, Barnard, say it and stop hinting."

"What?" Barnard asked, eyes wide with innocence.

"You know what. The references to kids. I know you want us to adopt but I'm not ready. Can you understand that? I'm not ready. Maybe we can have our own kids. The doctors haven't found anything wrong with either of us."

"We've been trying for three years, Serena. There may not be anything physically wrong, but something's not working right." God help him, but he'd almost said, "*You're* not working right." Barnard paused for a second to collect his thoughts. "Besides, there are a lot of kids out there who need a home and who need love. And I have a lot of love inside me to give a child. I want children, Serena. I want us to have a family."

"I want that, too, Barnard. Really I do."

Barnard looked at her, wondering if she understood the words she was speaking. "It doesn't seem that way, Serena," he said, choosing his words carefully. "Why won't you even consider adoption?"

"It's not that I won't consider it ever," she said. "Just not right now."

"Then when?" Barnard asked, his voice rising.

"I don't know," she said, matching his tone. "Have you thought that maybe God doesn't want us to have kids now? If there's nothing medically wrong with either of us, then maybe my not getting pregnant is God's way of saying we aren't supposed to have children, at least not yet."

Or maybe it's because you don't enjoy lovemaking, Barnard thought, but he couldn't bring himself to say the words. He knew they would hurt her too much, and despite everything that was wrong between them, he didn't want to hurt her. "Is that what you really think, Serena?" he asked instead. "That God doesn't want us to open our hearts and our home to a child, to children, who are homeless and in need of love? That's not the God I serve."

Serena shook her head. "You're not understanding me."

"Then help me to understand."

Tell him about Preacher, a still voice told her. Tell him now. Serena opened her mouth in obedience, but the words wouldn't come.

"Help me to understand, Serena," Barnard repeated.

Serena lowered her eyes to her plate. "I can't explain it," she said. "I just know how I feel."

Barnard sighed deeply. "And I know how I feel, so where does that leave us?"

Serena didn't give an answer and Barnard didn't expect one. They finished their meal in silence and Barnard knew that tonight as they slept each would hug their respective side of the bed.

Preacher couldn't believe it but he was about to lose his religion and he hadn't even been home one day. Tanya was acting like a witch. She'd arrived at the prison so late that even he'd begun to worry. He'd felt Barnard's rising fear, and later G-Money's, that she was going to be a no-show and he'd been embarrassed. He didn't want the brothers thinking he couldn't handle his business. Back in the day, Tanya never would have disrespected him the way she had tonight. In fact, no woman would have dared treat him the way Tanya had. And if a sister had tried, she'd have been kicked to the curb so quickly she'd . . . But that was the past, the old Preacher, he reminded himself. The new Preacher had a longer-term outlook. It wasn't only about today, it was about eternity. It wasn't only about him. It was about him and God and his family. That was the reason he wasn't going to do anything about the name G-Money had given him. And it was the reason he'd tolerate some of Tanya's jive. But he drew the line at letting her walk all over him. He was still a man, after all.

His sole joy for the day was Jake and Mack, now sound asleep in the backseat. Tanya hadn't spoken more than ten words to him. She'd kept her eyes on the road for the entire drive home and only responded to his attempts at conversation with mumbled one-word answers. Not wanting to beg her for conversation, he'd kept his mouth shut. But his temper had raged within.

By the time Tanya pulled the car into the garage and he'd gathered both boys in his arms, he was ready to have it out with her. "I want to talk to you after I put the boys to bed," he said. "So wait downstairs for me."

"Whatever," she mumbled as she unlocked the door so they could all enter the house through the kitchen.

Preacher's joy returned as he climbed the stairs to the room his sons shared. He eased the older Jake onto his bed, and then he put Mack on his. He pulled off Mack's shoes, shorts, and shirt and put him under the covers in only his underwear and socks. After tucking Mack in, Preacher did the same thing with Jake. He kissed both boys on their foreheads and then he stood looking down at them. As he did, tears fell from his eyes. These boys were his flesh. "Thank you, Lord," he whispered. "Thank you for keeping them safe and for being their father when I couldn't be with them. Teach me to be a father to them. Help me to show them by example how to live a godly life, a life that is pleasing to you. Amen."

Wiping his eyes, he turned to see Tanya standing in the doorway looking at him. "So now you're going to be praying over everything and everybody?"

Preacher nodded. No longer angry with her, he said, "Let's talk downstairs so we don't wake the boys."

Outside the boys' door, she said, "We can talk in the master bedroom. In case you've forgotten, we did our best work in there."

Preacher glanced toward the bedroom they'd shared for more than five years. "Not until we're married," he said.

She pressed her body against his. "You think you can hold out against me?"

Preacher had to force himself to move away. "Let's talk downstairs," he repeated. He heard Tanya's laugh as he turned, but she followed him and that was what he wanted.

Preacher waited in the living room until she entered, dropped into the oversized upholstered club chair, and folded her legs akimbo. He watched her and remembered the first time he'd seen her. It had been the Hawks season opener. A season ticket holder, he'd spotted her in the section he knew was typically reserved for friends and family of the players. It was her eyes—a greenish brown color that he had never seen before—and her smile—more open than any he'd seen on a woman as beautiful as she was. That she had legs a mile long hadn't hurt, either. Trying not to show how much she intrigued him, he'd gotten her name from one of the players and, on the evening of the Hawks first playoff game in six seasons, he'd introduced himself and asked her out. Of course, she'd turned him down. He'd expected it, since he'd also found out that she was dating T. J. Walker, at best an eighth man on a team with no real stars. Preacher couldn't see that the guy had much of an NBA career ahead of him, and he knew a woman like Tanya—high maintenance and proud of it—would soon figure that out for herself. By the time the season was over, T.J. had been traded and Tanya was free. He'd asked her out again and she'd said yes. As he seated himself on the oversized ottoman in front of her chair, he cleared his head of any thoughts of similarities between T.J.'s situation then and his now.

Instead of confronting Tanya about her attitude as he'd planned to do, Preacher said, "I know things haven't been easy on you while I've been away and I know it's going to take some time for us to find our rhythm as a couple, but I want you to know that I appreciate what you've done in taking care of our home and our boys while I was away. It was a lot on you and I'm sorry you had to do it alone."

Preacher sensed his words had surprised her. "It was hard," Tanya said. "And I didn't like it one bit. I didn't get involved with you to end up having to fend for myself and be alone."

"I know," Preacher said. "I didn't plan to get arrested. I didn't want to be separated from you and the boys. I'll never say I liked prison, but I can say that going there may have been the best thing that ever happened to me."

"You've got to be kidding," she said. "Well, it wasn't the best thing for me or for the boys."

"Hear me out," Preacher said. "It was a rough two years, but those days are behind us and I believe I'm a better man for them. I'm a better man because I know now that the way I was living my life was leading us—you, me, and the boys—down a dead-end road. I want more for us than that, Tanya. I want us to be a family."

"But how are you going to support us?" Tanya asked. "You say you're not going back into the business, so how are we going to live?"

"I have some opportunities lined up," Preacher said, though Tanya's words had touched the spot that was softest in him. The work-money issue concerned him greatly. "I won't be able to generate a lot of income right away, but I have skills and given a chance, I'm sure I can make a decent living for us."

"Decent?" Tanya folded her arms across her chest. "I didn't sign up for decent."

"I know, but can you honestly say you want me to go back to the drugs? Do you want our life based on that?"

Tanya didn't answer.

"Give me a chance," Preacher said. "I want to be your husband. When I gave you that ring—" he inclined his head towards the 3-carat diamond solitaire he'd put on her finger in exchange for her promise not to abort Jake "—I said I wanted to marry you. I'm not sure I did then, but I do now. I want to marry you and I want you, me, and the boys to be a family."

"I don't—"

He pressed two fingers against her lips. "You don't have to answer now," he said. "Just promise to think about what we have and what we can have as a family. I'll be a good husband to you, Tanya. I promise I will."

"Are you sure you want to move your knight there?" Dante Griggs asked Natalie. They sat on the floor on opposite sides of the coffee table in her living room, the chessboard on the table between them.

Natalie peered up at him. "Wanna help a sister out?" she asked, all the while thanking God that she had this game to focus on. There was something about Dante's dark good looks that could have her sitting here staring at the man like she was a teenager. She didn't kid herself that it was only his looks that attracted her though. She knew it was more the way he made her feel when he was around. With Dante, she felt wanted and cherished—two things that, after Benjamin, she wondered if she'd ever feel again. His double betrayal had undermined her self-confidence. How could it not? She'd never forget the way she'd felt the day she'd seen Benjamin and his girl Moesha arguing in the mall. He'd tried to lie his way out of it, but there was no lie he could put to the "Daddy" that had come from the lips of the little boy holding Moesha's hand.

Dante smiled, but shook his head. "I distinctly remember you saying you wanted to play this game on your own."

Natalie frowned. "You know reminding people of what they said is not an admirable personality trait."

Dante chuckled. "Sounds to me like a poor loser talking. But if you need help, I'll help you."

Natalie rolled her eyes. "Please, I don't need help." She put her knight back where it had been and studied the board. "I can beat you on my own."

"In your dreams."

Natalie looked up at him. "Hey, you're supposed to be trying to win me over. If you are, I hate to tell you but you're doing a pretty poor job of it."

Dante chuckled again. "Some women might be won with empty words, but not you. You like honesty. You like forthrightness. A lot of fake sentiment from me and you would've shown me to the door a long time ago."

Natalie moved her knight. "You've got that right."

"I know because I'm a smart man. And I've also got you in checkmate."

Natalie's eyes widened. "What are you talking about? I don't see checkmate."

"Look closer."

It didn't take a long study of the board to see Dante was right. Natalie slapped her palm against her forehead and leaned back against the couch behind her. "I can't believe you beat me again. You must have cheated."

"What's that? Sore loser talk again?"

Natalie pouted. "Any other guy would let me win at least one game."

As Dante set the board up again, he said, "That's just it. I don't want you to see me as just another guy. I'm special, unique. You'll never confuse me with the other guys you've led around by the nose."

"Now you're hurting my feelings," Natalie said, but he wasn't. He was saying the words she wanted to hear. "You make me sound like a difficult woman."

Dante shook his head. "Not difficult, headstrong. Now don't get all ruffled. I like a strong woman, a woman with her own opinions. I like you," he said, meeting her eyes. "A lot. More than I expected to."

"You really know how to flatter a woman," she said with a tad of sarcasm.

"Just want to be honest with you. One thing I'll promise you, Nat, is that I'll never lie to you. This thing, this relationship we're building, is important to me. I don't know where it's going but I want to make sure I don't mess it up. You feel me?"

She nodded. "I don't want to mess it up, either. I admit that I've been known to do that in the past."

"I know."

"And how do you know?"

"I'll tell you later," he said. "A man has to protect his sources."

"I don't know what I'm going to do with you," she said. "So I guess I'll get us something to drink. Coke all right with you?"

"Fine," he said. "But hurry back. I miss you when you're out of my sight."

"Now you're getting it," she said with a smile. "Those are words a woman loves to hear."

Dante got up from the floor and sat on the couch. When Natalie returned, she handed him a Coke and sat next to him. "I'm going to beat you next time," she said.

"I'm glad there's going to be a next time," he said, wrapping an arm around her shoulders and pulling her close.

"Okay, now you're pouring it on a bit thick." Contrary to her words and tone, she snuggled against his side.

"I couldn't think of anything to say, since I know you're not going to beat me next time."

"Don't be so sure," she said. "I have a secret weapon."

He looked down at her. "Secret weapon? Are you taking chess lessons?"

"I'm not telling. You have secrets and so do I."

Dante stared at her for a long minute and Natalie thought that he was going to kiss her. Instead, he said, "It's getting late. I think I should go."

Natalie glanced down at the gold Rolex he always wore. It was indeed getting late. She didn't want him to go, not yet, but she knew he needed to leave.

As if he could read her thoughts, he brushed his finger down her cheek and said, "I don't want to leave, but I'm honoring this relationship like I haven't in the past. You and I have different views on how God looks on the expression of love between two unmarried people who care deeply for each other. I hope you'll come to trust me enough to know that I'll never hurt you and that anything we do together would be an expression of love. The way I'm feeling right now and the way I think you're feeling, we may end up doing something we'll regret in the morning. I don't want that for us, so I'm leaving. Understand?"

She nodded, hating to admit that there was some truth to his estimation of her feelings, yet hating even more how much his words reminded her of Benjamin's. He hadn't pressured her sexually, either, but she knew now that was because he was getting his so-called needs met elsewhere. She wondered if Dante had someone else, too. Before her imagination could get the best of her, Dante took her hand and pulled her up from the couch with him. He walked her to her door with his arm around her shoulders.

When they reached the door, she still wasn't ready for him to leave, so she asked, "Have you thought any more about the prison ministry? I'd really like for you to talk to my brother. He could give you statistics and other information to help you to make a decision about hiring an ex-convict at your dealership. Most of them really do want to turn their lives around and will work very hard for you. My brother's organization does a great job of screening candidates."

Dante pressed his lips softly against hers for a moment. When he lifted his head, he said, "I know how important this is to you, so I'll talk to my partner about it and let you know, okay?"

She nodded.

"Good night, Nat," he said. "Sleep well, but think of me."

Natalie didn't answer but she knew she would do as he asked.

CHAPTER 3

Thank you, Lord," Preacher said when he awakened in his garage apartment the next morning. His first taste of freedom yesterday had been overshadowed by his irritation with Tanya, but he was making sure to start this day off the right way. He got out of bed, opened a window, and breathed in the fresh morning air. *No bars,* he thought, physically or spiritually. "Thank you, Lord."

Preacher grabbed his grandmother's Bible and spent some time in meditation before taking his shower and getting dressed. He was eager to see his children, so he didn't waste any time. He frowned when he turned the knob on the door in his kitchen that led to the stairway down to the kitchen in the main house. It wouldn't turn. *Tanya!* "Help me, Lord," he prayed, "not to get upset."

It's all good, he thought. Even though one of the apartment's best features was the inside access to the house and his boys, he would gladly take the longer outside route. He made his way to the front door and jogged down the outside stairs leading to the far side of the garage. He trotted around the house and rang the doorbell, shaking off the irony that he was doing this in his own home.

He rang a couple of times before Jake appeared in the sidelights, still wearing the socks, T-shirt, and underpants he'd been wearing when Preacher had put him to bed. Preacher's shock at his son answering the door was surpassed only by the joy that flashed on his son's face at seeing him.

He listened as Jake struggled with the lock, and then he scooped the boy into his arms when the door opened. Preacher held him close, too close, he guessed, since Jake squirmed a bit. Preacher relented and eased the boy to the floor, but not before giving him a kiss on the forehead and a second hug. He rubbed his hand across his son's head, love filling his heart. "Morning, champ," he said. "Where's your momma?"

Jake rubbed his eyes. "Bed," he mumbled.

Preacher caught the time on the foyer clock. Seven o'clock. Shouldn't Tanya be up and getting the boys ready for school or day care or camp or something? "Come on then," Preacher said. "Let's go get dressed so we can get some breakfast."

Preacher headed to his boys' room, pausing a long moment outside their bedroom to glance down the hall at the master bedroom door. He moved toward the master bedroom with Jake on his heels. He debated entering his old sleeping quarters without knocking but decided instead to rap on the door. "Tanya," he called. "You all right in there?" When he got no answer, he knocked again.

"Go back to bed, boys," she mumbled. "Momma's still sleeping."

Still sleeping on a weekday? Preacher rapped again. "Tanya, it's me, Preacher. It's time to get up and get these boys ready for the day." When she didn't respond, he said, "Tanya, do you hear me?"

"The whole neighborhood probably hears you," she said, pulling open the door.

Preacher's eyes roamed her scantily clad body; she hadn't bothered to put on a robe over the short pajamas. Before he could stop them, memories of the nights he and Tanya had shared in this room and that bed filled his mind. The smug grin that he saw when his eyes made their way back to her face told him she knew exactly where his thoughts were.

Tanya leaned down and kissed Jake, giving Preacher an extended view of her cleavage in the process. "Morning, baby," she said. "Go put on some pants so we can have breakfast." She patted her son's backside and sent him off. Then she looked up at Preacher. "See something you like, Preacher boy?" she teased. She opened the door wider and inclined her head toward the bed. "I'll make you a deal. You put the boys back to bed and I'll put you back to bed."

Preacher recognized temptation for what it was and he was reminded of Barnard's skepticism at his plan to move back in with Tanya. He had discounted his friend's concern then, but now he saw the wisdom of it. It was going to be difficult to stay in this house with Tanya and not sleep with her. It'd been two years since they'd been together, a lifetime ago and a minute ago all rolled into one.

Tanya's laugh brought him out of his thoughts. "You're a trip, Preacher. You know you want me. It's been two years since you've had a woman." She tipped her head to the side. "Or maybe you prefer a man these days?"

Whatever desire had been building within Preacher fizzled

with those words. He counted it a blessing. "Get dressed. The boys need breakfast and they need to get to school."

"School's out."

"I thought you had Mack in day care and Jake in year-round school."

"Well," Tanya said, with a toss of her hair. She turned and went back toward the bed. "That was when we had money."

Preacher widened his eyes. "What's this about money?" he asked, following her. "I left more than enough money in your account to last you two years. What did you do with it?"

Tanya plopped down on the side of the bed. "I had expenses, Preacher."

"What kind of expenses?" he demanded, standing over her. "What expenses were more important than our children's welfare?"

Tanya lifted defiant greenish brown eyes to him. "You knew what kind of woman I was when you hooked up with me, Preacher. I need things, nice things, and nice things cost money. I need to go to nice places, and nice places cost money. I need to pamper myself, and that costs money. The cash you left was gone before you were settled into your cell."

"I don't believe it," Preacher said, thinking of the sum he'd left. "How could you spend that much money?"

"It was easy. I was lonely, and the lonelier I was, the more I spent. I didn't sign up for this kind of life, Preacher. I need parties, fun, people. Not this."

"What are you saying, Tanya?" Preacher asked.

"You heard me."

"Are you threatening to leave me, take my kids?"

She shook her head. "I'm not threatening anything. As long as you can take care of me and the kids, we're here, but when you can't, we'll have to find someone who can." She tossed her long mane of hair over her shoulder. "I'm not getting any younger, so I don't have a lot of time to waste. I don't understand why you're trying to start a new life when you could easily go back to your old one."

Preacher leaned back against the dresser. "You actually want me to pick up where I left off when I was arrested? You've got to be joking. Why would I take that kind of risk with my future, your future, our kids' futures? Can't you see I want to build something good with you, Tanya? I want to give you more than I promised you, but this time I want to do it legally, in a way that you and the boys can be proud, in a way that doesn't bring violence and danger and possible imprisonment to our door. I want to be a good husband to you and a good father to our kids. Are you telling me you don't want that?"

Tanya pulled the covers up on the king-sized bed. "That sounds all well and good," she said, "but how are you going to do it? What's your plan? How long is it going to take?"

"A little longer now that we don't have the seed money I thought we had," he said. He still couldn't believe she'd spent all the money. He hoped she was lying—he wouldn't put it past her—so he'd check the balances himself.

"You can always get money from Loretta," she suggested.

Preacher shook his head. "No money from Loretta. I've told you and I've told her. It's no good. You know I want my sister out of the business. I'm not taking money from her."

"Hmmph," Tanya said.

"And neither will you, Tanya," Preacher ordered. "Nobody in this house takes money from Loretta. Do you hear me?"

"I hear you, but it's too late. Loretta's already been helping us out."

"What?"

She stood and headed toward the master bath. "You heard me. She's been helping out. She's been good to me and the boys even though you haven't been that nice to her since you found God or whatever. Loretta's your sister, and she loves you. She's been there for you through all of this. I don't see how you can cut her off the way you have. She'd never do that to you."

Preacher didn't bother giving an explanation because he knew Tanya wouldn't get it. He wondered if she even wanted to. "I'll get the boys ready," he said, "and we'll meet you downstairs for breakfast. I'll cook."

"Whatever."

Preacher gave her one last look and left the room. As he bathed and dressed the boys, he prayed for the Lord's hand on his family.

Barnard closed the door of his office in Faith Community Church and came back to join his prayer partner and Preacher's soon-to-be business mentor, Luther Brown. "Preacher and Wayne should be here in about an hour," he told the sixty-five-year-old man who'd been like a father to him since he and his sister had moved to Atlanta seven years ago. He sat across from Luther at the oval table.

"How you holding up?" Luther asked with a knowing glance that was very familiar to Barnard.

"I'm good," Barnard responded. Even as he spoke the words, he knew Luther wouldn't accept them at face value.

Luther leaned back in his chair and raised a brow. "So things with you and Serena are getting better?"

Barnard sighed. *What was the use in trying to scam Luther?* A few months ago, Barnard had summoned the courage to tell Luther about his problems with Serena. Both problems: the bedroom and the adoption. "Not really," he said. "But they aren't getting any worse."

"That doesn't sound too good," the older man said.

"Well," Barnard said, "it could be worse."

Luther leaned forward, all serious now. "I don't see how," he said. "From what you tell me, your relationship with Serena is missing a critical element. Sex is not the be all and end all of a relationship, but it's important."

"I love her," Barnard said in defense of both him and Serena.

"I know you do," Luther said. "But I also see a growing resentment in you."

Barnard closed his eyes, sighing again. *Was he that transparent?* "I'm handling it," he said. "The Lord is giving me the strength to handle it."

Now Luther sighed. "Have you told Serena how you feel?"

"I've talked to her about adoption."

"And the other?"

Barnard looked away. "I can't," he said.

"You have to," Luther encouraged. "You both need to talk this through, maybe talk it over with a counselor. You aren't the first couple to have problems in the bedroom and you won't be the last."

"It's not that serious, Luther," Barnard said. "Things will work out."

"Don't fool yourself, Barnard," Luther said. "And don't turn away from the help that God provides. You don't have to suffer this way."

Barnard gave a dry laugh. "You make it sound like I'm dying."

Luther shook his head. "No, you're not dying, but I wonder about your relationship with Serena. Is it strong and viable? Are you growing closer to her every day?"

"I love her," Barnard repeated, refusing to have his marriage examined any further.

It was Luther's time to sigh. He checked his watch. "Wayne and Preacher will be here shortly. Why don't we pray before they get here?"

Barnard nodded and bowed his head.

"Father," Luther began, "we come to you in the name of Jesus, our Savior, giving you all honor and glory for who You are and for what you've done for us. We thank you, Lord, that the challenges you put before us are not insurmountable. Father, I pray now for my brother Barnard, and my dear, dear sister Serena. I pray Lord that the physical intimacy you designed for marriage might be realized in their lives. I pray that whatever barriers hinder their physical closeness be identified and removed. I pray that the unity of spirit they share as one in marriage might be demonstrated in a physical relationship that celebrates that unity. I pray these things in Jesus' name. Amen."

Preacher was fuming when he reached the church later that morning for his meeting with Barnard, Wayne Dixon, his probation officer, and Luther Brown, his new business mentor. As soon as he'd opened the garage he'd seen where Tanya had spent much of their money—cars. A Benz G55 SUV that had to cost a hundred grand and a Porsche 911 convertible that must have cost even more. Was the woman crazy? Even when he was in the business, he'd kept a low profile. Nice cars like the Acura he was driving now—the one she'd driven to pick him up in yesterday—a nice home in a moderately upscale neighborhood, but nothing that would draw undue attention to him and his business dealings. Apparently, Tanya didn't share his restraint. She'd gone over the top, and he'd have to deal with her and her purchases soon. He'd counted on the money she'd spent to buy them into a legitimate business of some kind. The business skills he'd once used for evil, he now planned to use for good. He'd excelled at his old profession and he knew he'd do as well at a legit one, maybe even better, since he was dedicating his new work to the Lord. Now he faced his first glitch. No, correct that, his first two glitches. Tanya had spent the money and then she'd gone to Loretta for more. He'd have to deal with both women. Soon.

Barnard met him at the door to the Living and Learning Center at Faith Community Church. "Morning, man," he said. "Nervous?"

"A little," Preacher said, realizing he was.

"Don't be. Luther and Wayne are both Christians and good people. We're all here to help. Okay?"

"Okay." As Preacher followed Barnard down a wide hallway he wondered at the transition of other ex-convicts. He knew he was fortunate to have Barnard and the Faith Community Prison Ministry on his side. Their counseling and support coupled with the computer and business classes he'd taken on the inside gave him better odds than most. He was determined to make the best of his opportunity.

When he followed Barnard into an office off the wide hallway, he immediately recognized Wayne Dixon, the young brother who was his probation officer. They'd met before at the prison. Preacher still thought Wayne looked much too young and soft to be a probation officer. His look said grade-school teacher more than it said probation officer.

"Good to see you, Preacher," Wayne said, before Preacher could greet him. "I like the new clothes."

All the men laughed, which caused Preacher to relax a bit. "I sorta like 'em, too," he said. He was more than happy to be back in his old street clothes. Fortunately, he was a conservative dresser—tan linen slacks and a light shirt—so his clothes didn't go in and out of style. "I think the color fits me better."

When the second round of laughter died down, the man Preacher knew had to be Luther Brown extended his hand. "Good to meet you, Preacher. I've heard a lot of good things about you."

Preacher shook the older man's hand. Now this guy had the look of a successful entrepreneur, from his pinstriped tie to his 'gator shoes. "Same here. From Barnard's description, I sorta expected to see you walking on water."

Luther chuckled. "He must have been referring to my wife. I'm a mere mortal and don't do much water walking."

Preacher decided he liked this man and he knew he wouldn't have a problem working with him. "I appreciate what you're doing for me," he said to Luther. Then including the other men, he added, "You all, too. I want you to know I'm not going to blow this second chance I've been given. I want to make the Lord proud of me and y'all, too."

"Well, that's what we like to hear," Barnard said, ushering the men to a small table in the corner of his office. "Attitude is half the battle with the transition back to the outside." He inclined his head toward Wayne.

"I'll start first," Wayne said, handing a probation fact sheet to the others at the table. "This sheet outlines the general terms of your probation," he said to Preacher. "We went over it in detail before you were released, but I want to reiterate a few points for the four of us. First, no contact with anyone in your old business, anyone involved in illegal activity, or anyone with a criminal past."

Preacher nodded. He had heard all this before.

"Second," Wayne continued, "no travel outside the jurisdiction of the Court without my knowledge and permission. Third, your home and your workplace are subject to be searched at any time. No cause needed. It's a term of probation."

"A term which causes many prospective employers to balk at hiring people on parole or probation," Barnard interjected. "Who am I kidding? Prospective employers balk at hiring anybody with a criminal history. The search condition just makes them more wary."

"You're right," Wayne said, "but that's the way it is. On the one hand the criminal justice system is saying that imprisonment is for rehabilitation, while on the other hand, it's saying that it has very little faith in its ability to rehabilitate."

"I don't mind the premise searches much," Luther said. "I like the idea of the employer knowing that Big Brother is watching. It gives everybody incentive to keep their noses clean—employer and employee. Since I have nothing to hide, it doesn't bother me at all."

"You're in the minority, Luther," Barnard said. "The premises search is the biggest hindrance I face when lining up prospective employers."

"I hear you, man," Wayne said, "but there's nothing I can do. Workplace and home searches are core to criminal supervision services." He turned to Preacher. "Even more invasive than the workplace search, Preacher," he said, "is the home search. Your living premises are more likely to be searched and more often."

Preacher nodded. "I know that and it's one of the reasons, though not the primary reason, I'm living in an apartment above the garage in my former home. I don't relish the idea of the cops coming in and scaring my children."

Wayne grimaced. "I hate to tell you this, but because of the layout of that garage apartment, specifically that interior door in your kitchen that opens to the stairs down to the kitchen in the main house, the entire house is subject to search."

"What? I thought we had agreed—"

"I know," Barnard said, "and I'm sorry. I didn't think that door would be a problem, especially since it has a lock on both sides. I'm sorry, man."

Preacher wondered what more bad news they had for him. "There's nothing we can do?"

"Nothing short of walling in that door," Barnard answered, "and I'm not sure that's something you want to do, especially since you and Tanya plan on getting married soon."

"She's not going to like the idea of the home searches. I know this one is going to lead to an argument."

Luther chuckled. "I feel you, brother."

Preacher tried to keep his spirits up as he listened to the rest of Wayne's rules, including the mandatory monthly trips to the probation office, but it was hard not to see the next two years of life on the outside almost as confining as life on the inside.

When Wayne wrapped up, it was Luther's turn. "Barnard told me about your entrepreneurial bent, and your desire to start a legitimate business," he said to Preacher. "After talking with Wayne here, we think the best way to get you to the point of buying into a business or purchasing a franchise is for you to work in the business as an employee first."

Before he found out Tanya had spent their ready cash on cars they didn't need, this news would have crushed Preacher's spirits. As it was, all he could think was "thank you, Lord." He now had time to sell the cars and recoup at least some of the money for investing in a business. "That works for me," he told Luther. "When and where do I start?"

"We'll decide that together. I'm an entrepreneur myself but I enjoy building businesses, not running them long term. I have a couple of small concerns that are ripe for selling and I'm willing to give you an option to buy."

"Why would you do that? You don't even know me."

"That's right, I don't. I'm doing it because I believe in this program. When Barnard came to me with the proposition a few years ago, I was skeptical but we've had success. As a businessman myself, I understand that if you have a knack for running one business, you can translate that knack to different kinds of businesses. You were good at running a narcotics enterprise and I believe some of those skills will serve you well in a legitimate business. I'm here to help you make that transition."

Preacher began to praise God in his mind as he listened to Luther describe the businesses he'd bought—car dealerships, car washes, cleaning services, sandwich shops, athletic gyms, bookkeeping services, even a funeral home—you name it, he seemed to have his hand in it. The car dealership caught Preacher's interest, while the funeral home gave him the willies.

"How did you get involved in so many things?" Preacher asked Luther.

"It's my way of giving back," Luther said. "I've been blessed to accomplish a lot in my life, and now I have the luxury of working because I love it and not because I need the money. I get enjoyment out of starting new businesses and salvaging existing ones. I also know that business ownership is the way to genuine wealth in our society. God's put it on my heart to help others share in that wealth. We need to be givers, and the more we have, the move we can give."

Preacher nodded.

"We'll get together next week," Luther continued. "You need

some time to get settled, and then you can pick a couple of businesses that interest you. We'll arrange for you to spend some time working in each one before you decide which one you want to buy into. How does that sound?"

"It sounds great," Preacher said. "I appreciate the opportunity. I really don't know what to say."

"There's nothing to say," Luther told him. "Just be obedient to God and when He puts you in a place to help somebody, you be sure to do it. That's all I ask." He glanced around the table. "That's all any of us ask."

"Well, I can do that," Preacher said. "But I have to tell you that my funds aren't at the level I thought they would be and—"

Luther stopped him with a raised palm. "Did you earn that money in a way that would glorify God?"

Preacher shook his head.

"Then maybe it's a blessing. I was going to talk with you about your plans for financing. You don't want to start your new business with money from your old life. There are other options, better options that we can discuss. Your timeline to ownership is going to be extended, but in the long run, you'll be better off."

Preacher didn't like the idea of extending his timeline and he was sure Tanya wouldn't, either, but he didn't have any other options. Though he hated to think of his money as tainted, it was. That reality didn't sit well with him.

"I'd rather not get into the details now," Luther was saying. "I'm working with you because I believe the Lord brought us together for a reason. He'll give us the wisdom to work out the details. Agreed?"

What else could Preacher say? "Agreed."

With that settled, Barnard pulled out a calendar and they began to schedule the next couple of months of Preacher's new life. When that was done, Luther and Wayne left, leaving Preacher alone with Barnard.

"I don't believe what just happened, man," Preacher said. "Are you telling me this is what you do for everybody released into the program?"

Barnard shook his head. "It's a different process for every person. We look at your skills, your attitudes and aptitudes, your personal goals, and we ask the Lord for direction. That's what we did with you. Isn't this what you told me you wanted?"

Preacher nodded. "But—"

"But it's one thing to want it and another thing to have it happen," Barnard finished for him.

"Yeah, that's it," Preacher said. "I've always felt I had to fend for myself in life. My motto was, 'Nobody's gonna help me but me.' I didn't expect this, even though we've talked about it."

Barnard clapped him on the shoulder. "You're not alone, Preacher. Not now. Not anymore. You have a brand-new family of Christians who're with you every step of the way and a Father who loves you unconditionally. Everything you face may not be easy, not even with all our support, but if you remember that you're not alone, you'll make it through the tough times. Got it?"

"Got it," Preacher said. "This morning I was stressed and feeling down because Tanya had spent more money than I expected, but now I feel a glimmer of hope. I have to keep reminding myself to think eternally, not just for the now."

"You've got that right. And you've got to be strong where Tanya is concerned. She's not a Christian and she doesn't know what to expect from you, since you're not the same man who went into prison. She'll need time to adjust . . . if she adjusts."

"She'll adjust," Preacher said. "God is giving me everything else I asked for, so I have no doubt He'll make Tanya, me, and the kids a family. I just have to hang on and not get upset with her so quickly."

"That reminds me," Barnard said, "Serena and I would like to invite you all over for dinner one evening this week, or whenever you get the time. It might help your cause if our women meet and hit it off. Serena could be a good witness to Tanya. What do you think?"

Preacher wasn't sure what to think. Guilt gnawed at him. He needed to talk to Serena and together they needed to decide what to tell Barnard about their past and when. They both owed the man that much. "I'll talk to Tanya," he said. "Can I let you know later in the week?"

"Fine," Barnard said. "It goes without saying that you're invited to church on Sunday. Invite your sister, too. I'd like both of you to meet my sister, Natalie. Why don't you plan to come over for dinner after church?"

"Don't you need to check with Serena?"

"Your coming over won't be a problem with Serena. We're already having my sister and her friend, so we'll throw a few more steaks and burgers on the grill."

"You don't think like a woman, man," Preacher said. "Check with your wife first."

Barnard cocked a brow. "You think Serena might have trouble cooking for more people?"

Preacher nodded because that was part of his concern, though not the major part.

Barnard chuckled. "Serena's not much of a cook," he said, "so I'll be the one adjusting recipes for the additional guests."

"Tanya's not much of a cook herself, but I'm not man enough to allow you to tell her or anyone else that I said it."

Barnard chuckled again. "Now our women have to meet. They already have something in common."

They have more in common than you know, Preacher thought. "Speaking of Tanya, I'm gonna head on back home and spend some time with her and the kids." He extended his hand. "Thanks for everything, man."

"Don't thank me," Barnard said. "Thank Him. Now if you'll hold on a minute, I'll walk out with you."

"You don't have to do that," Preacher said. "I can see myself out."

Barnard grabbed a portfolio from his desk and tucked it under his arm. "I'm on my way over to Circle Autos. You know the place?"

"Don't think so. You buying a new car?"

"Nah, I'm going to talk to them about participating in our prison jobs program. Natalie knows one of the owners and she set it up for me."

"So your sister is as committed to prison ministry as you are?"

"Maybe even more so. Seeing our father in prison had a big impact on her. Most of her memories of him are when he was inside. She was devastated when he died there. Sometimes I think this ministry has been her salvation. Helping other people make the transition he would have had to make is sort of her tribute to him."

"The same way it is for you?"

Barnard glanced at him. "I guess it is. You can always count on the Lord to provide a way to help ease your pain. I'm grateful this is the way he provided for me and Natalie."

"I am, too," Preacher agreed. "I hope it goes well with this dealership."

"Me, too," Barnard said. "The hardest part of the program is lining up employers."

"Well, I'm looking to sell a couple of cars—" At Barnard's raised brow, he said, "Don't even ask. Let's just say Tanya got carried away when I was locked up. Anyway, I may check out this dealership. If they're considering joining the program, the least I can do is give them my business."

"That's the spirit," Barnard said. "We want to reward companies for joining the program and what better way to do it than sending them new business. Be sure to tell them I sent you. In fact, ask for Dante Griggs and tell him personally."

When the men reached Barnard's car, Preacher asked, "Should I tell this Dante that I'm in the program?"

Barnard shook his head. "That's not necessary. It's not his business. You want to be honest with people when the issue comes up, but you don't have to take a probation card to every encounter you have. Listen to your heart. The Lord will show you when you need to tell your story."

Preacher clapped Barnard on the back, and as Barnard got into his car, he headed toward his. Even though he'd had a good meeting and his future was looking bright, Preacher drove away from the church with a heavy heart. He dreaded the upcoming confrontation with Tanya about selling those cars. He knew he had a fight on his hands.

CHAPTER 4

Andre Davis shook his bald head in amazement as Barnard Jenkins exited the dealership. He turned and pointed a diamond-studded finger at his partner. "You've got to be out of your mind, Dante, man. You know we can't sign up for this prisoner release jobs program."

Dante ignored his partner's words and headed back to his office. Andre followed him. "Do you hear me, Dante?"

"I'm not deaf. Of course, I hear you. You'd better close that door or everybody in the dealership is going to hear you."

Andre closed the door and then turned to his friend. "I know you want to get in this guy's sister's pants, but this is going too far."

"Don't talk about Natalie that way," Dante said.

"Man, that woman has you whipped. You're going to put both of us at risk, get both of us sent to prison, and for what? So you can get—"

"Don't say it," Dante warned. "Don't talk about Natalie."

Andre sat in the chair in front of Dante's desk. "Look, Dante," he said. "I know this woman is special to you. I'll give you that, but we can't participate in this jobs program. You heard what Barnard said about impromptu searches of places of employment. We can't subject ourselves to that kind of scrutiny. You see that, don't you?"

Dante shook his head. "What I see is you acting like a scared little girl. Nobody's going to prison. We can hire a guy, put him in repair or something. What's he going to find out?"

"He could find out a lot," Dante explained. "We've got trailers coming in and out of here weekly moving hundreds of kilos of drugs. It's too risky, man."

"You're the one who put us at risk, Andre, not me," Dante accused. "I told you before and I'm telling you now, I want out. We don't need the money anymore. The whole operation is a risk we can no longer afford."

Andre slumped back in his chair. "You're talking like a crazy person. You don't just get out. It's not that easy."

"All I know is that you got us into this situation and now you need a plan to get us out of it."

Andre wagged his finger at Dante. "Don't get all high and mighty on me, partner. You were as open to this operation as I was."

"You have a faulty memory, Andre. You brought this deal to me. It was your idea."

Andre shook his head. "Okay, these accusations are getting us nowhere. We both knew we were in trouble and needed a quick infusion of cash. Yes, I brought this deal to you but you have to admit you didn't take much convincing."

Dante leaned back in his chair. "I'm serious, man," he said. "Natalie's very important to me. I can see myself building a life with her. I want to come to her with a clean slate."

"Clean slate? Come on, this is me you're talking to, Dante."

"And I'm telling you I want out."

"And I'm telling you it's not happening."

"If you don't do something," Dante said, "I will."

Andre sat up straighter. "Look," he said, "don't do anything crazy. I'll see what I can do, but you've got to give up this idea of joining this jobs program. It's too risky."

"I hear you," Dante said, getting up from his desk, "but now I've got work to do."

Andre took the hint and stood, too. "Don't do anything stupid," he said. "We both have a lot to lose if you do."

When Dante didn't say anything, but just sat back down and began studying the papers on his desk, Andre had no choice but to leave. He headed to his own office and picked up the phone. He dialed the digits he knew by heart and when she answered, he said, "We've got to meet. Now."

Andre beat his guest to the restaurant. He asked for a booth in the back and waited. He smelled her perfume before he saw her. He looked up at the petite chocolate sweetie coming toward him and his racing heart told him that he was as whipped as he'd accused Dante of being. He'd fallen for her during his freshman year at Morehouse, when she'd sold him his first nickel bag, and he'd never gotten her out of his system.

He stood and greeted her with a kiss on the check. "You're looking good, Loretta," he said. "But then you always do."

"I think you're biased," Loretta said, flashing those glistening whites at him. "But I accept the compliment all the same." She leaned across the table toward him, all business. "Now what was so important that we had to meet immediately?"

Andre knew she wasn't going to like the news, so he dreaded

telling her, but he dreaded more her finding out on her own. "Dante wants to enroll the dealership in a prisoner release hiring program sponsored by a local church."

Loretta leaned back in the booth, her eyes alert with interest. That look comforted Andre. Unlike Dante, Loretta recognized the seriousness of the situation. "Prisoner release hiring program?"

"Yes. A local church sponsors recently released prisoners and puts them in jobs with businesses enrolled in their jobs program."

"And the problem is?" Loretta looked as though she were waiting for the punch line.

"Is everybody around me crazy today?" Andre asked, waving his arms in frustration. "The problem is that businesses enrolled in the program are subject to random searches by the Department of Probations."

"Oh," Loretta said.

"Yeah, a big oh, if you ask me. We can't do it. I tried to tell Dante it was too risky, but he's not listening. He's got the hots for the program director's sister and he's not thinking logically. We have to do something."

"What do you mean *we*? Dante is your problem. It's up to you to keep him in line. You've done well with him so far. I don't see why you won't this time."

"I'm not so sure about this time, Loretta. My boy isn't thinking straight. This woman's got him all twisted. He's starting to sound guilty, talking about getting out. She's a church girl and I think she may be rubbing off on him."

"Please," Loretta said. "He's not the only one. It must be in the water you men are drinking." She closed her eyes for a few short seconds. "What's this woman's name and what's the church?"

"Her name's Natalie. I can't think of her last name, but hold up."

He leaned forward and pulled his wallet out of the rear pocket of his pants. "Her brother left us his card." He opened his wallet and pulled out a business card. "Her last name is Jenkins. Her brother's name is Barnard and the church is Faith Community."

Loretta flashed her whites at him again. "Could be things aren't as bad as they seem."

"What? Are you crazy? Didn't you hear me say that if we participate, the Department of Probation can make random searches of our premises?"

"I heard you," she said, looking all relaxed now. "Just because they can doesn't mean they will."

"Look, I don't want to end up in prison like your brother, so I'd rather not take the risk if you don't mind."

"But I do mind," she said. "You're not thinking clearly, Andre. We could work this opportunity to our advantage."

"You and Dante must be taking the drugs in addition to transporting them. That or you're both crazy."

"Could be that you're just scared. You know that's not a trait I find attractive in a man," she said. "A man can't think smart if he's hampered by fear. That's when he makes mistakes."

Andre didn't fall for Loretta's attack. "A smart man knows when to follow his instincts. And it doesn't take a lot of instincts to know that when you're involved in illegal activity, you don't want the police sniffing around. That is, not unless you want to go to prison." He lifted a brow. "I don't know. Maybe you like your men in prison. Is that how you get rid of them when you get tired? Is that what happened with your brother? Send big bro to prison and li'l sis becomes the top dog?"

Loretta sat back against the booth and gave him a coy smile. "Why all this interest in Preacher? Jealous?"

"Of a jailbird? I don't think so." No way would Andre admit

that Preacher was the only man in Loretta's life who worried him. Though he tried hard to hide it, his attraction and desire for Loretta had grown over the years, and now he wanted her all to himself. She didn't know it yet, but they were destined to rule an empire together.

"I don't believe you. Just think, Andre. If you sign up for this program, you could end up being Preacher's boss. Wouldn't you like that?"

He shook his head. "I bet you would though." He grinned at her audacity. "You're a dangerous woman, Loretta. A man would have to be a fool not to see that. I'm not a fool."

"Then stop thinking about Preacher and the police and start thinking about this opportunity."

"Risk, you mean?"

She leaned forward. "Think, Andre. Having an ex-con on the premises could be perfect. If anything went down, who do you think the cops would blame? Certainly not two upstanding men in the community like you and Dante. No, the cops would look at the ex-con." She tapped a finger against her temple. "This could be the perfect cover for us."

Andre grunted. "Or it could be the nail in all of our coffins."

"But you'll think about it. For me?"

Andre had never been able to deny her anything, and he knew this time would be no different. "I'll think about it."

She smiled and blew an air kiss in his direction. "Good, now buy me lunch. I'm hungry."

Loretta was practically giddy after her lunch with Andre. An idea had begun forming in her mind as soon as he had mentioned the jobs program. Preacher didn't know it yet but soon he'd be back in business with her where he belonged. She'd never let him be set up to take the fall as she'd suggested to Andre, but then Andre didn't need to know the details of her thoughts. She'd keep him in line and she'd get her brother back by her side. It was only a matter of time. The thought of it made her heart race. She picked up her cell phone and punched in Tanya's number. When Tanya answered, she said, "I'm on my way over to talk with Preacher. Make yourself and the boys scarce when I get there."

"You don't tell me what to do, Loretta."

"Please, I'm not even going there with you again. I need to talk to Preacher alone. I'll be there in fifteen minutes."

Loretta parked her Chrysler 300 in Preacher's driveway a short while later. She took the outside stairs to the apartment over the garage where he now lived. She hated the thought of her brother living over a garage like some poor relation, especially when that money-hungry Tanya was living large in the main house like some queen of the manor. When she reached the top step, she stopped and took a deep breath. She knew she had to remain calm if she was going to get Preacher to see things her way. She knocked twice and waited.

When Preacher opened the door and saw her, his eyes widened with joy and Loretta saw flashes of her old brother in them. "You look happy to see me," she said, stepping into his embrace.

Preacher hugged her close, tight actually. She felt the strength she'd always experienced in his arms, but this time the barely restrained violence that usually marked his touch was gone. She'd taken comfort in that violence, knowing that it meant Preacher could protect them; she missed it. Confused, she stepped away from him. "You've changed." She said the words aloud though she hadn't planned to.

Smiling at her, Preacher took her hand and pulled her fully

into the apartment. "I've been trying to tell you that," he said, "but you wouldn't listen."

"You didn't need to change," she said, her eyes taking in him and the cramped space that was his combination living room, dining room, and kitchen. She'd done a good job in picking the furnishings, but a garage apartment was still a garage apartment. "You were fine the way you were."

Preacher sank down in the leather recliner in his living room. "No, I wasn't, and we both know it. A Bible-toting, drug-dealing thug. That's what I was and I needed help."

"You weren't a thug," she said, sitting on the matching leather couch across from him.

"Yes, I was. A thug in a suit, but still a thug. It's all about the attitude. I thought I was the man, but then I met the real man. He changed my life, Loretta. Sitting in that prison cell I found what I've always been looking for."

"How can you say that, Preacher? You had everything. *We* had everything."

"Yeah, we had things, but when I was sitting in that cell all by myself, those things didn't mean much. What meant something was the people I love, especially my kids, and I realized that what I was giving them was going to land them in prison, too. I didn't want that for them, I don't want it for myself, and I don't want it for you."

To avoid the look of pity she thought she saw in his eyes, Loretta focused on the Varnette P. Honeywood painting above his head instead of looking directly at him. Why should he pity her? From where she sat, she was better off than he was. Turning her gaze back to him, she said, "So you're afraid of prison. Is that what this is all about?"

"I won't lie to you, 'Retta. I didn't like doing time. It's not for me.

I had to find some peace in that place and what I found was Jesus. So in a sense, it was worth it. But I don't want to repeat it."

Not wanting to hear those words from her brother, Loretta got up and walked to the bar that separated the living area from the kitchen. "What about our business?" she asked. "What about all we've built?"

Preacher followed her to the bar and stood beside her. "I don't want it."

She looked over at him. "You say that now, but how are you going to take care of your kids and keep Tanya in the style to which she's become accustomed? Jobs don't come easy to ex-cons, not good ones."

He smiled down at her. "I'll be all right. God has my back and He's put some good people in my life."

"What about me?" Loretta asked, turning so they faced each other. "We used to have each other's backs. Are you turning your back on me now? I need you, Preacher. You're all I have. You're my brother."

Preacher took her hand in his. "I love you, 'Retta. You want out and I'm here for you, but I can't go back to the life. I can't."

Loretta jerked her hand away. "You're afraid, Preacher. You won't have to do any more time," she said. "I can promise you that."

Preacher shook his head. "No, you can't. I thought we were too smart to get caught, but I got caught."

"It was a setup, Preacher," Loretta said, pacing in front of him. "We both know it had to be. No way would you be driving a car with drugs in it. Somebody put the kilos in your trunk and then called the police to tip them off. Together, we can find the person and make him pay."

Preacher shook his head, unwilling to share with her the name

G-Money had given him. He knew all too well what she'd do if she had it; the same thing he would have done two years ago. "I've thought about it and you're probably right about me being set up, but it doesn't matter," he told her. "Prison was where I needed to be, even though I didn't realize it at the time. If we found the person who set me up, I'd have to thank them."

Loretta laughed. "Come off it, Preacher. You're taking that 'turn the other cheek' stuff a bit too far. You can try to tell somebody else that story, but not me. I know you."

Preacher shook his head. "You knew the old me, 'Retta, but you don't know the new me."

Loretta relaxed against the bar. "You know I've never been a church person and I've never trusted church people. Sister Lillie Mae taught me all I need to know about church folks. The government says drugs are illegal, but if you ask me, churches ought to be illegal. Nothing but a racket if you ask me."

"Everybody's not like her or the other people you and I knew growing up. That was church, 'Retta. I'm talking about a real Jesus who's as close to you as I am now, who loves you more than I ever could, and who'll be a better friend to you than I've ever been. Think of how Big Momma loved us; well, Jesus loves us more."

Loretta scrunched up her nose. She couldn't believe her Preacher was spouting this mumbo-jumbo.

"I know you don't believe me, and I can understand, because I wasn't a believer at first. You're as hardheaded as I was, but I hope you don't have to fall as far as I did before you ask for help."

"Okay, Preacher," Loretta said. "You're going too far now. I've been taking care of myself for as long as I can remember. When I needed God as a child, He wasn't there, and now I don't need Him."

"Yes, you do," Preacher said. "I know you better than anyone, Loretta, and I know you need Him as much as I did, as I still do. Do you still cry yourself to sleep at night?" he asked softly.

The words whipped at Loretta's heart and she shot a fiery glance at her brother. "Don't go there with me, Preacher. We both have our demons. You know mine, but I know yours, too."

"But now I sleep at night, you don't. That's the difference between us."

Loretta shrugged off Preacher's words, but her eyes locked on his. "Just because you need the crutch of some god you can't even see doesn't mean I need it. I can take care of myself, and in case you don't know it, I've been taking care of your family too. God didn't do that, Preacher," she said, thumping her chest. "I did. I was there for your kids after Tanya blew your cash. I kept those shops in the black when Tanya was spending money like there was no tomorrow. That was me. Not God. And you should be thanking me, not telling me what I need."

"Tanya told me today what you did. She shouldn't have come to you. I left her more than enough money."

Loretta laughed. "You don't know the woman you've taken up with very well, do you, Preacher? Tanya is about the dollar, always has been, always will be."

"I know you don't like Tanya. You've made that very clear."

"I think you can do better than her. Tanya doesn't want you. She wants what you can give her. You're a smart man about everything except her. I don't get it. What is it about women like Tanya that make normally smart men like you act like fools?"

"She's the mother of my children," Preacher told her. "And she's going to be my wife."

Loretta raised her arms in frustration. "You've got to be kidding, Preacher. Do you really think Tanya's going to marry a broke ex-convict? Get real. Sister girl needs money and lots of it. Something tells me your girl is going to be as gone as your money."

Preacher rapped his fist against the bar top and Loretta knew she had touched a nerve. "I can take care of my wife and my family, Loretta. I appreciate what you did for Tanya but we no longer need or want your help." He walked to the door and opened it.

"You're kicking me out?" she asked.

He shook his head. "I think we've said all we have to say. You've never liked Tanya and you've never liked me with her. I have a new life now and the only way I know to make the new one work is to let the old one go."

"And that includes the people in the old life, too?" she asked, barely containing her despair at the callous way Preacher was treating her. "People who've known you and had your back for most of your life? You're going to choose that money-grubbing Tanya and some new people you've met at church over me? I'm your sister, Preacher," she pleaded, "the only family you have. I've always been there for you and you've always been there for me. Things don't have to change."

Preacher shook his head sadly. "They already have, 'Retta. How can we be as close as we were when we're living different lives? I'm on probation and you're trafficking drugs. Nothing good can come of it. Either you'll get caught and sent to prison, or I'll be charged with violating probation and be sent back there. I don't want that for me, and as much as I want you out of the drugs, I don't want you to end up in prison. You don't wanna go there, 'Retta."

"So I have to choose?"

Preacher nodded.

She walked toward him. "If you really loved me, you wouldn't make me choose."

"I'm doing this because I love you," he countered. "If you really loved me, I wouldn't have to make you choose."

Loretta bit down on her lower lip, making Preacher wonder if she was fighting tears. But when she spoke, her words were strong. "You'll need me, Preacher. We're a part of each other. You may think we aren't right now, but I know we are, and soon you'll know it, too." With no more words, she brushed past him and out of the apartment.

Preacher looked after her, his heart filled with love and concern. He closed his eyes and prayed, "Help her to see that she needs you, Lord. Make her nights restless and show her the emptiness of her life. But, in all things, keep her safe in the dangerous life she's chosen for herself. Show me how to love her in the way you want her to be loved. In Jesus' name. Amen."

His prayer finished, Preacher picked up the phone and dialed a number he hadn't dialed since he became a Christian, a number he didn't think he'd ever have to call again. But he had to make the call if he was going to keep his sister from doing something stupid. He knew her. Once she got an idea in her head she wouldn't let it go. They were alike in that way, or had been.

"Boss?" the voice on the other end of the phone said.

"I'm not your boss anymore, Big Boy," he told the man who'd been his sometimes driver and bodyguard. Next to Loretta, Big Boy was the only one of his crew that he really trusted.

"Old habits die hard, boss," Big Boy said. "You'll always be boss to me."

Preacher didn't bother trying to convince Big Boy otherwise. "I need a favor," he asked.

"It's done," Big Boy, the always loyal soldier, said.

Preacher sighed. "I need you to arrange a private meeting. No firepower."

"You got it. Give me the name, place, and time. It's done."

"Sooner rather than later," Preacher said. Then he gave Big Boy the name G-Money had given him.

CHAPTER 5

Sean decided to sit while he waited to be called into the Boss's office this time. His Gucci shoes were getting worn down with all his pacing. To keep his mind off his impending thrashing, he checked out the receptionist. He'd been too wrapped up in his own problems to take much notice of her on his previous visits, but now that he took the time to study her he saw that she was a cutie. He cleared his throat to get her attention. When she looked at him, he gave her his best smile.

Without an answering smile, she said, "You can go in now."

Sean would have been insulted that she'd ignored his attempt at flirting, but his anxiety over entering the Boss's office over-rode all other emotions. He found the Boss seated at his desk, the white earbuds to his iPod clipped to his ears, his head bobbing. Now this was a first for Sean. He'd never seen the Boss kicking back like this before. He began to relax. Things couldn't be so bad if the Boss was in such a good mood. He cleared his throat, causing the Boss to glance up at him.

The Boss waved Sean to a chair in front of his desk and kept bobbing his head. Sean relaxed even more. Maybe he was going to get some praise this time. He'd been working hard on Preacher and his family. The report he carried in his portfolio showed his progress.

With a broad smile still on his face, the Boss took off his earbuds and handed them to Sean. "Want to hear some real music?" he asked.

Matching the Boss's smile, Sean reached for the earbuds. This was the first time the Boss had shared anything with him like this. The day was looking up. Full of anticipation, Sean placed the white buds in his ears. When he didn't hear anything, he lifted questioning eyes to the Boss.

"Oh," the Boss said. "I forgot to turn up the volume. I keep forgetting your senses aren't as sharp as mine."

Since that was a well-known truth, Sean didn't think much about it as he waited for the music to fill his ears. His smile turned into a frown as wailings and screams blasted from the iPod. It sounded as though people were being tortured. He lifted questioning eyes to the Boss again as he pulled the earbuds out.

"Now that's music," the Boss said.

Sean wasn't sure what to say. He didn't know if the Boss was joking or what.

"What do you think of my music?" the Boss asked.

"I'm not sure I heard music," Sean said, deciding it was best not to lie.

"That's because you're an idiot with no taste and even less discernment," the Boss said, all remnants of his smile gone. "That was the sound of Third Hades. You'd better get used to it."

Sean slumped back in his chair. "Third Hades?"

"You heard me," the Boss said. "At the rate you're going, that place is going to be your new home real soon."

Sean flipped open his portfolio and handed the Boss his written report. "Things aren't as bad as they seem. I've been busy. It's all here in my report."

The Boss snatched the report, his smile now a snarl, and scanned the first page. "You got Preacher that information about who set him up," he said finally, "but you aren't doing enough with it. Get Preacher to start thinking about revenge. You understand?"

Sean nodded, making a note on the legal pad that was in his portfolio.

The Boss turned to the next page of the report. "The groundwork you're doing with that Natalie is interesting. She's the typical, been-done-in-by-a-bad-man desperate single woman, which makes her an easy target, like most single women. Send them a decent-looking guy with some cash in his pockets and we can get them to believe he's the second coming of His Son. Keep letting her think Dante is what He wants for her. Don't let her see him for what he really is until it's too late."

Sean made another note. "Got it, sir."

The Boss flipped another page and then he slammed his fist down on his desk. "What do you think you're doing by letting that Barnard have prayer time with Luther? Luther is nothing but trouble. Always going around praying for people. I've been trying for years to shake his faith and nothing works."

"I didn't know," Sean said.

"You didn't need to know so you can't use that as an excuse. You should never give those Christians time to pray. Let them talk themselves silly, but don't let them pray. We want Barnard's marriage to crash and burn, and here you are letting him pray with Luther. I'm not even going to talk about Preacher. He's praying when he gets up, when he goes to bed, and all through the day. How do you expect our negative thoughts and lies to have any impact if he's praying all the time?" The Boss rocked his head from side to side as he studied Sean. "Tell me that."

"I'll rectify the situation," Sean said. "I promise you."

The Boss eyed him skeptically. "Your promises don't mean squat to me. You must have me confused with Him. He's the one who gives second, third, and fourth chances, not me. Maybe we should end this now and send you to Third Hades. You don't have what it takes."

"I do have what it takes," Sean declared, feeling sweat beading on his brow but not daring to wipe it off. "I can win Preacher back and get you the collateral damage you want."

The Boss stared at him for what seemed like hours, but was probably only minutes. "Make it happen, Jones." He tossed Sean's report in the wastebasket next to his desk. "Now get out."

Thoroughly soaked with his own sweat, Sean headed for the door. He opened it, and then turned back and said, "I won't let you down, sir."

The Boss snorted. "You've already let me down. Now get out of here and stir up some conflict and confusion in Preacher's life before I have to stir up some in yours."

CHAPTER 6

Preacher entered the vestibule of Faith Community on Sunday with a heavy heart. He'd spent the previous night alone because Tanya had taken the boys to visit her mother. He wasn't upset because Tanya had gone; he was upset because she hadn't told him she and the boys planned to stay overnight. He'd only been home a few days and he missed his boys. He didn't like them being away from him. It was too soon.

Tanya had tried to explain her reasons and Preacher had to accept that she had some valid points. Her mother had never liked him and now that he had some clarity about his life, he knew he couldn't really blame her. After he'd become a Christian, he'd written her of the change in his life but she had returned his letter unopened. He'd have to visit her soon to let her see that he was a new person, though he felt it was going to take more than one trip to convince her.

He shook off his sad thoughts as he slid into a pew about midway down the sanctuary. He'd wanted the boys and Tanya with him this morning, but that was not to be and he had to accept it. There was always next Sunday, he told himself.

"There you are."

Preacher turned at Barnard's voice and saw his friend striding toward him. "Good to see you, man," Barnard said. "I'm glad you could make it."

Preacher stood up and greeted Barnard with a loose man hug. "I'm glad, too. You know I had to spend my first Sunday in God's house. There's no other place I'd rather be."

"Did you bring Tanya and the boys?"

Preacher shook his head. "It's a long story, man," he said. "I'd rather not talk about it now."

"No problem," Barnard said. "Praying is always better than talking and that's what we'll do this morning. Since you're by yourself, how about Serena and I join you?"

Preacher nodded. Though he dreaded his first meeting with Serena, he thought he was prepared to see her. What he had done to her still weighed heavily on him.

"All right then," Barnard said. "Hold tight here while I find Serena. She's probably with my sister somewhere. I'll track them down. I want you to meet both of them."

Preacher watched Barnard stride out of the sanctuary in search of his family and then he sat back down. "Prepare Serena's heart to see me, Lord," he prayed.

"Preacher?"

Preacher looked up into the most gorgeous set of brown eyes he'd ever seen. "Yes?"

She extended a slim hand. "Welcome. I'm Natalie, Barnard's sister. He's told me a lot about you."

Preacher stood and took her hand. "He's told me a lot about you, too, Natalie. Thank you for your work in the prison ministry. It's important work, but I'm sure you already know that."

"Thanks," she said, but he sensed she was uneasy with the praise. "I hear that your transition is going smoothly."

Preacher wasn't sure *smoothly* was an accurate description but he didn't bother to correct her. "I'm blessed," was all he said.

"Aren't we all," she agreed. She pointed to the space where he had been sitting. "Sit back down," she said. "And if it's okay, I'll sit with you. Barnard's gone to find Serena and I need to see her before service starts."

"That's fine," Preacher said, moving over so she could sit. "I'd appreciate the company."

"Barnard tells me you have two children."

"Yes, boys. Mack is four and Jake is six. Do you have kids?"

She shook her head and lifted her bare ring finger. "Not married."

She smiled but Preacher could detect sadness in her. He wondered why such a pretty woman was not married, but he knew it wasn't his place to ask. He thought about his relationship with Tanya. "Marriage isn't always a prerequisite for children."

"I know," she said, "I want children, but I've never wanted to be a single parent. I'm learning that all things come in God's timing."

Again, Preacher detected an underlying sadness. "Well, I didn't exactly do things God's way, but I'm working on it."

"What do you mean?"

"My kids' mother and I are planning to get married soon."

"Good for you," she said. "You'll have to bring her and your kids next time. We have a strong couples' ministry and the kids will love Children's Church. We even offer preschool and after-school programs through our Children's Center. Oh yes, and the pastor does premarital counseling."

Preacher smiled. "Are you sure you're not a plant to help visitors learn about all the services and programs in the church?"

"Sorry," Natalie said. "I get carried away. This is a great church. Barnard and I moved here about seven years ago when our father was incarcerated at Jackson, and the people have been wonderful to us. I'm sure you and your family will find a home here."

"If everybody is as nice as you and Barnard, I'm sure we'll fit right in."

Natalie responded but Preacher couldn't stay focused on what she was saying because he was distracted by a familiar voice—Serena's. He turned his head toward the sound and their eyes met briefly before Serena lowered her gaze. "Don't let my little sister talk your ear off," Barnard said as he leaned in to give his sister a kiss on the cheek. "I'm teasing," he told her when she bristled at him.

"You'd better be," Natalie said. "I've done a good job of keeping you company, haven't I, Preacher?"

"A very good job," Preacher said.

"Well, you've met one woman in my life. Now it's time for you to meet my better half." Barnard reached behind him to bring Serena to the forefront. "Serena, this is Preacher. Preacher, this is my wife, Serena."

"Hello, Preacher," Serena said as if they were meeting for the first time. "It's nice to meet you. Welcome to Faith Community."

"Nice to meet you, too, Serena." Preacher hated lying to Barnard but the plea in Serena's eyes made him go along with her. He owed her that much, but they needed to talk. Soon. He'd hurt her in the past, and if possible, he would never hurt her again. But he knew the lies couldn't continue. They would only lead to more pain for all of them, especially Barnard.

"Now you've met both the women in my life. What do you think?"

Preacher grinned. "How'd you get so lucky?"

"Good answer," Natalie said to Preacher. Then she punched her brother's shoulder. "What kind of question was that?"

"Look who's talking." Barnard rubbed his shoulder before turning to Preacher. "Did she even let you get a word in edgewise?"

Natalie glanced at Preacher, her eyes daring him to agree with Barnard. "I think we'd better change the subject," Preacher said.

Natalie smiled. "I knew I was going to like you," she told him.

"Nat," a male voice called, interrupting their banter.

Preacher watched Natalie's eyes brighten as she turned to the man who'd called to her. She waved him over and pressed a kiss on his cheek. "I've been waiting for you," she told him.

"I didn't know I was late," the man said, looking into her eyes.

She reached for his hand and pulled him into their circle. "Everybody, I'd like you to meet Dante Griggs."

Barnard extended his hand. "Good to see you again, Dante," he said. He inclined his head towards Serena. "This is my wife, Serena." After the two greeted each other with a handshake, Barnard introduced Dante to Preacher and they also shook hands. "Dante is one of the owners of Circle Autos," Barnard told them. "I met with him and his partner the other day to discuss their possible involvement in our jobs program." He looked at Dante. "I hope you've been thinking about it."

"A lot," he said. He smiled at Natalie. "I don't know who's more persistent," he told her. "You or your brother."

"Told you," Natalie said. "We Jenkinses are a single-minded bunch."

Dante smiled at her. "As long as there's room in your mind for a few other things, it's okay with me."

"No, you two are not flirting right here in the church," Barnard teased. "Dante, do I need to have the big brother talk with you?"

Dante's face sobered. "Anytime man, anytime."

With those words, Preacher understood the seriousness of the relationship between Dante and Natalie. Though he'd only just met Barnard's sister, he liked her and hoped this Dante was worthy of her.

The worship leaders came to the front of the church, ending the group's banter, and they took their seats. Preacher immersed himself in the worship, thinking about all that God had done for him. Surely, he was the most blessed man in the entire congregation. By the time the minister came to the pulpit, tears were already streaming down his cheeks.

"The scripture for the morning," Pastor Thomas began, "is one that's very familiar to most of us, First Corinthians, chapter 6, verses 14 through 15. If you brought your Bibles, I want you to turn there with me. I'm sure many of you know the scripture by heart, but I want you to turn there anyway."

Preacher wiped his eyes and opened his Bible. He was very familiar with the "unequally yoked" scripture.

"I'm going to read from the New Living Translation," Pastor Thomas said, "so there may be a few different words in the version you're using. Rest assured, the words may be different but the meaning is the same. Say Amen if you've found the scripture." After a chorus of amens from the congregation, Pastor Thomas read, "'Don't team up with those who are unbelievers. How can goodness be a partner with wickedness? How can light live with darkness? What harmony can there be between Christ and the Devil? How can a believer be a partner with an unbeliever?'"

Preacher settled in to listen to the sermon. Barnard had showed him this passage soon after he'd become a Christian to give Preacher an opportunity to look at his relationship with Tanya from a scriptural perspective. Given the life he and Tanya had lived, Preacher considered another passage in the same book more fitting, the one that talked about the believing spouse being able to save the unbelieving spouse. Right now, he and Tanya were not walking on the same path, but Preacher believed God could use his life to show Tanya what it really meant to be a Christian. He believed it with all his heart.

"Girl, you're turning into a real heathen."

Tanya heard her mother's call right before she felt the bedcovers whipped away from her body. She opened one eye, saw Maylene standing over her with her hands propped on her hips, and quickly closed her eye again before pulling the covers back up. "Please, Momma. Not this morning."

Maylene pulled the covers back again. "'Please, Momma' nothing. I know I raised you better than this, Tanya. Lying in bed on Sunday morning. You're becoming more trifling every day. Now get up."

Tanya buried her head facedown in one of her pillows. There was a time she had liked going to church but that all ended when Maylene decided that she and the pastor's son would make a fine couple. Odd as it was, Maylene was the first person to make Tanya feel like nothing more than a piece of meat. Maylene had put her daughter on the market to be the pastor's daughter-in-law, and everybody at Mt. Nebo had known it. Tanya had felt sorrier for Dexter, the pastor's homely son, than she'd felt for herself.

"Hiding your head is not going to solve anything, Tanya. You know you need to get up."

Tanya flopped over on her back. "I'm a grown woman, Momma. I think I can decide when I want to go to church."

"Grown my foot," Maylene said. "You're acting worse than the boys. I don't have this kind of trouble getting them ready for church." She stared down at Tanya, shaking her head. "But then they didn't stay out all night."

"I wasn't out all night," Tanya mumbled. *Maybe half the night,* she told herself. But then, she'd needed a break from the stress of dealing with Preacher and his issues. She'd deliberately misled him into thinking that she and the boys would be back home last night, when her plans all along had been to leave the boys with her mother and spend the night clubbing. It had been a long time since she'd gone out by herself looking to have fun. And she'd found it.

"Tell that to Wilford."

"Preacher is not the boss of me, Momma," she said, all the while knowing she didn't dare tell Preacher what she'd been up to. All he needed to know was that she and the boys had spent the night at her mother's. "I do what I want, go where I want."

Maylene shook her head. "Big talk now, but tonight you're going right back to that drug dealer."

"It's my home. I picked it out. I decorated it. Why should I leave?"

Maylene sat down on the side of the bed. "For once in your life, Tanya, will you use your head for something other than a hat rack? You're right. That is your house. No judge in Georgia would make you and those boys leave, but they'd sure make Wilford leave. Put him out, Tanya, so you can move on with your life."

Tanya rolled over and faced away from her mother. "Not again. I'm not having this conversation again." She pulled a pillow over her head.

Maylene sighed. "You're throwing your life away, Tanya. You've already wasted enough years on Wilford. Pastor Green's son has always been sweet on you and I bet he's still interested. You know he's still not married."

"And I know why," Tanya muttered into her pillow.

"Don't believe that gossip. There's nothing wrong with Dexter Junior," Maylene said. "There are plenty of women after him. He's the one being picky. You know, one day he's gonna have his own church, maybe even Mt. Nebo once his father retires. You could do a lot worse, Tanya." She sighed again. "But then I don't have to tell you that. Look at the men you've picked. First, that no-talent basketball-playing T.J. and then the drug-dealing Wilford. At the rate you're going, you might as well go straight to the prison and pick out your next man."

Tanya turned over and faced her mother. She didn't like it when Maylene hit close to the truth. T.J. had been a bad pick, but how was she to know his knee was going to go out on him? He'd been a hot prospect when he was drafted. Another reason T.J. had been a bad pick was that he turned violent when he got a little drink in him and started comparing the life he could have had as an NBA star with the life he did have as someone slipping out of the league altogether. Preacher had been a welcome change after all that drama. "Why are you so concerned, Momma?"

"I'm worried about you and the boys, especially the boys."

Tanya rolled her eyes. "Right." She had a feeling Maylene was more concerned about herself and how Preacher's new financial situation was going to affect her.

"What does that mean?" Maylene wanted to know.

"Nothing, Momma," Tanya said. "Just leave me alone so I can get some sleep."

"You're really not going to church?"

Tanya shook her head into her pillow.

"You don't have to be embarrassed," Maylene said in a soothing voice that surprised Tanya. "The talk will die down as soon as you leave Wilford. That's why you should have left him as soon as he was arrested. The longer you stay with him, the more people are going to think that you knew all along."

Tanya turned back over and faced her mother. "I did know."

"Don't be ignorant. People don't have to know that."

"Like they don't have to know that Preacher and I are living together?"

Maylene waved off that comment. "Please. You aren't the only one at Mt. Nebo shacking up, or whatever your generation calls it. As long as you don't flaunt your situation, nobody's going to say anything. People understand how things are today."

"Okay, Momma, whatever you say."

Maylene finally stood up. "I say you ought to go to church, but since you won't listen to good advice, I hope you'll get up and have dinner ready for us when we get back." With those words and without waiting for an answer, Maylene turned and left the room.

Serena could feel the heat of Preacher's eyes on her. She knew he hadn't liked having to lie about knowing her, but this wasn't the way she wanted Barnard to find out. How thick her lies had become in such a short time! How was she going to get herself out of it? Help me, Lord, she pleaded silently. Please help me to tell Barnard the truth. She glanced up at her husband, and despite the problems between them, the smile he gave her told her how much he loved her. She squeezed his hand in hers, willing him to feel her love, and leaned closer to him. He put his arms around her shoulders and hugged her close.

"You all right?" he whispered.

She nodded against his shoulder, unable to give voice to another lie. She stayed tucked against her husband's side for the duration of the sermon, reliving the past and undoing her mistakes in her mind. When the service was over, Barnard asked again, "Sure you're okay?"

She smiled at him. "Fine," she said.

"I don't feel like cooking," he said. "Let's take everybody out. Are you up for it?"

Though Serena didn't look forward to sharing a meal with Preacher, she couldn't very well change her story and say she didn't feel up to going out. "Why not?" she said, hoping Preacher would turn them down. She knew he would be as uncomfortable as she was.

She watched as Barnard asked Preacher.

"Let me check and see if Tanya and the kids are back," Preacher answered, disappointing Serena. He pulled out his cell phone and moved over to a quiet corner so he could talk.

"You two are going with us, right?" Serena asked Natalie and Dante. The more people at the table the less likely she'd have to talk to Preacher.

Natalie shook her head. "Dante already made plans," she said. "But we should get together for dinner one evening. Let's talk about it next week."

"Sounds good to me," Serena said. She leaned forward and hugged her sister-in-law. "Enjoy yourself," she said. Then she turned to Dante. "It was nice meeting you. Don't be a stranger."

"I don't plan to be," Dante said, taking Natalie's hand in his. "I know a good thing when I see it. Natalie's very special to me and I hope to be around for a long time."

"Then we definitely have to get together," Barnard interjected. "Man-to-man."

"Oh, please, Barnard." Natalie rolled her eyes and tugged on Dante's hand, pulling him away from her family. "I'll see you all later."

Serena watched the couple as they left the church hand in hand. She could see what attracted Natalie to Dante: good looks and an easy charm. Unfortunately, she could also see what attracted Dante to her: her openness and innocence.

"So what do you think?" Barnard asked.

"I don't think he's right for Natalie."

Barnard chuckled. "Okay, mother hen, tell me why."

Serena eyed him. "Did you see that watch?"

Barnard whistled. "How could I miss it? How do the kids say it—man's got the bling-bling."

Serena smiled and then she leaned up and kissed him on the cheek.

"What's that for?" he asked.

"For being you."

Before Barnard could respond, Preacher returned. "Tanya and the kids are at her mother's, so if the offer still stands, lunch would be great."

They quickly made their way out of the church and to their cars. Preacher drove his own car, following Serena and Barnard. They reached the restaurant and, in short time, they were seated in a quiet booth, Serena and Barnard on one side, Preacher on the other.

"I'm hungry," Barnard said. "What about you?" he asked Preacher.

"Man, I'm always hungry. Good food may end up being my downfall."

Barnard chuckled, but Serena could only muster a smile. "We'll have to have you and your family over one weekend. I grill a mean steak and I'm not too bad with ribs, either. Tell him, Serena."

"He's a good cook," Serena said. "Much better than I am."

Barnard winked. "I told you."

Serena looked at her husband. "You told him what?"

Preacher chuckled. "I warned you, man."

The ringing of Barnard's cell phone saved him from Serena's interrogation. He leaned forward and pulled the phone out of his pocket. Looking at the caller ID, he said, "I need to take this." He excused himself from the table, leaving Serena alone with Preacher.

"It's been a long time," Preacher said.

"Not long enough."

"I want to apologize—" Preacher began.

Serena glanced over in the direction Barnard had gone. "Not now, Preacher."

"Then when?" Preacher asked. "I can't keep lying to Barnard. *We* can't keep lying to Barnard."

"And you want to tell him what?" she accused.

"I want to tell him we knew each other."

"In the biblical sense, you mean?" She shook her head. "It would hurt him."

"It was a long time ago, Serena," Preacher reasoned. "Barnard's a good man. He won't hold your past against you."

Barnard returned before Serena could respond. He didn't sit, but stood looking down at them. "I have to leave. That was Wayne. He needs some papers that I have at home."

"Then we'll go," Serena said, reaching for her purse.

Barnard pressed his hand against her shoulder, keeping her seated. "No, you and Preacher go ahead and eat. It'll only take a few minutes. Wayne's going to meet me at the house and I'll drive straight back." He pressed a kiss on Serena's forehead. "I'll be back before you miss me," he said. "Besides, this will give you and Preacher a chance to get to know each other." Barnard lifted his eyes to Preacher. "She's my most precious asset, man. Take care of her while I'm gone."

Preacher nodded. "I'll do my best."

"Get the prime rib," Barnard suggested, backing away. "It's excellent."

The waitress came to take their orders just as Barnard was leaving. Serena took as long as she could with her selection, wishing that she could prolong the task until Barnard returned.

"What do you recommend?" she asked the waitress, after Preacher had placed his order.

"The prime rib is always good, and I like the salmon."

Serena pretended to think about it. "How's the rib eye?" she asked. She and the waitress went back and forth for about five minutes before she made her selection. "And a glass of iced tea, unsweetened," she added.

"She deserves a big tip," Preacher said, causing Serena to look directly at him for the first time since Barnard had left them alone. "The smile she wore when she came to the table was genuine," he explained. "The one she wore when she left was pasted on. You wore her out with your questions."

"I couldn't decide what I wanted." She picked up a pink packet of sweetener and twisted it between her fingers.

"Right."

"What does that mean?"

"Nothing," Preacher said, lowering his voice. "I'm sorry, Serena."

"Sorry for what?"

"For everything," he said. "I tried to explain it to you in the letter. Didn't you read it?"

Did she read it? She couldn't get the words out of her mind. "I read it."

"I understand if you're not ready to forgive me, but I'm so sorry for everything I put you through, for the pain I caused you."

"Words, Preacher," she said. "Talking is easy."

"Tell me what you want me to do," he pleaded. "Tell me and I'll do it."

"Get out of our lives, Preacher," she said. "That's what you can do."

Preacher slumped back against the booth. "Anything but that, Serena. You know my probation is contingent on my participation in the jobs program. There's no way I can get out of your life. Barnard's my sponsor."

Serena smirked. "Like I said, words are easy. You asked and now I've told you." She leaned toward him. "Can't you see that it's no good for either of us? Barnard's going to be crushed when he finds out. You'll be a constant reminder to him."

"Because I'm a constant to reminder to you?"

She nodded. "Yes."

"And none of those memories are good?"

Serena gave a harsh laugh. "What was good about it? I was a naive girl who thought the town bad boy was in love with her. I gave up too much with you, Preacher. It hurts to remember how much."

"I'm sorry," he said again.

"You may be sorry, but it doesn't help. I have to live with what I did. You don't."

Preacher shook her head. "Oh, but I do. I live with it, Serena."

She smirked again.

"Okay, I admit that I didn't think too much of it at the time. I didn't want kids. I didn't want to be married. I didn't want to be tied down."

"I, I, I," Serena interjected. "It was all about you." She thumped her chest with her forefinger. "What about me?"

Preacher sighed. "You're right. It was all about me. I'm sorry for that. If I could go back and relive that time, I promise you I'd do it differently but I can't. And I grieve, Serena," he said. "I grieve for our child."

Serena shook her head. "Don't," she said. "Don't talk about it. I don't want to talk about it. I can't."

Preacher leaned back against the booth and Serena closed her eyes to keep her tears at bay. Their baby was dead and it was Preacher's fault. He'd encouraged her to have the abortion, demanded it really. He'd driven her to the clinic and, after the procedure was over, he'd driven her back home. It had been the first time he'd come to her house. Because she knew her parents wouldn't have approved of their relationship, they'd kept it secret. It had been an exciting time for the normally straitlaced Serena. Nobody would have ever guessed that she was seeing Preacher. She only dated boys who shared her Christian beliefs, boys who came to her house and met her parents. But Preacher, with his grandma's Bible, had been different. She'd met him at the mall, of all places. He'd been a charmer them. And it hadn't taken long for him to charm her. She often wondered how she'd been so gullible.

She kept her eyes closed and her mouth shut until the waitress brought their food. She and Preacher ate in silence, the past looming between them.

CHAPTER 7

The morning service replayed itself in Natalie's mind, starting with her conversation with Preacher and ending with Pastor Thomas's scripture reading. The love in Preacher's voice when he spoke of his kids made her think of Benjamin and the horrible way he'd kept the news of his son hidden for two years. Then Pastor Thomas had preached about being unequally yoked and she'd thought about the question Serena had asked her about Dante's spirituality.

"I hope your silence doesn't mean you're getting tired of me," Dante teased Natalie. They were seated at an outdoor restaurant on downtown Atlanta's Peachtree Street.

Her thinking disturbed, she looked over at Dante. "Sorry," she said. "What did you say?"

Dante chuckled. "I know I'm losing my touch now."

Natalie smiled. "No, really," she said. "I have a lot on my mind."

"I'm a good listener," he told her. "Want to share?"

Natalie wasn't sure what to share. She was about to make something up, when out of the corner of her eye, she saw a man she readily recognized striding toward their table. Beyond him, she glimpsed his soon-to-be wife hiding behind a menu. She turned her focus back to Dante, hoping against hope the man wouldn't stop at their table.

"Hello, Natalie," an alto voice that was as familiar to her as her own said.

She glared up into those dark, almost black, eyes she had once loved, saw his wide smile and deliberately did not return his greeting. How could he? How could he walk up to her as though nothing had happened between them?

His smile faltered a bit. "I saw you over here and I wanted to say hello."

When she didn't speak, Dante jumped in. "Dante Griggs," he said, extending his hand. "I'm a friend of Natalie's."

"Benjamin Towles," he said. "I used to be a friend of Natalie's." He inclined his head toward the table where the woman was sitting. "I saw you sitting over here and I thought I'd say hello."

"Well," Dante said, "maybe that wasn't a good idea. If you'll excuse us, Natalie and I are trying to decide what to order."

"Oh," Benjamin said, looking bewildered. "I'll go then."

"Good idea," Dante said with a smirk. When Benjamin was gone, he looked at Natalie and said, "Old boyfriend?"

"You could say that."

He eyed her closely. "I take it the relationship didn't end well."

Now that was the understatement of the decade. Natalie would have laughed if she didn't hurt so much. "No, it didn't."

Dante reached across the table, covered her hand with his, and squeezed. "I'm sorry," he said. "The man was a fool to let you go."

She looked up at him. "Yes, he was, wasn't he?"

He nodded. "Given that his loss is my gain, I can't help but feel a little sorry for the brother. His coming over here like that makes me think he's beginning to realize what he lost. Should I be concerned?"

Natalie shook her head. "No way. There's nothing left between Benjamin and me. Whatever feelings I had for him died a long time ago and I'm not sure he ever had feelings for me."

"He did," Dante said with certainty.

"How do you know?"

"A man knows these things. I could tell by the look in the brother's eyes. He regrets losing you. Why'd you dump him—another woman?"

"You could say that." She looked directly at Dante. "He was engaged to me but having sex with her." She inclined her head to the table Benjamin shared with Moesha.

Dante looked stunned for a moment and then he laughed riotously.

"What's so funny?" Natalie asked.

When Dante stopped laughing, he said, "No wonder the brother looked so pitiful coming over here. He picked her over you? He must be crazy."

Natalie felt a calmness and self-confidence settle over her. Being with Dante was right. He gave her a strong sense of self-worth. Benjamin hadn't wanted her, but Dante did. And Dante saw her value; Benjamin had thought her stupid.

"The man is a fool, Natalie. He had some nerve coming over here like that. I shouldn't have been nice to him."

Natalie chuckled. "You weren't exactly nice, Dante," she said. "You practically ordered him to leave us alone."

"Yeah," Dante said, "but I didn't hit him."

Now Natalie laughed. "You're good for me," she said.

"Keep reminding yourself of that and we'll do well together."

Natalie thought again about Pastor Thomas's sermon. Maybe she and Dante were more equally yoked than it looked on the surface. So what if he wasn't into organized Christianity as much as she was. He had a good heart, and a good heart had to come from God. Besides, she wasn't into organized Christianity as much now as she had been before the relationship fiasco with Benjamin. She had experienced a brutal truth with him: going to church does not make one a Christian. She bet Dante had a better chance of getting into heaven than Benjamin did. "You know what I want to do?" she asked Dante. "I want to forget they're here and enjoy our time together. Benjamin is of no interest to me and no threat to you."

Dante lifted his glass of white wine. "Your wish is my command."

"You've been awfully quiet today," Barnard said to Serena as they changed their clothes upon returning home from their meal with Preacher. "You sure you're okay?"

"I'm fine," she said. "A little tired."

"I think it's more than that," he said.

She turned to him. Dressed only in her slip, she said, "What?"

"I think it's more than that. You don't like Preacher, do you?"

She turned away. "It's not that," she said. "He's all right."

Barnard came to her and placed his hands on her bare shoulders. His touch both warmed her and made her ashamed. She stepped away.

Barnard sighed. "Something's wrong," he said. "Talk to me."

Her back to him, Serena closed her eyes. "You're worrying for no reason. Everything's fine."

He went to her again. Placing his hand on her shoulder, he turned her to face him. "Are you sure it's not Preacher? I know you don't approve of his old lifestyle, but I think he's sincere in wanting to follow the Lord and our support will mean a lot. He's going to need all the help he can get to keep from turning back to his old life."

"Why us?" she finally asked. "Aren't there other families out there who can befriend him and his fiancé? I really think they'd be better off with a couple with children."

Barnard dropped his hands. "We could be a couple with children if you'd change your attitude about adoption."

Serena refused to be baited into their age-old argument. Barnard didn't know how hard it was for her to think about adopting a baby. The thought of holding another woman's baby, of knowing another woman had the courage to have her baby with the hope that someone else would take care of it, reminded her of her own decision. She knew the doctors hadn't found anything physically wrong with her, yet she couldn't help but believe her inability to conceive was God's punishment for her aborting her first child. "I can't argue about this today, Barnard."

"Who's arguing? I'm talking."

Serena pulled on a pair of Capri sweats and a light shirt. "Well, I can't talk right now," she said. "I'm going to take a run. Clear my head."

"Wait. I'll go with you."

She shook her head. "I need some alone time, Barnard. I won't be gone long."

"You can't run away from this."

"I'm not running away. I'm going for a run."

As she reached the door, Barnard said, "Don't go."

She pressed her forehead against the cool oak door. "I need to get out."

He came up behind her, wrapped his arms around her waist, and rested his chin against the top of her head. "And I need to be with you. We're pulling away from each other too much, and I don't like it. I don't like what it's doing to us. We used to be best friends and lovers as well as husband and wife. We were one in every sense of the word. I don't feel that now."

The past came back to bite me, and you got caught in it, she thought, but she couldn't force the words through her lips. She thought she'd dealt with the past, but Barnard's talk of babies and adoption followed by Preacher's reentry into their lives brought it all back.

"Serena?" Barnard said.

Her name on his lips brought her thoughts back to the present. "You think I like the way things are between us?" she asked, turning to face him. She placed her hand against his cheek. "I don't like it, but I don't know how to fix it." *Or I don't have the courage to fix it.*

"Going running won't help."

"Neither will arguing about it."

"What about counseling then? We have to do something."

Serena knew counseling wouldn't help. Been there, done that, years ago. "Please, let's not do this. Not now."

"Okay," Barnard said. "For today, let's call a truce. Let's not think about those things that separate us. No talk of Preacher or of babies. It's just you and me."

Preacher and babies, the two thoughts were intricately linked in her mind. "Think you can do that?" she asked.

He pressed a kiss against her lips. "I know I can. How about you?"

She wrapped her arms around his waist and held on tight, wanting more than anything to push away the demons that separated them. "I love you so much that it scares me sometimes."

He pulled back and looked at her. "You have nothing to fear with me. I'll never hurt you. Don't you know how much I love you?"

She bit back tears. "I'm afraid that one day you'll stop," she whispered, holding him tighter.

"I won't," he said, even as the concerns Luther had expressed about his marriage filled his mind.

"I love you," she said again, still holding tight to him.

"Show me," he encouraged, backing toward the bed with her in his arms. When his knees hit the bed, he fell back with her on top of him. He pushed her hair away from her face. "I do love you," he said.

She tried, but that was the problem. She shouldn't have to try so hard. He didn't know what was worse: no lovemaking or dutiful lovemaking. Both left him feeling empty.

Preacher speed-dialed Tanya's cell phone number again when he reached his home and saw her car was not in the garage. He was beginning to get upset. He'd been calling her since he left the restaurant, and she hadn't picked up her phone. Calls to her mother's house went unanswered, leaving Preacher clueless as to where they were. Tanya finally answered on the fifth ring. "Where have you been?" he asked. "I've been calling you for the last half hour."

"Hello to you, too, Preacher," she said. "Momma and I took the boys to see some kids' flick. 'Bout bored me to death, but they wanted to see it. I couldn't very well keep my cell on during the movie, now could I?"

Preacher didn't even suggest that she could have kept it on

vibrate, which she used to do back in the day when she didn't want to take a chance on missing a call from him. It seemed those days were long gone. "When will you and the boys be home?" he asked.

"We're going to get a bite to eat first. We should be there in a couple of hours."

"Why don't I drive over and join you."

"There's no need for that," she said. "By the time you get here, we'll be finished anyway. I'll see you in a couple of hours. You can wait that long, can't you? Now if you have romantic plans for the two of us, I could put a rush on it."

Preacher couldn't help but smile. Tanya was nothing, if not persistent. "Just get home soon," he said. "I miss you and the boys."

"I know," she said. "See you soon."

Preacher clicked off the cell phone. He looked at the empty house before him and knew he didn't want to go in because he didn't want to be alone with his thoughts. He was a man with woman problems, three women to be exact: Tanya, Loretta, and Serena, and he had no idea how he was going to handle them. Tanya was totally out of hand, treating him like he wasn't even there and had no say-so in their lives. Loretta couldn't take no for an answer and Serena wanted him to disappear. He'd known he'd have challenges when he got out of prison, but he had no idea the first ones to surface would all involve women. He guessed his player days were catching up with him.

When he looked at his relationship with each woman, he knew in his heart he owed something to each of them. He'd strung Tanya along with the promise of marriage for more than six years. To be honest, he hadn't really planned to marry her. He'd only given her the ring to shut her up and to keep her from aborting Jake. He owed her. He'd been Loretta's only family for as long as he could remember. He'd taught her to lean on him, taught her that her life revolved around him. And now that he wanted out of her orbit, she wouldn't let go. At least, not easily. He owed her. And Serena. Lord, Serena. He'd taken an innocent girl and made her a woman before her time. And when she'd gotten pregnant, he'd turned his back on her. He owed her. He owed them all and he had no idea how he was going to repay them.

Knowing he wasn't going to come up with any answers today, he backed up the car and headed out with no particular destination in mind. Even though he missed his boys, he took great satisfaction in being able to drive down the familiar streets taking in the old and the new.

After driving around for about an hour, he got the idea of driving by Circle Autos and taking a look at some of the cars. He thought he might get an idea of how much cash he could expect to get from those money pits Tanya had bought. Ten minutes later, he pulled into the lot. It was closed, of course, so he was free to roam. He whistled at some of the sticker prices, realizing costs had certainly gone up in the short time he was in prison. He also saw a few new body styles. The new Chrysler really got his attention. She was a beaut! Now this car better suited the lifestyle that he and Tanya lived than did that Benz and Porsche she had blown money on. He hoped he'd be able to convince her of that. But even if he couldn't, keeping those cars wasn't an option. Simply put: they couldn't afford them.

Preacher checked his watch and then looked around for a few more minutes before getting back in his car and heading home. Tanya still wasn't back but he expected her any minute so he entered the main house instead of going to his apartment. To pass the time, he went into the den, turned on the computer, and surfed the Web, looking for used-car prices. In a short time, he found a site that gave resale prices for used cars. He was pleased to see he was even able to print out a price sheet to tape to the car window. He quickly printed one for both the Benz and the Porsche. Looking at them, he knew they'd be great conversation starters for him and Tanya. He smirked. Make that argument starters.

That done, he headed up the stairs, and since he was in the house alone, he took some time to browse the bedroom he had once shared with Tanya. The bathroom was the same, and so was her closet. Well, almost the same. He didn't think it was possible but she had more clothes than when he'd left. He shook his head. Now she took up her space and the space that used to be his. How could one woman buy so much, much less wear it?

He glanced at the bed, and again, the memories flooded him. On a whim, he took a seat on the side that had been his and bounced a bit, telling himself he was only comparing the mattress to the mattress in his apartment. Tanya's was definitely better. He checked his watch again and then he stretched out, just for a minute. He yawned, closed his eyes, and was soon asleep.

He slept and he dreamed. In his dream, he and Tanya were married and happy. She'd come to share his faith and they were finally one. No longer was he living above the garage and sleeping alone. Now he was sleeping with his wife. And their loving was so much better than it had been in the past.

"Wake up, sleepyhead," Tanya's silky voice whispered.

Preacher's eyes fluttered open and he saw her standing before him clad in nothing but her bare loveliness. She was even more beautiful than he remembered.

"You were waiting for me, weren't you, Preacher boy?" she purred as she slipped in next to him. "I've been waiting for you, too," she said, pulling his mouth to hers.

"I love you, Tanya," he whispered before losing himself in her kiss.

"I love you, too, Preacher," she whispered back. "And I love what you do to me."

Her softness in his arms coupled with his long-term celibacy made their celebration of love that much more explosive. Loving her was wonderful, holding her close afterward was even better. Preacher closed his eyes, fighting back reality, but his eyelids fluttered open.

"I knew you couldn't hold out against me," Tanya said, looking down at him.

Preacher blinked a few times. "Tanya?"

She grinned. "Who did you think it was?"

Preacher pushed her away and sat up in the bed. "This shouldn't have happened."

"I'm not complaining," Tanya said. She lay back, her hands folded under her head, and winked at him. "I guess you do still like women."

Preacher closed his eyes as the realization of what he had done, had wanted to do, and had enjoyed doing, washed over him. *Forgive me, Lord.*

"Please don't tell me you're feeling guilty," she said.

"I wanted to wait until we were married, Tanya. I wanted to show you and the Lord that much respect."

She leaned up on her knees and kissed his ear. "Hey, you can disrespect me like that anytime."

Disappointed in himself, he pushed her away. "Stop it, Tanya."

"I think it's too late for that now, Preacher. As the old folks say, the horse is already out of the barn."

As Tanya laughed at her own joke, Preacher reached around the bed for his clothes and hastily tugged them on. "Forgive me, Lord," he muttered. "I didn't mean to."

Tanya laughed harder. "Sure did seem like you meant it to me. I'm not too sure God's going to fall for that excuse. You might want to come up with something else." She snapped her fingers. "I've got it. How about 'The devil made me do it'?" She fell back on the bed, laughing at her own wit.

Preacher found nothing funny. Dressed, he slipped into his shoes.

"Where are you going?" Tanya asked. "You're not being much of a gentleman if you're going to leave without saying thank you or good-bye or something."

Preacher couldn't even look at her, his guilt was so strong. "I'm going to see the boys," he said, heading for door.

When he pulled it open, she said, "They're not here."

He turned to face her. "What do you mean they're not here? Where are they?"

Tanya lay back in the bed. "They're at my mother's."

"What?"

"You heard me. They're at my mother's. She keeps them for me."

"What are you talking about? I want my kids at home. You know that. Why did you leave them at your mother's?"

"Because I have to work, Preacher," she explained. "And I can't afford a sitter. We can't afford a sitter."

"Work? You? Since when?"

"Since my man became unable to support me."

He strode back to the bed and stared down at her. "What are you talking about? Where are you working and when did this start?"

"I'm back in the salon every day," Tanya said. "Somebody had to bring money into this house. Since you couldn't, Loretta and I had to step up. You'd better be glad you have hardworking women in your life. Some women would have left you when you got locked up, but not me and Loretta. We stuck by you. And how do you show your appreciation? You kick Loretta to the curb and you pooh-pooh everything I've done. From the cars to the job to the boys to my wanting to love you. Well, I'm doing the best I can do. We all are. Too bad you're too perfect to see it."

Preacher dropped down on the side of the bed. "I'm not perfect, and I'm not pretending to be. But there are some things that I know are right and some things I know aren't."

"And what happened in this bed between you and me is not right? I give myself to you, to show you how much I care, and you take it and then you throw it back in my face. How do you think that makes me feel?"

Preacher thought he saw tears in Tanya's eyes, but he couldn't be sure. She was such a player and an actress that he found it hard to believe her words were sincere. "I'm not throwing anything back in your face. I just wish you would work with me instead of against me."

"Yeah, right. What you mean is that I should do what you tell me to do. Well, that's never been me and it's never going to be."

Maybe she was right, Preacher thought. She really hadn't changed; he had. And now he expected her to fall into line with his change. "I want the boys back home," he said. "We can take care of them."

"How? You'll be working and I'm working. How are we going to take care of them? "

Preacher didn't have an answer. "I want them home."

Tanya folded her arms across her chest. "You can want them home all you want, but until you can put some dollars on the table to pay for their child care while we work, they stay at my mother's. Thank God, she's willing to keep them. She gets joy out of it, always has, so I don't see any reason to change things now."

Preacher didn't like Tanya's defiant attitude and he searched for the words to put her in her place. "Look," he said, seizing upon the one thing he had going for him, "we'd have the money if we got rid of those cars. They're too expensive. We're putting them up for sale tomorrow and we're going to get our kids."

The look Tanya gave him told him that she didn't appreciate his command. "You can sell the Benz but you're not selling my Porsche."

"We're selling them both and you're getting something less expensive. You never should have bought them in the first place. What were you thinking?"

"I was thinking I was about to marry a man on the move and I ended up with a jailbird. That's what I was thinking."

Preacher took a deep breath. "Tomorrow the boys come home and tomorrow the cars go up for sale. You can get something less expensive, but those cars go tomorrow." He turned and headed for the door.

"I hate you," she said, flinging a pillow at him. "I wish you'd stayed in prison."

Preacher ducked. Then he forced himself to leave the room before he said something he'd regret. "Tomorrow," he said. "My boys come home tomorrow."

CHAPTER 8

Feeling guilty about his inability to resist Tanya for even a week, Preacher endured a restless night. When he got up the next morning, he knew he had to take charge of his household situation and he knew where he had to start. After taking a quick shower and a few minutes for his morning meditation, he headed out to get his boys. He didn't bother letting Tanya know his plans for fear she'd call her mother. An unprepared Maylene would be easier to deal with.

He pulled into his mother-in-law's driveway about thirty minutes after leaving home. He got out of the car, and surveyed his surroundings. Maylene had done a good job keeping the place up. The yard was alive with colorful flowers and the lawn was immaculate. Yes, Maylene had transitioned well from her apartment in Perry Homes, one of the oldest and most dangerous housing projects in Atlanta, to her four-bedroom ranch in a middle-class

South DeKalb neighborhood. Preacher knew Maylene was living better than she'd ever lived, and Maylene knew it, too. She'd never admit it though. Just as she'd never admit that it was "drug money" that bought the house, the furnishings, and the car she drove. She told herself the money Tanya gave her came from the salons she and Tanya ran. What a joke that was! The money that started those salons was the same drug money that bought the house.

He rang the bell and waited. Maylene peeped out the side-lights, frowned, and then pulled open the door. Instead of inviting him in, she stepped out.

"What are you doing here?" she asked, in the same tone of disdain she'd always used with him.

"Good morning, Ms. Maylene," he said.

"Don't play games with me, Wilford," she said. Since she learned of his drug-dealing ways, she'd refused to call him Preacher. "I want to know what you're doing here."

So much for good manners, Preacher thought. "I'm here to get my boys."

"Those boys aren't going anywhere."

Preacher prayed for strength. "They're my boys and they're coming home with me."

Maylene folded her arms across her stomach. "What does Tanya have to say about this? She's their mother and she left them here with me. God knows, they don't need to be with you. There's no telling the kind of people you'll have around those boys. You're not fit to be a father."

Preacher took a deep breath. "That may have been true at one time, but it's not true anymore. I've changed, Ms. Maylene. I've decided to live my life for God."

Ms. Maylene spat. "Please. Everybody who goes to prison finds God. Who you trying to fool, boy? I wasn't born yesterday."

"I did find God," Preacher said. "My life has changed."

"Tell that to your probation officer, but I know better. Jailhouse conversions are a dime a dozen, Wilford. First, you go around calling yourself Preacher and doing every evil thing a person can think of. And now you're talking about a conversion. Boy, you better be glad God doesn't strike you dead."

Preacher gave up. There was no explaining anything to Maylene. "I want to get my boys," he repeated. "Are they up?"

"They're eating breakfast," she said.

Preacher moved around her to enter the house but she caught him by the sleeve. He looked down at her hand on his arm and then back up at her eyes. "Don't forget who paid for this house," he told her, hating to go there, but seeing no other way.

Maylene dropped her hand from his arm. "You're no good for those boys. Can't you see that? Do you want them to end up the way you did?"

"That's exactly what I don't want, Ms. Maylene. That's one reason I changed my life. I know the way I was living was leading me to prison or a coffin. I thank God it was prison. I don't care whether you believe me or not, but I'm going to get my boys and I'm taking them home. I need them and they need me."

"Don't be selfish, Wilford," Maylene said. "Leave the boys here. I've taken care of them most of their lives, even before you went to prison. Neither you nor Tanya ever had time for them."

"That was then," Preacher said. "Things are different now. They're my boys. I love them and I want them with me."

"But—"

"There's nothing you can say. I'm taking them home."

Ms. Maylene moved aside, out of his way. "Go ahead, then. You're going to do what you want anyway, you always have."

Preacher stepped into the house and called to his boys. He heard the patter of their feet before he saw them. "Daddy! Daddy!" they said, and then both of them launched themselves into his arms. Preacher fell back on the floor on his behind and held them in his arms. Nobody was going to keep him from his kids. Nobody.

Preacher wasn't surprised that the Porsche was no longer in the garage when he and the boys returned home. Tanya was out but he doubted she was at work. She was probably with one of her girlfriends, spending more money that she didn't have. Well, he was going to deal with one of her expenditures this morning. He turned to his boys. "How'd you two like to help Daddy wash Mommy's car?"

"Yeah," they said. Preacher grinned and they went to work. When they finished, the vehicle was clean and the boys were soaked. To extend their fun, he turned the hose on them and let them play in the water. When they were good and soaked as well as good and tired, he tossed big towels to both of them and had them dry off a bit. Then he took them upstairs and dumped them both in the bathtub. While they continued their play in the bath, he went looking for the title to the SUV. He found it on the top shelf of Tanya's closet, in the metal box where she kept most of her important papers. Keeping track of important paperwork was a habit he had forced upon her, and to his relief, she'd kept at it. Title in hand, he went to the computer and printed out two copies of the used vehicle price sheets he'd found yesterday. He stacked the printouts on Tanya's dresser and went to get his boys out of the tub.

Once the boys were clean and dressed, Preacher took them back outside and let them tape the price sheets to the passenger-side windows. "Good job, men," he told them when they finished, giving each a pat on the head. "Now we've got to go sell this baby."

With the boys in car seats in back, Preacher drove to Circle Autos. He entered the dealership, the boys trailing after him. "I'm Preacher Winters," he said to the well-groomed salesman who greeted them at the door. No doubt the guy had gotten a glance at the Benz and saw Preacher as a good prospect. "I'm here to see Dante Griggs. He's expecting me."

The salesman looked disappointed as he turned and led them to the bullpen in the middle of the floor, where he had the man sitting there page Dante. Preacher and the boys roamed the showroom while they waited. "Which car do you like best, boys?"

The boys scrambled from one car to the next.

"That one," Mack said, pointing at a Ford Escort.

"Not that one." Jake pointed to a Ford Expedition. "This one. I want this truck."

Before Preacher could pick sides, Dante joined them. He extended his hand. "Good to see you again." He looked down at the boys. "And who are these little men?"

Preacher introduced the boys. Mack, a little shy, hid behind Preacher's legs, but Jake imitated his father and extended his hand for a shake. Dante chuckled and shook Jake's hand. Preacher knew then that Dante had sold a lot of cars in his day. He had no doubt the man could sell about anything he wanted to sell. Making nice with the kids was straight out of Car Sales 101.

Finished with the kids, Dante looked back up at Preacher. "What can I do for you three men today?"

"I brought in the car I told you about yesterday," he said. "Thought you'd give me an estimate on it."

"Let's see it," Dante said.

Preacher and the boys led Dante to the car. Dante whistled. "This is a beaut. How old?"

"Less than two years," Preacher said. "Less than ten thousand miles."

Dante strolled around the car. When he came back to Preacher, he said, "You'd better be glad it's a Benz or you'd lose a lot of money on this. You're in luck though because the Benz SUV is on our 'most wanted' list. You may get that asking price you have on the price sheet."

"You really think so?"

Dante nodded. "We have a used lot a couple of miles down the road." He reached in his pocket and pulled out a card. After scribbling on it, he handed it to Preacher. "Show them this card and they'll give you their best deal."

"Just like that?" Preacher asked.

Dante nodded. "It's a Benz, man, and this is Atlanta. It'll probably be sold before you get back home."

Preacher laughed. "Maybe I should have put a sign on it and parked it in my front yard."

"Not a good idea," Dante said. "Just because a lot of people want it doesn't mean they can pay for it. You'd get a lot of people stopping by your house who were nothing but lookers." He clapped Preacher on the back. "No, your best bet is to leave the sales to the professionals. Don't worry. We'll give you a good deal, better than you'll get anywhere."

Preacher wasn't sure he believed Dante. Why would this guy give him such a good deal? He didn't even know him.

"Hey," Dante said, "you're good friends with Natalie's brother and I'm trying to make a good impression on Natalie. I'm going to see that you're treated right. Trust me."

Preacher grinned. "I'll trust you," he said. "Do me wrong and I'll tell Natalie."

Dante chuckled. "I sorta expected that."

Tanya sat in the restaurant that housed Loretta's office and grinned at Maurice even though she wasn't interested in him. She just wanted to get back at Preacher. When she'd arrived home from work, her Benz had been missing from the garage along with the title that she stored in her closet. Preacher had made good on his word and sold her Benz. That was bad enough, but he'd gone through her personal papers to get what he needed. For her, this was the beginning of the end.

"I can't believe Preacher lets you out all by yourself," Maurice said. "If you were my woman, looking like you do, I don't think I'd let you go anywhere without me."

Maurice was fooling himself if he entertained any notions of having a woman like her, but Tanya let him dream. "With a man like you," she teased, "maybe a woman wouldn't want to go out by herself."

Maurice grinned, flashing his gold grill. "So, Preacher lost a step when he was in the joint?"

There was a bit too much satisfaction in Maurice's voice. While Tanya gave herself permission to talk about Preacher, she didn't appreciate other people doing it. When they put him down, they were putting her down, since she was still technically his woman. "Nothing wrong with my man's steps," she said. "A man like Preacher doesn't have to track a woman to make her come home. She wants to go." With a flip of her hair, she blew Maurice off and headed to the back of the restaurant to Loretta's office.

She remembered a time when a thug like Maurice wouldn't have had the nerve to speak to her, Preacher's woman, but word of Preacher's conversion had spread fast and far. At the smell of weakness, the sharks had come out in full force, ready to take Preacher's woman and his business. Loretta had kept both safe for him. Tanya couldn't help but admire her longtime combatant for the way she'd handled everything. She'd quickly shown that she intended to keep what she and Preacher had built, even if Preacher no longer wanted it. Word on the street had always been that she was the brawn of the team, while Preacher was the brains. Loretta had proven she was both.

"It's about time you made it back here," Loretta said, when Tanya entered her office. "You're really going low if you're flirting with Maurice."

"Every man needs a dream," Tanya said, sitting in the leather chair in front of the desk from which Loretta ruled her empire. Some people might think she was a simple bookkeeper who rented a back office in this restaurant, but her real work was managing the books, and now the business, of the drug enterprise she and her brother had run together.

"And some end up with a nightmare," Loretta retorted. "Speaking of which, what's up with you and Preacher?"

"He sold the Benz today."

"You can't be surprised by that. You know as well as I do that he never would have allowed you to buy that Benz if he'd been there." She lifted a brow. "That Porsche is gonna be next."

Tanya pouted. "Over my dead body. He'd better not even think about it."

Loretta just stared at Tanya. "You're a piece of work," she said. "Other than selling your Benz what else is Preacher doing?"

"He went to church on Sunday."

She frowned. "That figures. He's determined to see this God thing through. I think he's being stubborn. I could strangle him."

Tanya grinned. "Well, he wasn't thinking about God or church Sunday night."

"What do you mean?"

Tanya cooed at Loretta. "What do you think I mean?"

"Preacher slept with you?"

"Please," Tanya said. "Don't sound so surprised. It was only a matter of time. I knew it and Preacher knew it. Preacher has never been able to resist me and no religious conversion was going to lessen his desire for what I have to offer." She looked up at Loretta. "You should have known that."

"What I know is that Preacher is a fool when it comes to you. So that's it? Preacher slept with you."

"That's a lot. Preacher was making all these speeches about how he wanted to honor God and be celibate until we got married. Well, we see who got honored and I don't think it was God. Girl, Preacher's not going to be able to stick with this religious goo-goo. He's a passionate man—about everything."

"You may be right," Loretta reluctantly agreed.

"There's no maybe in it. You know I'm right. Little by little, Preacher will turn around. He probably doesn't realize it but he's already falling away from his newly found faith."

"By sleeping with you, you mean?"

"That, and him selling the Benz, too."

Loretta folded her arms across her chest. "Yeah, right, Tanya, I must have missed that commandment about not selling thy girlfriend's car."

Tanya smiled. "What about 'Thou shalt not steal' and 'Thou shalt not lie?' Well, Preacher either lied or stole or both when he sold my car."

"And how do you figure that, Ms. Moses?"

Tanya laughed. "I don't have to be Moses to figure out that

Preacher had to forge my name on the title in order to sell the Benz." At the light of understanding that dawned in Loretta's eyes, Tanya added, "What? You thought I signed it over to him? You've got to be kidding me."

Loretta dropped her folded arms. "Forgive me, Tanya, I forgot for a moment who I was dealing with."

"I'm not exactly stupid, you know," Tanya said. "Preacher is going to realize the straight-and-narrow life is not for him and I'm going to help him by pointing out how big a hypocrite he is. It won't be long before he sees the light, as the church folks say. We just have to put up with him until he does." She cast a wary glance at Loretta. "It's going to be hard to do, though, with our limited income and all."

Loretta rolled her eyes. "How much do you want?" she asked.

"I need to put those kids in day care," Tanya said, hating that Loretta could read her so well. She brushed off her pique. Loretta was paying her for a service—reining Preacher back in—and she was providing that service.

"I thought your mother was keeping them."

"Preacher was up first thing this morning to go get them. He was angry last night when I told him I'd left them with Momma."

"I can't believe you were surprised."

"Look, Preacher can't expect me to sit at home all day."

"You used to."

"That was when we had money. Now I have to work. I can't stay at home and take care of those kids."

"You're going to put them in camp and day care," Loretta said. "You're not going to be taking care of anybody but yourself."

"You know what I mean."

"Yeah, that's the sad part. I do." She opened her checkbook. "How much do you need?"

Tanya gave a figure that caused Loretta to lift a brow in her direction. "Now who's dreaming?" She scribbled a figure on the check, signed it, and handed it to Tanya. "That's all you get. You bring Preacher back into the fold and you may get more."

Tanya took the check, frowned a bit at the amount. "Do I get a bonus if I get him back within the next six months?"

Loretta couldn't believe the gall of Tanya. "No, you don't get a bonus. What do you think this is—the NBA?"

Tanya stood. "I'm following your lead, Loretta. You've got a reputation for being a tough businesswoman. I want to build my own reputation."

Loretta leaned across the desk toward Tanya. "Don't mock me, Tanya."

Tanya lifted her hands in defense. "I'm not mocking you," she said. "I'm complimenting you. You're doing business in a man's world and holding your own. If what you did were legal, you'd be businesswoman of the year, an example to young black women everywhere."

Loretta laughed. "You know you're full of it, Tanya."

CHAPTER 9

After Preacher put his boys to bed, he went back downstairs to wait for Tanya. He needed to talk to her again about selling the cars and whatever else she'd bought when he'd been away. He'd thought that sleeping with her was his low point, but when he found himself about to forge her name on the title to the Benz so he could sell it, he knew he was headed down the wrong road. "Forgive me, Lord," he said, his eyes closed. "And please help me to be an example to Tanya and the boys. I've gone so wrong in such a short while, but please don't let my mistakes keep them, especially Tanya, from seeing that You've changed my life."

"Is that all you do?"

Preacher snapped his eyes open at the sound of Tanya's words. "I should be doing more of it," he said. He wanted to ask where she'd been, but knowing the question would lead to a fight, he asked instead, "How are you?"

Tanya stepped out of her heels and walked toward him. "Tense," she said. When she stood directly in front of him, she asked, "Want to help me relax?"

Preacher stood and moved away from her. Though his heart knew what she was offering was not his to take, his body didn't seem to care. "That's not going to happen again, Tanya, not until we're married."

She dropped down in the chair, a smug grin on her face. "If you say so."

He could tell by the tone of her voice that she didn't believe him. She thought she had him. "We need to talk," he said, reminding himself why he'd waited up for her.

"So talk."

"About the Benz and Porsche."

She stared up at him. "What about them?"

"I need you to sign the title to the Benz so I can sell it."

She laughed. "Why didn't you sign my name yourself? That's what I thought you'd done when I came home earlier this afternoon. I was surprised but pleased to see the Benz back in the garage tonight."

"I thought about forging your name," he admitted, "but then the Holy Spirit stopped me."

"Right," Tanya muttered.

Preacher pretended he didn't hear her. "The vehicles are in your name, which makes them yours to sell or not sell. So it's your decision, Tanya. You either want to contribute to making this relationship and this family work or you don't."

"Don't put this on me, Preacher," she said. "You're the one who's not upholding his end of the bargain."

He shook his head. "That's not true. If I hadn't been in prison, you never would have bought either of those vehicles. It was wrong for you to buy them and you know it."

"I don't know any such thing. You weren't here and I needed something."

He walked over and knelt down in front of her. "Well, I'm here now, and I want to be here for you and the boys. I want that more than anything, but I need you to work with me, not against me."

She looked directly into his eyes. "I'm not going to become some religious fanatic and I'm not going to live like a pauper."

"I don't expect you to do either, but I do expect you to be rational." When she looked away, he lifted his hand to her chin and turned her face to his. "This is not about me, and it's not about you. It's about us as a family. I want to marry you, Tanya. I want you, me, and the boys to be a family. You used to want that, too."

"Times change and so do people," Tanya murmured.

"Change can be good," he said. "All I'm asking is that you give me a chance."

"I can't make you any promises, Preacher," she said. "You knew the kind of woman I was when you met me. You can't expect me to change now."

Though Tanya's words hurt, Preacher accepted them. He wanted her to change, knew she could change, but she didn't know it. At least not yet. He wasn't ready to give up on her, though. If God could change him, then He could change Tanya. "Are you going to sign the title?" he asked.

"If I do, will you stay out of my personal papers? I don't like that you went though my files, Preacher. I don't think that was very Christian of you."

Preacher moved back away from her. "You're right," he said. "I was wrong to go through your papers. I won't do it again."

Tanya nodded. "Okay then."

"You'll sign the title?"

She nodded.

"To both the Benz and the Porsche?"

"You're pushing it."

"You can get another car, Tanya, a cheaper one, but the Porsche is unreasonable. You have to see that. You couldn't drive it if I were back in the business and you know it."

Tanya sighed loudly. "All right, already. I'll sign them both over, but you'd better get me something good in return."

Thank you, Lord. He smiled at her. "You can pick it out yourself. We'll make it a family event. You, me, and the boys."

"Yes, the boys. Did you go get them from my mother's?"

He nodded. "They belong here with us."

"So you said."

"And now that we're selling the cars, we have the money for the school and the home day care, if that's what you want."

Tanya stood, yawning. "Do we have to decide tonight? I'm tired."

Preacher shook his head. "I have a few days before I start work, so I'll keep them for the rest of the week, but we have to decide soon."

"Okay," Tanya said. "Are you sleeping with me tonight?"

"You know the answer to that, Tanya."

She brushed a kiss against his cheek as she walked past him. "Your loss," she whispered, and then she picked up her shoes and headed up the stairs to her bedroom.

Preacher dropped down in the chair she'd vacated. "Thank you, Lord," he whispered. "Thank you, Lord." As he continued to sit there, a thought occurred to him and he frowned. *Hadn't*

Tanya given in a bit too easily? He pushed the thought away with a shake of his head, deciding to trust that Tanya's easy compliance was God at work.

After Tanya headed to the salon the next morning, Preacher packed up the boys and got started on the full day ahead of them. First, they would head over to the church to meet with Barnard, maybe surprise Tanya by taking her out to lunch, and then meet with Luther later in the day about a business that he thought was a perfect fit for Preacher. After coming clean with Tanya last night, Preacher was again encouraged about the future. As he pulled into the church parking lot he still felt guilty for his sexual encounter with Tanya, but he tried not to let it consume him. Barnard pulled up next to him.

"Morning, bro," Barnard said to him, when they were out of their cars. Stooping down to the boys' level, he asked, "And who are these young men?"

Proudly, Preacher introduced his sons. Barnard extended a hand to each of them. "Hello, boys," he said. "Your dad is a good friend of mine and he's told me a lot of good things about you. I'm glad to finally get to meet you in person." He looked up at Preacher. "They look exactly like you."

Preacher beamed, he couldn't help himself. "They do, don't they?"

Barnard laughed as he stood up. "Proud papa, huh?"

Preacher put a hand on each boy's head. "Can't help it, man."

"I understand fully," Barnard said, with what Preacher thought was a tinge of sadness. Before he could pursue it, Barnard added, "I spoke with Natalie about watching the boys in the Children's Center while we talk. If it's okay with you, they can stay with her.

The Center is around the corner from my office. We don't have a school yet," Barnard explained, "but we do have a preschool and daily child care."

Preacher and the boys fell into step with Barnard as he led them to the Children's Center. "I didn't know Natalie worked at the church."

"My sister is a busy woman," Barnard said. "She works with the prison ministry and with the Children's Center, but her real business is the health club she and Serena run together. She's a volunteer in the Center and today happens to be one of the days she works."

"Lucky me," Preacher said.

Barnard chuckled. "Your boys are lucky. I hate to say this about my sister, but she's a pushover where kids are concerned. Once she gets to talking with them and playing, she can't seem to stop."

"I'm going to tell her you said that."

Barnard cut him a quick glance. "You wouldn't dare. Besides, what I meant to say is that she loves kids and she's really good with them."

Preacher laughed. He was still laughing when Barnard opened the door to the Children's Center and Natalie greeted them. "What's so funny?" she asked. Instead of waiting for an answer, she smiled down at the boys and introduced herself. They immediately took to her, or was it the lollipops she offered them? When she took them around the corner and the boys saw the other children and the toys, Preacher knew they'd be okay.

"Would you boys like to stay here with me while your dad and Mister Barnard go have a talk?"

The boys looked up at their father. "Can we, Dad? Can we?"

Preacher smiled down at them. "If you promise to obey Miss Natalie."

"We promise," both boys said.

"Okay, then," he said to them. Then he looked up at Natalie and added, "Thank you."

"No problem at all. You've got a couple of good ones here," she said to him. She winked at the boys. "Come along," she said, "let's join the fun."

Preacher watched as his sons followed Natalie into the circle of children. She introduced them to each of the kids and then suggested they join the little boys playing with trucks.

"You ready?" Barnard asked, forcing Preacher's attention away from his boys.

Preacher nodded and followed Barnard back to his office. After they were settled in chairs in front of Barnard's desk, Barnard asked, "So how's it going?"

Preacher shrugged. "Things are going great, man. A glitch here, a glitch there, but overall I'm encouraged."

Barnard lifted a brow. "Glitch? What happened?"

"What makes you think something happened?"

"This is me you're talking to, Preacher. I know you. So tell me."

"It's Tanya," Preacher finally said.

"You slept with her."

Preacher jerked his eyes up to Barnard. "What makes you think that?"

Barnard looked at him a long moment before asking, "Am I right?"

Preacher nodded. "I don't know how it happened, man."

"I don't believe that," Barnard said. "You were in prison for two years without a woman. I bet you can tell me very clearly what happened. Let's not play games here, Preacher."

Preacher stood and shoved his hands into his pockets. "All right, man," he said. "It happened. I let it happen. I wanted it to happen, and God help me, I enjoyed it. I thought I could handle it, her, myself, but I was wrong." He rubbed his hand down his face. "Boy, was I wrong."

"Yeah, you were," Barnard agreed.

Preacher turned to look at his friend. "You don't sound surprised."

Barnard shrugged. "I'm not."

Preacher sat back down. "Well, I am. I thought God could keep me safe. I thought I trusted Him more than I did."

Barnard shook his head. "Do you remember the story of Jesus going into the wilderness to be tempted by the devil?"

Preacher nodded.

"Well, one of the temptations was for Jesus to toss himself off a mountain to prove that God would send his angels to protect him. That's sorta what you did."

"I don't get it."

"You deliberately put yourself in a situation with all sorts of potential for a bad outcome."

"No, I didn't," Preacher declared.

"Come on, man, at least be honest. You'd been in prison for two years without a woman, and then you move back into the house with the woman who has shared your bed for more than six years and you tell yourself you're not going to sleep with her. I don't know what kind of dream world you were living in. It was only a matter of time. Sure, God gives us an escape every time, but why put yourself in a situation that you know is so full of temptation? It didn't make a lot of sense then and it doesn't make a lot of sense now."

"Fine time to tell me," Preacher said.

"I tried to tell you before you left prison, but you weren't hearing me. You had it all figured out."

"I wanted to be close to my boys," Preacher said in his own defense.

Barnard rested a hand on Preacher's shoulder. "I know you did, man, and I'm not trying to beat you up about it. But I want you to be honest about what happened and why. If you're not honest with yourself, it's going to happen again and again."

Preacher closed his eyes as he accepted the truth of Barnard's words. Yes, he could see it happening again. When he opened his eyes, he asked, "What makes you so smart?"

"I figured out a long time ago that God treats all His children the same. If He's a certain way with me, I figure He's that way with you, too."

"But you're married."

Barnard laughed. "Yes, I know."

"You know what I'm saying."

"I wasn't always married," he said, "and marriage doesn't mean the bedroom problems go away."

Preacher didn't want to hear that Barnard and Serena were having those kinds of problems. It seemed to add to his sin of omission to even probe, but it appeared Barnard wanted—needed—to talk about it. "You and Serena having problems?" Preacher asked, all the while praying the answer was no.

"Let's just say that things could be better."

"I'm sorry, man," Preacher said. "I thought everything was great between you two. You seem so happy together."

"Looks can be deceiving."

Preacher didn't know what to say. Given the huge secret that lay between him and Serena, how could things be great between them? Not knowing what else to do, he placed his hand on Barnard's shoulder. "What can I do, man?" he asked.

"Pray," Barnard said. "Pray that my wife realizes how much I love her."

"I'll pray," Preacher said, feeling like a big hypocrite. His past with Serena loomed before him so large as to be suffocating. He wanted to unburden himself and tell Barnard the truth, but the truth wasn't his alone to share. No, it was his and Serena's. He sighed deeply. He'd tackled Tanya; now he had to tackle Serena. He didn't look forward to it. "Let's pray now," Preacher said.

Barnard lowered his head and began. "Father, we come to you in Jesus' name, thanking you for the life you've given us and asking forgiveness for the many ways we've fallen short of what you want for us. I pray for my brother, Preacher, that you forgive him for his fall and show him how to live godly among Tanya and his boys. If it means moving out, Lord, please give him the courage to do so. Teach us to be grateful for what we have, even as we yearn for more. Take the desires that stem from what we want and turn them into desires for what you want for us. Help us, Lord, to see the difference. We love you, Lord, and we want to do your will. Guide us in your way. Amen."

Preacher cleared his throat, still not as comfortable praying aloud as Barnard was. "Father, I thank you for my brother, Barnard. I thank you for the example of a godly man He has been for me. I pray now for his marriage, Lord, knowing that you already recognize the need. I pray that you bind Barnard and Serena's hearts even closer, that they might experience the full joy of marriage. I pray, too, Father, that one day Tanya and I can have a godly marriage. Help me to be a better example to her. In Jesus' name, Amen."

When Preacher opened his eyes and lifted his head, Barnard said, "We have to get Serena and Tanya together. I think Serena will be a good influence on her."

Preacher didn't doubt that Serena could be a positive influence on Tanya, but he did doubt that his friend's wife wanted to spend time with Preacher's girlfriend. That was asking a bit too much. "I'm not too sure about that," Preacher hedged. "Tanya's not very open to things of God yet. I'm afraid she might feel she's being cornered and I definitely don't want that."

"If you say so, man. Then what about your sister? How are things on that front?"

"Not much better." He thought of Loretta's penchant for revenge and Big Boy's lack of progress in locating the guy G-Money said set him up. He certainly hoped Big Boy found the guy before Loretta did. Unfortunately, there was no way Preacher could share any of those happenings with Barnard.

"Do you think Loretta would like to meet Natalie? They're both single women, about the same age, accomplished. They might hit it off."

Again, Preacher wasn't too sure, since Barnard wasn't aware that Loretta was in the drug business. He'd met Natalie and liked her a lot. He didn't want to chance putting her in an uncomfortable position with his sister. No, if the two women met, he'd have to warn Natalie of his sister's business. It was the least he could do. "Let's not rush it," Preacher said. "I think they're going to need some time." And Preacher knew he needed some time to deal with the secrets that lay between him and Barnard.

"All right, then. Just let me know when. By the way, what plans do you and your boys have for the day?"

Preacher grinned. "We're going to surprise Tanya and take her to lunch, and then I'm taking them with me when I meet Luther this afternoon."

"So Luther's found something for you?"

Preacher nodded. "A funeral home. He's pretty excited about it but I'm not sure." He shook his head. "A funeral home?"

Barnard laughed. "Luther's a wise man. Hear him out. He's never steered me wrong. If he sees you in this business, I'd wager God wants you there. Keep your heart open."

"I'll try, man."

"You're taking the boys with you?"

"No other choice. I promised Tanya I'd care for them this week, so that's what I have to do."

Barnard stood. "Let's talk to Natalie. She may be able to keep them this afternoon."

"I don't want to put her out. She's already helped me out by keeping them for this short time. The entire afternoon would be asking too much."

Barnard waved off his concern. "Don't worry about it. If she can't do it, she'll tell us. Let's go ask her."

Sitting in her lawyer's office, Tanya thought about the lie she'd told to start the day. After having breakfast with Preacher and the boys, she'd headed off to work, or so she'd told Preacher. She'd gone to the salon, all right, but it wasn't to work; it was to make a few phone calls. She wasn't as stupid as her mother, Loretta, and Preacher thought she was. And one day soon they'd find out. Two hours later, here she was, seated in her lawyer's office, listening to the options that lay before her.

"He has no legal claim on any of your assets," Allan Richards explained. "He'd only have a claim if he gets custody of the kids, which is highly unlikely given his criminal record and probation status. I don't see any court awarding him full custody."

"You're sure? He can't touch my money?"

Allan shook his head. "The only money he can touch is the account with his name on it. The other accounts are untouchable.

You took my advice and moved your accounts to a different bank, so I'm assuming you also kept this information from him."

Tanya nodded. Her mother would be proud of the way she'd schemed against Preacher while he was in prison. That is, if Tanya would tell her, which she wouldn't. She had plans for her mother, too. "What about the house in Decatur and the salons?"

"Preacher has no claim on them, either. The house in Decatur is yours, your salon is yours, and you have a fifty-one percent interest in the salon your mother owns." He closed the folder in front of him. "Why are you asking me these questions, Tanya? We've gone over all of this before."

Ignoring him, Tanya asked, "What if Preacher bought into a new business. Would I have any claim on that?"

"It depends on how he finances it and how he sets it up. If he uses funds from your joint account, you might have some legal standing. Of course, it would be better if you or your boys were listed as co-owners. Then again, as long as you have custody of the boys, there's not much Preacher's going to get that's not going to come through your hands first. The child support laws in Georgia are clear. So what's this about, Tanya?"

"Just double-checking my options," she said.

"You have more options than Preacher's leavings. I hope you know that."

Tanya wanted badly to roll her eyes, but she fought the desire. She'd met Allan at some party. He'd pursued her, but she hadn't thought much of it, since men always pursued her. She enjoyed the game, but she hadn't really been interested. In fact, she hadn't really thought that much about him until one of her girlfriends told her he was a hotshot family law attorney. After that, she'd begun to give him enough attention to make him think there might someday be a chance for the two of them. "Preacher is the father of my kids," she reminded him, as she always did, when he pushed for more of a relationship with her. "I have to think of my boys."

"Your concern for your children is admirable, Tanya, but you have to think about yourself. I know your children's happiness is your primary concern, but you have to know that kids are happiest when their parents are happy."

"I know that, Allan," she said, "but it's hard, especially now that Preacher's back. The boys love him so much. I can't bear to separate them. Not now."

"But soon?"

She nodded, hating that begging tone in his voice. "I'm making sure that everything is ready when I make that decision."

"Are you sleeping with him?" Allan asked.

Like it was his business, Tanya thought. "Of course not," she lied. "I told you I'm not interested in him that way. I'm only there for my boys. Preacher understands and accepts the boundaries of our relationship."

"You're a beautiful woman, Tanya," he said. "Preacher would have to be crazy not to be attracted to you."

"Well, he can be as attracted as he wants. He lives in the apartment above the garage and I make sure he stays there. Now, are you going to keep asking me questions or are you taking me to lunch?"

A broad smile spread across Allan's face. He looked like a big dumb dog. "I've reserved a private dining room for us upstairs in the Terrace Restaurant. I'm ready when you are."

She nodded. She could do much worse than Allan, she thought. She might have to start treating him better.

CHAPTER 10

Sean took a covert glance at his watch. It felt as though he'd been sitting in front of the Boss's desk for hours. After his snooty secretary had told him to go in, the Boss had told him to sit and had then gone back to whatever he was working on. It looked like a game of some sort, since the Boss was using joysticks, but he wasn't about to inquire. Since the incident with the iPod, he figured he was better off not knowing. He certainly didn't want to see a visual of Third Hades. Sean glanced at the Boss, then quickly looked away, not wanting to be caught staring.

Given all the Boss wanted him to do, sitting here in the office wasting time didn't seem to be a good use of either of their energies. Of course, Sean would never share that observation with the Boss. The man didn't appreciate advice. He looked in the Boss's direction again when he heard the man clear his throat. He found the Boss leaning back in his chair, arms folded across his stomach, watching him. Sean swallowed.

"Jones, I've been looking at your work, and for the life of me, I don't understand what you're doing."

Sean swallowed. *Here we go again*. "Sir, I'm working on Preacher, his family, and his church friends the way you told me."

"Not the way I told you," the Boss snapped. "I said I wanted results. I don't see results. All I see is a bunch of activity with no payoff."

Sean took a deep breath. "Things are moving along, sir. My plan is working. I got Preacher to have sex with his fiancée," he added with pride.

The Boss turned a hot stare on him. "That was a fiasco," the Boss said. "I can't believe you're stupid enough to brag about it. Getting Preacher to have sex was the easy part, dummy. Our power is in what happens afterward. And what happened next with Preacher? He felt guilty for all of five minutes, confessed to his friend, and then they prayed for forgiveness." The Boss lifted his hands in frustration. "What did we get out of that? Nothing," he answered for himself. "Absolutely nothing."

"But—"

"No, buts," the Boss said. "I thought you understood the power of secrets, Jones. Apparently, I thought wrong. How hard did you work to keep Preacher from confessing to Barnard?"

Sean looked above the Boss's head, unable to meet his eyes. "I'll have another chance," he said, hoping he sounded confident. "The girlfriend is going to keep after him. She'll get him back in bed again. The guilt and shame game will be easier after he falls the second time."

"You may have a point," the Boss said. "I hope so for your own sake. Preacher is looking to me like the worst case of 'almosts' and 'what-ifs' I've seen in a very long time. *What if* he went on a revenge trip to find the person who set him up? He hasn't. He *almost* forged his girlfriend's name on the car titles so he could sell them. *Almost*, but he didn't. You seem to be able to get close, Jones, but you don't seem able to close this deal. I don't know if you can."

"I can," Sean said, wanting to bring up the sex again but resisting the urge. Even if the Boss discounted it, Sean knew it was major. The Boss was just too ornery to give him the credit he deserved on that one. "You'll see the results you're looking for very soon. All I need is a few more days."

The Boss wagged his head from side to side. "I've heard that before. What difference will a few days make anyway? What are you working on?"

"I'm leading Dante and Natalie to the altar and Barnard and Serena to divorce court. And Preacher's going to help me with both. He doesn't know it yet, but he will. After he does, I'll lead him directly back to his sister and her business. I really do have a handle on this situation."

"You'd better," the Boss said. Then he lowered his head and went back to his joysticks. Since he hadn't dismissed him, Sean didn't move. He hoped it didn't take another couple of hours before the Boss let him go.

CHAPTER 11

Preacher headed off alone for a surprise lunch with Tanya. His boys were more than happy to stay at the Center. In fact, they were so happy that Preacher was a little hurt. He would have enjoyed taking them for lunch, but they preferred hot dogs at the Center with the other kids and Miss Natalie. He shook his head. Barnard's sister had done a job on his kids in no time flat.

In short order, he was pulling into the parking lot of Tanya's Curl and Weave. It was the first time he'd seen the place since he'd been out, and it brought back memories of the excitement Maylene had shown the day she'd brought him and Tanya to this place. The salons were all Maylene's idea: Maylene's in southeast Atlanta and Tanya's in Buckhead. Tanya hadn't been too hot on the idea, but she'd gone along with the deal because she would own both shops–sole owner of hers and part-owner of her mother's. Of course, Preacher put up all the money. A grim smile crossed Preacher's face when he considered Maylene's hypocrisy. As much as she derided his old lifestyle, she hadn't hesitated to reap its benefits.

He had to give Maylene credit, though. The business brought in a steady stream of money. At least, it had before he'd left for prison. Preacher knew Maylene worked hard at her shop every day, but Tanya had a manager who did most of the work in hers. Tanya was truly a figurehead, which was why it was hard for him to believe she had turned into this hands-on owner during the time he was in prison.

Preacher felt a bit of trepidation as he reached the entrance to the shop. He realized this visit would be his first to his past since he'd been released. Until today, he'd spent his time at home with Tanya and his kids, or with Barnard and the people from church.

Walking through the door was like stepping back in time. A lot of things had changed but apparently beauty shops weren't one of them. Tanya had stuck with her original blend of silver, black, and white, which made for a pristine look. Wisps of old school R&B floated in the air and mingled with the varied conversations among the customers and stylists. Wanda, the stylist-manager, who'd been there when he was sent up, saw him first.

"Preacher!" she called. "Is that you?" Without waiting for him to answer, she stopped pressing her customer's hair and rushed to him, giving him a big hug. "It's so good to see you."

"It's good to see you, too," he said, stepping back and looking at her. "Still looking good."

She grinned. "And you're not so bad yourself. It looks like you spent some time in the weight room."

He took a quick glance around the room at her reference to his time in prison, self-conscious of his status in the eyes of Tanya's customers. He caught a few whispers and some sly, and not so sly, glances shot his way. He guessed he'd have to get used to the uneasiness he felt. Returning his attention to Wanda, he said, "I had to do something with my time."

"You got that right," she said. "My cousin LeRoy did a hard four at Jackson and I swear that boy blew up like a balloon. First man I ever seen to get fat in prison."

Preacher almost winced at her mention of prison and again his eyes scanned the room to see who may have overheard her. After giving Wanda the chuckle he thought she expected, he asked, "Tanya here?"

Wanda shook her head. "Nah, she's been gone all morning. Said she had to run an errand."

Preacher's disappointment must have shown on his face because Wanda added, "Cut Tanya some slack, Preacher. She had a rough time of it right after you got sent up. You know how some people can be. There was some talk," she said. "The police came around a lot in the beginning."

Preacher remembered that now, but he realized he had pushed those thoughts from his mind. Since the cops knew Tanya was his woman, they had tried very hard to connect her business with his. Fortunately for both him and Tanya, they had agreed to leave her alone on the condition that he turn over all his liquid assets. He'd done it, too. Except for the money that was technically Tanya's, he'd left prison a broke man. He didn't like to think about that because the entire incident left a bad taste in his mouth. He'd feared for his family and he knew that his illegal actions had almost ruined them. He promised himself he'd never put them in that situation again and he meant it. "I'm sorry they involved the shop," he finally said to Wanda. "Thank you for sticking with Tanya. I know she can be a pain sometimes."

Wanda rolled her eyes. "What do you mean sometimes? Tanya's always a pain; I just know to keep my Advil on hand, so she doesn't get to me the way she gets to other folks. Anyway, like I was saying, she held up better than I thought she would in the aftermath. You know, Tanya never struck me as a fighter or someone to depend on for the long haul, but she fooled me. She toughed it out."

Preacher realized Wanda was right. Tanya had endured a lot because of him, so he needed to be more patient with her and her attitude. "Well," he said to Wanda, "so much for my plans for a surprise lunch for Tanya. I should have called her on her cell to find out her schedule."

"Nah, you shouldn't have. A woman likes to be surprised. You'll have to come up with something else."

Preacher nodded. "I guess I will. Anyway, tell her I was by and I'll catch her later this afternoon."

"Will do," Wanda said, backing toward her client. "You take care of yourself, Preacher," she added as he reached the door. "And don't be a stranger."

Preacher went back to his car and tried to reach Tanya on her cell, but she wasn't answering. Her business was probably a trip to a spa somewhere, so he tried not to let his inability to reach her bother him. He didn't want to eat alone and let thoughts of Tanya's whereabouts drive him crazy, so he decided to get fast food at the nearest drive-through and then head over to the funeral home early.

After the nightmare that Sunday had been—starting with the failed lunch with Preacher and ending with a less than satisfactory bout of lovemaking—Serena was happy for the chance to hide out at her gym. The stress of taking a teen's measurements was about all she could take today. She wished Preacher would disappear from her life. She wished Barnard would stop pestering her about adoption. She wished—

"What's the verdict, Miss Serena?"

Serena read the numbers on the measuring tape she'd placed around Bertice's waist. "You're down another inch, girl," she told the teenager, who'd been coming to the gym religiously for the last six months. "You should be proud of yourself."

Bertice's round face lit up in a smile. "I am, Miss Serena," she said. "I can even tell it in my clothes. I've gone down three dress sizes."

"Good for you," Serena said, glad somebody was getting good news. "We're going to have to make you the poster girl for the gym."

Bertice chuckled. Then she sobered. "But I still have so far to go," she said.

"Don't think about the distance, Bertice," she advised the still-chubby girl. "Focus on feeling better and being active. Thinking about how far you have to go is only going to make you depressed."

"You're right," the girl said. "But sometimes it's hard. All the other girls are so skinny and I'm always the biggest one. I'm tired of being the big one. I want to be a normal size like everybody else."

Serena's heart went out to the girl. "I understand, Bertice."

"How could you?" Bertice said. "I bet you've never had a weight problem."

Serena forced a smile for the teen, even though memories of the time during which she'd gained the weight were painful. It had been right after she'd had the abortion, the most difficult time in her life. Why did everything these days seem to go back to that period? She couldn't help but blame Preacher. "Well, you'd lose your money. I was never heavy as a teenager, but there was a time before I finished college that I gained a lot of weight."

The girl's eyes widened. "You did?"

Serena nodded.

"How did you lose it?"

Serena grinned. "The same way you are, exercising and cutting back on the junk food. I felt as awkward as you felt, probably more awkward, since people kept commenting on how much weight I'd gained, like I didn't know it."

"People can be so mean."

Serena rested her forehead against the young girl's. "Yeah, they can be."

"You know," Bertice said, "sometimes I wonder if I'm too fat to even call myself a Christian. I feel like I've let God down. Did you ever feel that way?"

Serena knew the feeling very well, but this wasn't about her. "I did and sometimes I still do. But you know what, Bertice? It's not true. If we all waited until we were perfect to call ourselves Christian, then very few of us would ever get the chance. The Lord is proud of you for what you're doing to get yourself healthy. He's the one who's giving you the desire to make the change and the courage to do the hard work to make it happen. Yes, you may stumble or fall off the plan, but you get right back on it. God doesn't care whether you're fat or thin, but He does care that you're using food the wrong way or if you're not taking care of yourself. He cares because He loves you."

"I know, Miss Serena. Sometimes I just get down on myself."

Don't we all? "Well, that's not God who's telling you to get down on yourself. God is the one who's building you up, who's encouraging you to continue on the path you're on. God is the one who's trying to tell you how beautiful you are in his sight exactly as you are. You aren't making yourself good enough for God with the exercise and all, Bertice. You're only doing your part in keeping the temple in which He resides healthy. No more. No less. Got that?"

Bertice smiled. "Got it."

"Okay, then, now you'd better get started on the machines. Your mom will be here to pick you up in a little while."

Bertice walked away encouraged, but Serena felt like a hypocrite. She could give advice to others about accepting God's love, but she didn't follow her own advice. If she did, her life wouldn't be so messed up now. She wanted to blame Preacher, but there was only so much she could lay at his feet. The lies to Barnard were hers and hers alone and she'd have to deal . . .

"What's got your nose all scrunched up?" a deep baritone voice asked.

Serena turned and saw her husband standing at her side. "What are you doing here?" she asked.

He leaned down and kissed her softly on the lips. "I came by to have lunch with my wife."

She smiled. "That was a sweet idea but you know I can't go out for lunch."

He took her hand and led her to the front of the club. She gasped when she saw the lunch he had laid out for them on the table in the anteroom, the only place men were allowed. He'd stopped at the Chinese restaurant down the block and picked up her favorites. "You shouldn't have," she said, even though she was glad he had. She leaned up and kissed him on the cheek. "I'm such a lucky woman to have you."

Barnard chuckled. "Perfect response," he said, kissing the tip of her nose.

After letting her assistant know where she was going to be,

Serena sat in one of the wicker chairs and he took the one next to her. Following a quick blessing, they dived into the containers.

"This is so good," she said, licking sweet-and-sour sauce from her fingers. "But my customers are going to kill me for eating here."

Barnard dug into his orange chicken. "Tell them it's healthy Chinese."

Serena laughed. "Yeah, right. I'm sure they'll go for that."

He lifted a spoon of fried rice to her lips. "Or you could tell them that I made you eat it."

"Like they'll believe that. Most of them already know you're a softie."

He chuckled. "How's your day, so far?" he asked.

"Typical. Good. Yours?"

"Interesting."

She stopped eating to look at him. "What does that mean?"

"I met with Preacher this morning."

Serena froze at his words. She didn't want to talk about Preacher. "Something happen?"

"Not really." He leaned close to her. "He's still having problems with Tanya. She seduced him."

"Yeah, right," Serena said, before she could stop herself. "It takes two to tango, Barnard. Don't make excuses for Preacher. He's a grown man."

"I know, and that's what I told him. But he had such honorable intentions."

Serena's food felt like it was sticking in her throat. She couldn't put Preacher and honorable in the same sentence. *"Hmmm . . ."*

"We talked about what happened and what he could have done to prevent it."

"Preacher has two kids," she said. "I'm sure he already knew."

Barnard put down his fork. "You really don't like him, do you?"

At that question, Serena knew she'd gone too far. "It's not that I don't like him," she said. "It's more that I don't trust him." At least that was true.

"How can you trust him, when you don't know him and won't give yourself a chance to get to know him? This isn't like you, Serena. Are you sure there isn't something else about him that bothers you? He hasn't been inappropriate or anything, has he?"

Serena shook her head. "No, no," she said, trying to think of a way to extricate herself from the conversation. "It's not that."

"Then what is it?"

Serena knew this was an opportunity to tell Barnard the truth, and she considered doing so for a brief moment, but then decided that this was not the right place. "It's nothing, Barnard."

Barnard didn't look like he believed her, but thankfully he left the topic alone. "I invited him and his fiancée to dinner."

Serena sucked in her breath, almost choking on her egg roll.

"But Preacher declined the offer."

Serena breathed a sigh of relief before taking another bite of her egg roll.

"Something tells me you could be a positive influence on her. Any chance of your dropping by her salon and introducing yourself? Nothing formal, no pressure. Just extend the hand of friendship."

No, Serena thought, *there was no way she could do that.* "If Preacher wants us to leave her alone, I think we should honor his wishes. No use making Tanya even more uncomfortable with his newly found faith."

Barnard popped the tab on one of the cans of diet soda he'd brought. "I don't see how offering friendship can hurt. Preacher is keeping his family too close to him. He needs to let them interact with other Christians so they'll know what Preacher's gotten himself into. Take today for instance. He brought his boys with him to the church, and they spent the morning with Natalie and the other kids in the Children's Center. In fact, they're still there and they're having a ball. Until today, I don't think it ever occurred to Preacher that he could put his kids in day care right there at the church. You know as well as I do that it's the services that first bring many people to church. It could work that way with Preacher and his family if he'd allow more interaction."

Serena knew Barnard was right, and if they were talking about anybody but Preacher she'd be hustling herself right over to Tanya's shop. But given the circumstances, she wasn't sure she could pull it off. "What you're saying makes sense, Barnard. Why don't we pray about it and see where the Lord leads. Maybe Preacher will make a move and we won't have to."

"Okay," Barnard said, "but we can't just let this hang. Preacher needs our help with his family even if he doesn't realize it yet."

Serena nodded. Preacher wasn't the only one who needed help.

Luther, Preacher, and George, a man about Luther's age who was one of the funeral home caretakers, finished their tour of the facilities in about an hour's time. Preacher had no idea of all that went into running the place. While he still wasn't sure if he wanted his life's work to be managing a funeral home, he now had a greater appreciation for the work they did.

"So what do you think?" Luther asked him when they entered the office that Luther had commandeered for himself after purchasing the place a few months back. Apparently, the owner had only sold because his son had no intention of continuing the family business. The way Preacher understood it, the old man was still pretty angry with his son for turning his back on his inheritance.

"It's more interesting than I thought it would be."

Luther chuckled. "I know what you mean. I never thought I'd be into funeral homes, either, but there is a lot of potential here. I'll be honest with you, I have some other businesses you might think you'd like better, but this is the one the Lord has put on my heart for you." He lifted his palm when Preacher tried to interrupt. "Before you say anything, I'm not so arrogant that I think the Lord will put it on my heart and not put it on yours as well. That's why I brought you down here today. I wanted you to see the place, begin to get a feel for it and the people. This is the kind of place that would allow you to dig deep roots into the community, Preacher. Funeral homes have always been, and I believe the good ones will continue to be, a cornerstone of the African American community. These guys perform a service and touch a family in a way that few businesses do. Just think about it."

"I will," Preacher said. "When do I need to make a decision?"

Luther leaned back in his chair. "I'd like to know in a day or so. If you want to give it a try for, say, six months, we can start next week. If you're not interested, we can start looking at other options. How does that sound?"

Preacher nodded. "I can work with that."

"Good," Luther said. He pulled a green folder out of the middle desk drawer. "I had this packet put together for you. It gives you some information on the formal training you need for the mortuary business. Yes, you have to be licensed and to get a license you have to have formal college preparation." He pushed the folder toward Preacher. "It's all in there. Take a look at it and we can talk more when we meet again."

Preacher picked up the folder, opened it, and skimmed its contents. This folder represented his future and the future of his family. He thanked God he'd taken those classes while he was in prison. Otherwise, the idea of going to college would be more daunting than it was. "I'll give it some serious consideration."

"That's all I ask," Luther said, standing up. "If you have any questions, give me a ring. Anytime. Also, if you want to drop by again between now and next week, you're free to do that, too. I'll let George know to give you the run of the place when you're here. Sound good?"

Nodding, Preacher took the hand that was offered him. "Thanks again, Luther. I appreciate the way you've extended yourself to me and the genuine concern you've shown for my future."

"You're welcome," Luther said, "but don't thank me. Thank God. He's watching over both of us."

"Well," Preacher said. "I thank God for you. How's that?"

"Sounds good to me."

With that, the men said their farewells and Preacher left the office. As he strolled to his car, it settled in his spirit that he would try the funeral home for six months the way Luther had suggested. He had nothing to lose by doing so, and if Luther was right about God's hand in this, Preacher didn't want to miss out on a blessing.

"Hey, Preacher, hold up."

Preacher turned at the sound of his name and saw a young man about nineteen or twenty jogging toward him.

"It *is* you," the boy said when he reached Preacher. "I didn't know whether to believe George or not when he told me you were here."

Preacher searched his mind but couldn't place the young man. "And you are?" he asked.

"I'm Patrick Owens," he said. "I've heard a lot about you and I wanted you to know that if you need anything, I'm your man. I've always admired you and the way you handled your business, man, and I want to run with somebody like you, somebody who knows what's what."

Preacher stared at the boy for a long second, but the boy didn't back down. "You know I just got out of prison, right?"

The boy nodded. "It's cool, man. You did two easy. And kept your business running all the while. You're the man, Preacher."

Preacher shook his head. "I'm no longer in the business," he said. "I've left the life."

The boy took a sly glance around. "I know you have to lay low while you're on probation. That's why I wanted you to know that I'm your man. Anything you need done, I'll do. I'll take the risk for you, man. You won't get sent back up if I'm around. I'll take the fall for you."

Preacher's heart ached at the young man's words. This was a line he'd been given many times before and what made it sadder was that it wasn't a line. This young man was ready and willing to turn his life over to Preacher to do whatever he wanted with it. There'd been a time when he'd welcomed this blind loyalty, required it even. Knowing there was no use trying to make this kid believe he was no longer in the business, Preacher asked him, "You work here?"

"Off and on," he said. "One time I thought we were going to be doing business here, but it didn't work out. The old man wouldn't go for it, but now that you're here, we could turn that around. Make this place a distribution and drop center. Do a lot of business. The police would never suspect."

Preacher shook his head. "No business will be done out of here," he stated. "None. Do you hear me?"

"I hear you, man, I was just saying—"

"I know what you're saying and I want to be clear. You tell

everybody who asks exactly what I told you. No business will be done here. Got that?"

The boy practically stood at attention. "I got it," he said. "Whatever you say. I'm with you however you want to roll."

What Preacher wanted to do was roll this boy upside his head, but he knew it would do no good. "Well, right now, I'm rolling home and you ought to roll home, too. You want to hang with me, you have to keep yourself out of trouble. You got that?"

"Got it."

"Good."

Preacher turned to get in his car. "When you coming back?" the boy asked.

Preacher looked over his shoulder. He didn't have much experience in signs, but he knew that meeting this boy was one. "Tomorrow," he told the teen. "I'll be back tomorrow."

CHAPTER 12

Preacher hoped against hope that Barnard was still at the church when he returned there after leaving the funeral home. He wanted to share his excitement about the sign he'd received from God and his resulting enthusiasm about the funeral home gig. He made a beeline to Barnard's office, even before stopping to check in on his kids. That's how eager he was to share his news. Disappointment reigned when he found Barnard's office door closed and he got no response to his knock.

"Man," he said in frustration.

"Something wrong?" Natalie said from behind him.

He turned to her. "Nah, nothing's wrong. In fact, I wanted to talk to Barnard because something is so very right. It's news he'd appreciate."

She smiled at him. "Well, I'm not Barnard, but I like good news as well as he does. How about telling me instead?"

Preacher hesitated for a moment, not really sure of the reason for his reluctance. He brushed off his concern and said, "I think I had a sign from God today."

Natalie tugged on Preacher's hand. "I want details," she told him as she led him to a small room directly to the left of the Children's Center. "Lots of details."

As they passed the Center, he waved in the direction of his sons, who were actively engaged in serious play, but he didn't even get a notice from them. "Guess they're okay without me," he murmured.

Natalie finally got him to a chair and pushed him down in it before sitting herself down in one facing his. "They're fine. Now tell me about this sign of yours."

Preacher began to laugh, a full belly laugh, the first he'd had with an adult in as long as he could remember. Natalie's enthusiasm was refreshing and freeing.

"What's so funny?" she asked. "Was the sign funny?"

Preacher laughed harder, and then forced himself to sober a bit. "You're wonderful. Do you know that? You're absolutely wonderful. Your response to my news couldn't have been better if I'd asked God to plan it for me."

Her smile told him that she understood. "Sometimes we don't have to ask. He just answers. That's the kind of guy He is."

"You're right," he said. "You're so very right."

Natalie slid toward the edge of her chair. "Now gimme those details before I have to hurt you."

Preacher forced himself not to give in to a fresh bout of laughter. Instead he told Natalie about Luther, the funeral home, and Patrick, the teenaged boy he'd met there. "As that kid was talking to me, Natalie," he said, hearing the awe in his own voice, "I knew, I just knew the funeral home was the place God wanted me to be. I was going to give it a try anyway because Luther was so sure it was right for me, but I didn't have to go on Luther's word. God let me know directly."

Natalie placed a hand on his. "I'm so happy for you, Preacher."

"Then you think it was a sign, too?"

Natalie nodded. "I think God gives us physical assurances sometimes, and this was one He gave you. He won't always be as blatant as He was this time, but you'll still be sure it's Him. He has that way about Him. We really do learn to hear His voice."

Now instead of laughing Preacher felt like crying. Tears of joy were building behind his eyes but the man in him forced them back. He couldn't sit there crying like a baby in front of Natalie, could he?

She patted his hand. "It's okay, Preacher. I've never thought tears meant weakness in a man. Actually, I think it shows strength and depth of character for a man to shed tears of joy at what God is doing in His life."

Preacher laid his hand atop hers and they shared a smile. "You know," he said, "I've often wondered, why me? Why did God choose for Barnard's path to cross with mine and why was I ready to hear what he had to say? There are better men than me that God could use, men who have done far less damage to others than I've done. So why me?"

Natalie moved her hand and cupped his chin with it. Looking directly into his eyes, she said, "There's no use asking yourself those questions, Preacher. God chose you because He loves you. He chooses us all because He loves us. It's just that some of us are ready to follow Him and others of us aren't. But make no mistake about it, He's always there choosing."

Preacher placed his hand on top of hers again. "Thanks for reminding me, Natalie. I'm glad you were here today."

She slid back in her chair and he allowed her hand to fall from his face. "I'm glad I was here, too. I get encouragement from hearing what God is doing in other people's lives. Those things remind me that He can work through the trials in my life as well."

"I doubt you even have trials."

She glanced away. "We all have trials, Preacher, and we will as long as we're alive."

Preacher leaned forward and turned her face to his. "I didn't mean to make you sad or discount what you go through."

She shook her head. "I'm not sad," she said, but he didn't fully believe her. "Not now. I'm coming out of a bad time and into a good one. I'm seeing hopeful possibilities again. That's a good thing for me. For a while there, I was afraid to even think about possibilities."

Preacher grinned at her. "Something tells me this good thing has to do with your friend that I met on Sunday."

To his joy, she blushed. "Am I that transparent?"

He shrugged. "It looked serious. On both sides."

"Dante's genuine. With him, what you see is what you get. I like that," she said. "It's what I like about you as well."

He lifted a brow at those words.

She chuckled. "Okay, maybe I draw conclusions about people a bit quickly. But it's true, I do get that vibe from you, that you're not trying to be anything but what you are—a loving parent and husband-to-be, and a man who's truly trying to serve the Lord with his all."

Preacher pushed away thoughts of the contradictions in his life. The way Natalie saw him was the way he wanted to be deep in his heart. He wished Tanya saw him the way that Natalie did. A man could go far with that kind of faith by his side. "I'm trying," he said.

"And you'll be successful," she said. "With God's help we both will."

He squeezed her hand. "From your mouth to God's ears."

There was a relaxed shared silence between them that had Preacher feeling he'd known her for a very long time. It was similar to the feeling he had about Barnard, but different.

"Your boys have had a great time here today," Natalie said, breaking the silence. "Why don't you bring them back tomorrow, or better yet, enroll them for the summer? They'll enjoy themselves and be introduced to some basic Christian teachings at the same time."

"I like the idea," he said, "and I'll talk to Tanya about it tonight."

She nodded. "Why not bring her over and let her see for herself? Once she meets the staff and sees how much the children enjoy themselves, she'll be sold. I know she will."

Preacher couldn't stop the grin that spread across his face. "Are you always this positive?"

"Only when I know I'm right." She winked. "And that's most of the time."

Preacher laughed. "That guy of yours is one lucky dude. I hope he knows what a gem he has in you."

"I think he does," Natalie said confidently. "And I know what a gem I have in him. It goes both ways, which makes it all the better."

"Don't I know it," Preacher said, thinking about his relationship with Tanya. The two of them had a long way to go to reach the level of mutual respect Natalie apparently shared with her guy.

Natalie stood and drew Preacher up with her. "Bring Tanya by the Center tomorrow," she said, as if she knew his thoughts.

"Your kids will make friends and through them, you and Tanya will make friends with other couples in the church." When he didn't immediately respond, she said, "It's a start, Preacher, and you have to start somewhere. Now let's go get your boys. I have a feeling they're going to want to extend their time here."

"And that's bad?"

Natalie chuckled. "Actually, it's funny. Some of my best laughs have come from watching parents trying to drag their kids away from here."

Natalie had been right and Preacher had the headache to prove it. He also had a greater appreciation for the staff at the Children's Center. Not only had his boys begged to stay longer, their new friends had joined in with them. That was too much noise for any one man, so naturally he'd given in to their wishes. The upside was now the boys were tuckered out and getting them down for a nap after they'd gotten home had been pretty easy. He wouldn't let them sleep too long though, or he'd be up all night with them. Ah, the joys of parenting.

He was about to start worrying about Tanya's whereabouts and what he was going to do about dinner when he heard her car pull into the garage. She breezed into the house, kissed him full on the lips, and then stepped back and said, "I heard you came by the shop today to take me to lunch. What a nice idea! You should have called first though. I had a meeting over at Bronner Brothers."

"Bronner Brothers, huh?" Preacher didn't really believe Tanya had a meeting at Bronner Brothers, one of her hair product suppliers, but he decided not to challenge her on it. Besides, he could be wrong. Maybe Wanda was right and Tanya had grown more responsible while he was away. Maybe, but he doubted it. His instincts told him she'd spent the time shopping or out gossiping with her girlfriends. "Well, I hope the meeting went well."

She flashed him her best smile. "Very well." She went to the fridge, pulled out a Coke, and handed him one. She winked. "Don't want to tempt you with alcohol. You might think I was trying to seduce you. Again."

Preacher felt the sting of her words as he followed her into the living room and watched her slip out of her shoes and sink into her favorite chair. "I'm glad your day went well," he said after he was seated on the couch next to her chair.

Undaunted, she asked, "How was yours? Anything new on the business front?"

Preacher felt renewed excitement about what had happened today and began to tell her.

"A funeral home?" she repeated when she heard the words from his mouth. "You've got to be kidding me, Preacher. Not a funeral home."

Since Tanya's reaction was pretty much the same as the one he'd had when he first heard the news, he didn't take exception to it. "Yes, a funeral home. It's a solid business."

Tanya chuckled. "If you mean because people are always dying, then I guess you're right, but where's the glamour in it, Preacher? Funeral directors and their families either drive those big Cadillacs or those big Lincolns. Neither one of them are really my style." She eyed him closely. "You're kidding me, right? You're not really considering investing in a funeral home."

Preacher stood, stuffed his hands in his pockets, and looked out the living room window, away from Tanya. His mind couldn't help but go back to the conversation he'd had with Natalie. He was now doubly glad she'd been there to hear his news and to give some words of encouragement and support. Tanya sure knew how to rain on a man's parade. He turned to her. "It's more than a funeral home, Tanya. It's like a calling. I believe this is the place God wants me to be. I think He wants to use me to bring hope and help to some lives."

Tanya looked up at him. "Uh, it's a funeral home. The only people you're going to see are dead ones." She laughed at her own wit. "Don't tell me you're going all *Sixth Sense* and *Ghost Whisperer* on me. You don't see dead people, do you?"

"You're really funny," Preacher said, hating that she didn't get what he was trying to tell her. He realized then how much it would mean to him if she did.

"Look," she said, "you're praying over everything and everybody and then you come and tell me how God is going to use you to help dead people. What am I supposed to think?"

Preacher took a deep breath. "He's not going to use me to help dead people. It's the living ones, the families of the deceased, the people who work at the funeral home, and the community." He thought about Patrick but decided not to tell Tanya about him. She wouldn't get it and her lack of understanding would only frustrate him.

"Oh," Tanya said. "But still, a funeral home? Why not something like a restaurant or supper club?" Her eyes lit up. "How about a car dealership? Something imported. That way, we'd always have the latest cars. Have you thought about something like that? If you had a BMW or Porsche dealership nobody would question our driving one of those cars. I'm being real, Preacher. I think that's the way to go."

Preacher could only stare at her. How could two people be on such opposite pages, he wondered? How could they ever meet? He didn't see it, but he certainly hoped and prayed it would happen. He had seen today with Natalie what could be between a Christian man and woman and that's what he wanted with Tanya.

"So what do you say?" Tanya asked. "Will you look into a car dealership?"

"The funeral home—"

"I thought you said we were in this together, Preacher. Well, it doesn't look like we're in it together if you make all the decisions by yourself. If you're doing this for the family, then the family ought to have a say. Do you really want your boys growing up around a funeral home? You know most of those funeral directors live right next to the funeral home. Some of them even have their house connected to the funeral home. How creepy is that?"

"I can promise you our home won't be connected to any funeral home," Preacher said, "but I can't promise about the dealership. I'll mention it to my sponsor but I don't hold out any hope. We don't have that kind of cash and without some backing, which we don't have, I don't see us raising it, unless we have more money than you told me we did."

Tanya quickly began shaking her head. "That's all we have, Preacher. Now I'm almost sorry I spent so much if it means we're going into the dead people business. All my girlfriends are going to think that's hilarious." She eyed him. "You don't expect me to start going to a bunch of funerals, do you? You know black is not my best color."

As Preacher listened to Tanya, he tried not to focus on how shallow she sounded, but it was a difficult task. Had she always been like this? If she had, how in the world had he tolerated it? He decided to change the subject. "I found a summer spot for the boys today."

She looked up at him. "You did? Where?"

"The Children's Center at the church I went to on Sunday. I left the boys there today when I went to the funeral home. They had a really good time."

"That's nice," she said, her lack of interest apparent.

"I thought we could both go over there tomorrow so you could see it for yourself. It's a decision we should make together."

She smiled at him. "You are getting the hang of it, aren't you?" she said. "I guess I'd better go see this place. I don't want my boys around some crazy religious fanatics."

Preacher had to bite his tongue to keep from responding to that one. What was the point anyway? "Okay, we'll go over tomorrow and decide. Sound good?"

Tanya placed her empty Coke can on the coffee table. "Works for me. Now what are we gonna do about dinner? I say we take the boys out for pizza."

An exhausted Preacher climbed the steps to his apartment later that night. He, Tanya, and the boys had ended up at Mickey Dee's instead of the pizza place because the boys wanted to play on the gym. Now a McDonald's franchise was a great business venture. That's where the money was.

After entering his apartment, Preacher headed straight for the bathroom. His plans for the evening included a long, hot shower followed by a long, restful night of sleep. A knock at his door put his plans on hold. Who could that be? His first thought was a home inspection by the Department of Probations. That thought was incorrect. He opened the door to find a smiling Loretta.

"What's up, big bro?" she asked, coming in like he had been expecting her. "I caught the boys before they went to sleep. They look more and more like you every day. I guess you don't have to wonder if they're yours."

Preacher rubbed the back of his neck. First Tanya, and now Loretta. What had he done to deserve them both in one day? Thank God for the reprieve he'd had with Natalie. Having no other option, Preacher closed the door and followed his sister to the couch, where she'd already settled in.

"Tanya tells me you've found a business opportunity."

Preacher nodded, wondering how much Tanya had told his sister.

"I know she's spent most of your money, but I can easily get my hands on some more for you, and with no trail back to me."

Preacher began shaking his head.

"Oh, hear me out," Loretta said, "before you break your neck saying no."

"There's nothing you can say that will convince me to take money from you, Loretta. Nothing at all."

Loretta squinted up at him. "You're beginning to sound a little too self-righteous. Isn't there a scripture in that Bible of yours about pride leading to a fall?"

She was close enough, Preacher thought. "I'm not being self-righteous, merely doing what I know is right. Taking money from you would be the same as being back in business with you."

"And that would be so bad?"

Preacher sighed deeply. "We've been through this before, many times. You have to accept my position."

Loretta folded her arms and sank back into the couch. "Go ahead and be that way, if you want. I'm only trying to help. I'm your sister, remember?"

Preacher brushed his hand across his head. "Of course, I remember, 'Retta, don't talk crazy."

She pouted. "Sometimes you act like I'm some stranger, or worse, that I'm some demon trying to corrupt you. I only want to help. I love you, and I love those boys. You're the only family I have."

Preacher sat next to her. "I know you love us and I know you want to help, but the help you want to give me is not the help I need."

Loretta lifted her arms in mock defeat. "So how I am supposed to help you then? What's this business you're going into?"

"Tanya didn't tell you?"

Loretta shook her head. "Miss Motor Mouth held back this time, believe it or not. Surprised me, too. She smiled and said she'd let you tell me, so spill."

"I have an opportunity to buy into a funeral home."

Loretta blinked twice, fast. "What?"

"I have an opportunity to buy into a funeral home."

"You mean funeral home, like with dead people?"

Preacher found this reaction a bit tiring. "Yes, a funeral home with dead people. What other kind is there?"

Loretta started laughing. "First you run a narcotics business and now you want to run a funeral home?" She laughed harder. "Let's see, this could work. If the drugs kill them, you can bury them. Hey, we could even do some joint marketing. I could put a label on my product advertising your services. What do you think?"

Preacher got up from the couch and walked away from his sister. "I think you missed your calling. You should be on tour with Mo'Nique."

Loretta tried to stop laughing. "Oh, okay, don't get all bent out of shape, Preacher. I was only having a little fun. But you have to see how silly this is. Why would you want to go in the funeral home business? It's so, so, dead." She started laughing again.

Preacher could only shake his head. What was he going to do with Loretta and Tanya?

"Okay, Preacher," Loretta said, sobering a bit. "I'll stop with the jokes. I just don't want you to end up in some business that bores you to death. You need something more exciting, something that will have you around the living. You're so good with people. Have you thought about buying a car dealership?"

Preacher eyed her a bit. "Did Tanya put that idea in your head?"

Loretta turned her lips down in a frown. "You're joking, right? Me get ideas from Tanya? You've got to be joking."

Preacher wasn't sure he believed her. What was the likelihood of the two of them coming up with the same idea independent of each other? It was too much of a coincidence. Then again, it was hard for him to imagine the two of them working together on anything.

"Look," Loretta said, "I've got connections at a local dealership and one of the owners may be looking to get out. It would be a nice place for you to land. That would be more your style than some old-fogy funeral home."

"What do you mean you have connections at a local dealership? What have you gotten yourself into, Loretta?"

"Oh, calm down, big brother. Your little sister has been taking care of business while you were away. I saw an opportunity and I took it."

"What kind of opportunity? Stop talking in circles."

"Let's just say I brokered a deal between a group in New York and a group in Miami that included a connection with a local dealership here in Atlanta. Not a lot of risk for us, but a lot of cash."

"I told you we shouldn't get in bed with that New York–Miami crew. How many times did I tell you that? How many times did I turn them down?"

Loretta walked over to him. "It's easy cash."

Preacher looked at her, remembering the times he'd justified his own actions with those same words. "And your grand plan is for me to become part-owner of a dealership that's moving product for the New York–Miami connection. You must really want to see me back in prison."

Loretta recoiled as if he'd hit her. "Don't say that. Don't even think it. You know that's not what I want."

"What else can I think when you put out an idea like that? How can any good come of it?"

"It's a clean operation. Circle Autos has a great reputation. Nobody knows what's going on there."

Preacher's brain stopped working for a moment at the name Circle Autos. "Did you say Circle Autos?"

Loretta nodded. "So you've heard of them, huh? I betcha it was all good, too."

Preacher stared at his sister as Natalie's lovely face flashed through his mind.

CHAPTER 13

Tanya studied the smile tugging at the corners of Preacher's lips as he watched Jake and Mack run ahead of them up the walkway to Faith Community Church. "So you're not upset anymore, huh?"

He glanced in her direction. "Upset?"

She bumped his hip with hers. "Yeah, upset. You haven't spoken more than ten words to me since we left the house. I figured you were upset because it took me so long to get ready."

"Not hardly, Tanya."

She shrugged. "Well, I knew you had no reason to be upset, since I only wanted to look my best for you. This is the first time I'm meeting your church friends and I wanted to make a good impression."

Preacher laughed, shaking his head at her. "You're a trip, Tanya. Since when have you started dressing for me?"

Tanya gave a pretend pout. "I've always tried to look nice for you. You used to appreciate it. You used to compliment me on the way I dressed. You haven't given me one compliment since you've been back."

Preacher stopped walking and turned fully to her. She waited as his gaze traveled from the top of her head, where she'd pulled her hair back off her face in a severe style that she reserved for her few conservative outings, to the multicolored sundress that fit looser than her usual garb, on to her bare legs, to her feet clad in a pair of flat, silver sandals. She had to admit that the shoes were a welcome relief from her normal three-inch heels. Since she knew she looked good, though not as good as she could have looked—she didn't want to scare the church folks—she wanted his appreciation and approval.

"You know you look good, Tanya," he told her as he leaned in to buss her cheek. "You always do."

She smiled at him. "I guess that'll do for a compliment. So if it wasn't my tardiness, what had you all in a twist?"

"A lot on my mind," he said, as they reached the boys at the top of the steps to the church. He pulled open the door so the boys and Tanya could enter. After following them in, he said, "I'm sorry for making you worry."

Tanya frowned. "I wouldn't say I was worried, but I did wonder where your mind was. You haven't exactly been 'Christian Preacher' this morning. I was hoping that maybe my guy was coming back to me."

The twitch in Preacher's jaw told her he didn't like the conclusion she had drawn. "I'm still Christian Preacher, as you put it," he told her, "just got some stuff on my mind. I was thinking about going over to the funeral home after we leave here."

"I thought we were going to look at cars—," she began, but she was cut off as the boys began running ahead of them, calling to a "Miss Natalie." A young woman about her age stooped down and greeted her sons with a hug.

Tanya turned to ask Preacher who the woman was but he had speeded ahead of her. Left with no choice, she picked up her pace, her personal antennae going up, and joined the group.

"So I see you brought them back," Miss Natalie was telling Preacher. "I'm glad you did."

"Just taking your advice," he said with the biggest smile Tanya had seen on his face this morning. As though he'd just remembered her presence, he pulled her to his side and said, "I also brought Tanya with me so she could see the place. Natalie, this is Tanya. Tanya, this is Natalie. She works at the Children's Center."

Natalie beamed at her like she was a rap star or something. "It's so nice to meet you," Natalie said. "Welcome to Faith Community. We're happy to have both you and Preacher."

Tanya couldn't tell if the woman was faking it or not because you really couldn't tell with church people. "Nice to meet you, too," she said. "Preacher has raved about this place and I can see the boys feel really comfortable here." She looked down at her sons, each holding on to one of Natalie's hands. "You like coming here, don't you boys?" she asked.

"Yeah," both boys said.

"Can we go play now?" Jake asked.

Tanya turned to Natalie for an answer.

Natalie stooped down so she was eye level with the boys, still holding their hands. "Do you remember where the Children's Center is?" she asked them. Jake nodded. "Then run along. We'll be there in a while."

Tanya watched her sons scamper off with a bit of envy. How had this woman become so close to her kids so quickly?

"You have great kids," Natalie told her. "You and Preacher should be proud."

"Yes, they're good kids and, like most parents, we like seeing them happy. They seem happy here."

"We try to make everyone feel welcome," Natalie said, "so I'm glad to see our efforts are bearing fruit. How would you like to go on a tour of the facilities and meet some of the workers? I'll show you around." She turned to Preacher again. "You're welcome to join us but it's going to be a repeat of what you saw yesterday."

"I don't mind," Preacher said.

Well, Tanya minded. Preacher and this Natalie were a little too familiar with each other for her comfort. That the woman wasn't wearing a wedding ring only made matters more suspect. "Oh, that's not necessary, Preacher," Tanya said. "You said you wanted to go over to the funeral home this morning. Why don't you go over there now? I'll call you when I'm ready and you can pick me up and then we can head for the car lot." She turned to Natalie. "We have quite a few errands to run today." Then, turning back to Preacher, she added, "How does that sound?"

Preacher looked at Natalie, who nodded, and then back at Tanya. It grated on her that he looked at Natalie first, as if asking permission. "If you're sure?"

"I'm sure, Preacher," she said. "Natalie will look after me. Won't you, Natalie?"

Natalie waved her arms toward Preacher, shooing him away. "I'll take good care of Tanya. You go over to the funeral home so you can get started on your destiny." She turned to Tanya. "Have you been to the funeral home yet?"

Tanya shook her head.

"Well, why don't I give you a ride over there after we finish here. I don't want you to miss out on seeing the place."

Tanya opened her mouth, but Preacher spoke before she did. "How nice of you," he said to Natalie. "But I can pick her up. Like she said, we have some errands to run today."

"Okay, but if you change your mind, my offer's still open."

"Thanks," Preacher said. Then he gave Tanya a hug, whispering in her ear, "Behave." He smiled at Natalie and then he left.

Tanya turned to Natalie. "I didn't think he was ever going to leave."

Natalie chuckled. "It's sorta nice having a protective guy. You've got a good one."

Tanya looked down at her. "So you noticed?"

"Noticed what?" Natalie asked.

"That Preacher's mine."

Natalie's eyes widened, like she was surprised. "I don't think I understand what you mean."

"Oh, but I think you do," Tanya said, not buying her surprise. "Are you and Preacher becoming friends?"

"I'd like to think so," Natalie said.

"Well, I have a problem with men in committed relationships having friendships with single women. Nothing but a disaster waiting to happen."

Natalie rested her hands on either side of her waist. "Look, Tanya, I don't know what point you're trying to make here, but Preacher is only a friend and I'd hoped you and I could be friends, too. If it puts you at ease any, I'm seeing someone myself so you don't have to worry about me having designs on Preacher. And I can tell you that he doesn't have designs on me. All he talks about are you and those kids. You're a lucky woman. No, scratch that, luck has nothing to do with it. You're a blessed woman to have a man like Preacher who holds you in such esteem. I recognize that, but let's not get it twisted. I've got my own man who holds me in high esteem so I don't need or want yours. Are we clear?"

Tanya tucked one of her arms in Natalie's and let her lips relax in a smile. "Very clear," she said. "You know what?" Without waiting for a response, she said, "You're my kind of woman. I think we're going to become very good friends. What do you say to you and your guy going out one evening with me and my guy? I think we'd have fun."

Natalie seemed to study her, as if gauging her sincerity before she answered. "I like that idea. Let me talk to Dante and I'll get back to you on a date. I'll get your number when we're completing the paperwork for the boys to enroll in the Center. That work for you?"

"Perfectly," Tanya said, with a smile. "Now show me around so I know what I'm getting my boys into." Though Tanya kept her smile in place, she also knew she had to keep a watch out for this Natalie chick. Tanya might be thinking of discarding Preacher, but there'd be six inches of snow in Atlanta before she'd let anyone steal him from her.

Preacher pulled into the funeral home parking lot and eased into an open space near the entrance. He removed the key from the ignition and pressed the handle to open the door, but he couldn't complete the action. He searched his heart for the enthusiasm he'd felt for this place yesterday, but all he could find was anxiety about Loretta, the dealings at the car dealership, and Natalie.

How did he end up in the middle of this mess? he wondered. All he wanted to do was get out of prison and make a good life for his family. Now Loretta had put all of that in jeopardy with her wheeling and dealing. Of course, he could go on as if he knew nothing and let the chips fall where they may. But Natalie deserved better. Preacher didn't want to see her hurt, but the sinking feeling in his chest told him that no matter how this played out, she would be one of the losers.

But how could he warn Natalie without fingering Loretta? He knew his sister was in the wrong, but though he wanted her out of the business, he didn't want to see her in prison. His instincts told him Natalie would feel compelled to go to the authorities, especially since Dante had been willing to drag the jobs program into his mess. Though Preacher knew it was unfair, he felt no sympathy for the man. He didn't know him well so friendship didn't factor in. All he saw was a liar using Natalie. He couldn't tolerate that kind of abuse. He had to do something.

Getting out of the car, he flashed back to Tanya asking him if he were angry at her for being late. He would laugh if he could summon up the emotion. Her tardiness hadn't even registered with him. He had real problems that Tanya's minor irritations couldn't touch. He had to plan his next steps carefully, he decided. Then he heard his name called, turned and saw Patrick, the kid from yesterday, jogging toward him.

"I was waiting for you, man," the kid said when he reached Preacher. "I'm ready for work. What we doing today?"

Preacher really didn't have the energy to deal with this kid, but what choice did he have? This boy was determined to stick to Preacher like glue, and Preacher knew that if he turned him away, the kid would only align himself with somebody else and end up in a world of trouble.

"Come on inside," he said.

Preacher greeted George with a handshake. "Morning," George said. "Mr. Luther cleared out the office for you. Let me know if you need anything."

"Thanks, George," Preacher said. "Why don't you do me a favor and give Patrick here a short tour? Let him know what we really do around here."

George raised questioning eyes to Preacher. "You sure?"

Preacher nodded, clapping the kid on the back. "He's going to be working with us. Let's talk after you show him around and we'll figure out what he can do."

"Whatever you say," George said, eyeing the kid skeptically. "Come on, boy," he said to the kid.

Patrick bristled as if he were about to hit George.

"Don't even think about it," Preacher said. "You treat George with the same respect you treat me. Got it?"

The boy quickly backed down. "Got it."

Preacher nodded. "Good. I'll see you and George when you finish."

Nodding, the kid followed George down the hallway. After they had gone about ten steps, George turned around and said, "I forgot. A guy is waiting for you in the office."

"Lord, I hope you know what you're doing," Preacher said aloud, after George and the kid were out of earshot, "because things seem to be spinning out of control."

When Preacher opened the door to Luther's office, he was taken aback to see Big Boy sitting in one of the chairs flipping through a magazine. "What are you doing here, man?" Preacher asked. "How did you even know I'd be here?"

Big Boy inclined his head toward the door. "That kid has a big mouth. Everybody in Atlanta knows you're here. I didn't believe it at first, so I had to come check it out for myself."

Not again, Preacher thought, bracing himself for the negativity.

"You really are going straight, aren't you?" Big Boy said.

Preacher relaxed, he wouldn't have to explain himself again.

"That's the plan, man." He walked to Big Boy and gave him a man's embrace. "It's good to see you. How things shaking for you?"

"Trying to keep my nose clean, too, man," he said, "but it's tough. The life is always calling to me. And it's hard not to heed it. But my old lady is good at keeping me straight. Even got me this job at UPS. Imagine it, me on a nine-to-five."

Preacher laughed. "It's different, huh?"

Big Boy laughed, too. "You're telling me. The good thing is I drive a truck, so I'm out all day by myself. It's hard work, but it's good work."

"I'm proud of you, Big Boy."

"Well, don't be too proud. My hands aren't as dirty as they used to be, but they still aren't totally clean." He gave a self-deprecating grin. "The business ain't like it used to be, man. I think it's getting more dangerous every day. I'm glad I had a chance to get out. I'm just sorry it took you getting sent down for it to happen."

"It's all good, man," Preacher said. "Things happen for a reason."

Big Boy sat back down, and Preacher pulled up a chair next to him. "I assume you're here because you have some news for me."

"Yeah, I do," Big Boy said, "but I'm not sure you gonna like it."

"What?"

"I couldn't find him. From all accounts, he dropped out of sight around the time you got clipped."

Preacher nodded. G-Money's information must have been right. "Any idea where he went?"

Big Boy shook his head. "None. It's like the dude vanished. Disappeared. I'm sorry, man, but that was all I could find out."

"It's all right. I appreciate your help."

"So you think this guy was involved in you getting arrested?"

Preacher met Big Boy's gaze. "Is that what you think?"

"Looks like it. Besides, I heard your sister's been looking for this dude, too."

Preacher put on his game face, hiding all emotion. "How long?"

Big Boy shrugged. "Don't know. Her guys came to the same dead end that I came to, but she hasn't given up. You know Loretta. She ain't gonna give up until she finds him."

"That's my sister."

"So what you gonna do? Loretta ain't playing. That dude gonna wish he was dead if she finds him."

Preacher knew he had to try to save his sister from herself. "I'm gonna find him first."

"How you gonna do that? I told you the guy done disappeared."

"Takes a lot of cash to disappear like that. We need to figure out where he got it. Besides, he's not smart enough to have pulled this off by himself. I'm sure he was working for somebody. That's the person we need to find. Any ideas on that?"

Big Boy laughed. "I'm already on it, man."

Preacher pointed his index finger at Big Boy's chest. "Just don't get yourself in trouble. The goal is for both of us to keep our noses clean. So don't cross any lines that could get you in trouble. Got it?"

"Now you're sounding like my old lady. I hear ya." Big Boy stood. "Well, I'd better get outta here. Today's my day off and I'm supposed to be mowing the grass. Women!"

Preacher laughed. "Sounds like you got a good one there. You'd better hold on to her."

"I'm trying, man," he said. "I'll ring you when I find out something. I figure it's best we don't meet again."

Preacher nodded, understanding fully that their friendship

could not be a public one until Preacher was off probation. "Thanks again."

Big Boy waved his hand behind him as he closed he door.

Preacher dropped his head in his hands, wondering what other troubles the day would bring.

"Thanks again for giving me a ride over here, Barnard," Tanya said as she got out of his blue Taurus. While this brother didn't have the style or the cash to make him attractive to her, Tanya acknowledged that he was, in fact, a good catch. Handsome face with a nice body, though a little heavier than she liked her men, but by no means fat, and a charming smile. She'd bet he kept the little woman at home happy. "I can wait here by myself until Preacher gets back from dropping some kid off at the train station. It's only a short trip and he said the caretaker would be here."

"Not a problem at all. I don't mind waiting for Preacher with you," Barnard said, closing the car door behind her. "In fact, it seems fitting."

She looked back at him. "What do you mean by that?"

Barnard chuckled. "I waited with Preacher for you at the prison the day he was released."

"The day I was late, you mean?"

"Yeah, that day."

"I'm sorry I was so late."

"I'm only sorry I didn't get to meet you that day. I've wanted to for quite a while now." He turned up the wattage on his smile. "I'm glad that we'll be seeing more of you."

"Me, too," Tanya said. "Thanks for letting me steal your cook-out idea. I'm really excited about it since it will be the first time Preacher and I have hosted an event since he's been back home. We used to entertain a lot, so I'm really looking forward to it."

Barnard nodded. "So am I. I can't wait for you to meet my wife. I think you two are really going to hit it off."

"If she's anything like your sister, we'll become fast friends," Tanya said, even though she still didn't trust Natalie with Preacher. "Natalie's very easy to know. She seems serious about the guy she's dating. What does big brother think about him?"

Barnard pulled open the door to the funeral home and allowed Tanya to enter before him. "I've met the guy, talked some business with him," he said. "He seems all right. Your cookout will be the first time we've been together in a social setting though. That alone should win you points with Serena. She's been trying to get those two over for dinner for a while now."

"I'm glad I could help," Tanya said, already losing interest in the topic. She looked around for the caretaker, but she didn't see him. "So this is Preacher's new business, huh? A funeral home."

"Yeah, it is," Barnard said. "Natalie told me he's really excited about it, but I guess you already know that. So what do you think?"

Tanya sat on the bench in the foyer, unsure where else to go. She certainly wasn't going to go searching around the funeral home looking for the caretaker. "It's a funeral home, Barnard. It's not exactly the business I wanted for Preacher. This seems like a business for an old person. Preacher is a young man and he needs a young man's business."

Barnard sat next to her. "This business will be what you and Preacher make it, Tanya. It'll only be old if you're old, and you're not old. You two can breathe life into this place, and serve a lot of good in the community in the process."

Tanya stood and walked down the hallway a bit. "I don't know, Barnard. I just don't see it." She turned back to him. "Can't you help Preacher find something else? I was thinking of a car dealership, preferably an import. That's more Preacher's style, and mine. I can see us building that business together, but not this one." She looked toward the door when she heard a car drive up. "I hope that's Preacher."

Barnard got up and went to the door. "Yeah, that's him." He opened the door. "Hey, man, good to see you." They two men clapped each other on the back. "I've been taking good care of Tanya for you."

Preacher gave Tanya a questioning smile. "Been enjoying yourself?" he asked, extending his hand to her. "Let's go in the office."

"I've got to leave," Barnard said. "I have a couple of errands to run before heading back to the church." He turned to Tanya and gave her a brief kiss on the cheek. "I enjoyed meeting you and I look forward to seeing you again. I'll have Serena get back to you with a date."

Tanya bussed his cheek. "Sounds good. Thanks for everything."

"What's this about Serena getting back to you?" Preacher asked after he and Tanya were seated in the office.

"Just me trying to be the good fiancée. I've invited your friends over for a cookout. Barnard and Serena and Natalie and Dante. All we need to do is coordinate schedules. What do you think of that?"

I think you're playing with fire, that's what I think. "I think you've been busy."

"Is that all you have to say? I thought you'd be happy about this. Or maybe you don't want your friends over? Maybe you want to keep them separate from me? Is that it?"

Preacher could already feel the tension mounting around this cookout. Him and Serena with their secret. Him knowing what was going on at Dante's dealership. He wasn't sure he was up for it. "You're talking crazy, Tanya."

"Don't try to play me, Preacher. I'm the master player, not an idiot. I saw the way Natalie looked at you and the way you looked at her. The chick will have to be cold-blooded to go after you after she visits the home we share and sees how loving we are."

Tanya was so far off base, Preacher didn't know whether to be glad she didn't know the truth or sad he didn't feel he could share the truth with her. "Don't blame me or Natalie because you're having evil thoughts. There's nothing going on between us. Maybe you're the one with something on the side."

"Don't try to turn this on me," Tanya said. "Though if you want to get technical, since you're not taking care of business at home, I'd be within my rights to look elsewhere."

"Not as long as I'm living and breathing," Preacher said, growing tired of this conversation. "I've told you what I'm trying to do for us. You either stand with me on it or you don't, but you don't run around on me. You don't even think about it. Do you understand?"

Tanya sat back down. He knew she realized she'd overplayed her hand and pushed him too far. "Look," she said, "what do you expect me to think? You and this chick are mooning over each other—"

"We were not mooning over each other. She's Barnard's sister. We're friends, Tanya. That's it."

"Don't be obtuse. Yours wouldn't be the first platonic friendship to grow into something more. Before you know it, you'll be comparing me to your little Miss Perfect Christian and thinking that she's everything I'm not. I won't put up with it."

"Then why did you invite them over?"

"I told you. I want her to see us as a family and I wanted her man to see her with you. He'll probably tell her the same thing I'm telling you."

"Here we go with the games."

"It's not a game to me," she said. "I'm fighting for my family. You may think these church people can do no wrong, but I'm here to tell you they can."

"I can see there's no telling you anything. We'll have your cookout and you'll see what you need to see. All right?"

She nodded.

"Okay, now do you want to see the funeral home operation?"

She started shaking her head before he finished the question. "Not now. If we're going to check out new cars today, we need to get started. We have to pick up the Porsche, drive to the dealership, and get back to the church in time to pick up the kids. We're really pushed for time."

Preacher accepted her excuse even though it wasn't valid. They had plenty of time. Tanya just wasn't interested in seeing the funeral home. How in the world was he going to get her to change her mind? He could feel his faith that she would change wavering. What would he do if she didn't? He didn't even want to think about it. He had enough problems for today. The most pressing were finding out how deep Dante was in with Loretta and figuring out what, how, and when to tell Natalie about him. "Okay," he finally said to Tanya. "Let's take care of the cars. At least, we'll get that out of the way."

CHAPTER 14

Serena put down the bottle of disinfectant she'd been using to clean the gym equipment and checked her watch. Her sister-in-law was over half an hour late. Natalie was supposed to close tonight, but she hadn't called and she wasn't answering her cell. Serena had called the church, so she knew her sister-in-law had left there over an hour ago. Where was she?

Serena pulled her cell out of her pants pocket and punched in Natalie's number. She answered on the second ring. "Where are you?" Serena asked. "I've been worried."

"Out front. Open the door and let me in."

Serena peered around the corner and, sure enough, there was Natalie. She closed her phone and rushed to the door. "Are you all right? What happened? It's unlike you not to call."

Natalie hugged her. "I'm sorry I worried you, sis. I have no excuse; time just got away from me."

Serena watched as Natalie stashed her shoulder bag behind the counter. "I know you're ready to go home," Natalie said, "so why don't you head on out. I'll be okay. The security guard is still in the lot."

"I'm in no rush," Serena said. "Barnard called and he's going to be late tonight."

"So you've spoken to Barnard," Natalie said, as she made her way back to the gym area, disinfectant and a cleaning rag in hand. "I guess he told you then."

Serena followed after her. "Told me what? Natalie, you're acting strangely. What's going on?"

Natalie glanced up at her and then focused her attention on the leather seat of the leg extender she was cleaning. "Preacher's girlfriend came by the Children's Center today."

Why was Natalie being so cryptic? "And?"

Moving to the next machine, Natalie said, "She's planning a cookout for the six of us."

Serena dropped down on the seat of the leg extender machine. "Cookout? Six of us?"

Natalie glanced up at her. "Yes, cookout with you and Barnard, me and Dante, and her and Preacher. Sounds like fun, huh?"

It sounded like a nightmare to Serena but she didn't understand why it seemed to sound the same way to Natalie. "So what was she like?"

"Who?"

Serena rolled her eyes. "Tanya, Preacher's girlfriend. Who else?"

Natalie stopped cleaning and looked at her. "Tall, thin, attractive."

"That's how she looks. What's she like?"

"Well, she's bold. I have to give her that."

Serena went to Natalie and pushed her down on the seat of the arm press. She sat on the seat of the chest compression machine next to it. "What's going on?"

Natalie wiped her hands down her face. "I can't believe I let her get to me. Lord, forgive me."

"Start at the beginning and tell me everything."

"She practically accused me of trying steal Preacher away from her." Natalie stood and began pacing in the small space between the two machines. "Me? Steal her man? Please! You know what happened with me and Benjamin. I'd never do anything that cruel."

"I know you wouldn't," Serena said, "but what makes her think you would?"

Natalie stopped pacing for a moment. "Who knows what goes on in that woman's mind? Preacher and I are friends and that's what I told her."

"Friends?" Serena repeated. "When did you and Preacher become friends? I thought you were just acquaintances."

Shrugging, Natalie sat back down. "We're becoming friends. I like him, Serena."

"You don't even know him." Serena wanted to knock some sense into Natalie's head. "How do you know you like him? I didn't even know you'd talked to him other than at church that Sunday."

"Well, I've seen him a couple of times since then. He came by the church the other day with his boys and Barnard brought them down to the Children's Center. The boys spent the day with me there while Preacher ran errands. Later, when he came back, he was looking for Barnard to tell him his good news about this business opportunity the Lord had given him. Since Barnard wasn't there, he shared it with me. We ended up encouraging each other. That's when I learned what a nice, genuine guy he is. I like him, Serena. Is that wrong?"

Not wrong, but not wise, either. "No, of course it's not wrong."

Natalie took a deep breath. "I know it's not wrong, but Tanya's accusation made me feel . . . I don't know, dirty. It makes no sense."

Serena knew she had to be careful with her next words. She placed her hand on Natalie's knee. "But I can see Tanya's concern. You're an attractive woman and Preacher's an attractive man. Things happen."

"We're brother and sister in Christ, for heaven's sake. Besides, I'm happy in my relationship with Dante, and Preacher's definitely committed to his family and that means Tanya. I can't believe I have to explain this to you, of all people. You know me."

But Serena also knew Preacher. "It's not your intentions I'm worried about."

Natalie looked up at her. "Preacher is not interested in me that way."

Serena shrugged, trying to ease into her position. "Maybe not now. You have to remember that he's a new Christian, involved in a relationship with a non-Christian who doesn't appear interested in becoming a Christian. It doesn't take a giant leap to think that one day he's going to start wishing Tanya were more like you."

"Are you saying I shouldn't continue my friendship with Preacher?"

That's exactly what I'm saying. "Not really. What I'm saying is that you have to respect Tanya's wishes. You can be friendly with both of them, but if it makes her uncomfortable, the friendship can't really go any further than that, can it?"

Natalie sat there for a few moments, eyes closed. Serena respected her enough to give her time to sort through her feelings.

When Natalie opened her eyes, she said, "You're right. I have to be careful with Preacher for Tanya's sake." Now she placed her hand on Serena's knee. "So I need a favor from you, Serena."

Serena covered Natalie's hand with her own, very pleased her sister-in-law had come to the right conclusion. "Whatever you need."

"I need you to be a friend to Preacher and Tanya."

"But—"

"Wait," Natalie said, "and hear me out. I know in my heart that Preacher needs friends. You didn't see him the other day when he came by to tell Barnard his news about working at the funeral home. He was crestfallen when Barnard wasn't there. When I offered to lend an ear, I could tell he was reluctant, but he gave in and shared with me. It was wonderful, Serena. For me and for him. I want him to have more opportunities like that. He needs them if he's going to grow as a Christian."

"But why me?"

"Not only you, really, you and Barnard. You two could sort of adopt Preacher and Tanya until they get to know and feel comfortable with other Christian couples. I'm sure Tanya would be more comfortable with you than she is with me. And there'd be lots of opportunities for the four of you to do things as a couple. Please, Serena. They need you."

"I don't know."

Natalie slid her hand away. "I don't understand your reluctance to give Preacher a chance. He's a good man. All I'm asking is that you let him show you."

Serena couldn't believe the conversation had turned on her this way. Her goal had been to get Preacher away from Natalie and now Natalie was asking her to become his best friend. That was impossible. But what choice did she have. "I'll try," she finally said, all the while wondering how she would pull it off. She'd have to find another couple for them; her mind was already going through the church roster.

Natalie leaned over and kissed her cheek. "Thanks, sis. I knew I could count on you. The first thing we have to do is give Tanya a couple of available dates for this cookout of hers." She stood. "I'll get our purses and we can do that now. I want to get started making Tanya feel welcomed and not threatened."

Natalie walked away with a bounce in her step that hadn't been there when she'd arrived at the gym. Serena was left plotting to extricate herself from the promise she'd just made.

Preacher had gone to bed worrying about Natalie and he'd awakened the same way. It was like knowing someone was about be involved in a car crash, and having no way to save them. All he could do was remind them to wear their seatbelt to limit the damage. In Natalie's case, he still wasn't sure how to do that.

Natalie had been nothing but good to him and his family, and he was about to bring pain into her life. While a part of him knew it wasn't his doing, another part of him felt fully responsible. He'd brought Loretta into this business a long time ago, and the business that he started was going to hurt somebody he cared about, somebody who cared about him.

Early on in the business, he'd learned to harden himself to how his actions affected others. How else could he run a business that exploited people's helplessness? After getting saved, he'd found he couldn't dwell on his past sins, for doing so was debilitating. He didn't like to put faces on the money he made. He didn't want to think about the broken lives and broken homes his business had created. It hurt too much.

But this thing with Natalie was something he couldn't run from. He'd have to face this head-on, except he wasn't sure how. He wished he could talk to Barnard or Luther or even Wayne, his probation officer, but he couldn't talk to them because he didn't want to put his sister in jeopardy.

He'd convinced himself to stay away from Natalie until he had a plan. Then he'd dropped the boys off at the Children's Center and run into Barnard. In his excitement about the upcoming cookout, Barnard had told Preacher that Natalie was working at the gym today while Serena was taking the day off.

That bit of information was why Preacher was parked in front of Serena and Natalie's gym now. He needed to talk to Natalie, if only to apologize to her for Tanya's accusations yesterday. As he pulled open the door to the gym, it occurred to him that his presence in a women's gym might be awkward. He walked up to the unmanned counter, looking for a bell or some way to make his presence known. Not seeing one, he stood there with his hands stuffed in his pockets.

"You did good today, Bertice," came a voice from around the corner that Preacher recognized as Serena's, not Natalie's. He considered making a run for the door.

"Thank you, Miss Serena. I'll see you tomorrow."

Serena and a young girl rounded the corner and Preacher's escape plans evaporated. Serena's eyes widened when she saw him, but she kept a smile on her face until the young girl left the building. "What are you doing here, Preacher?" she asked, once they were alone.

Preacher felt like a child caught with his hand in the cookie jar. "I dropped by to see Natalie."

Serena began shaking her head. "I don't understand you,

Preacher. Can't you leave Natalie alone? You have a fiancée. Isn't one woman enough for you?"

Preacher pulled his hands out of his pockets and clasped them together. "Natalie and I are friends, Serena. I'm sure you understand friendship."

Serena stared him down. "Maybe I do, but apparently Tanya doesn't."

Preacher dropped his hands. "So Natalie told you. How bad was it?"

"It was bad, Preacher. Your girlfriend left Natalie feeling as though she'd done something wrong. You should never have put her in that position. You should have stayed away from her, but you couldn't, could you?"

Preacher had no comeback because Serena was right. How could he explain to her that he valued his friendship with Natalie, despite Tanya's evil thoughts? "Maybe you're right."

He could tell his words surprised her by the way she eyed him. "Then why don't you leave Natalie alone? Why are you here today?"

"I was sure Tanya's words had hurt her and I wanted to apologize," he said. "That's the only reason I'm here."

Serena studied him, as if trying to decide whether to believe him. "You know, I almost believe you, Preacher."

"Almost?"

"Yes, almost. If you really cared about Natalie, you'd stay away from her. Can't you see you bring pain and sorrow wherever you go? Leave her alone. Let her be happy."

Preacher squeezed his hands into fists to fight the pain Serena's words caused. They hurt so much because they were so true, truer than she even knew. "I can't relive the past, Serena. I can only do what I can in the present. I want to make things right with Natalie, with you, and with Barnard. I want you all to be happy."

"What does Barnard have to do with this?" Serena asked, sounding like a momma bear protecting her cubs.

"It's what we've done to him. Serena, we have to tell him the truth."

"Not that again."

"If Natalie told you about Tanya's accusations, then I'm sure she also told you about this cookout that Tanya has planned. We need to tell Barnard before this cookout. There's no way we can spend another evening behaving the way we did at the restaurant that Sunday. Barnard's not stupid. He's going to know something's wrong. It'll hurt him less if we tell him now. The longer we hold on to this secret, the more damage it's going to do."

"I'm not telling him," Serena said, her eyes hot with defiance.

"If you don't tell him before the cookout, I'll tell him after."

"Why do you want to hurt me?"

He shook his head. "I don't want to hurt you or Barnard, but the reality is that both of you are going to be hurt. I'm only trying to lessen the pain." He paused, unsure if he should add these last words. He loved Barnard like a brother and he wanted to show Serena how desperate the situation was. "Serena, Barnard has told me about the problems you're having in your marriage."

"He wouldn't!"

"He did, and that tells me how much he's hurting. Besides feeling like a hypocrite when he confides in me, I also feel that some of your problems are related to our secret. You have to tell him so you can begin to work on your issues."

Serena gave him a hard look. "Stay out of my personal life and family, Preacher, and get out of my place of business."

He opened his mouth to say more but she cut him off.

"Leave. Now. Or I'm calling the cops."

He believed her, so he left.

Loretta drummed her fingers on the table of the booth at McDonald's while she waited for Tanya and the boys. Her table faced the window so she could see them when they drove up. If the chick didn't show up in the next five minutes, Loretta was leaving. She'd have to see the boys another time.

When Loretta saw the tan Lexus crossover SUV with the vanity plates that read "TANYA1" pull into a space across the lot from the door, she shook her head at Tanya's notion of scaling back on cars. A few minutes later, Tanya breezed into Mickey Dee's sporting dark sunglasses and a micromini. Evidently, she thought she was in Hollywood.

"You're late," Loretta said as Tanya slid into the booth across from her.

Tanya slipped off her sunglasses. "Not that late."

Loretta ignored her fake smile. "Where are the boys?" she asked. "I thought you were bringing them."

Tanya shrugged. "I thought I was, too, but Preacher ended up picking them up from the church and they're going to some Little League game or something. I passed, since I preferred to spend time with you."

"Yeah, right. What do you really want, Tanya? I hope you didn't come here just to show off your new ride. Unlike you, I have things to do."

"No need to be mean, Loretta. I just wanted to see you. Have some girl talk."

"Tell me anything," Loretta said. "Like how you got Preacher to buy you that Lexus. I thought you were scaling back."

"We did scale back. I gave up a Benz and a Porsche and I'm left with that thing." She waved her hand in the direction of her vehicle. "I wanted the premium SUV, the LX model, but Preacher wasn't having it. That thing out there is the bottom of the line Lexus SUV. I'm almost embarrassed to drive it."

Loretta's dislike of Tanya gushed up in her like lava in a live volcano. "Girl, you've got some nerve complaining about a Lexus, especially when none of the money came out of your pocket." She sighed deeply. There was no sense chastising Tanya about her spending. She didn't get it. "Now tell me why we needed to meet before I get up and leave."

Tanya leaned back in the booth, lifted her right hand, and studied her nails. "Guess who's giving a cookout?"

Loretta rolled her eyes. "Guessing games are for kids. Out with it, Tanya."

Tanya frowned. "You certainly know how to take all the fun out of things, Loretta. You really do need to lighten up. You're going to end up with high blood pressure or a heart attack."

Loretta drummed her fingers on the table and stared at Tanya, saying nothing.

"All right, already. I'm hosting a cookout for Preacher and his church friends this weekend."

"That's it? I don't see why you're bragging about it. You're supposed to be getting Preacher away from those folks, not entertaining them, or have you forgotten? Maybe you're turning like Preacher did?"

"No way," she said. "I'm only trying to keep things lively. I thought it might be fun to have them over. Get to know them a little bit. You know what they say, keep your friends close and your enemies closer."

Loretta considered Tanya's words. The airhead might have

a point. It'd be nice to check those jokers out. Preacher was so blinded by them that he couldn't see them clearly. She, on the other hand, could spot a faker from a mile away. "So who all's coming to this cookout of yours?"

"I knew you'd be interested." Tanya leaned forward, a gleam in her eyes. "Preacher's sponsor, the guy who worked with him at the prison, and his wife. The guy's sister and her man. And me and Preacher. So there'll be six of us."

Loretta began shaking her head. "No," she said. "There'll be eight of you. Add me and my date to the guest list."

Tanya sat back. "You and a date? Who is he? I knew there was somebody."

Loretta rolled her eyes again. "Focus, Tanya. We're talking about this cookout of yours. I'm coming and I'm bringing a date. I hate to admit it, but you had a good idea about getting to know these people. We need to help Preacher see them for who they truly are."

"I know what you're talking about, girl. I had to put one of those church sisters, that Natalie, on blast. She was pushing up on Preacher."

Loretta wasn't sure she believed Tanya, but it was an interesting development. She'd have to watch this Natalie. She remembered Andre telling her that Dante was dating the woman. What an interesting little gathering this was going to be. "You'd better watch out," she told Tanya just to irritate her, "Preacher is into all things church these days. His finding a church woman is the logical next step."

"No man steps out on me, Loretta. Preacher is no different. Besides I have something that church woman doesn't have."

Loretta eyed her. "And what's that?"

"Jake and Mack. Preacher might think—and I do mean think—

about another woman, but he won't think long because those boys are mine, and if I go, they go, too."

Loretta leaned across the table. "Don't push it, Tanya. Those boys are my nephews. You'll regret it if you even think about taking them from their father. You got that?"

Tanya smirked. "I'm just saying."

"Well, you've said enough. Now I've got to go. Keep me updated on the cookout and don't tell Preacher I'm coming. Something tells me he'd try to talk me out of it."

As Loretta moved to slide out of her seat, Tanya touched her arm. "There's one more thing," she said with a smile.

"What?"

"The cookout. You know I don't like to cook."

Loretta started to roll her eyes, then stopped herself. She'd be cross-eyed if she spent too much time with Tanya. "So why'd you offer to host a cookout?"

"You know church folks and cookouts. I knew they'd go for it."

"And you're telling me this because. . ."

"I was thinking about catering the event. You know, we want something nice. We don't want those people feeling sorry for Preacher."

Loretta felt a bitterness like lemon twist her lips. She should have known. She pulled out her checkbook. "How much?"

CHAPTER 15

"You're looking good today." Sean did a double take at the normally snooty secretary sitting outside the Boss's office. Since the woman had never given him the least personal of comments, he took a quick glance around the reception area to make sure she was talking to him. Still unsure, he said, "I beg your pardon."

"You're looking good," she said, with what could only be described as a flirty smile. "I like that suit."

Sean cast a wary eye at her. Like any man, he wasn't immune to the flirtations of a pretty woman, but her sudden interest struck him as odd, especially since the suit he wore today was no different than the suits he'd worn on his previous visits. "Thanks," he said. If the woman hadn't been so pretty, he might have called her on her past behavior, but he was not one to look a gift horse in the mouth. "You're looking good yourself," he said. "You always do."

"Thanks," she said. "But you seem to be the man of the hour."

Sean leaned against her desk. "Do you know something I don't know?" he asked, hoping for a bit of inside information. Who knew the Boss's plans for him better than his secretary?

She gave him a coy smile. "If I told you," she said, "the Boss might ship me off to Third Hades."

Sean laughed at her wit and she laughed with him, though both of them knew there was a lot of truth in her words. When they stopped laughing, she scribbled something on her note pad. She tore off the top sheet, and handed it to him. "Call me sometime," she said, with a wink.

Sean grinned as he took the sheet of note paper. "Jessica Bell," he said looking at the name and number she had scribbled. "A pretty name for a pretty woman." He folded the paper carefully and put it in his wallet.

"My friends call me Jessie."

"Well, then, Jessie Bell," Sean said. "Is it all right if I call you tonight?"

"Don't tease me, Sean," she said, batting her eyelashes. "Now you're going to have me sitting by the phone all night waiting for your call."

Despite his uneasiness about her sudden interest in him, Sean puffed out his chest a bit. It had been a long time since a woman had come on to him so strongly and it felt good. "I wouldn't do that," he said. "I'm definitely calling you tonight. Maybe we can go out sometime soon."

"Definitely," she said. "Now you'd better head in the Boss's office. He's ready for you."

Sean had a bounce in his step when he entered the Boss's office. He realized that, unlike on his previous visits, the chatter with the secretary had kept his mind off the meeting with the Boss. As a result, he wasn't as nervous today as he'd been on previous visits.

He'd have to thank Jessie for her help, he thought, as he took his regular seat in front of the Boss's desk.

The Boss cleared his throat. "So what's happening with Preacher?"

Feeling a confidence he knew was rooted in his conversation with Jessie, Sean slipped open the buttons of his suit jacket and relaxed in his chair. "It's all good," he said. "That Serena is playing right into my hands. For someone who is supposed to be a strong Christian, she's falling fast. Looks like we can count her as collateral damage."

"Not so fast, Jones. Tell me more about this."

"Well, Serena and her husband are supposed to be guiding Preacher in his new life, but because of the secret past Serena has with Preacher, that plan is not working too well. The more I bombard her with thoughts of the past, the more she refuses to accept Preacher and his new life. She's so far gone that now she's pushing her sister-in-law into the arms of one of ours and away from Preacher who belongs to our enemy."

The Boss laughed. "Some of those church people really are easy prey. It can be fun to watch them fall into our arms, but we can't get too confident. You have to keep on top of her. Keep up those negative thoughts of her past with Preacher. The more she focuses on the past, the less likely she'll be to see Preacher as the godly man he is." The Boss eyed Sean. "That brings up a question, Jones. Why is Preacher still a godly man? He's supposed to be falling into our hands as well."

Preacher was a major irritant that Sean couldn't wait to see fall—hard. His confidence slipped a bit as he gave the Boss his status. "Preacher is falling and he doesn't even know it yet." Sean rubbed his hands together and licked his lips, as he'd seen the Boss do. "I'm squeezing him from all sides. He's not going to know what hit him. My strategy is to go for the collateral damage first. After Serena, I've got my eye on Natalie. She already thinks she's in love with Dante. Since Serena's helping, all I have to do is keep supplying Natalie with negative comparisons between Dante and her old boyfriend, Benjamin. Serena will do the rest. Once Natalie marries Dante, she's all ours."

The Boss stared at Sean for a long moment, a slow smile forming on his face. "You may be on to something, Jones," he said. "You're about to make a believer out of me. Be careful though. When we get this close, the enemy sends in reinforcements."

"I'm being diligent," Sean said, very familiar with how the enemy operated at this point in the battle.

"Good work," the Boss said, causing Sean to do his second double take of the day. He'd gotten an actual compliment from the Boss! Then the Boss turned stern again. "Now get back to it."

Sean slid out of his chair. "Yes, sir," he said. He thought about saluting, but he didn't want to press his luck. He strode out of the office with an extra bounce in his step.

He'd have to buy flowers for Jessie. Winning her to his side could be very helpful in his ongoing relationship with the Boss. Just because the old man was complimentary today didn't mean he wouldn't be threatening Sean with Third Hades at their next meeting. Yes, he reaffirmed to himself, he needed someone like Jessie on his side.

CHAPTER 16

Jake! Mack! Calm yourselves down and stop all that screaming," Preacher called to his sons, who were running around the backyard playing horse with some old plastic horse heads on a stick Tanya had dug up from somewhere. He sat back in the redwood chaise lounge in his fenced-in backyard and closed his eyes. *They're driving me crazy.*

A soft hand squeezed his shoulder and he opened his eyes to see Tanya drop down into the chaise next to his. She sipped from a glass of iced tea. "You're really worried about this cookout, aren't you?"

Worry didn't adequately describe how Preacher felt. It was as though he were sitting on a keg of dynamite waiting for it to explode. "What makes you think I'm worried?"

She eyed him skeptically. "Your impatience with the boys. It's a beautiful sunny day and they're playing the way kids play. I can't believe I'm saying this because I'm usually the one who's hard on them, but give them a break, Preacher. It's summer and they're having fun."

Preacher knew she was right. He looked over at his boys. They'd stopped running for a moment while Jake doctored Mack's horse. Preacher was about to offer his help, when the boys galloped off again, whooping and hollering. He smiled. "I didn't realize I was being impatient with them."

"I know you didn't. So tell me why you're so worried about this cookout? These people are your friends, right, your new Christian family? I'd think their coming over would make you relaxed, not anxious." She leaned toward him and nudged him with her shoulder. "I promise not to do anything that will embarrass you."

He cut a glance at her. "What? You won't accuse Natalie of trying to steal me away from you?"

She sat back in her chair and sipped her tea. "I don't know why you were embarrassed by that. Natalie is a woman. She understood where I was coming from. We're straight. There are no hard feelings on either side."

Preacher didn't respond because he knew there was no sense engaging Tanya in a conversation on the topic. Besides, Tanya's turf issues with Natalie were the lesser of his concerns today.

"I can't wait to meet this man of hers," Tanya said. "The man a woman picks tells you a lot about her."

Preacher couldn't resist asking, "What does your picking me say about you?"

The doorbell rang and Tanya got up. "Saved by the bell. Besides that's a bedtime question. Ask me the next time you're with me in bed." She winked and then opened her palm to him. "Come with me. Let's greet our guests as a family."

Preacher stared at her hand a long moment before taking it. He wasn't sure he was ready to greet guests. He got up anyway. He turned and called to the boys, "Come on, boys, let's go greet our guests." Horses and all, the boys galloped after him and Tanya.

Instead of going through the house to answer the bell, they came around the outside of the house and through the gate. Natalie and Dante stood on their front porch, with Dante playfully kissing Natalie along her neck.

"You're hurting my hand," Tanya said to Preacher, her voice tight. With a smile pasted on her face, she added, "You'd better not embarrass me by acting jealous over a woman being kissed by her man. I won't have it."

Before Preacher could respond, Tanya called to the couple, "Hey, you two, there are kids around here."

Dante flashed them a smile and Natalie blushed. The couple walked toward her and Preacher. Natalie leaned in and kissed Tanya on the cheek. "It's good to see you again," she said. "Thanks for having us over."

Tanya accepted the kiss, though she didn't give Natalie one in return. "And who's this handsome man with you?"

Natalie stepped back. "This is Dante Griggs. Dante, this is Tanya, Preacher's fiancée. And you and Preacher have already met."

Dante stepped forward and gave Preacher a two-fisted shake. "Good to see you, again, man. I hope you got everything all worked out with your car."

Tanya extended her hand to Dante. "So you're the guy who helped Preacher get rid of my vehicles," she said in what Preacher recognized as her flirting voice. "Shame on you."

Dante lifted his open palms in her direction. "Hey, I'm innocent. A man comes to me and tells me my girl says treat him right. I give him what he wants."

Tanya laughed, that open laugh of hers that was meant to enthrall a man. Preacher wanted to tell her to ratchet it back a notch. He glanced at Natalie, whose face told him nothing of her assessment of the situation. She only smiled at him, a smile with nothing hidden. He smiled back.

"Where are the boys?" Natalie asked.

Preacher turned and saw them standing by the gate. Jake apparently doing more doctoring on Mack's horse. "Boys," he called to them. "Miss Natalie is here."

The boys got on their horses and galloped toward Natalie. "Look at us, Miss Natalie, we're riding horses," Jake said.

"Riding horses," Mack chimed in.

"So I see," Natalie said, leaning down to press a soft kiss on each head.

Preacher smiled down at her until he felt Tanya bristle up next to him. "Let's head out back," Tanya said, "where we'll be comfortable." She took Dante's arm, Natalie followed with a boy on each side, and Preacher pulled up the rear alone.

"What a lovely home you have, Tanya," Natalie said, after the boys had gone back to their play. "This yard is wonderful. Did you do the landscaping yourself?"

"Please," Tanya said. "I'm not one for getting dirty. We hired a guy from Lithonia."

"You'll have to give me his name and number. My yard needs help."

"I've volunteered to get a little dirt under my fingers for you," Dante said, pulling Natalie close.

Natalie patted his shoulder. "You work all day the same as I do. I don't want you working when we're together. Besides, I think Tanya has the right idea."

Tanya put an arm around Natalie's shoulder. "See, Preacher, I told you Natalie and I would become fast friends. Come on, Natalie," she said. "Let me show you the rest of the house." She turned to Dante. "Something tells me you'd rather sit here with Preacher and talk sports or something equally boring."

Dante pressed his hand to his heart. "You wound me. What man would rather stay with an ugly mug like Preacher when he could follow two beautiful women?"

Natalie and Tanya laughed. "He's a keeper, Natalie," Tanya said, her eyes on Dante.

Natalie leaned up and brushed a kiss on Dante's jaw. "I know."

"*Uh-oh,* Preacher," Tanya said. "They're in love and it's new. We may have to get towels to cover Jake's and Mack's eyes."

Dante and Natalie laughed, but Preacher could only force a smile.

Tanya tugged Natalie away. "Cold drinks are in the cooler on the patio," she called back to Preacher and Dante. "Have at 'em."

Giggling, the two women entered the house. Preacher didn't know quite what to make of either of them. He supposed Natalie had bounced back from her run-in with Tanya and was displaying her typical Christian charity. He wasn't sure what Tanya was up to.

"I think I will have something to drink," Dante said. "You want something?"

"Where are my manners?" Preacher said. "I'm the host. I should be asking you."

"No problem," Dante said, following Preacher to the patio. "It's a cookout. The only rule is every man for himself."

Preacher laughed, but it sounded hollow to his ears. He wondered how it sounded to Dante.

"So did the car thing work out?" Dante asked again after they reached the patio.

"Yeah, it did." Preacher lifted the top off the cooler. "Help yourself."

Dante reached in and pulled out a soda can and Preacher did likewise. "So what did you end up getting?" Dante asked.

"A Lexus."

Dante laughed. "I thought you were scaling back."

"Well," Preacher said, "there's scaling back and then there's Tanya scaling back."

"I know what you mean, man. The good news is she's worth it. I have to say it. I think we both did extremely well in our selection of women."

"Yeah," Preacher said. "Sometimes we get more than we deserve."

"That's exactly the way I feel about Natalie. I know I'm not good enough for her, but I'm still not letting her go."

Preacher eyed him sideways. "I know Tanya was teasing you, but you really do sound like a man in love. Is it serious?"

"I want to marry her," Dante said.

Preacher didn't know what to do with that bit of information. Asking Dante if he were crazy was definitely not the appropriate response. "Marriage is a big step," Preacher said. "Make sure you're ready for a wife before you take one on."

"That's what I'm doing, man," Dante said. "I'm almost there. I've even picked out the ring. I'm just waiting for the right time."

Preacher turned his soda can up to his lips to give himself time to think of a suitable response. Soon the can was empty. He lowered it and let the question on his heart fall from his lips. "Would that be before or after you stop transporting drugs through your dealership?" He thought Dante would choke on his soda. He clapped the brother on his back. "You okay?"

Dante glanced back at the door to the house. "What are you talking about, man?"

Preacher stepped closer to him. "Don't play dumb with me, Dante. Atlanta is a small town in a lot of ways, so news spreads. You're a businessman, surely you know that."

Preacher watched as Dante's throat contracted in a swallow, even though he wasn't drinking anything.

"What do you want?" Dante asked.

"I don't want Natalie to get hurt," he said.

"I won't hurt her."

"You already have. Your lies have hurt her, and when she learns the truth about you and your business, she'll be hurt even more. How could you bring her into this, man? How can you even think about asking her to marry you? That's not the life you want for the woman you love. I know. Believe me, I know."

Dante stepped back. "I'm not a drug dealer."

Preacher heard the unspoken "like you" loud and clear. "Keep telling yourself that," he said, "but leave Natalie alone. Get out of her life."

"Is that a threat?"

Preacher shrugged. "Consider it good advice from a reliable source. Do you really want to see her face when she finds out who you really are? How about when she and all her friends read in the papers that the cops raided your dealership?"

Dante opened his mouth to speak.

"There's nothing you can say, man," Preacher said. "If you love her, prove it by letting her go."

Dante stepped up to him. "And if I don't?"

"I'll have to tell her." Preacher paused to let those words sink in, a tactic he'd used to great effect in his past life. "I'll have to tell her, anyway, but I'll wait awhile after you break it off with her. That'll be easier. At least then she'll think you cared enough about her not to involve her or the prison ministry she cherishes in your dealings. What's she going to think when she realizes you were going to involve the prison ministry in your drug activities?"

"I wasn't going to do that," Dante said. "I'm getting out."

Preacher shook his head. "Either you're stupid or naive. You don't decide to 'get out' from the guys you're dealing with. They hold all the cards. You should have checked before you got in bed with them."

"How do you know so much about it?" Dante asked, a smirk on his face. "Could it be that I'm not the only one with secrets?"

Preacher lifted his hands. "These are clean, man, but like I said, Atlanta is a small town, and I know a lot of people. I hate to say this, since I'm a man, but men gossip more than women. Your business is common knowledge." Preacher knew he was overstating his case, but he wanted this guy out of Natalie's life.

"I don't like threats," Dante said.

"I don't make 'em," Preacher shot back.

At the sound of the women's voices coming from the house, both men turned toward the door. Natalie came out first. "You were right, Tanya," she said. "They were missing us."

Preacher watched as Dante pulled Natalie close. "I always do," he said.

Tanya strolled over to him. "You need to take notes, Preacher. Dante is making you look bad."

Preacher met Dante's eyes over the women's heads. "Don't worry. I've been taking notes for a while now." Dante's frown told Preacher he got the message.

* * *

Dante wanted to leave. He didn't know how much longer he could sit here pretending to concentrate on this inane conversation of Tanya's while Preacher silently reissued his threats. He hoped the other guests would hurry up and arrive so he could get away from Preacher's piercing eyes.

He needed to talk to Andre. How many other people knew about their illegal business dealings? He'd left all of that in Andre's hands, telling himself that the less he knew, the less culpability he would have. It had been a lie then and it was a lie now. He was in this up to his eyeballs. He knew it. And Preacher knew it.

Dante breathed a relieved sigh when he heard, from beyond the fence, a female voice call "Where's the party?"

"Auntie Loretta!" the oldest of the boys said. Then he and the younger boy galloped toward the gate. Tanya got up and followed them. When Preacher rose, she pressed her hand against his shoulder. "I'll get it. You stay here with our guests."

"So, is Loretta your sister or Tanya's?" Natalie asked Preacher, after Tanya had gone.

Preacher swallowed. "Mine."

Natalie beamed. "Great. I've wanted to meet her."

Dante took note that Preacher didn't share Natalie's enthusiasm at his sister's arrival. "Preacher," Tanya called, "your sister has brought her beau for you to inspect."

Preacher's sister said something in response but Dante didn't hear what it was. His eyes were fixed on the sister's beau, his partner, Andre! What in the world was Andre doing with Preacher's sister?

"Let me do the introductions," Tanya was saying. "Natalie and Dante, this is Preacher's sister, Loretta, and her friend, Andre Davis."

posed to be a party, remember? Why don't you get drinks for our new arrivals?"

Loretta followed Preacher to get the drinks, while Dante sat next to Andre.

"Momma," Jake called. "Mack tore up his horse."

Tanya said, "Emergency time. Excuse me."

Dante pressed her back down in her seat. "Fixing horses is a man's job. Let me and Andre take care of it."

"Since you're helping me out," Tanya said, "I won't take exception to that sexist comment. What about you, Natalie?"

She shook her head. "No, let 'em work now. They'll pay later."

Dante and Andre headed off toward the boys, the laugher of the women behind them.

"What's going on, man?" Dante asked, between clenched teeth. "You're dating Preacher's sister? How long has this been going on?"

Andre shrugged. "For a while now."

Dante stopped, as understanding dawned. "Don't tell me she's the go-between on our illegal transportation project."

"I won't tell you then," Andre said, striding ahead of Dante so he could reach the boys first. In short order, they had the horse repaired and the boys were back at play.

"Is Preacher in on it, too?"

Andre shook his head. "No, he was in prison when we got involved. It's Loretta's gig, all by herself."

"But he knows about it."

"I'm not sure," Andre said. "Since he's been out of prison, things have been strained between them. He's trying to go Christian on her. Why all the questions about Preacher?"

"I wasn't asking a question. I'm telling you, Preacher knows."

Andre shrugged. "So, he knows."

Loretta extended her hand to Natalie. "It's so nice
some of Preacher's friends. I appreciate the way you've su
my brother. I don't know how we'll ever repay you."

"No repayment needed," Natalie said. "We love Preache
I can't tell you how much I've wanted to meet you."

"Well," Loretta said, "if we hadn't met through Preache
certainly would have met through Circle Autos."

Dante cleared his throat. He looked down at Natalie. "And
my partner," he said. "I've told you about him. I didn't know
was going to be here. It seems he's been keeping secrets." He too
Loretta's hand in his. "Pretty secrets, at that."

Loretta tapped Andre in the belly with her elbow. "Andre's been a bad boy. He certainly should have introduced us before now. But don't blame him for today. He didn't know we were coming until a couple of hours ago. I thought it would be a nice surprise." She looked up at Andre. "Surprised?"

"You know I am." He extended his hand to Natalie. "Nice to meet you," he said. "Even though we've never met, I feel I know you. My partner talks about you all time. What have you done to the man?"

Natalie chuckled. "Nothing but good, I hope."

Dante smiled, casting a brief glance in Preacher's direction.

Andre then extended his hand to Preacher. "Nice to meet you, man."

"Same here," Preacher said. He turned to Loretta. "It seems my sister is full of surprises today."

Loretta laughed as she hugged him. "I asked Tanya to keep my coming a secret. I wanted to surprise you. It worked, didn't it?"

Preacher glanced at Tanya. "It worked, all right."

"Lighten up, Preacher," Tanya said, full of gaiety. "This is sup-

"He's threatened to tell Natalie if I don't end our relationship. He even mentioned police raids."

Andre laughed. "Empty threats. Think about it. Whatever happens to us, happens to his sister. What's he going to do?"

Dante relaxed a bit. "He could still tell Natalie."

Andre clapped Dante on the shoulder. "That, my man, is your problem. We know how far Preacher will go with his information, but I'm not sure about your girl. Maybe we need to hurry and lock down our participation in her brother's jobs program."

Dante eyed him. "The one you've been against since day one?"

"Hey, I'm flexible. We need some leverage against your girl. Having that jobs program linked to the dealership is as good a way as any to assure that she stays in line."

When Andre started to walk away, Dante grabbed his arm. "I can't do that to her."

"I don't care what you do, man. I tell you like you tell me. She's your problem. Take care of her."

"This is all your—"

"I'm not even listening to that lie today. I'm here with my woman. It's a beautiful day. I'm going to enjoy myself." With that, he shrugged off Dante's arm and headed back toward the group. Dante had no choice but to follow him.

Serena cast a sideways glance at her husband as he pulled into Preacher and Tanya's driveway behind the two other cars parked there. She had never known Barnard to be this angry with her. He hadn't spoken to her since he'd accused her of using delaying tactics to get out of coming on this outing. She couldn't help it if she hadn't been able to find anything to wear, could she? Nor could she help it if her parents called just as they were leaving.

Well, Barnard thought those things were deliberate. Unfortunately for her, he was right. She should have realized how transparent her actions would be, but she hadn't been thinking clearly. No, all she'd been thinking of was ways to get out of spending an afternoon with Preacher and his family. A root canal sounded more inviting.

Barnard got out of the car, still not speaking to her. She sat waiting for him to open her door until she realized he wasn't going to open it. Her husband was already headed toward the side of the house. Serena thought about stubbornly sitting in the car, but decided against it. She scrambled out of the car and rushed towards her husband.

"You trying to leave me?" she asked.

Barnard frowned down at her. "I should have left you at home. You've made it clear you don't want to be here."

Serena had no answer for her husband. He was right.

Barnard started shaking his head. "I don't understand why you won't give Preacher a chance. This is so unlike you."

"I'm here now," she said. "That's all that matters."

"Don't fool yourself, Serena. It's like something evil comes over you when the subject of Preacher comes up. I think you need to pray about it. I don't think the Lord approves."

Serena felt her own anger rise. Barnard was chastising her? She couldn't believe it. If he only knew—but he didn't know. And that was her fault.

"It's about time you two got here," Natalie said, when Serena and Barnard walked through the gate into the backyard, where the other six guests were seated around a big redwood picnic table.

The woman sitting between Natalie and Preacher stood. Serena assumed she was Preacher's girlfriend, Tanya. "Welcome," the woman said. "I was beginning to worry."

The tall, sleek woman pressed her cheek first against Barnard's cheek and then against Serena's. "So this is your wife, Barnard?" she asked.

Serena thought Barnard did a good job with his fake smile. "Yes, this is the little lady. Serena, this is Tanya, Preacher's fiancée."

"Thanks for inviting us over, Tanya," Serena said. "I'm sorry we were late. My parents called before we left and you know how parents can be."

Tanya laughed. "Don't I ever. You'll have to meet my mother some day. Until then, we'll have to settle for trading horror stories."

Tanya's openness put Serena at ease, but that vanished when Preacher approached. He patted Barnard on the back and squeezed her shoulder with his hand. She fought back a wince at his touch. "Good to see you two," he said. "Come on. Let me introduce you to everybody."

"I'll get you something to drink," Tanya said.

"Barnard and Serena," Preacher said, "I'd like to introduce you to Loretta, my sister, and her date, Andre Davis, who's also Dante's partner at Circle Autos."

Barnard gave Andre a hearty handshake. "Small world, man, small world." He inclined his head toward Dante. "What's it going to take to get you guys to sign on with the jobs program? The paperwork is ready. All we need are your signatures."

Andre lifted his hands. "No business talk today," he said. "But I think you'll be hearing from us soon. Dante and I were just talking about how much we want to get involved." He turned to Dante. "Weren't we, man?"

Serena couldn't help it, but her gaze kept straying to Preacher. Something was going on between him and Dante. For the second time, she caught Dante glancing at Preacher when he was asked a question. She wondered what that was about. She hoped Dante hadn't picked up on Preacher's interest in Natalie. She turned a hot stare on Preacher, telling him with her eyes what she thought of him. He turned away to say something to Andre.

"You know," Loretta chimed in, "Tanya has a couple of salons. You may want to sign her up as well."

Tanya joined them with glasses of lemonade for Serena and Barnard. "Did somebody call my name?"

"No business talk today," Andre said again. "Loretta and I are trying to get to know Serena and Barnard. Aren't we, babe?"

When Loretta smiled, Serena thought she looked familiar. She was sure she had seen Preacher's sister before but she couldn't remember where. "Have you and I met before?" she asked Loretta.

Loretta studied her face. "I was wondering the same thing," she said. "Your face does look familiar."

"Maybe you've been to our gym?" Natalie offered. She gave the address.

Serena's eyes widened. Now she remembered where she'd first met Loretta.

"I've been there," Loretta said. "But only once." She smiled at Serena. "You have a good mind for faces, if you remember every one that comes into your gym."

Serena glanced at Preacher again. His strained expression told her that he knew how she knew his sister as well. Loretta had been the courier for the letter Preacher had sent to Serena. Serena wondered how much Loretta knew about her relationship with Preacher. She prayed she knew nothing, and if she did know something, Serena prayed she'd keep it to herself.

"Serena's good with faces and names," Natalie added, "much better than I am. She's strong in a lot of areas where I'm weak, and vice versa, so we make good business partners."

"It's the same way with me and Dante," Andre said. "He's the number cruncher; I'm the front man. We operate in different roles, but we're always on the same page in our decisions. We're a great team, aren't we, man?"

Again, Serena saw Dante glance at Preacher before nodding. Natalie only smiled at her man, rubbing her hand down his arm. Serena doubted her sister-in-law saw the exchange between the two men.

"Partnerships have always fascinated me," Loretta said. "I wish Preacher and I could go into business together."

Serena forced herself not to look in Preacher's direction.

"Maybe you can," Barnard offered. He glanced at Preacher. "You and Loretta should really think about it. A lot of people complain about going into business with family, but it's worked well for Serena and Natalie."

"It sure has," Natalie said. "I trust Serena and she trusts me. I can't think of a better arrangement."

Serena agreed because it seemed to be expected of her. "It works for us, but then we run a small business."

"It works for me and Dante," Andre said. "We've known each other since college. We're more brothers than friends, wouldn't you say?"

"Brothers," Dante repeated.

Andre tipped back his drink. "Remember when we were thinking of a name for the dealership. We were going to call it Brothers Auto. Remember that? Then we decided people might interpret Brothers the wrong way, so we went more generic. There's nothing like being in business with someone who has your back. I'm lucky to have Dante at my side. This business would be nowhere without him."

"Okay," Tanya said, "enough of the mutual admiration society. I'm ready to eat. Who else is hungry?"

Preacher called the boys to the table. Then he asked Barnard to bless the food. After he finished, Tanya said to the group, "I just realized that Preacher and I are the only ones in this group with children." She nudged Serena, who stood next to her, with her hip. "What are you and Barnard waiting on, girl? You'd better get busy."

Serena met Barnard's gaze and forced a smile. "Soon," she said.

"Well, it'd better be," Tanya said. "You two aren't getting any younger. Kids will run you ragged. Trust me—have them now so you will still have some time for yourself after they're out of the house."

"Amen to that," Natalie said.

"Did you hear that, Dante?" Andre teased. "I think somebody is sending you a message."

Natalie took Dante's hand in hers before saying to Andre, "Stop causing trouble. You're going to scare my guy away."

Andre shook his head. "This guy is not going anywhere, Natalie. You want him; he's yours."

"Remind me to stop telling you my secrets, Andre," Dante said. "A man has to have some leverage with his woman and you're giving away all of mine."

Tanya chuckled. "Rarely does a man have the upper hand with a woman." She winked at Serena. "We just let you think you do. Isn't that right, Serena?"

Serena glanced at her husband. "What do you say, Barnard?"

"In the better relationships, the upper hand shifts depending on the situation."

Tanya laughed. "Good answer, Barnard." She turned to Serena. "Good going, girl. You've trained him well." Then she turned to Preacher. "You've done a great job picking friends, Preacher. I think we're on to something good."

Serena marveled at how far off base Tanya was in her analysis. Preacher's eyes told her his bewilderment matched hers.

CHAPTER 17

Keeping his attention focused on the conversation between Andre and Natalie, who seemed to have become fast friends, Preacher resisted the urge to check his watch again. The last time he'd done it, Tanya had sent him one of her "I can't believe you" glares. No doubt, in her eyes, this little get-together was a major success. He just wanted it over before some major catastrophe occurred.

Serena had been covertly watching him all afternoon. So he'd been covertly watching Barnard to make sure that he wasn't watching Serena watching him. Tanya may have been having a good time, but he felt as though he'd worked a double shift in a factory.

If his instincts were right, Loretta was the powder keg. He knew his sister, so he watched and waited for her to make her move. She'd spent a little time talking with Natalie and joking with Barnard and Dante. They all loved her. His sister could be charismatic when she wanted.

She smiled at him now as she made her away around to Serena. Preacher put his drink on the table and stood, preparing to follow her. Barnard intercepted him before he reached them. "Nice party, man," he said.

"I'm glad you and Serena could make it."

From the sour look on Barnard's face, Preacher knew he'd made the wrong comment. "I'm sorry we were late," he said. He began shaking his head. "I don't understand it, but Serena absolutely doesn't like you."

Preacher braced himself. He wasn't sure how to respond, so he didn't.

"I know you've felt it and I apologize."

"No need for apologies." He shrugged. "Sometimes people don't click."

"But this is so unlike Serena. I have to be honest with you and tell you I've asked her if you've gotten out of line with her."

"Barnard, I'd never—"

"I know," Barnard said. "She told me you hadn't. But she's my wife and it's not like her to be unreasonable about a person, so I have to ask you, do you have any idea what her problem is with you?"

Until this point all of the lies between Preacher and Barnard were lies of omission, things he'd kept from his friend. To lie now would be a bald-faced lie, man-to-man, face-to-face. To tell the truth would betray Serena. "Look, Barnard," he said. "You need to talk to Serena. The answers you want are hers to give, not mine."

"Is that a yes or a no?"

"It's neither. It's merely some advice from one friend to another. Serena's your wife. You should be having this conversation with her. I'm sure she'd be upset if she knew you were having it with me."

"You're right, man. I know you're right, but I don't seem to be able to get through to her. She has put up a wall where you're concerned and she won't take it down."

"She's here," Preacher said. "That's a step. You have to give her credit for trying."

"Maybe," Barnard said, but he didn't sound too convinced. "So many things aren't right with us lately. This is only one of them."

Preacher didn't want to hear this. "Have you thought about seeing a counselor?"

Barnard nodded. "We've talked about it, but that's as far as it's gone."

"Maybe you need to pursue it, for your marriage and for your sanity."

"I hear you, man," he said. "I'm sorry to bring this up when we're supposed to be relaxing."

Guilt overwhelmed Preacher. "Don't worry about it," he said, making a show of his smile. "Hey, I've got some horseshoe stakes and horseshoes. How about we set up a court and challenge Dante and Andre to a game? They look entirely too smug after beating us at darts."

Barnard answered with a smile.

Before heading off to the game, Preacher glanced in Tanya and Serena's direction to make sure all was well with them. Upon seeing the two of them laughing together instead of glaring at each other, he allowed himself to relax a bit. A quick look in Loretta's direction indicated that she was also on her best behavior. "The challenge is on then," he finally said to Barnard. "Let's beat them like they stole something."

* * *

"Your husband and my brother get along like they've known each other for years," Loretta said to Serena. The two women sat alone at the picnic table. Natalie and Tanya had joined in the game of horseshoes.

"Well, if you want to be technical about it, they have known each other for about two years. But I know what you mean. Preacher's friendship means a lot to Barnard."

"And vice versa. But I'm surprised."

"I guess their friendship is odd. A straitlaced guy like Barnard and the anything-but-straitlaced Preacher. They make an odd couple."

Loretta shook her head. "That's not what surprises me."

Serena didn't want to do it, but she had to. She met Loretta's gaze. "Then what surprises you?"

Loretta chuckled. "Let's not play games, Serena. I'm surprised your husband doesn't know about your past relationship with Preacher. He doesn't know, does he?"

Bile rose up in Serena's throat and it was all she could do to keep from spitting it at Loretta's feet. "I don't know what you're talking about."

"Sure you don't. I knew something scandalous was going on in this pious little group of Christians trying to take my brother away. Isn't there a commandment about lying? I'm sure there's one about adultery."

"Adultery? What are you talking about?"

Loretta laughed. "It doesn't take a genius to figure it out. There has to be a reason you haven't told your husband about a relationship that supposedly ended years ago. Maybe you still have a thing for Preacher. Or maybe it hasn't ended between you two. You've been watching my brother all night. I hope your husband hasn't noticed."

"You're talking crazy."

"Deny. Deny. Deny. Now I don't think that's in the Bible."

Serena moved to get up. "I don't have to sit here and listen to this."

Loretta gave her a fake smile. "You sure don't. Why don't we both go join the others? I'm sure they'd be interested in this conversation, especially that husband of yours and the sister-in-law business partner who trusts you so much."

"You wouldn't dare!"

"Why wouldn't I?"

"Preacher's your brother."

"Tell me something I don't know."

Serena sat back down. "What do you want from me?"

Loretta leaned close to her. "I want you hypocrites to leave my brother alone. I want him out of your church and out of your life."

The hypocrite moniker stung, but Serena couldn't refute it. That she and this woman who called her a hypocrite wanted the same thing left a bitter taste in her mouth. "I can't control Preacher," she said. "You ought to know that."

Loretta sighed. "So you've already tried to get rid of him?"

Am I that transparent? "Let's just say my life would be a lot less complicated if Preacher were not in it."

Loretta eyed her. "*Ahh,* so what went on with you and Preacher was pretty serious." Serena's surprise must have shown on her face because Loretta added, "All I knew was that it ended badly. I have no idea why, though you can fill me in on the details if you like."

Serena didn't even bother to respond. "If you're finished, I'd like to leave now."

"For now," Loretta said. "But this conversation is far from over."

* * *

"Are you sure you have to go?" Tanya asked Natalie, who had told her that she and Dante would be the first to leave. In reality, Tanya couldn't wait for Natalie to get out of her sight. She wanted them all off her property, had wanted them all gone since she'd overhead the conversation between Loretta and Serena, and it took every ounce of self-control she had not to kick them out. Preacher had disrespected her by bringing his women, ex-women, whatever, to her home. That she would not tolerate. Had it not been for her ego, she'd have put him on blast in front of these so-called saints and let the chips fall where they may. But she had too much self-esteem to let the men here know what Preacher had done to her. Besides, Loretta would have taken too much satisfaction in seeing her react to Preacher's misdeeds. She had other ways, better ways, of getting back at her fiancé. He'd regret the day the thought even crossed his mind to disrespect her.

"I'm sorry," Natalie said. "Dante needs to go in to work for a few hours and I don't like it when he works late."

"I understand," Tanya said, tired of the fake smile she wore. "You'll have to come over again."

Natalie shook her head. "Next time, you, Preacher, and the boys will come to my place. It's not as nice as yours but I think you'll be comfortable."

Over my dead body. "I look forward to it."

"Okay, everybody," Tanya called to the group. "The first party poopers are leaving. Say good-bye to Natalie and Dante." She hoped the others would follow their lead and pack up as well.

As luck would have it, that first departure started a round of good-byes that ended with Loretta saying, "We'd better get out of here as well. If Dante's going to work, I know Andre is going, too."

Tanya wanted to wipe that smug smile Loretta gave her off her face. She knew Loretta took great satisfaction in thinking she knew something Tanya didn't know. Tanya couldn't wait to return the kindness. "Not everybody at one time," she said, unable to summon up a stronger protest.

"Serena and I will stay and help you and Preacher clean up," Barnard offered.

If you don't get that wife of yours out of my presence now, you're going to see something that'll make WWF SmackDown *seem like a kid's game.* "I want you to stay," she forced herself to say, "but cleanup isn't necessary. I hate to admit this but we catered the event and the cleanup crew will be arriving any minute now."

"Then I guess we should take our leave as well," Serena said.

Tanya couldn't look at the woman, had no graceful words to give her. She was relieved when Preacher stood next to her and said, "We've certainly enjoyed having you two. We hope you come again."

"Next time you'll have to come to our place," Barnard said.

When the two men clapped each other on the back, Serena took a step toward her. Unable to take her acting any further, Tanya took a step back and seared the woman with her stare. Serena wisely stepped back and turned with her husband to leave.

Tanya walked alongside Preacher as their last two guests got in their car. Preacher waved to them as they drove away; she didn't bother. "What's up with you and these church women?" she asked Preacher before Serena and Barnard's car was out of the driveway.

"I don't know what you're talking about," Preacher said, heading back to the backyard.

Tanya followed him. "I thought I'd dealt with this problem when I put Natalie in her place. Now this Serena comes to my home and spends the entire afternoon watching you. At first, I didn't think she liked you too well, since she had a frown on her face most of the time. But now I'm thinking that look meant something else. You've slept with her, haven't you?"

Preacher's eyes widened in surprise and his response was a couple of beats too late in coming. "You're letting your imagination get the best of you."

"Don't try to play me, Preacher," Tanya said, grabbing his arm and forcing him to stop and deal with her. "You didn't answer my question. Have you slept with Serena, who's supposed to be your new Christian sister?"

"Get your mind out of the gutter, Tanya," he answered, but he didn't meet her eyes when he did.

"You lying hypocrite," Tanya said. "You dirty lying hypocrite." She lifted her hand and slapped him with an open palm. "You have the nerve to bring your women up to my home, like I don't matter. I've told you before and I'm telling you again, Preacher, I won't have it."

Preacher rubbed his jaw. "You're crazy. I don't have any women. How many times do I have to tell you that?"

"Talk is cheap," Tanya said, itching to slap him again. "Actions are what counts. The next time we have a cookout I'll invite some of my male friends and old boyfriends and see how you like it."

"I can't believe you're jealous."

"I'm not jealous, Preacher, but I'm not going to let you disrespect me in my own home. That will never happen again. If you want to pursue other women, let me know and me and the boys can make other arrangements."

Preacher's hand stilled on his jaw. "What are you talking about—make other arrangements? This is your home, the boys' home."

"Well, if that's true, then maybe *you'll* have to make other arrangements. You're not going to live here with me and the boys, even in the garage apartment, if you're seeing or pursuing other women."

Preacher sat down in the nearest chair and pulled a resisting Tanya down on his lap. "I'm going to tell you this for the last time. I'm not interested in any woman but you. I don't know how else to make that clear to you." Tanya stiffened at his words. "What can I do to put you at ease?"

"You can get those church people out of our lives," she said. "Can't you see they're causing trouble between us?"

Preacher shook his head. "I can't do that. You know that Barnard is my sponsor. You've got to get over these suspicions of yours. These people are in our lives, at least until my probation is over."

"Ask for a new sponsor."

"It's not that easy."

Tanya scoffed. "I bet it'd be easy if that Barnard knew you'd slept with his wife."

"I'm not sleeping with Serena," he told her. "How can I get that through your thick skull? You're the only woman in my life, the only woman in my heart."

Tanya decided to change tactics. She leaned in close to Preacher, resting her head on his shoulder. "You can come to bed with me tonight. Maybe all this sexual electricity I'm seeing is a result of my own frustration."

Preacher brushed his hand down her hair. "When do you want to get married?" he asked her. "I wanted to wait until my financial situation was more stable, but if we're going to live like married people, we may as well get married. What do you say?"

"I've already said yes."

"Then why don't we just do it. We can go down to the courthouse tomorrow."

Tanya sat up and away from him. "Courthouse? Tomorrow? You've got to be joking. I'm not getting married in some stupid civil ceremony. I want a big wedding, with all my family and friends and a few of my enemies. I want the grand white dress and the huge wedding party. I want it all." With her eyes, she dared him to question her choice of white.

He picked up her left hand and kissed the finger wearing the engagement ring he'd given her. "How about we compromise and have a medium-sized wedding here at the house?"

Tanya pouted the way she always did when she was determined to get her way. "I'm going to have to think about that. You know I've always wanted a big wedding, Preacher. You seem to want to change everything up now. You promised I could have a big wedding and now you're reneging."

"I'm not reneging," he said, releasing her hand. "I'm only trying to speed things up."

Tanya got up from his lap. "I'd rather wait until I can have the wedding I want, the wedding of my dreams. We don't have to wait until we're married to sleep together again but if that's the way you want it, that's the way it'll be. I'm not giving up my wedding."

Preacher nodded. "We'll have the big wedding then."

Tanya left him sitting there and went into the house. She knew he thought he'd gotten her back in line with his lame concessions about the wedding. Unfortunately for him, marriage was the last thing on her mind. No way was she going to tie herself up with a broke ex-convict who had so little respect for her that he'd lie straight to her face. Preacher may have thought she was a fool, but she'd show him.

* * *

Andre waited until they got back to Loretta's townhouse to question her. "So what was today about?" he asked, following her down the hallway to her bedroom.

She kicked off her shoes and stretched out on the bed, fully clothed. He lay down next to her and she turned to him. "What did you ask me?"

She was such an audacious woman, he had to smile. "You heard me. I want to know what game you were playing today."

She grinned. "It was fun, wasn't it?"

"If you call your brother almost sending Dante into cardiac arrest, then yes, it was fun."

"What are you talking about?"

Andre lay back on his pillow and folded his hands under his head. "I'm not telling," he said. "You're not the only one who can keep a secret."

Loretta put her hands on his chest, and he thought she was going to try to kiss the truth out of him. Instead, she snaked her fingers up his chest to his underarms and began to tickle him. He convulsed with laughter. "Stop!"

"Tell me!"

More laughter. "Stop and I'll tell you."

More tickles. "Tell me and I'll stop."

He tried to roll away from her but she followed him, still tickling. He gave in. "Preacher told Dante he knows about the drugs going through the dealership."

Loretta stopped tickling him and sat up.

He sat up, too. "I figured that would get your attention. Did you tell him?"

Loretta nodded. "But why did he bring it up to Dante?"

"Apparently, he doesn't want Dante seeing Natalie. He told

him that if he didn't break it off with her, he'd tell her what we were doing. You don't think he will, do you?"

"What else did Preacher say?"

"I'm not sure. Dante said something about police raids, but I didn't think much of it. I figure your brother is yanking his chain to get him away from Natalie. Your brother must have some rap. Living with one woman and threatening the boyfriend of another."

"You sound envious of my player brother."

Andre nipped her shoulder with his lips. "I have the woman I want. Doesn't mean I can't admire another brother's game, though."

"So what did Dante tell my brother?"

Andre moved to her cheek. "I'm not sure he told him anything." He stopped kissing Loretta. "But this woman is important to him. I've told you he wants out because of her."

"Then let him out."

Andre pulled back so he could look into her eyes. "You're joking, right?"

"Not at all. Tell Dante I'll buy him out."

"What?"

"You heard me. Tell Dante I'll buy him out."

"So you and I can become partners?"

"Something like that," she said.

Andre liked the idea of being partners with Loretta. In fact, he had often dreamed of the two of them presiding together over their own business empire. That dream had seemed far-fetched when her brother occupied that place in her life, but now that he'd chosen another path, Andre was hopeful for a more permanent relationship—business and personal—with her. "Why are you really willing to buy Dante out?" Andre didn't expect an answer. Loretta usually kept her plans to herself.

"Don't look a gift horse in the mouth. Take my offer to Dante. He can name his price, as long as it's a reasonable one."

"When Dante said he wanted out, I'm sure he didn't mean this way."

She lay back on her pillow and closed her eyes. "I don't care what he meant. Now I want him out. He doesn't have much choice. He either sells his share to me at his price or I take it at my price. It's up to him."

"I hear you," Andre said. "I'll tell him tomorrow."

She opened her eyes. "Why not tell him tonight? You heard him say he was going to the office."

He nipped at her neck again. "I have other plans for the evening."

Loretta pushed his head away. "I'll be here when you get back. I want his answer tonight."

"There's no need for me go anywhere," Andre said, reaching for her phone on the nightstand behind the bed.

Loretta grabbed his hand. "Not over the phone," she said. "This has to be done face-to-face."

Dante got up from his desk and looked out his office window on the car lot that represented years of hard work on his and Andre's parts. "I don't want to sell," he said, after Andre laid out the details of Loretta's offer. "I want them out."

"That's not an option, Dante," Andre said, slumping casually in the chair in front of Dante's desk with his legs stretched out in front him. "Things have gone too far. The only way to get out is to sell."

"I'm not doing it."

"You don't have a choice."

Dante spun around to face Andre. His friend's apparent calmness irked him. "What do you mean?"

Andre sighed. "Loretta has decided she wants your share of the dealership. She's not taking no for an answer."

"Why, that's crazy!" Dante kicked the side of his desk and began pacing in front of the window. "She can't come here and strong-arm me into selling."

"Yes, she can."

Dante stopped pacing. "You can't be serious, Andre."

"Sit down, Dante. You've got to wake up to the truth. Either you want to be in the New York deal for the long haul or you sell. There's no middle ground."

Dante stuffed his hands in his pants pockets. "I could call the cops." When Andre sat up a bit straighter in his chair, Dante took satisfaction in finally getting a reaction from his partner.

Andre shook his head. "You don't want to do that."

"I want the business we built back. I want these people out. I ought to call the cops."

"That's not going to get you what you want. What makes you think the cops are going to let you keep this business? What makes you think you won't end up in prison?"

"I could turn state's evidence."

Andre laughed. "You've been watching too much television, or maybe not enough. In order to turn state's evidence, you have to have some evidence. You don't know enough about what's going on to have anything to offer to the cops."

"But you do."

Andre slumped back in his chair. "You'd turn me in?"

"No, man, that's not what I'm saying. We could go to the police together."

Andre shook his head. "You're not thinking clearly. Focus on what you want, Dante."

"I want our business back the way it was before we got involved with these hoodlums."

"Too late for that. What else do you want?"

"I don't like the idea of giving up what I've worked so hard to build. I won't do it."

"Not even for Natalie?"

"Don't bring her into this," Dante said.

"What do you mean, man? She's already in it. We wouldn't be having this discussion if it weren't for her. If what you want is a life with her free of this business, your choice is easy: sell to Loretta. If you want to hold onto the business, then you've got to let her go or get her so deeply involved that she has as much to lose as we do if something goes wrong."

Dante took some time to dissect his partner's words. He wanted his business back but at what cost? "What if none of those options work for me?"

Andre stood, checking his watch. "Life sucks sometimes. What else can I say? You have to play the hand you're dealt. You can always use the money to start another business. Then you and Natalie can have a real fresh start."

Though there was logic to Andre's advice, Dante didn't see why he had to start over because some thugs wanted what was his. Preacher and Loretta didn't control his destiny, even if Andre thought they did. He wouldn't give up his business without a fight.

CHAPTER 18

Natalie awakened the next morning refreshed and excited. "Thank you, Lord." The cookout with Preacher's family had gone very well, in her opinion. Tanya had been the perfect hostess and Natalie had detected little of the hostility from their first meeting. There had been a moment there when she and Dante were leaving that she'd sensed a bit of impatience from Tanya, but she attributed it to the stress of acting as hostess for a new group of people.

What made her happiest was that Serena had done a good job with Preacher's girlfriend. Natalie had seen them in conversation a couple of times during the afternoon. Now she wouldn't have to worry about the couple. Serena and Barnard would take good care of them.

She'd miss her growing friendship with Preacher, but Serena had been right. She'd sensed some tension between him and Dante that made her wonder if Dante saw what Serena saw. Whatever. She'd done her best to make Dante feel secure. She'd been openly affectionate with him so he wouldn't have to worry about where her interests lay.

She got out of bed, quickly showered and dressed for work at the Children's Center. She hoped she would see her brother so she could compare notes with him about the cookout. As she was putting on her earrings, the doorbell rang.

"Who could that be at this hour?" she said aloud, heading down the hallway. She put on her second earring and opened the door. "Dante?" she said. "What are you doing here?"

Dante leaned in and brushed his lips against her cheek. "That doesn't sound very welcoming."

"Forgive me," she said, stepping back and opening the door wider. "Come on in. Is something wrong?"

Dante sat on her couch and patted the space next to him. She hesitated, then sat. "You're scaring me, Dante. What's wrong?"

He pulled her close. "Let me hold you for a few minutes," he said. "I just want to hold you."

Natalie leaned into his embrace. "Talk to me, sweetie."

"In a minute. Just let me hold you."

Natalie's anxiety grew but she kept quiet and let him hold her. She prayed a silent prayer that whatever he had to tell her wasn't bad. She couldn't help but think of Benjamin and that failed relationship. She pushed those thoughts out of her mind. This wasn't Benjamin; this was Dante. The two men were as different as night and day.

Dante tipped her chin up. "I love you," he said.

She batted her eyelashes, fighting tears. Her instincts told her his news wasn't good. "I love you, too, Dante."

"How much?"

Natalie pulled away from him. "Don't do this," she said. "Just tell me." Dante didn't say anything and her anxiety soared. "Is there another woman?"

Dante shook his head and pulled her close again. "Never that," he said. "You're the only woman for me. That's why this is so hard."

She pulled back and looked into his eyes. "You're scaring me, Dante. Just tell me."

Dante sighed. Then he pulled away from her. "I should do this like a man." He stood and sat on the coffee table so he faced her. "We can't see each other any more."

"What? Why?"

Dante took her hands in his. "Believe me, it's for the best." He brought her hands to his lips and kissed them. Then he held them against his heart. "I haven't been honest with you about something," he said, "something big."

Natalie felt the pain of betrayal. She tried to pull her hands from his but he held on tight. "Hear me out," he pleaded.

"Why should I?" Natalie asked, blinking at the tears pooling in her eyes. "I trusted you, Dante. You told me I could trust you." She looked away from him. "I thought you were different. What a fool I was!"

Keeping her hands in one of his, he used the other to turn her face back to him. "I told you it wasn't another woman, and it isn't. There is no secret girlfriend, no secret child, no secret wife. You are the only woman in my life."

The burden that had embedded itself in her chest lightened at his words. "Then what is it? Tell me."

He dropped her hands and stood. Turning away from her, he

said, "A couple of years ago, Andre and I got in a major financial bind at the dealership." He turned back to her. "To fix it, we diversified, I guess you could say, to increase our cash flow."

Natalie didn't think that sounded so bad. She ran a business, so she knew about financial binds and cash-flow problems. "Is that all?"

Dante shook his head and sat on the coffee table again. "Now my business associates are trying to force me out."

"Can they do that?"

"Not legally."

"Well, get a lawyer and fight them."

Dante met her eyes. "I can't."

"Sure you can," Natalie said. "We'll find an attorney. Barnard knows a lot of people. I'm sure he'll know the perfect person. Let's call him right now."

When she would have gotten up to get the phone, Dante pressed her back down. "This is not something I can fight through legal means because the business relationship wasn't a legal one."

Natalie's heart contracted violently. "What does that mean?"

"It means Andre and I got the money through illegal means."

"You went to a loan shark? Oh, Dante, how could you and Andre even think about going that route? Still, I think you can fight them legally."

"We didn't go to a loan shark."

Natalie's frustration rose. "Then where did you get the money?"

"We started transporting goods for Preacher and his sister."

Natalie rolled his words around in her head, trying to make sense of them. "Preacher and his sister?"

Dante nodded.

Natalie merely stared at him, still unable to make meaning

of his words. “What kind of business do Preacher and Loretta have?”

Dante didn’t answer and he didn’t look away.

Understanding finally dawned for Natalie. “No,” she said, shaking her head. “NO!”

Dante reached for her but she eluded his grasp and stood. “You’re telling me that you’re transporting drugs for Preacher and Loretta?”

He looked up at her with the dreamy brown eyes she loved. “I’ve been trying to stop, to get out,” he said, “but Preacher and his sister are ruthless. They want me out so Preacher can have a legal business to run now that he’s out of prison.”

Natalie started shaking her head. “Preacher’s going into the mortuary business,” she said, remembering the pure joy in Preacher’s face when he told her about the opportunity God had given him. Dante had to be wrong. “He’s not interested in your dealership.”

“Listen to me, Natalie,” Dante said. “He’s interested. He told me so himself yesterday.”

Natalie folded her arms across her chest and began pacing. “This is too much,” she said. “It’s too much.” She stopped pacing and stared at this man she thought she loved and realized she didn’t even know him. “You’re a drug dealer,” she said, trying to get her mind around the truth of the situation. “You’re a drug dealer.”

Dante went to her and tried to pull her into his arms. “Natalie—”

“I don’t want to hear it!” she screamed. “Get out!”

“But—”

She strode to the door and jerked it open. “Get out,” she said. “I don’t even know you.”

Natalie knew her words hurt him by the crestfallen expression on his face, but she couldn't think about his pain now. All she knew was that she'd trusted him and he'd let her down.

Outside the door, he called her name again. She closed the door in his face and then collapsed in tears in front of it.

Preacher sat at the counter in his apartment drinking a cup of coffee. Tanya had taken the boys to school this morning, so he took a few moments for himself before diving into the day's tasks. He'd awakened this morning feeling as though he'd barely dodged a bullet. The cookout and the fight with Tanya that followed it only served one purpose for him. It told him it was time to come clean with Barnard, Natalie, and Tanya. He was tired of lying. He wanted to fix things and he knew he needed help to do it. The only person he considered turning to was Barnard, but he couldn't go to Barnard with his problems until he came clean about his past with Serena. He'd give her a final chance to tell her husband and then he'd tell him. He had to. He'd also tell Barnard about Loretta and Dante and the dealership. He was sure Barnard would know what to do. Preacher surely didn't. Then he'd have to sit down and explain everything to Tanya. He saved her for last because he knew there'd be drama, and he didn't want to drain all his energy dealing with her before he dealt with everybody else. He'd talk to her tonight when he hoped he'd have more answers than he did now.

He had to do one thing before he went to Serena and Barnard though. He had to give Loretta one last chance to give up the business. She could do it because there were people lined up to take her place, eager for the power and position she held. The same power and position he once held. It was ironic that it would be easier for Loretta to get out than it would be for Dante. It was unfair, but that's the way the narcotics business worked.

Preacher finished his coffee, grabbed his keys, and left the apartment. When he was about halfway down the stairs, Natalie turned the corner, ready to come up. Seeing him, she stopped and said, "We need to talk."

"Okay," he said, guessing her visit had something to do with Dante. He wondered what the brother had told her.

Natalie didn't say a word until they were both in his apartment and the door was closed behind them. He offered her a seat.

"I prefer to stand," she said. He saw it then, the pain in her eyes and he knew Dante had told her something.

"Is it true?" she asked.

"Is what true?"

"The dealership, the drugs."

Preacher hated the pain he saw in her usually happy eyes. "I'm sorry, Natalie."

Natalie dropped down in the recliner as if a boulder had landed on her. Her purse fell to the floor beside the chair. "How could you?" she asked.

"I wanted to tell you," he said, "but I didn't want to hurt you."

"That sentiment seems to be going around this morning," she said, "but it doesn't help. It doesn't help at all. How could you do this to Dante? To me? To Barnard? Especially Barnard, after the way he put himself out there for you."

Preacher frowned. "What are you talking about?"

She flashed accusing eyes at him. "You know what I'm talking about. You and your sister forcing Dante into your drug business and now trying to force him out and take his dealership." She shook her head. "You certainly had us fooled. Tell me, Preacher, did you and Loretta sit around and laugh at how naive we were? I bet we gave you both a good laugh."

Preacher squatted in front of her, his stomach churning at the betrayal and disgust in her voice. "I don't know what Dante told you," he said, "but I didn't force him into anything."

"Yeah, right. I'm getting good at parsing what people say and what they don't say. What about your sister? Did she force him?"

Preacher glanced away, unable to bear the guilty sentence in her eyes. When he turned back to her, he said, "It happened while I was in prison. I didn't know anything about it until a few days ago. And my sister didn't force Dante, he willingly joined in with her."

Her eyes widened in disgust. "Are you trying to make excuses for your sister?" she asked. "You've got some nerve."

"I'm not trying to make excuses. My sister is guilty, too."

"And so are you. You knew and you did nothing. Were you going to let Barnard get the jobs program mixed up in that mess? After all he's done for you, were you going to let him do that?"

Preacher shook his head. "I wasn't going to let that happen. That's what I told Dante yesterday at the cookout."

"I don't believe you. Dante told me you threatened him because you want to push him out of the dealership so you and your sister can have it."

"That's a lie," Preacher said. "Dante is lying to you."

Natalie took a deep breath. "It seems to me you're both liars. How am I supposed to know who to believe? All I know is that Dante came to me with the truth but you didn't."

"I wanted to. I was going to. Today."

"Right. Now isn't that convenient? You must really think I'm an idiot."

Preacher knew her reaction was reasonable given what she'd just learned, but her words still pierced his core. He remembered the day she'd told him she knew he was a good guy. That seemed like a long time ago now. "I think you're wonderful," Preacher said. "You and Barnard have been nothing but supportive of me. That's why I spoke to Dante yesterday. I asked him to put some distance between you two so you wouldn't be hurt by his business dealings. I wasn't going to sit on the secret for long, Natalie. You have to believe me."

She shook her head. "But I don't believe you. That's what a lie does, Preacher. It erodes all trust."

"I know but I am telling the truth now."

She met his gaze. "Why didn't you come to us when you first found out? How did you find out anyway?"

Preacher didn't say anything.

Natalie breathed out a sigh. "No need to answer. Of course, your sister told you. So is that what you were doing, protecting your sister?"

Preacher nodded. "She's guilty but she's my sister and I don't want to see her in prison."

She lifted her arms and Preacher thought she was about to whack him. He didn't move because he felt he deserved her attack. But she didn't hit him. She let her arms fall to her side. "I understand about your sister, Preacher, but I don't understand how you could throw us under the bus to help her."

"I was trying to figure out how I could both protect her and tell you. I couldn't find an easy answer."

Natalie's sorrow-filled eyes met his. "You could have come to us, Preacher. We're not some people you met on the streets. We're your brother and sister in Christ. Together we would have come up with something. We would have tried to help Loretta, if she wanted to be helped."

That was his worry. Loretta hadn't wanted to be helped, but

maybe now she would. "I'm sorry," he said. "I thought I could take care of it myself."

"It doesn't matter now," Natalie said, reaching down for her purse.

When she stood, Preacher asked, "What are you going to do?"

"I'm going to tell my brother what's going on."

He followed her to the door. "I know I don't deserve to ask anything of you, Natalie, but if you have any compassion in your heart left for me, I ask that you let me tell Barnard. He's been a real brother to me and he deserves to hear the truth from me. Will you give me that?"

Natalie didn't answer immediately. While he waited for her response, he felt the bullet he thought he'd dodged settle into the chamber of his heart. He bled on the inside.

"I'm doing this for my brother, Preacher, not for you. You get today. I'm calling him from the car and telling him I need to see him before he talks to Dante or Andre, just to make sure they don't try to pull a fast one and sign up for the program. I'm telling him tonight. If you haven't told him by then, too bad for you."

He opened the door for her. "I'm sorry, Natalie. You don't know how sorry I am."

Natalie's lips turned down in a frown. "You're right, Preacher, you are sorry. You know what hurts most? I didn't just believe you, I believed *in* you. I have to ask, was your conversion real or was it just an act to get yourself out of prison?" Not waiting for an answer, she turned and headed down the steps.

No sooner had Preacher closed the door, sat down on the couch, and dropped his head in his hands in despair when he heard footfalls coming up the inside stairway. It had to be Tanya. He waited while she unlocked the door from her side and let herself in without knocking. She came in blazing. "What's going on here, Preacher?" she asked. "Are you sleeping with Serena *and* Natalie? Tell me I didn't just see Natalie coming from your apartment. What was she doing here?"

Preacher really didn't need this now. "It's not what you think, Tanya. She needed to talk to me about some business."

Tanya propped her hands on her hips. "What business? Last I heard you weren't in the gym business and she wasn't in the funeral home business, so what kind of *business* did she need to talk to you about?"

Preacher wiped his hands down his face. "I'll tell you all about it tonight," he told her. "But right now I need to run a couple of important errands."

"Errands more important than your family? You'd better get your priorities straight, Preacher."

Preacher couldn't deal with Tanya's ranting right now, so he grabbed his keys and headed for the door.

"Don't walk away from me when I'm talking to you," she called after him. "Who do you think you are? Who do you think I am?"

Preacher turned back to her. "Be patient until tonight. I can't deal with this right now. I promise I'll tell you everything."

Tanya rolled her eyes. "You've made me a lot of promises," she said. "And a lot of them have been broken."

Preacher couldn't take anymore. "Tonight, Tanya. We'll talk tonight." He closed the door behind him, leaving her standing there in the middle of his living room talking to herself. There'd be hell to pay when he came home tonight.

Preacher called Loretta and had her meet him at a park near the funeral home. She grinned when she saw him sitting in one of the swings. "Reverting back to your childhood," she said, taking a seat in the swing next to his.

"Things are getting out of hand, 'Retta," he told her, seeing no need to waste time with niceties. "Dante has told Natalie and Natalie's going to tell her brother."

"Tell them what?" Loretta asked.

"About the drugs going through Circle Autos and about our involvement in it."

"You're not involved." *Yet.*

"The way Dante's telling it, you and I forced him in and now we're trying to force him out." He stopped swinging. "Are you trying to force him out, Loretta?"

"He wants out," she told him. "So I thought buying his share would be a good opportunity for you. It was a win-win situation."

Preacher shook his head. "Have you heard anything I've been telling you over the last two years, 'Retta? I don't want back into the life. I want to be as far away from it as possible. Why are you so determined to drag me back in?"

"Look, Preacher," Loretta said. "I've listened to your salvation mumbo jumbo, but I'm not buying it. I don't know what game you're running, but I know it's a game. I just can't figure out why you won't let me in on it. Don't you trust me anymore?"

Preacher sighed. Talking to his sister was like talking to a brick wall. Nothing penetrated. "It's not a game, Loretta. I'm a changed man."

Loretta smirked. "Then why are you lying to your buddy Barnard about your relationship with his wife?"

Preacher closed his eyes.

"Didn't you think I'd remember her, Preacher? I'm not senile, you know. How long have you two been boldly seeing each other right under her husband's nose?"

Preacher was taken aback at how his lies looked from the perspectives of others. "I'm not seeing her."

"That's not what she said."

"What are you talking about? What have you said to her?"

"Calm down, Brother. I just let her know she wasn't fooling me. I saw the way she watched you at the cookout yesterday. I'm not stupid; there's something going on between you. And right under your supposed best friend's nose? If that's Christianity, sign me up. It sounds like a better racket than what I've got going."

How low had his lies brought him? Preacher thought. The sister he'd so wanted to see Christ in him only saw a man playing a game. "It's not how it looks, 'Retta," he said lamely.

She shrugged. "Looks like a duck, sounds like a duck, must be a duck. That's all I'm saying."

Preacher had no idea how to reach her, so he stopped trying. For the moment. "What are you going to do?"

"About what?"

"Aren't you concerned about what Barnard and his sister are going to do?"

She shook her head. "All they're going to do is get Dante and Andre sent to prison. That's on them. Not on me."

"What about the New York folks?"

"What about them? You know as well as I do that some low-level expendable person is going to take the fall for this. They're not worried. I'm not worried."

Preacher's heart ached at the ruthlessness he heard in his sister's voice and saw in her eyes. With every word she spoke, the distance between them widened. He wondered if they'd ever be able to bridge the gap.

CHAPTER 19

Serena pounded around the track at the gym this morning. She'd left early, before Barnard had gotten out of bed. She couldn't look at her husband's face again with the lie between them. Not with the threat of Preacher's sister looming. Not with the damning look Tanya had given her as she and Barnard were leaving the cookout yesterday. Tanya knew something and Serena could only guess that it was about her past relationship with Preacher. The time had arrived for her to tell the truth, something she should have done a long time ago. She just didn't know how to do it.

As she rounded the track for the fourth time, she rehearsed in her mind her fourth scenario for how she would tell Barnard about her past with Preacher. Unfortunately, all four had the same ending: her marriage in trouble. She increased her pace, hoping the adrenaline that fueled her physical body would increase her mental capacity. She needed ideas!

"You're at it early," Natalie said, as she fell in beside her.

"I could say the same for you," Serena said. Natalie was not a runner, so Serena knew something was up with her sister-in-law. She welcomed a break from her own dire situation, so she asked, "What's going on?"

"Need to clear my head," Natalie said, maintaining Serena's pace. "This seems to help you, so I thought I'd give it a try."

Serena let the next lap pass in silence, sensing Natalie needed the quietness of her own thoughts. After another lap, Serena glanced at Natalie out of the corner of her eye. The tears she saw streaming down her sister-in-law's cheeks stopped her in her tracks. She pulled Natalie's arm to get her to stop. "Nat, what's wrong?"

Natalie shook her head. "I can't talk about it, Serena."

The two of them were too close for Serena to accept those words. "You can talk to me about anything." She lifted her hands to Natalie's cheeks and wiped her tears. "Now tell me what's wrong? Did something happen between you and Dante?"

Natalie tried to smile, but failed. "How'd you guess?"

Serena smiled. "When a woman cries, a man is usually the cause."

"You couldn't be more right," Natalie said, sighing deeply. "This morning I can do without all of them." She glanced at Serena. "Sometimes I'm so jealous of you and Barnard. Don't get me wrong. I love you both and I love that you're happy. But I so want what you have and it doesn't seem that I'm ever going to get it. All I get are imitations. First, Benjamin. And now, Dante. What is it about me that I attract and fall for the wrong men? Is something wrong with me?"

"Nothing's wrong with you," Serena said. Natalie's praise for her marriage made her feel like the worst of hypocrites. She leaped at the opportunity to change the subject. "Now tell me what happened with Dante."

Natalie shook her head. "You wouldn't believe it. I'm not even sure I believe it. I thought I knew him." She laughed. "Like I thought I knew Benjamin. And like I thought I knew Preacher." She turned to Serena. "Maybe I'm called to be single and I just don't know it or won't accept it. There's no other explanation for my poor track record with men."

Serena's focus zoomed in on Preacher. "What's Preacher got to do with this?" She prayed Loretta hadn't gotten to Natalie with her suspicions.

"Don't go ballistic on Preacher," Natalie said. "I can't take 'I told you so' this morning."

"Then tell me what's going on," Serena repeated. Natalie's reaction suggested that her problem with Preacher had a source other than his past relationship with Serena. While Serena experienced a bit of relief that her secret was still safe, it occurred to her that if she'd been honest about her past with Preacher, he wouldn't have had the opportunity to hurt Natalie the way he obviously had. She wondered what Natalie would think when she realized that truth as well.

"I'll tell you," Natalie said. "But I need some time."

"Natalie—"

Natalie took her sister-in-law's hand in hers. "I really need this time to try to get some clarity on my life. Given the series of bad decisions I've made, it's clear I'm not hearing the Lord's voice and I need to figure out why. Give me the day and I promise to drop by your house tonight and tell you and Barnard all. I'm going to need to tell both of you and I don't want go through it all twice.

Will you do that for me—wait until tonight? It may be late, but I promise to come by."

"If you're sure?" Serena asked, ashamed for being relieved that Natalie's visit this evening would give her an excuse for waiting a day longer to come clean with Barnard. It wouldn't be fair to hit him with her past with Preacher and Natalie's problem on the same evening.

"I'm sure," Natalie said.

Nodding, Serena took the reprieve she'd been given. She left for the shower counting all the ways Preacher's presence had damaged her relationships and hurt those around her. She'd do tomorrow tonight what she'd been too much of a coward to do before. She'd tell the truth and pray she still had a husband and a sister-in-law after she did.

Tanya rarely complained about her looks, but today was one rare day when her beauty might work against her. Before her little run-in this morning with Preacher about Natalie's visit, she'd planned on looking her best for this meeting. Now she thought she'd be better served by looking a bit worse for the wear.

Despite feeling naked and exposed without her makeup, she climbed out of her car and headed across the parking lot and to the church. Barnard hadn't been in when she'd brought the kids to the Children's Center this morning, but he was here now and he was waiting for her. She had plenty to tell him, too. Preacher might think he was playing her for a fool, but she'd show him who the fool really was.

Barnard's door was open when she reached it, and she stood for a moment looking at him sitting at his desk immersed in paperwork, before she interrupted, "Barnard."

He looked up, giving her a huge smile. "Tanya," he said, getting up and coming to her. "It's so good to see you. I'm sorry I wasn't here when you came by earlier." He pointed to the round table in the corner of his office. "Have a seat," he said. "Can I get you something to drink?"

Tanya shook her head. "No, thanks," she said. "I'm fine. I'm just happy you had some time for me this morning."

He sat next to her and gave her that smile again, causing her to feel a tinge of regret at what she was about to do. Collateral damage, she thought they called it, that's what he was.

"After yesterday," he said, "I consider us friends. Friends always have time for friends. Besides, you said you needed a favor and I want to help."

"Thanks, Barnard. I hope you'll feel that way after you hear what I have to say."

"I'll always consider you a friend," he said. "Now tell me what I can do to help you."

Tanya put her folded hands on the table, holding them together tightly. She hoped she came across as timid and upset. "I don't know how to say this but to say it." She glanced up at him and quickly glanced away. "I want you to keep your wife away from Preacher."

She saw confusion cloud his eyes, so she wasn't surprised when he said, "I don't understand."

She dabbed at her eyes with her knuckles, wishing she could force some tears. "I know you don't, Barnard," she said. "You're a good man. You don't deserve what they're doing to us and neither do I." Tanya waited for understanding to dawn in eyes, but the question in them remained. *How could any man be so dense?* she wondered. So much for hints. "Serena is sleeping with Preacher."

Barnard began shaking his head. "That can't be."

Tanya understood his denial and felt a twinge of pity for him.

"But it is. I know it is. I don't know how long it's been going on, but I know for a fact they've had and are probably still having a sexual relationship."

She watched as his confusion turned to fear. "You're wrong," he said. "It's impossible. Not Serena. Not Preacher. I don't believe it."

She reached over and covered his hand with hers. "I felt the same way when I first heard, but it's true."

Barnard snatched his hand away from hers, as if he'd been burned. "I'm not going to believe these lies," he said. "I know you don't like that Preacher has become a Christian, Tanya, but you're going too far with this lie."

She leaned close to him. "I overheard Serena and Preacher's sister arguing about it yesterday at the cookout."

"I don't believe you. Why didn't you say something then?"

Tanya went in for the kill. "Because, like you, I was in denial. I didn't want to believe Preacher was cheating on me. Not after all that garbage he'd given me about becoming a Christian and wanting to make a family with me and the boys. I overheard it, but I couldn't believe it."

"So why do you believe it now?"

"Because I asked Preacher."

Barnard looked as though he'd been punched in the gut. "And he told you he was having an affair with my wife?"

Tanya thought about lying here, but in her opinion the truth was damning enough. "Of course he didn't. I asked him and he lied."

"Maybe he was telling the truth."

Tanya knew Barnard was reaching for any excuse to keep from accepting what he already believed on some level. "I know Preacher. Can't you tell when your wife is lying to you?" When he didn't correct her by saying he and Serena didn't lie to each other,

Tanya knew she had him. "Think about it, Barnard," she said, pressing her advantage. "They say there are always signs when your partner is cheating. Can you honestly say there haven't been signs?"

Barnard didn't answer immediately, so Tanya waited. She could imagine the thoughts going through his mind. Thoughts about his wife with Preacher, and all he'd done for the man. "I know you're probably wondering if this is partly your fault for bringing Preacher into your lives, but I don't blame you and you shouldn't blame yourself. Serena and Preacher are adults. They decided to cheat on us and they have to decide to stop cheating. I've told Preacher I won't put up with it. Now I need you to do the same with Serena." Tanya looked away again. "I know you must think I'm a pathetic woman coming here begging you to keep your wife away from my husband, but you have to understand. I have children to think about, children who need a father who's committed to their family. Believe me, if it weren't for the boys, I wouldn't be here fighting for my marriage."

"You've spoken to Preacher about all of this?" Barnard asked, as if coming out of a daze.

Tanya nodded. "Yesterday and this morning. I'm willing to forgive him and try to go on, but this thing between him and Serena has to stop if we have any chance of making our relationship work. I know you probably hate me for coming here, but I didn't see any other way of getting this done. I thought about going to Serena, but I don't think I can have a rational conversation with her. I know you don't understand this, being a good Christian and all, but right now all I want to do is scratch out her eyes." She paused for effect. Then she reached for his hand again, this time holding on tight. "Please, Barnard, you have to help me."

Barnard didn't answer. He sat there, a beaten man, the huge

smile he'd worn earlier long gone. All that Tanya saw now was sorrow—deep, deep sorrow.

"I'll talk to Serena," he said. "That's all I can promise."

Tanya squeezed his hand and then released it. "Thanks, Barnard. I'm so sorry that Preacher has brought all this trouble to your doorstep."

She took his slight nod as evidence he'd heard her.

"There's more," she said.

"How can there be more?" Barnard murmured. "What can you possibly add to what you've already told me?"

Tanya sighed. "I know you want me to get out of your face, but I feel I owe you this." She took a deep breath, stretching out the moment. "Preacher's sister, Loretta, was his partner in the drug business. She took over for him when he got locked up."

Barnard looked up at her, meeting her eyes. "What are you trying to tell me, Tanya?"

She shrugged. "If this thing with Barnard and Serena hadn't come up, I never would have thought anything about this because I believed Preacher's conversion. Now that I'm unsure about that, I can't help but wonder what else he's lying about."

"You think Preacher is still in business with his sister?"

She bit her lip. "I hope not, for my sake and the sake of the boys, but I'm not sure. I just thought you should know, since Loretta is dating your sister's boyfriend's partner."

"Are you saying Andre's involved with Loretta's business?"

She lifted her shoulders in a half shrug. "I don't know the answer to that. It would make my life easier if I did. I just wanted you to know so you and your sister could be careful."

Barnard rubbed his hands down his face. "All of this is too much. It's too outrageous."

Feeling her work here was done, Tanya stood. "I'm sorry to

bring all this to you, Barnard, but I figured you'd rather know than be in the dark. I wanted you to have the chance to take care of your family the way I'm trying to take care of mine."

Barnard pressed his palms on the table to push himself out of his chair. It was as though the news she'd given him had weakened him. Instead of reaching out to comfort him, she murmured "I'm sorry" and left the room. Once in the hallway, she smiled broadly. *If I can't find a man to take care of me,* she thought, *I should give acting a try.* There was big money in Hollywood, and given her performance a few minutes ago, she definitely had talent.

When Barnard heard the garage door go up, he knew Serena had arrived home. He didn't know how long he'd been sitting here on the bed he shared with her, thinking but unable to make sense of anything. He'd left the church soon after Tanya had, and he'd been sitting here since. It had been light outside when he first entered the room, and now it was dark, as dark in the room as it was in his soul. He knew this was the darkest moment of the darkest day of his life. How many times did a man question his life's work and his marriage on the same day? Wasn't there some rule somewhere that said when one went bad, you were supposed to rest on the other? Well, he had no rest. He couldn't even pray. He didn't know where to start.

"Barnard," he heard Serena call from the floor below. He wanted to answer her, but he couldn't force his mouth to open. He continued sitting in the dark. He heard her footfalls up the stairs and then down the hallway to their bedroom. He squinted when she switched on the bedroom light.

"I didn't know you were up here," she said, coming fully into the room. "Why didn't you answer when I called you?"

He watched as she slipped out of her shoes and then walked

over to him in her stockinged feet. She pressed a kiss against his forehead. A typical act for a very atypical day.

"So how was your day?" she asked.

He looked at her wondering if what Tanya had told him were true. Could this woman he'd loved more than he loved himself be cheating on him with a man he thought had become a close friend? He didn't want to believe it. He sighed deeply. "Tanya came to visit me today."

Serena, headed to the closet, turned back with a deer-in-the-headlights expression in her eyes. He knew then what Tanya had told him was true, or close to it.

"Is there something you need to tell me, Serena?" he asked, his voice calm though his heart raced.

Serena padded back to the bed. "What did Tanya say?"

Barnard shook his head and repeated his question.

"I was going to tell you tomorrow night," she said. "I know now I should have told you a long time ago."

Barnard closed his eyes in response to the pain in his heart as much as to the tears in her eyes. It was true!

"How long has it been going on?" he asked, his eyes still closed.

Serena pressed her hand against his chest. "Look at me," she pleaded. "Please look at me."

He opened his eyes. The woman in front of him looked like his wife, the woman he'd married, but he didn't know who she was.

"Thank you," she said.

"I need to know, Serena. I need to know how long it's been going on and I need to know how you could lie to me about him. At least now I understand your reaction to Preacher. It was all an act, right, to throw me off the track?"

"No no no," she kept saying, shaking her head so hard he wondered if she'd hurt her neck. "It's not like that."

"What's it like then? Tell me because I need to know."

"It's a long story."

"I've got nothing but time."

Serena turned away. "I can't talk to you when you're this cold toward me."

Hysterical laughter bubbled up in Barnard and roared out of him. "You're chastising me about my reaction to your affair? I have to give it to you, Serena, you do have some nerve! But I guess it takes nerve to sleep with two men at the same time." He couldn't stop his words. He wanted to hurt her. "What's amazing to me is that you're not really that good in bed." She blanched, but he took little satisfaction in the direct hit. "Then again maybe it's different with him."

Serena stood, turned away from him, and folded her arms around herself. After a couple of minutes, she turned back to him. "I know you're hurting, Barnard, and I'm sorry to be the cause of your pain. But you have to believe me, you have to believe that the only thing I did wrong was not tell you about something that happened years ago."

"Years ago?" he asked.

She came back to the bed and sat next to him. "My freshman year in college I had a relationship with Preacher. It goes without saying that it ended badly." She squeezed her eyes shut. When she opened them, they were clear, empty, a look he'd never seen in them before. "To make a long story short, I got pregnant, Preacher paid for an abortion, and we never spoke again until he came to church that Sunday." When he didn't immediately respond, Serena added, "It's the truth. I can give you details, if you want them, but that's the gist of it. The reason I can't tolerate Preacher is because he reminds me of a series of bad decisions I made in my youth, decisions that ended with my aborting the only child I may ever have."

Barnard felt the pain in her words and he believed her, but he wasn't moved to comfort her. "Why didn't you tell me?" he asked. "Why did you choose to lie to me? You lied every time I asked you about Preacher. Both of you lied. Why didn't you tell me? I'm your husband."

She looked away again. "I've been asking myself that question all day, Barnard, but I don't have an answer that makes any sense. I just couldn't deal with it. It was easier to block it all out than to deal with it."

"Is the abortion why we haven't been able to have children? Did you know this before we married?"

Serena shook her head. "No, I didn't know," she said. "You have to believe me. I would have told you if I thought we couldn't have children. I know it's hard for you to believe now, but I could not have married you without telling you."

She was right; it was hard for him to believe her. But somewhere deep inside him he wanted to, he needed to.

"The abortion didn't have any medical complications that should prevent my getting pregnant, but sometimes I wonder if God isn't punishing me for the abortion. I decided to end one baby's life, so God doesn't feel I'm worthy to be given another."

Barnard knew that wasn't the way God operated, but he had his own pain to deal with right now. He had nothing to give Serena.

"Aren't you going to say something?" she finally asked.

"I don't know what to say," he said. "What do you want me to say?"

She shrugged. "I know I don't deserve it, but I'd like some

assurance that this hasn't destroyed our marriage. I do love you, Barnard."

He wiped his hands down his face. "Those words coming from your lips don't mean what they used to mean. They no longer have value. I don't know what to do with them."

"You can take them and hold them in your heart," she suggested.

He shook his head. "There's no room in my heart, right now, Serena. Every corner of it is filled with despair and disappointment. I thought we had more than we have. I was wrong." He stood.

She reached for his hand. "We can get it back, Barnard," she said. "I know we can. It happened a long time ago. It doesn't have to affect us now."

He looked down at her hand on his and shook it off. "That's where you're wrong," he said. "If you had told me earlier, we could have dealt with it as something in your past, but you chose to bring it into our marriage and into our present and our future. I don't know how to deal with it. It hit me out of left field. I knew we had problems, but I never suspected something like this."

"What are you saying, Barnard?" she asked, and he heard the fear in her voice.

"I have a suitcase in the car. I need some time to think, to get my mind around all this."

"Don't leave, Barnard," she begged. "Please don't leave. We can work this out."

Barnard looked down at this woman he loved, but whom he no longer knew. "If we're to have any chance of working this out, I have to leave." With those words, he turned and walked away from her and the home they'd made together, unsure he'd ever return.

* * *

Preacher's heart lurched when he saw Barnard's car parked in his driveway. He'd tried to contact Serena all day but she hadn't answered her cell. He hated to admit it but he'd been too cowardly to go by the gym looking for her. He wasn't ready to see Natalie again. He'd also been trying to get in touch with Barnard, had even gone by the church looking for him. As he turned into his driveway and pulled up beside Barnard's car, he wondered what the brother knew and who had informed him. His instincts told him this wasn't a social visit.

Barnard was out of his car and waiting by the time Preacher cut the ignition. Preacher prayed for wisdom and favor to rule this conversation. "Hey, man," he said, when he got out of the car. "I've been calling you all afternoon."

Barnard met him near the Acura's hood. "Two questions," he said, ignoring Preacher's greeting. "Why didn't you tell me about your relationship with Serena, and why didn't you tell me that your sister was your partner in the drug business?"

Apparently, Serena *and* Natalie had spoken to him. He was glad Serena had gotten to tell her side first, but he was disappointed that Natalie hadn't waited as she'd said she would. "I wanted to tell you," Preacher began, but Barnard cut him off.

"I want the answers to my two questions," he said. "Nothing more, nothing less."

Preacher knew the betrayal Barnard felt and hated that he was its source. "The story of my past relationship with Serena wasn't mine to tell, Barnard. Believe me, I've wanted to tell you. I begged Serena to tell you since before I left prison."

"You were in contact with Serena while you were in prison? And you never thought to mention it to me? Do you even understand the concepts of trust and friendship? I thought we were friends, man."

"You're the best friend I've ever had, and that's the truth. Everything that's good in my life you had a hand in it. Don't ever doubt the sincerity of our relationship. I've never considered you less than a brother."

Barnard scoffed. "A brother wouldn't have lied to my face Saturday night at the cookout. I asked you straight out if you knew why Serena was so cold toward you and you lied."

Preacher wanted to argue that technically he hadn't lied, but he knew it was no use. He had lied in every way that mattered. "My only defense is that I owed it to Serena to let her tell you. I hurt her in the past, Barnard, and I couldn't bear to hurt her again. The only good thing that's come out of this is that she did get to tell you first."

"Serena didn't tell me first," Barnard said. "Tanya did."

"Tanya?"

"Yes, apparently your fiancée overheard some talk between Serena and your sister at the cookout on Saturday. She put two and two together and came up with you and Serena having an affair. She wants me to keep Serena away from you." Barnard shook her head. "Some example you've been to her."

"I know I was wrong, Barnard, but I had good intentions. I had decided to come clean with you and Tanya today, regardless of what Serena decided. I couldn't bear the lies anymore."

"How convenient for you! Do you honestly think I believe you? When I think of the times I've shared with you the things going wrong in my relationship with Serena, I feel like a fool. I trusted you, man."

Barnard's disappointment cut Preacher deeply. The opinion of this man, of his father in the faith, meant everything to him. "You weren't a fool, Barnard, and I never thought you were. I want you and Serena to be happy. Those times you talked to me made me uneasy as well. I felt like a hypocrite and worse, but what could I do? I was torn between my loyalty to you and what I felt I owed Serena. I may have made the wrong choice but it was for the right reason. You have to believe me."

"The only thing I believe that you've said tonight is that you're a hypocrite. Let's get on to my second question about you and Loretta. Why didn't you tell me about her?"

Preacher shrugged. "Because she's my sister and I wanted to protect her."

"Well," Barnard said, stepping closer to Preacher, "I understand about sisters and I want you to stay away from mine."

"I'd never intentionally hurt Natalie," he said.

"Did you know your sister's boyfriend was Dante's partner?"

Preacher shook his head. "I had no idea until the cookout."

"Is Andre involved in your sister's business?"

Preacher nodded.

"Is Dante?"

He nodded again.

"And you didn't tell us? How could you put my sister, me, and the jobs program in jeopardy that way? You knew I was trying to sign Circle Autos up for the program. Why didn't you say something?"

"I didn't know until a couple of days ago. Believe me, I struggled with it. I gave Dante a heads-up and threatened to turn him in if he didn't leave Natalie alone. You and Natalie are like family to me, Barnard."

Barnard shook his head. "From where I'm sitting the family you care about most is your sister. I can't pretend I don't understand because I do. What I don't understand is why you didn't trust me enough to tell me. What did you think I'd do, Preacher, turn her in?"

"I wasn't sure what you'd do," Preacher said, "and I couldn't risk it. I know my sister is wrong, and I want her out of the business, but I don't want her to go to prison."

"I see that very clearly," Barnard said. "I also see that you were willing to sacrifice me, Natalie, and the jobs program in order to protect your sister. As someone who's supposed to be your brother in Christ, I don't know how to assess that decision."

"I'm sorry, Barnard," Preacher said, knowing the words were not enough, but knowing too they were all he had. "If I had to do it over, I'd handle things differently."

"We have a God of second chances, Preacher. At one time, I was sure you knew that, that you had experienced it firsthand. Now I wonder."

"Don't say that, man. Don't even think it. You know my conversion was real."

Barnard stared at him for what seemed like a long time. "I have no idea what's in your heart, so I won't presume to judge you. I only ask that you stay away from me and mine, and that includes both Serena and Natalie. You've cost us too much already."

Preacher had no response and Barnard didn't wait for one. He turned, got in his car, and backed out of the driveway. As Preacher watched him speed away, he felt he was losing the better part of the man he'd become.

CHAPTER 20

Life was good, Sean thought, as he strolled in the Boss's reception area, and it got better when his eyes met Jessie's and her face lit up with joy. They'd had a wonderful evening together, an evening that hadn't ended until breakfast this morning. Sean's plans to use her for the information she could provide had changed and now he considered her his woman. She had proved she cared deeply for him by reading his personnel file and telling him what she'd learned, a deed that could mean Third Hades for her if the Boss found out.

They considered what she'd learned from the file well worth the risk. Sean now knew that the Boss's recent maltreatment was a test of his readiness for a promotion. According to notes in the file, Sean was passing with flying colors.

Sean glanced toward the Boss's door and seeing it was closed as it normally was, he strode directly to Jessie's desk, pulled her up and into his arms, and gave her what he hoped was a toe-curling kiss. "Miss me?" he asked when he ended the kiss.

"You know I did," she said, sinking into her chair. His kiss must have made her weak. "Will I see you tonight?"

"No doubt," he said. "Why don't I pick you up after work?"

She began shaking her head. "That's not a good idea. And neither was that kiss, though I enjoyed it. We've discussed this before. I don't want to take a chance on the Boss seeing us together. He's so unpredictable. I don't know if he'll be angry, or happy or indifferent."

Sean agreed with her, so they planned to meet at his apartment later that night. After they set a time, Sean headed into the Boss's office. The old man was seated at his desk, as usual, and, as usual, his head was bent in some activity. He didn't have his joysticks today though, which Sean considered good news.

The Boss looked up as if he read Sean's thoughts, but that was impossible since the Boss couldn't read thoughts. That was a trait of the enemy.

The Boss folded his arms across his stomach. "Update," he said.

"Good news on all fronts," Sean said, leaning forward in his chair. "Preacher's world is caving in. His past relationship with Serena has been exposed, so Barnard has turned his back on him. Barnard has also walked out on his marriage, leaving Serena alone to drown in the guilt of her past. The only setback we've had is that Natalie and Dante are over, so we'll have to find a new way to get her. The upside is that Preacher is no longer a potential romantic interest for her. Misinformation about his involvement with his sister's drug business has ruined his relationship with her and she's turned against him. Right now, the only people Preacher has in his corner are his sister and Big Boy. We have him right where we want him. And last but not least, Tanya is still ours. In fact, her scheming set Preacher's downfall in motion. She deserves some type of reward for what she's done."

"Don't worry about any rewards for Tanya," the Boss said, "I'll take care of her." He steepled his fingers across the bridge of his nose. "Good of you to think of it, though. You may be getting a handle on this, after all. You're beginning to think the way I think."

Sean thought those words were the highest praise the Boss could have given. They were so out of character that Sean would have questioned their sincerity if not for the information Jessie had given him from his personnel file. "Thank you, sir," he said. "I'm only doing as I was trained. I told you I wanted to prove myself to you."

The Boss tossed Sean's words aside with a wave of his hand. "We're at a critical point now, Jones. We're close to accomplishing our goal, so the enemy is hard at work to stop us."

Sean thought of Preacher and smirked. "He pulled Preacher back the last time, but He won't stop me now. He never should have given these people free will."

"I can't disagree with you there," the Boss said. "But the fact remains that it's not over until it's over. You have to be diligent. Now's the time to focus all your energies on this project. Don't let victory slip from your hands," he warned. "You've come too far to end up in Third Hades because you tripped up on the final lap."

"It won't happen, sir," Sean said. "I know what I have to do and I'm committed to doing it."

"Now that's what I like to hear," the Boss said. "You sound like a man who enjoys his work. I like that."

Even though he knew the Boss could start berating him again tomorrow, Sean felt himself grow taller under his praise. "Just following your example, sir," he said.

The Boss chuckled. "Get out of here, Jones, and get back to work."

For the first time, Sean left the Boss's office smiling.

CHAPTER 21

After his confrontation with Barnard, Preacher wanted to have a word or two with Tanya for being so malicious, and he wasn't talking about the Word of God. Back in the day, he would have read her up and down for such craziness. What was he thinking? Back in the day, Tanya never would have even contemplated such betrayal.

What was going on in the woman's mind? He knew the answer even as he asked himself the question. She'd been thinking of herself and getting back at him. She was not a complex woman by any means. With Tanya what you saw was all there was. Was this really the woman with whom he wanted to spend the rest of his life? His answer was only clear when he thought of his boys. They deserved a mother *and* a father. He didn't want to be a weekend dad. He wanted to be there for his kids. If being there meant putting up with Tanya, he'd do it. He'd asked God for a godly family and he refused to give up on it, despite what Tanya had done today. Though his church family had apparently given up on him—Natalie and Barnard had practically kicked him to the curb with very little thought and no discussion—he wasn't about to give up on the godly family he believed God had for him, Tanya and the boys.

Thoughts of his boys made Preacher yearn for the feel of their loving arms. The dark house told him he'd have to put his personal needs on hold. Apparently, Tanya had taken them out for the evening. Maybe it worked out for the best, he thought. Even though he could calmly and rationally think about what she'd done today and why, he didn't trust himself not to blow up at the nonchalant attitude she was sure to have when he confronted her.

Why couldn't she have waited? He'd told her he'd tell her everything tonight. Leave it to Tanya to go flying off the handle. He still needed to talk her; he didn't want her overhearing anything else and embarking on another path of destruction. No, the next truths she heard would come from him. He could only imagine the fallout. If things had been bad with Natalie and Barnard, they were going to be ten times worse with Tanya. He bounded up the stairs to his apartment, dreading his upcoming discussion with her but wishing she would hurry home so he could spend some time with his boys.

After getting himself a glass of iced tea from the refrigerator, he flipped open his cell phone and dialed Tanya's number. She picked up on the second ring. "Why are you calling me?"

Preacher pressed a thumb and forefinger against the sides of his nose. "What time are you coming home?" he asked, ignoring her rude question. He would not argue with her over the phone.

"I left you a note," she said. "You ought to read it."

"I didn't see any note," Preacher said. Now, after she'd made a mess of nearly all his relationships, she'd started being courteous and leaving him notes. A flag of suspicion went up in his mind.

"Well, look for it," she said, and clicked off the phone.

Preacher pulled his phone away from his ear and stared at it. The urge to give Tanya a word or two quickly returned. He flipped the phone closed and placed it on the kitchen counter. Then he walked through the dining area to the living room, looking for the note. He found it propped on the coffee table, his name scribbled in Tanya's bold hand. His apprehension escalated as he opened it and ran off the chart as he read:

Preacher,

I told you not to play games with me, but you didn't listen. Now you have to pay. The boys and I are gone. I will not live with a liar and a womanizer. You need to think about what you want. If you decide it's me and the boys, get in touch with my mother. I'll be calling her next week. You can call me on my cell, but I want you to do some thinking before you call because I'm only taking one call from you. Anything beyond that, go through my mother.

Tanya

Preacher dropped down on the couch, the note falling from his hand. He couldn't believe it. Tanya had taken his kids! She'd really taken his kids! Preacher felt as if his world had started spinning. His boys were gone.

He jumped from his seat and rushed to his cell, punching in

Tanya's number with quick strokes. She didn't pick up after the fifth ring and the call went to voice mail. He uttered a curse before leaving her a terse message, "You can't do this, Tanya. Bring my boys back home." Feeling helpless and hopeless, he slammed the phone closed and threw it back down on the counter. "Why is she doing this to me?" he cried aloud.

He rushed over and picked the note up from the floor, quickly reading it again. His first thought was to call Maylene but his instincts told him a personal visit would be more effective. He grabbed his keys, jogged down the steps, got in his car, and speeded over to her house. Throughout the drive, he prayed he would find Tanya and the boys sitting in her mother's house, safe and sound. A half hour later he was knocking on Maylene's door. She opened the door but made no move to let him in.

"Is Tanya here?" he asked, cutting through the normal courtesies.

Maylene twisted her lips in a frown. "Why are you looking for Tanya over here? She lives with you."

"She's gone," Preacher said. "Are the boys here?"

Maylene's frown eased into an expression of concern. "No, the boys aren't here. What's going on, Wilford? Where is Tanya? Where are those boys?"

Preacher's worry ratcheted upward. "I don't know, Maylene. Tanya has left me and taken the boys with her. I don't know where she is. Do you have any idea where she's gone?"

Maylene shook her head. "She took the boys with her? I don't believe that. She would have brought those boys to me if she was going somewhere. This is not like Tanya."

Preacher searched his mind for what to do. "Look, call Tanya on her cell. She's not answering my calls. Maybe you can find out where she and the boys are."

Maylene studied him as if deciding whether to do as he asked. “Wait here,” she said. “I’ll get my phone.”

When she turned away, Preacher let himself into the house. A part of him didn’t trust that Maylene would tell him where Tanya and the boys were, even if she knew. “Jake, Mack,” he called out. “It’s daddy.”

Maylene came back into the living room, her phone in her hand. “I told you they weren’t here,” she said, “so stop yelling in my house.”

Though still unsure of Maylene’s truthfulness, Preacher stopped calling for his boys and sat in the nearest chair while Maylene dialed Tanya’s number.

“What’s going on with you, Tanya?” the older woman said after a few moments. “Wilford’s over here telling me you’ve taken the boys and left him. What’s going on?”

Maylene stopped talking and Preacher assumed Tanya was answering her question. He wished he could hear what she was saying. He itched to snatch the phone out of Maylene’s hands and demand that Tanya bring his boys home, but he knew she’d only hang up on him. Right now, Maylene was his only hope of getting information.

“I can’t pretend I’m unhappy you finally came to your senses and left the drug dealer,” Maylene said, meeting Preacher’s eyes, “but why’d you take those boys? You know you should have left them with me.”

More silence as Maylene listened.

“Oh, all right,” Maylene said. She looked at Preacher. “I’m putting this on speakerphone,” she said to him. “She wants to talk to both of us.” Maylene pressed a button on the phone and placed it on the table next to Preacher’s chair.

“You’re on speaker, Tanya,” Maylene said.

"Can you hear me, Preacher?" Tanya asked.

"Come home, Tanya," he pleaded. "We can work out whatever's wrong, but you need to bring the boys home."

Tanya gave a hearty laugh. "You and Momma always seem to think you know what I need. You're alike in that way."

Preacher glanced up at Maylene, who frowned at him.

"But that's a conversation for another day," Tanya said. "I want you both to hear this loud and clear. These boys are mine and they go where I go. I'm their mother, not you, Momma, and I say where they go or not go."

"Stop talking crazy, Tanya," Maylene said in a no-nonsense tone. "Bring those boys here. You know I'll take care of them and you can do whatever you want. You're a grown woman; they're children. Bring them here, or tell me where they are and I'll come get them."

"Listen to me, Momma. For once in your life, listen to what I'm saying. These boys are staying with me. If you don't start respecting me as their mother, you may never see them again."

"Look, Tanya," Preacher said, jumping in. "I know you're the boys' mother. I want you all back home so we can be a family. Haven't I been saying that since I got back? Isn't it what I've told you I wanted?"

"Don't listen to this drug dealer, Tanya," Maylene piped in. "You leave those boys with me. You don't want them to grow up in a life of crime, do you?"

Preacher shot Maylene a threatening glare. Then he said to Tanya, "Please come home."

"It's too late for begging now, Preacher. You should have thought about your family when you were carrying on with your church ladies. You want me and the boys back, you do as I asked in that note. Then maybe, just maybe, we'll return home."

"Tanya—"

Preacher was cut off when Tanya ended the call.

"Well done, Wilford," Maylene said. "Now you've got those boys out there somewhere with Tanya. She's my daughter but you have to know that her maternal instincts are about at the zero level. What are you going to do?"

Preacher looked up at Maylene, and seeing only disdain in her eyes, he got up and left her house without responding to her question. When he got in the car, he dropped his head on his steering wheel and prayed for the safety of his children.

Alone in her living room, Serena paced. She'd been pacing since she'd heard Barnard back his car out of the garage. Her husband had packed a bag and left her! None of the scenarios she'd played in her mind had Barnard leaving their home. Nor had they included the pain in his eyes. She squeezed her eyes shut to block the memory, but it did no good. His expression was burned into her mind.

She wanted to blame Preacher for Barnard's leaving. In fact, she'd spent the last forty-five minutes doing exactly that. But sometime within the last fifteen minutes it had become abundantly clear to her that the fault was hers and hers alone. The abortion she still put at Preacher's feet, but the subsequent lie about her knowing him belonged to her. Why had it taken her so long to accept responsibility? Why did it take Barnard leaving her for her to see the light? Why? Why? Why?

Hearing a car pull in the driveway, she rushed to the door, praying Barnard had had a change of heart. Her excitement fizzled when she saw that it was Natalie, not Barnard. She remembered then Natalie's plan to come by tonight to tell her and Barnard about her problems with Dante and Preacher. Talk about bad timing!

She pulled the door open.

"Gosh, Serena," Natalie said, making her way up the walk. "I hope you haven't been standing around waiting for me all evening. I'm sorry I worried you."

Serena embraced her sister-in-law. "I wasn't really waiting," she said when she pulled back. "I heard the car drive up and looked out the window."

Natalie took a deep breath and asked, "Where's that brother of mine? I'm sure you two have spent the evening pondering my situation and how you were going to help me."

"Come on in and sit down, Natalie," Serena said. "I have some news of my own to share."

"Yes, let's hear yours. There's no way it can be as pitiful as mine." Natalie kicked off her shoes and plopped down on the couch. "I know Barnard heard me drive up. Where is he?"

"He's not here," Serena said, unsure how to break the news to her sister-in-law.

"Oh, he's working late. When do you think he'll be home? I really don't want to go through this twice," Natalie said.

"He's not working, Natalie," Serena said gently. "He's not staying here tonight."

"What? Is he out of town?"

"No, he's not out of town."

"Then where is he?"

"I'm not sure where he is. I thought he might be at your place."

"Why would he be at my place when I told you I was coming over here tonight?"

"Natalie, I don't know how to tell you this, so I'm just going to tell you. Barnard packed a bag and decided to sleep somewhere else tonight."

"Packed a bag? What do you mean? Why would he do that? Is

this about the adoption?" Natalie lifted her arms in frustration. "I can't believe Barnard. That's no reason to leave. If you two can't talk through a problem like reasonable people, then there's no hope for the rest of us. What's that brother of mine thinking?"

Serena placed her hand on Natalie's knee. "We didn't argue about adoption," she said. "He left because I told him about a relationship I had with Preacher when I was in college."

Natalie's eyes widened. "You and Preacher?"

Serena nodded. "I was in college."

"But I didn't think you even knew Preacher."

"Neither did Barnard. That's the problem. I never told either of you. Instead, I pretended I didn't know him."

Natalie began shaking her head. "I can't believe this. Why would you lie about knowing Preacher? It makes no sense, Serena."

Serena gave a dry laugh. "You're telling me. For months, I dreaded Preacher's release from prison, and then after he was released, the idea of spending any time around him made me ill."

"I thought you'd gotten over that. The other day you even agreed to take him and Tanya under your wing. You came to their cookout." She rocked her head from side to side. "All this time you and Preacher knew each other and pretended you didn't." She met Serena's gaze. "I gather it was a serious relationship."

Serena nodded.

"How serious?"

Serena brushed her hands down her jeans-clad thighs. "I thought I loved him, Natalie, and it ended badly."

"Are you still in love with him? Is that why you're still so angry with him?"

Serena shook her head. "Heavens, no, I'm not in love with Preacher. How can you even ask me that?"

"There's something you're not telling me. What is it?"

"I'm still so angry at Preacher because every time I look at him or think about him, I relive the abortion he forced me to have."

Serena watched as Natalie digested her news. Her changing facial expressions would have been comical were the situation not so dire. Natalie surprised her when she began to laugh. When the laughter turned to hysterics, Serena reached for her sister-in-law. "Natalie, please calm down. Barnard and I will work this out. I promise you we will. I love your brother. You know that better than anybody."

Natalie soon stopped laughing. "I don't know what I know anymore, Serena. My life seems to be spinning out of control. Things I could count on, like you and Barnard forever, like me and Benjamin forever, like me and Dante becoming forever, like Preacher loving God forever. Those things I can't count on anymore." She rubbed her hands down her bare arms as if to ward off a chill. "My brother and I are quite a pair. What did we do to deserve such betrayal?"

Serena winced at Natalie's words. Being lumped in with Benjamin was her worst fear coming to life. "I didn't set out to hurt you or Barnard. I was only trying to protect myself. I realize now how badly I handled it."

Natalie lifted a brow. "Good for you."

Serena had no response. She'd known Natalie would be hurt. If she could turn back the clock, she'd definitely handle all this differently. "I'm sorry, Natalie."

Natalie slipped her feet into her shoes. "I seem to be getting a lot of that lately. Dante, Preacher, and now you. What am I supposed to say? I really don't know what I'm supposed to say. You and Preacher have this whole long and complicated history and here you are pretending not to know each other. You made fools of us all."

"I don't blame you for being upset with me, Natalie," Serena said. "I should have been honest. I hate to admit this to you, but Preacher has been begging me to come clean about our past since before he was released from prison. I didn't have the courage to do it."

"Preacher lying was one thing," Natalie said. "We haven't known him that long, but you, Serena? Why? As close as we are, were, why?"

Serena shrugged. "The lie about Preacher was to cover up the abortion. I wasn't ready to deal with it; I'm still not ready. It hurts too much. For so long, I've tried to pretend it never happened. It almost worked. Then Barnard met Preacher at the prison and the past was brought back to me in living color and put on display. I couldn't deal with it."

"What made you finally come clean with Barnard today?"

"He confronted me tonight. Tanya came to see him today and she told him she thought Preacher and I were having an affair."

Natalie gave a dry laugh. "Leave it to Tanya to call a spade a spade." She stood. "Do you have any idea where Barnard went?"

"If he's not at your place, he's either at a hotel or the church."

Natalie nodded. "I'd guess the church." She headed for the door. "I'd better get over there. I know how he's feeling. We can commiserate together."

Serena stood by while Natalie pulled open the door. "I'm still here for you, Natalie, if you need an ear. Tonight was supposed to be about you, not me."

Natalie shook her head, turned away, and headed down the walk. Serena watched her until she pulled out of the drive. When she could no longer see Natalie's car, she closed the door and resumed pacing. This time with tears streaming down her face.

* * *

Natalie called Barnard on her cell while she walked to the back entrance of the church. "I'm out back," she said, when he answered. Not giving him time to respond, she flipped her phone closed. Barnard had the door open for her when she reached it.

"What are you doing here, Nat?" he asked.

"I needed to see my big brother," she said. "Is that still allowed?"

"Of course," he said, giving her a hug. "Rough day?"

She pulled back and looked up at him. "For you, too, I hear."

He nodded. "I guess you've seen Serena."

"I just left your house," she said, following him back to his office. He opened the door and she saw that he'd made himself a bed on the couch in the corner. She looked up at him. "You can't stay here, Barnard."

He dropped down on the couch. "Watch me."

She sat next to him. "By tomorrow afternoon everybody in the church will know you spent the night here. Do you really want your and Serena's business to become church gossip?"

He pinched the bridge of his nose. "I wasn't thinking."

She rocked against his shoulder a couple of times. "That's all right. Little sister can do your thinking for you this time."

He looked down at her. "We're quite a pair, aren't we?"

She chuckled. "You don't know the half of it." She gave her brother a sideways glance. "I hate to tell you this, Barnard, but I have more bad news to dump on you about Preacher, his sister, Dante, and drugs."

"I know what's going on with Dante and the dealership," Barnard said. "Tanya told me this morning when she told me about Preacher and Serena. I didn't know you knew. How did you find out?"

"Dante came clean this morning." She lifted her shoulders in a shrug. "Too little, too late."

"I'm sorry, Sis."

"So am I. I thought Dante was one of the good guys."

"Don't beat yourself up about it," he said. "There's nothing wrong with believing the best in people."

"That's nice of you to say, but you have to admit I'm piling up a pretty unimpressive track record here."

"Seems we both are."

"Don't even try it, Barnard. There's no way you can even begin to compare my relationship with Dante to yours with Serena. What you two have is real. It may be a bit tarnished right now, but you can shine it up good as new, if that's what you both want. Dante and I didn't have what you have. We're done."

"You sound sure."

"I am. Why shouldn't I be?"

He shrugged. "I don't know. When you care about somebody as much as you cared about Dante, it's hard to walk away."

"I'm not walking away, Barnard. I was given a hard shove, by both Dante's actions and his words. There's nothing there to build on. The foundation was a lie. Sad, but true."

"I'm sorry, Natalie."

She smiled at him. "Thank you, Brother. I've heard those words several times today but this is the first time they've meant something."

"I know what you mean," he said.

"You and Serena are going to work this out, aren't you?"

"It's a big deal, Nat. The abortion is big enough, but that was the past. This thing with Preacher is a whole other matter. She was lying to me on a daily basis. That's hard for me to understand."

"I can't help you because I don't understand, either. So what are you going to do?"

"I was going to stay here a few nights until I sort it all out, but I guess that's not a good idea. I'll find a hotel."

"No, you won't," she said. "You'll stay with me."

"I don't want to get in your way."

"In the way of what? My romance just died, so there is nothing to get in the way of. Besides, neither one of us needs to be alone right now, even though we want to be."

He rocked against her side. "When did you get so smart?"

"Just following my big brother's example." They sat silently for a few moments. "What are we going to do, Barnard?"

He shrugged. "What can we do? We have to go on," he said.

"But what are we going to do about Preacher and Dante and the drugs? Don't we have to do something?"

"At some point," he said, "but not tonight. We're both operating on raw emotion, and a lot of that emotion is anger and betrayal, so we can't think clearly."

"You can say that again. I've spent the whole day trying to figure out where I went wrong. It's not natural for someone claiming to be a Christian to miss the Lord's voice as frequently as I have lately. But I can't seem to pray."

"I know what you mean. Why not try something different? You pray for me and I'll pray for you. If I can't hear what God's saying to me, maybe He'll show you and vice versa."

Natalie pressed a kiss against his cheek. "I love you, Barnard. I'm blessed to have you for a brother."

"Same here, Nat. Now let's pray." Instead of praying from his sitting position as Natalie expected, Barnard got down on his knees, closed his eyes, and bowed his head. She joined him. "Father God," he began. "We thank you for the life you've given us and the people you've placed around us. Today has been a challenging day for me and Natalie. We've both been hurt by decisions made by people we love. This hurt is clouding our ability to see your purpose in those actions, so we come to you asking for patience and understanding. I specifically pray for my sister, Natalie, that you strengthen her heart. Help her, Father, to forgive the men who have hurt her in the past, so that her present and her future will be free from the influence of her unforgiveness. In Jesus' name. Amen."

Natalie choked up at Barnard's words. Her heart quickened when he mentioned forgiveness, and she knew that was the answer for both of them. "Father," she said, feeling lighter than she'd felt all day. "Thank you for answering our prayer. I understand fully, Lord, the challenge you've placed before me and Barnard. The lesson we have to learn, as Barnard prayed, is the lesson of forgiveness. Help us, Father, not to look at the wrong we feel was done to us, but to focus on your response to the wrong done to your Son, Jesus. Any pain and betrayal we feel pales in comparison. I pray a special prayer for Barnard and Serena, that you would restore their marriage to a higher level of intimacy than either have experienced. I pray that Barnard forgives Serena for her secrets and that Serena forgives herself for the mistakes of her past that still bind her. I pray, Lord, that the relationship you were building between Preacher and Barnard continues to grow. Help us to remember, Lord, that he is a new Christian, and that how we respond to him now will have a great impact on whether and how he continues to walk with You. I pray, Father, that You forgive me and Barnard for our self-righteousness today that made us unwilling to see anyone's pain but our own. I pray this in your Son's name. Amen."

Natalie turned to find her brother staring at her. "You see, that's why I wanted to be alone," Barnard said. "Alone I could suffer in my self-righteousness disguised as pain, but with you, I'm challenged to walk the path that Jesus would walk. I tell you, Sis, I'm not ready to forgive. I want more time to feel the pain."

Natalie hugged him close. "I know, Barnard. Tonight, we'll take that time, but tomorrow we start the healing process." Natalie patted her brother's back as he wept against her shoulder. Pretty soon her tears mixed with his. *Maybe,* she thought, *the healing would begin tonight.*

CHAPTER 22

Preacher knew it was a long shot but he had to give it a try. He sat in his car, parked about three blocks from the church, and waited. He'd been waiting for over an hour. After spending a sleepless night worrying about his boys, he had to do something and sitting here waiting, though not much, was something.

At first, he'd parked in the church parking lot, but considering Tanya's present state of mind, he didn't think that was a good idea. Even if she decided to bring the boys to the Center this morning, which was a longshot at best, he knew she'd change her mind if she saw his car parked there. So he'd moved a reasonable distance away and prayed he'd soon see his boys.

As his life fell apart around him, to his surprise, he found clarity. He'd come to the aching conclusion that marriage was not in the cards for him and Tanya, not the way things were now. Not only had she betrayed him by going to Barnard with her outrageous suspicions, she had done the unforgivable and taken his boys. He knew he'd never be able to trust her again.

He'd also gained some clarity about his new Christian family. Natalie and Barnard's swift judgment cut him deeply. Yes, he knew he'd been wrong to lie about his past with Serena, but he didn't think that was reason enough for the two siblings to doubt his conversion. Hadn't Barnard told him repeatedly that becoming a Christian didn't mean he'd never make a mistake again? How quickly Barnard had forgotten his own counsel!

It hurt him to think they believed he was still in the drug business. Okay, he admitted to himself, not telling them about Loretta's involvement in his business could look suspicious. Despite that, he thought they owed it to him to listen to his side of the story, and not automatically brand him a liar and a hypocrite.

All that paled with losing his boys though. Barnard, Natalie, and their opinions didn't really matter to him now. All that mattered was seeing his boys again. He checked the clock on the dash, and seeing it was an hour after the time the boys usually reported to the Center, he put his car in gear and made his way to the church parking lot. All the while, he prayed he'd find his boys there, playing happily.

Despite his continued prayer as he parked and got out of the car, Preacher's heart rate increased as he walked toward the Center doors. What would he do if his boys weren't there? What would he do if they were? What were his rights when it came to his children? He tossed those questions away because he didn't like the answers. Tanya was the boys' legal guardian and he knew his criminal history wouldn't serve him well in any custody battle. After closing his eyes and issuing a brief prayer, Preacher pulled open the door to the Center. As bad luck would have it, Natalie was the first person he saw.

"Preacher?" His name dripped like a question from her lips. The smile she usually had for him was conspicuously absent.

"I'm not here to cause trouble," he told her. "I just want to see my boys."

She blinked twice. "Your boys? They're not here."

Preacher's knees weakened and he dropped down in the nearest chair. He covered his face with his hand. Even though the odds had been against him, his disappointment was keen.

"Is something wrong?" Natalie asked.

The sincerity in her voice almost made Preacher confide in her. Almost. He stood. "Nothing," he said, fighting the urge to share his pain with her in much the same way he'd shared his joy after deciding to take on the funeral home gig. But things weren't the same between them. He already missed the relationship they had been building. "Thanks for your help."

When he turned to walk away, Natalie reached for his arm. "Preacher, where are your boys? When they didn't show this morning, I thought you'd kept them away on purpose because of all that's going on."

He studied her, calculating what he had to lose by telling her. Realizing that he'd already lost everything important to him, he said. "Tanya's taken them."

Her eyes widened. "What do you mean, she's taken them?"

"What I said. Tanya has left me and taken the boys with her."

"I don't understand," Natalie said, her brows scrunched up. "Why would she do that? Did you have a fight or something?"

Preacher shook his head. "There doesn't have to be a fight for someone close to you to turn on you. You ought to know that. Look how you and Barnard turned on me."

"Look, Preacher—"

Preacher shook off her hand. "I don't have time for this," he said. "I have to find my boys." Taking a small bit of pleasure at her obvious surprise that he'd turned the tables on her, Preacher opened the door and left the Center.

Serena crossed paths with Preacher as she entered the Center. He didn't acknowledge seeing her and she returned the favor. Now that the truth was out, all pretense between them was gone. She shook off the realization that the relief she'd expected to feel once he was out of their lives didn't materialize. Unwilling to analyze that observation further, she focused her attention on the task at hand: winning her husband back. When she saw Natalie coming toward her, her heart skipped a beat.

"Did you see Preacher?" Natalie asked.

Serena nodded. "He was walking out when I was walking in."

"How'd he look to you?"

Serena couldn't believe the concern in her sister-in-law's voice. "I didn't look at him closely," she said. "Why are you asking?"

"I'm worried about him," Natalie said. "Apparently, Tanya has taken the boys and left him."

Serena had no pity to give him. "That seems to be going around," she said.

"What?" Natalie asked, finally turning her attention away from the door Preacher had exited and toward Serena.

"Spouses leaving," Serena said.

"Tanya didn't just leave. She took his kids, Serena," Natalie said. "He loves those boys. He'll be lost without them."

Serena refused to stand there while her sister-in-law wailed about Preacher and his life, without showing the least bit of concern that Barnard had left her. "I've got to see Barnard," she said.

Natalie shook her head. "That might not be a good idea, Serena. He needs some time to process everything. He's still hurt and angry."

Serena closed her eyes against the pain she'd caused. When she opened them, she said, "I have to make him understand. Time is not the answer."

"Too bad you didn't come to that conclusion earlier."

Serena winced.

"I'm sorry," Natalie said. "That was out of line." She sighed. "That's what I'm trying to tell you. Talking to Barnard now is not a good idea. Things that don't need to be said will be said out of anger and pain."

"Even though you may be finding it hard to believe, Natalie, I love your brother. I also know him. Letting him stew about this is not the best thing for our marriage."

Natalie shrugged. "I'm just giving you some advice. I can't make you take it. But know this, Serena, I want you and Barnard to work this out. He loves you, even though he doesn't want to focus on that love at the moment."

Serena's heart lightened at her sister-in-law's words. "Thanks for telling me," she said. Bracing her shoulders back, she added, "Now say a prayer for me as I try to right the wrong I've done."

"I'm already praying," Natalie said.

Serena strode purposefully towards Barnard's office. Memories from their first meeting, their first date, their first kiss, and their wedding, all flashed through her mind and encouraged her to follow through with her plans. Her husband was worth fighting for.

His door was open when she reached it. She stood there looking at him, engrossed in the paperwork on his desk, thinking how much she loved everything about him. She loved his strength, those powerful arms that could protect her from any harm. She loved his heart, big enough to love her despite her faults. His big heart gave her hope this morning.

"Barnard," she called softly.

He looked up at her and, for a brief moment, his familiar smile greeted her. It faded quickly to be replaced by a flatlined look of suspicion. "Serena," he said with no emotion.

She walked into the room—asking for permission didn't seem a good idea—and closed the door behind her. She took a deep breath and prayed for mercy. "We need to talk," she said, pulling a chair to his side of the desk so the furniture didn't separate them. She wouldn't allow their emotional distance to be amplified by physical distance in this small room.

He leaned back in his chair and folded his arms across his midsection. "Okay," he said. "Talk."

She shook her head. She would not allow him to disengage. Too much was at stake, their marriage and their future. "Not like this," she said. "I want you to really speak to me. Tell me what you're feeling. Tell me what I can do to make things right again. I'm willing to do whatever you want, Barnard," she said. "I love you and I miss you. Last night was the first night since we've been married that we've slept apart in anger. I don't want another night to pass that way."

"Everything doesn't fix as easily as you seem to think it does, Serena. You'd better get used to sleeping alone for a while. I need time."

Serena's hands tightened on the arms of her chair. "How much time?" she asked, fearing his answer.

He rubbed one of his hands around the back of his neck. "I don't know."

"That's not an answer."

"It's the only one I have," he said. Then he looked directly at her and asked, "How long did it take you to forgive Preacher?"

"What are you talking about? What does Preacher have to do with this?" Serena sank back in her chair, wounded from the anger in his tone and the satisfied gleam in his eyes at her reaction. Maybe Natalie had been right.

He raised a brow. "You're not seriously asking me that question, are you?"

"The situations are totally different," she said. Surely he could see that there was no comparison between her and Preacher and him and her. Surely he saw the difference.

He leaned toward her. "They all boil down to the same thing in my mind, Serena," he told her. "You want forgiveness and I'll bet Preacher wanted it, too. What did you tell him when he asked?"

This conversation was not going at all the way Serena had planned. "Why are we talking about Preacher?" she asked. "We should be discussing us, our marriage, our future."

"Don't you see, Serena?" he asked. "Preacher is at the center of our problems, or rather your past with Preacher. You brought it right into our marriage and you have to get rid of it. We can't move forward together until you let go of the past. How can you expect me to forgive you when you can't forgive yourself or Preacher?"

Serena got up from her chair, unable to endure more of Barnard's scrutiny. "Why are you doing this?" she asked, pacing in front of his desk. "Why don't you come home so we can work this out?"

"We can't fix our problems, Serena, until you can admit what they are." He got up and stood in front of her, effectively ending her pacing. "Can't you see?" he said. "We both need time. I need time to accept the lie that's been between us all this time and you need time to figure out why you needed to lie."

"I know why I lied," she said. "I lied because I feared you'd judge me, and given what's happened, I was right."

Barnard leaned back against the desk. "You're wrong, Serena. You need to ask the Lord to show you the truth."

She scoffed. "Did the Lord tell you to leave me? Did you ask Him before you packed up and left?"

Barnard nodded. "I know you don't believe me, but I did ask. I was hurting so much though that I couldn't hear His answer. I had to leave to keep from doing or saying something that would cause even more damage to our relationship."

"So you haven't given up on us?" Serena held her breath as she waited for an answer.

"I can't," he said, meeting her eyes. In them she saw her own fear along with what she prayed was a glimmer of hope. "What we have was put together by God. I won't give up but I also won't go on with things as they are."

"That sounds like an ultimatum."

He looked away from her briefly. When he turned back, he said, "I'm being honest, Serena."

"So all I have to do is make nice with Preacher and you'll come home?"

He snorted and then he shook his head. "If you really think that's all you need to do, we're in more trouble than I thought. We can't work through this together if you won't even accept what the real problem is."

Serena bit down on her lower lip. "Preacher hurt me so badly, Barnard."

"And you hurt me," he said, placing his hand over his heart. "Does that give me the right to shut you out forever?"

Serena couldn't make sense of this conversation. She came here to talk about her marriage and here she was talking about Preacher. "I don't know how to forgive him," she finally said, choking back her emotion. She looked at Barnard and wished he would take her in those strong arms of his and tell her everything was going to be all right. She opened her arms to him in a desperate plea for understanding and help.

Barnard didn't move. "You can start by forgiving yourself. You've been blaming Preacher all these years for ruining your life, but look around, Serena. Your life isn't ruined. The longer you hold onto your negative feelings about him, the more you stunt our relationship. It can never grow into what God wants it to be if you don't forgive yourself. You sinned. We all have. We all do. Jesus died for those sins, but you have to let them go."

Serena turned to him, tears streaming down her face. "I don't know how," she said. "After all these years, I don't know how."

Barnard moved to her then and gave her the comfort she'd longed for since he'd walked out of their home. "I'll help you," he said, pulling her into his arms. "We'll help each other."

Preacher didn't know what to do with his anxiety so he went to the funeral home, hoping that being there would rekindle within him some excitement and hope for his future. When he pulled into the parking lot, he saw Big Boy standing outside waiting for him. His instincts told him Big Boy brought news that would only add to his already full plate of life's problems.

"Hey, man," Big Boy called. "What's shakin'?"

"You don't want to know, man," Preacher said. "Believe me, you don't."

Big Boy followed him into the funeral home and to his office. After the door was closed, Big Boy said, "You can tell me, man. I'm here for you. You know that, right?"

Preacher did know it. Big Boy, unlike his new Christian family, was there to support him in his time of need. He told him about Tanya taking the boys.

"That's low," Big Boy said. "A woman shouldn't pull no trick like that on her man. What you gonna do?"

"I have to find them, man," he said. "I have to get my boys back."

"I'm feeling you, man," Big Boy said. "Now that I've finished up the first job you gave me, I can help with this one."

"You found out who set me up?"

Big Boy nodded. "You'll never guess. Not in a million years."

Preacher didn't have time for games. "Who was it?"

"Andre Davis, the guy that owns Circle Autos."

Preacher opened his mouth, but no words came out.

"Word is he's been seeing your sister, but I guess you already know that."

Preacher nodded. *How could this be?* he wondered. "Why?" he asked. "I didn't even know the guy until recently."

Big Boy shrugged. "You'll have to ask your sister."

After giving Big Boy the okay to start looking for Tanya and the boys, Preacher headed over to his sister's. He could only imagine what she was planning. In their last conversation, she'd made it clear that Andre didn't mean that much to her. And that was before she knew of his betrayal. Preacher prayed he got to her before she got to Andre. He didn't need any more complications in his life.

Loretta greeted him warmly when he entered her apartment. "Come on in," she said, leading him to the couch. "What brings you by? Missing your little sister?"

He sat in the chair across from her. "What do you have planned for Andre?" he asked.

She got up. "I need a soda. Do you want one?"

He followed her into the kitchen. "Big Boy told me today that Andre was the one who set me up. He also told me that you know. What do you plan to do about it?"

She pulled two cans of Coke out of the refrigerator. She handed one to him and took one for herself. She popped the top and took a swallow. When she lowered her can, she said, "Don't ask me again if you don't want me to tell you."

Preacher lowered his can and set it on the counter. "Don't do something crazy, 'Retta. I know how your mind works."

She left the kitchen and he followed her back to living room, where they sat again. "Our minds used to work alike," she said. "I'm going to do the same thing you would have done, what you should have done."

Preacher pointed his finger at his sister. "I don't need this right now," he said. "Tanya has left me and taken the boys with her."

Loretta jumped up, eyes blazing. "No, she didn't. Tell me that crazy woman did not take your kids, my nephews. Just who does she think she's messing with?" She stared down at her brother. "She thinks you're weak, Preacher. She never would have done this a couple of years ago. Now she feels she has an advantage over you. What are you going to do about her?"

"I'm trying to figure that out, 'Retta. Don't you think I'm trying to figure that out?"

Loretta sat down. She leaned toward her brother. "Okay, look at where this church stuff has gotten you. Your woman has disrespected you in the worst way possible and you don't know what to do about it. Well, I know what to do about it. If you won't take care of this, I'll take care of it. Tanya knows not to mess with me."

Preacher didn't even consider telling Loretta that Tanya had dropped a dime on her to Barnard. That would surely send his sister off. He'd have to find a way to tell her to watch her back without revealing Tanya's role. "Leave Tanya and the boys to me, Loretta. I mean it."

"I hear you," his sister said, settling back against the couch.

"I mean it," he said again.

She tipped her can back and took another swallow. "You've got to handle your business, Preacher."

"I'm handling it," he said.

"Right."

Her sarcasm was too much for him to deal with. "I'm concerned about my kids, Loretta."

"So am I, only I'm willing to do something about it."

"Something like what?" he asked. "You'll do something that'll get my kids taken away from me for good. I won't risk it."

She set her soda can on the table next to her. "I'd never do anything to hurt you and the boys. I'll just put Tanya in her place."

"You don't get it, do you?" he asked.

"I get that somebody needs to give little Miss Tanya a reality check."

He pinned her with his eyes. "Maybe you're the one who needs the reality check."

Loretta sat forward. "What do you mean by that?"

"Look, Loretta, Tanya does have the upper hand. She has the law on her side. She goes to court and she gets sole custody of my kids. Easy. She may even get a restraining order or something. She's a loose cannon right now."

Loretta frowned. "It won't go that far."

"I won't risk it."

"Tanya's not exactly mother of the year material," Loretta said, with a sneer. "You could get custody."

Preacher sighed deeply, fighting impatience with his sister. "Be realistic, Loretta. Let's say Tanya and I went to court and the judge decided neither of us were great parents. Who do you think would get custody of my kids? You, my closest relative, who also happens to be a drug dealer, or Maylene, the beauty shop owner, Tanya's closest relative? And you know how much Maylene hates me. I don't want her raising my boys."

"It won't come to that, Preacher. I'll take care of Tanya."

Preacher leaned forward and put a hand on one of his sister's knees. "You will not have any contact with Tanya. You will leave her to me. I'm serious, Loretta. You go after her in any way and I'm no longer your brother."

She brushed his hand away. "You're not serious."

"I'm deadly serious," he said. "Your way doesn't work for me anymore. I've tried to tell you but you won't listen. Don't try to help me. Think about helping yourself. Get out of this business, Loretta, before it's too late. The walls are closing in," he said. "I can feel it."

"I don't believe you'd cut me off."

He met her gaze and held it. "For the sake of my boys, I would. I love you, Loretta, but not at the expense of my kids. I can't do it. I won't."

"But I'm your family, too."

"Then act like it," he said. "Act like we mean something to you. Do something to help me get my kids legally. You can't help me as long as you're walking boldly on the wrong side of the law. You're a danger to me and my kids. I've closed my eyes to it long enough."

"I guess I know where I stand then," Loretta murmured. "Never trust a man who says he loves you, even if it's your brother." She looked at him, her eyes damp with unshed tears. "Andre said he loved me," she said. "He set you up because he wanted me all to himself. He said I'd never give another man the time of day as long as you were around. He showed his love for me by betraying me. Crazy, huh? What's even crazier is that you're doing the same thing."

Preacher shook his head. "It's not like that, Loretta."

She stood. "It's time for you to leave, Preacher. You've been perfectly clear about where I stand with you. Nowhere."

"It's not like that, 'Retta," Preacher said, feeling his sister's pain.

She shrugged as if his words no longer mattered. "If it walks like a duck, you know the rest. Now get out." When he would have spoken, she screamed, "Get out NOW!"

With one last look at his sister, Preacher left her house. As he did, he realized he didn't have anywhere else to go or anyone else to turn to. Except Big Boy. And because he was on probation, he couldn't even go to Big Boy's house. He was alone. This was not the life he expected when he became a Christian. He began to pray.

CHAPTER 23

The first thing Preacher did when he got home was call Big Boy and tell him to cease looking for Tanya. During his prayer time in the car, he'd realized that the stand he'd taken with Loretta was a stand he needed to take with his entire past. Big Boy had been his bodyguard and the person who watched his back in the old life. Preacher realized he couldn't keep leaning on him for the same services if he really wanted the new life Christ had given him. He did want that life, even though it seemed the life didn't want him.

The more he thought about Barnard and Natalie, the more their desertion hurt. How could they deny the work Christ had done in his life and heart? In the old days, he would have walked away from them and the life they represented, but too much was at stake now. After realizing how close to death and hell he'd been, he wasn't turning back. Not only was his life and soul hanging in the balance, so were the souls of his boys. His old life paled in comparison to the small taste of Christian life he'd experienced. He wasn't going back. He'd tell Barnard and Natalie that tomorrow. What they did with it was up to them.

Preacher felt alone in one way, yet surrounded by God's love in another. His burgeoning joy had come out of deep grief and the seeming loss of all he cherished. He began to hum an old hymn he remembered his grandmother singing, "Precious Lord." As he hummed the words, his heart filled with the love that God had showered on him when he'd deserved death for the life he'd lived and lives he'd destroyed. His singing turned to prayer and soon Preacher was on his knees pouring out his heart before the Lord. "Thank you, Lord," he prayed. "These past two days have been the worst days of my life. Thank you for not allowing the challenges they brought to consume me.

"Thank you, Father, for Tanya and my kids. I pray for their safety and their safe return. Help me to trust you, Lord, that this situation is temporary. Give me wisdom in dealing with Tanya when they do.

"Thank you, Lord, for Loretta. Forgive me for taking so long to speak the words of truth you gave me tonight. Use those words for your purpose in showing her the futility of the life she's chosen.

"Thank you, Lord, for Barnard and Serena. Please forgive me for being selfish where Barnard is concerned. It's true that I didn't tell him about my past with Serena out of respect for her privacy, but as you already know, a part of me feared losing his friendship. Restore his marriage, Lord.

"Thank you, Lord, for Natalie. Forgive me for not telling her immediately about Dante. I pray that you encourage her during this rough time. Give her strength to go on without becoming jaded."

After a few minutes of silence, he continued, "Lord, thank you for not leaving me, for guiding me, for showing me how to live this life. Forgive me for the lack of faith that made me keep secrets that ended up hurting me and the people I love. Help me to face the consequences as a godly man should. In Jesus' name. Amen."

Preacher stayed on his knees after the prayer was over, taking comfort in being in the presence of God. He began humming his grandmother's hymn again.

With fresh bagels and hot coffee in the bag in his hand, Barnard knocked on Preacher's door bright and early the next morning. Over breakfast, he and Natalie had decided that one of them needed to talk to Preacher. Barnard wanted the task, as much for himself and Preacher as for him and Serena. When Preacher didn't answer, he knocked again.

A sleepy-eyed Preacher opened the door before Barnard knocked a third time. "Good morning," Barnard said, entering the apartment. "I bet you're surprised to see me."

Preacher closed the door and watched as Barnard spread out his breakfast goodies on the bar. "*Surprise* is a good word," he said. "What brings you by so early?"

Barnard stopped taking bagels out of the bag and met Preacher's eyes. "I came to apologize on behalf of me and Natalie," he said. "We were both wrong in how we handled the last couple of days. I know it's not much. I can only imagine how disappointed you must be by our reaction. My only excuse is that we were operating out of pain and anger, not Christian love."

Preacher, who had picked up a bagel and begun to spread on some cream cheese, ceased his motions. "I was coming by today to explain that to you. Leave it to God to bring you here this morning. He amazes me." Shaking his head, he resumed spreading the cream cheese on his bagel.

Barnard smiled. "You're not the only one He amazes." He followed Preacher's lead and spread cream cheese on his own bagel. "You were really coming over?"

Preacher grinned. "With guns blazing. You and Natalie left me swinging in the wind. I've never felt so alone."

Barnard's smile faded. "I'm sorry, man," he said again. "I hope you can forgive us."

"You're already forgiven," Preacher said, after taking a sip of his coffee. "Do you forgive me for lying about my past with Serena, and for not telling you about my sister's continued involvement in my old drug business?"

Barnard leaned against the counter, bagel in hand. "I forgive you," he said, "but I still don't understand. I guess I don't really have to. What I know is that your conversion was real, that you're my brother in the faith, and that we all have made wrong choices, sinned, and fallen short of God's glory."

"Thanks for saying that, man," Preacher said, feeling the sting of emotion in the back of his eyes. "I needed to hear those words, but I also need to try to make you understand."

"It's not necessary," Barnard said.

"It is to me," Preacher said, taking another sip of coffee. "I value our friendship, Barnard, and I'd like to resume it."

Barnard looked away and then turned back to Preacher. "I'm not sure that's possible."

Preacher coughed, almost choking on his coffee. "What? I thought you said you forgave me. I don't understand."

"It's not about me," Barnard said, after slapping Preacher on the back. "It's about Serena. She's still struggling with her past with you and I want to support her. To be honest, she's not ready to deal with you yet. I know that's not right, but that's the way it is. She's my wife and she has to come first. Do you understand?"

Preacher poured the dregs of his coffee down the drain, glad for the distraction. His lies had come full circle. He had to accept the consequences of his actions. "Do you think she'll ever forgive me?"

"Right now, it's not about forgiving you. Serena has to forgive herself."

"Ahh," Preacher said. "I sorta thought the same thing."

"Then you understand about our friendship?"

The regret that he heard in Barnard's voice eased the dismay Preacher felt at the direction their friendship was being forced to take. "I understand," he said, "but that doesn't mean I like it. In addition to being my spiritual mentor, you're also my probation sponsor. What's going to happen there?"

"Don't worry about it," Barnard said. "Contrary to what my recent actions showed, I won't leave you hanging. I've already spoken to Wayne and he's agreed that Luther can step in for me. He's drawing up the paperwork at the probation office today."

"How much do they know?" Preacher asked.

"I had to tell them everything I knew, Preacher. People can't support you if they don't know the truth."

"I can't believe they want to support me, given that they know the truth."

"What can I say? Their reactions were decidedly different from mine and Natalie's. They demonstrated that sustaining kind of love that Paul talks about in 1 Corinthians 13, a love that 'never gives up, never loses faith, is always hopeful, and endures through every circumstance.' They believed the best of you and asked for an explanation of the lies. Once they were told, they understood. They didn't agree, but they understood."

"Thanks for being my advocate with them," Preacher said.

"It's the least I can do for my brother," Barnard said. "We may not be able to share the same kind of friendship we shared before, but you're no less a brother to me. I want to be sure you understand that point."

"I understand," Preacher said. "I could have saved us all a lot of trouble if I'd been up front and honest from day one, couldn't I?"

Barnard nodded. "But don't beat yourself up about it. Learn from it. And remember it when something similar happens to someone else. Be better to them than I've been to you."

Preacher heard his own guilt in Barnard's voice. "Now I have to tell you not to beat yourself up. You had every right to be angry with me. I would have been angry, too."

Barnard waved off Preacher's words. "Natalie told us about Tanya and your boys. I told the pastor, and he has the whole church praying for you."

Preacher's eyes widened in surprise. "What? The entire church?"

"Not everyone knows it's you specifically, but the pastor knows and the prayer warriors know. They know and they're all praying. Your boys will be home soon, safe and sound."

"I don't know what to say."

"'Thank you, Lord,' will work," Barnard said, with a smile.

Preacher lifted his eyes upward. "Thank you, Lord." Then he looked at Barnard, "Thank you, brother."

At this moment, Natalie wished she'd gone to see Preacher and had her brother make this call on Benjamin for her. Even as the thought passed through her mind, she knew this was a task she had to do herself.

She walked through the bank's lobby and toward the row of offices. "Benjamin Towles, please," she said to the pert secretary seated outside the trio of offices. "Tell him Natalie Jenkins from Faith Community Church wants to speak with him."

"Have a seat, please," the young woman said, as she punched in a couple of digits on the phone on her desk.

Natalie sat in the soft leather chair to the left of the desk. Benjamin came out of his office within minutes. The question in his smile was matched by the one in his eyes. "Natalie," he said, coming to her. "What a surprise. What brings you by?"

Natalie stood. "If you have a minute," she said, "I'd like to talk to you about a personal matter."

His smile faded a bit. Natalie certainly understood why. They hadn't had a civil conversation since she'd learned of his betrayal. Despite his obvious misgivings, he escorted her to his office and closed the door behind them. He took his seat behind the desk while she sat on the other side facing him.

"I won't keep you long," she said. Then she took a deep breath. "Things ended badly between us, Benjamin, and I've harbored ill feelings for you since. You've asked me on several occasions to forgive you, and today I came to give you that forgiveness. I've withheld it too long."

Benjamin leaned forward and rested his forearms on his desk. "Thank you, Natalie," he said. "I don't know what to say. I'm sorry I hurt you. It was never my intention. I still wish we could have worked things out."

Natalie shook her head. "We weren't meant to be, for obvious reasons. But that doesn't mean we can't find happiness with other people. You've already found someone, and I want to be ready when my time comes. I know now I'll never be ready as long as I'm angry and unforgiving about what went on between us."

"I still love you," he said.

Natalie stood. There was no need to go down this road again.

"I pray those are just words, Benjamin," she said. "Don't make the same mistake twice. Love the woman you're with and stop looking for the next best thing. Allow yourself to be happy. That's what I plan to do." She smiled at him, able for the first time since their break-up to remember the good times they had shared along with the bad. "Good-bye, Benjamin," she said. "Be happy."

Later that afternoon, Preacher met with Wayne and Luther at the funeral home. The three of them sat around the table in Luther's office and planned Preacher's next steps. Since Barnard had already given them most of the information they needed, Preacher only had to fill in the details.

"Why do you think this Dante lied to Natalie about your involvement with your sister's business?" Luther asked.

Preacher lifted his shoulders in a slight shrug. "Maybe he thought it was true. Maybe he wanted to get back at me for forcing him to end things with Natalie. Maybe a little of both. I don't know."

"It doesn't matter," Wayne said. "What matters is that it's not true."

"It's definitely not true," Preacher said. "I've been extra careful about not involving myself with my sister or her business. I encourage her on every occasion to get out."

"But you never turned her in," Luther added.

Preacher winced. "I felt a certain loyalty to her," he said. "And I thought I could get her out, but I've had to accept that she doesn't want out. I don't like it but that's the way it is. What's going to happen to her?"

"I've got a call in to a lawyer buddy of mine," Luther said. "He's agreed to meet with your sister, get a read on what she wants to do with her life, help her all he can if she wants to be helped. He's the best. She'll probably have to do some time, but if she's willing to cooperate with the district attorney, my buddy will get her the best deal possible. In the end, though, it'll be up to her."

"It's her best bet, Preacher," Wayne said. "You can't keep protecting her. You can give her a hand, but she has to stand or fall on her own."

Preacher knew his friends' words were true, but he didn't like hearing them. Despite his best efforts, it seemed his sister was headed for prison. That felt like failure to him. "I'll call her and let her know to expect to hear from the attorney."

Luther shook his head. "That's not a good idea. You can't make this decision for her. You have to trust God that we are as concerned about her as you are. We're not going to turn our backs on you or her, not before giving it our best efforts."

"I don't believe this," Preacher said, his gaze traveling from the hope in Wayne's face to the wisdom in Luther's. "I don't believe how good you both are being to me and Loretta, and you don't even know her."

Luther placed a hand on Preacher's shoulder and squeezed. "We know you love her and we know you've been praying for her. That's enough for us. We're family, Preacher. We stumble sometimes, but we're family."

Preacher took a moment to absorb the truth of those words. Family. God had honored his prayer.

Wayne cleared his throat. "Now we turn our attention to the situation with your kids," he said. "When was the last time you heard from Tanya?"

Preacher told them about Maylene's call to her.

"Can't we trace her cell phone?" Luther asked Wayne.

"We need a court order to do that."

"She took my kids," Preacher said. "Isn't that a reason to get one?"

Wayne shook his head. "I'm afraid not. She's the custodial parent. Besides, she's only been gone a couple of days. I'm sorry, but there's nothing we can do except wait."

Preacher sighed. "That's easier said than done."

"If you really think she'd hurt the kids, we could pursue an order on those grounds. Do you think she would?"

Preacher was tempted to lie, but he shook his head. "She's using them to yank my chain. It's a power play. Nothing more. But things can go wrong. Anything can happen. I want my kids back home."

"We know it's hard, Preacher," Luther said. "Just hang in there a couple more days. If something doesn't give, we can go another route."

"I'm not hearing this," Wayne said, covering his ears with his hands.

"Whatever we do will be legal, Wayne," Luther said. "We just won't go through the courts."

"All right then," Wayne said, stacking his papers in front of him. "That's all I had. The paperwork's done to change your sponsor from Barnard to Luther," he said to Preacher, "and it should be signed off on in the next couple of days. So consider it done." Then to Luther he said, "You'll have your lawyer friend get in touch with Loretta today or tomorrow?"

Luther nodded. "He's trying to reach her today."

Wayne turned to Preacher. "We're done here, unless you have something else."

"That's it," Preacher said, reaching out to shake the men's hands. "Thanks. Both of you." Then his cell phone rang. "Excuse me," he said, pulling out the phone. "I need to take this. It's Tanya's mother."

Preacher stood and walked a few feet away from the table where they sat. "What is it, Maylene?" he asked. "Have you heard from Tanya?"

"Wilford, I don't know what I'm to do with that girl. She took those boys to Disney World for the week and calls me this morning crying about how they're driving her crazy. She wants both of us to come down there and bail her out. I could ring that girl's neck."

Preacher started laughing, releasing all the anxiety that had built up since he'd gotten Tanya's note. "Disney World?" he repeated.

"You heard me," she said. "I'm on a seven o'clock Delta flight tonight."

"But I can't leave—," he began, but she had hung up.

Preacher closed his phone and started to laugh again.

"What's so funny?" Wayne asked.

"Was it news about your kids?" Luther asked.

"Yes, it was news about my kids," Preacher said. "Tanya's taken them to Disney World and quickly figured out they were too much for her to handle. She's called in the cavalry—her mom and me—for support." Preacher started laughing again, and his friends joined him. His world had just righted itself! *Thank you, Lord!*

Natalie said a brief prayer before she entered the dealership. She needed closure on her relationship with Dante and she felt she owed him the truth of what she'd done with the information he'd given her. She didn't expect him to thank her.

She was headed toward the bullpen in the middle of the floor when she heard him call her name. She turned and her heart tripped at the sight of him. Her attraction for him had not faded, but sadly physical attraction wasn't a solid foundation for a relationship, not even a friendship.

When he reached her, he leaned in and kissed her cheek. "It's good to see you, Natalie."

"Can we talk somewhere, in private?" she asked after he pulled back.

"Sure. Why don't we take a walk outside? No sense sitting in a stuffy office on such a beautiful day."

He took her elbow and guided her outside. He led her to the shaded picnic area behind the dealership where he'd taken her when they first started seeing each other. He had been his most romantic that day, showing off his business with pride and later feeding her chocolate covered strawberries under the moonlight.

She sat at the picnic table and he sat next to her. "I'm sorry, Natalie. I don't know what else to say."

"There's no need to go through all of it again," she said. "I didn't come here to torture you."

He flashed those bright whites at her. "Thanks. Is it too much to hope that we can be friends, maybe even continue building on what we started?"

She shook her head. "That's impossible, Dante. You were smart to end it."

He looked away. "I know you're right, but I hate it." He turned back to her. "You're the best thing that ever happened to me," he said. "You know that, don't you? For you, I wanted to change. Only for you."

"Why didn't you then?" she asked.

"It's not that easy to get out and, when you've worked as hard as I have, it's too hard to give it all away."

Natalie gazed toward the sun. She guessed they'd said all that needed to be said. What an odd way to end a relationship she'd thought would last forever. "I have something to tell you that I don't think you're going to like."

"You told your brother?" When she nodded, he said, "I figured as much. So what's his plan? Is he going to report us, including Preacher? I can only imagine the bad publicity a move like that would generate for his jobs program."

I didn't really know him, Natalie thought as she listened to him, *and he didn't really know me.* "There's a lot more at stake here than the reputation of the jobs program," she said. "Barnard's spoken with Preacher and Preacher has spoken with his probation officer. He came clean about everything."

"I bet he did," Dante said, with a smirk. "So are they revoking his probation?"

Natalie shook her head. "He's not involved in Loretta's dealings. He gave all that up when he was in prison, after he became a Christian. He only found out about what was going on here at the dealership a few days ago when his sister told him. He was sincere when he came to you. He didn't want your business, Dante. He was trying to protect me."

Dante gave a dry laugh. "I can't believe you fell for that load of manure. That story doesn't even make sense. How can you believe it?"

"I didn't at first," she admitted. "But when I calmed down, I realized I had seen the evidence of Preacher's love for God. His conversion was real, Dante. I saw the fruit of it; I see the fruit of it. I know his story is true because I know his heart is true. I can't explain it any better than that."

Dante scoffed. "You and this extreme view of God. I never did understand it. How can you live your life that way?"

Sadness settled over Natalie. In her haste to find a romantic partner to heal the pain Benjamin had inflicted, she'd forsaken the opportunity to show a lost soul the way of Christ. She'd carry that burden a long while. "I can't explain it to you, Dante," she said. "Not today but maybe someday." She stood. "I've said what I came to say. Take care of yourself."

He looked up at her with that smile again. "I always do, Nat. I always do."

Natalie walked away, leaving her past behind her.

CHAPTER 24

Preacher waited for Tanya in the lobby of Disney's Grand Floridian Hotel and Spa. Leave it to Tanya to go first class all the way. He knew she had to have money stashed away somewhere in order to be able to foot the bill for such opulence. He'd have to get over it. Tanya could have the money and everything else that had been his as long as she didn't try to deny him access to his kids.

Tanya had been nowhere to be found when he and Maylene had arrived earlier tonight. She'd left a note at the front desk telling them the kids were in the Mouseketeer Clubhouse, the hotel's official child-care service. The boys had been happy to see Preacher and Maylene, who'd rounded them up, fed them dinner, and put them to bed. Preacher grinned at the memory of the stories the boys had told of things they'd seen and done and wanted to see and do. He had a full day ahead of him tomorrow and he couldn't wait to get started. His instincts told him that he'd probably have more fun than the boys.

He thanked God he'd even been allowed to make this trip. He knew Wayne had gone out on a limb by giving him permission to leave the state. The kindness and support of his Christian family after his confessions awed him. If only he'd trusted them enough to tell the truth from the beginning. He wondered how different things would be if he had. But this was not the time for "what-ifs." No, this was a time for rejoicing. And rejoice he would.

"What are you grinning about?" Tanya asked, interrupting his thoughts. He'd been so engrossed in them that he hadn't heard her walk up. She sank into the plush upholstered high-back chair next to his.

"Thinking about the boys," he said. "They're in bed, in case you wondered."

"Nothing to wonder about." Dressed in a black sheath that hugged her body and with diamonds glittering from her ears, neck and wrists, she crossed her long legs and swung her feet, designer sandals and all, back and forth in his direction. "The attendants in the Mouseketeer Clubhouse take very good care of the kids. In fact, you and Momma wouldn't even be here if those stupid people had better hours. The Clubhouse is only open from four thirty to midnight. What do they expect people to do until four thirty in the afternoon? You know Jake and Mack—they were up and raring to go at some ungodly hour every day. It was too much. And forget about after midnight. You know the parties are only beginning at that hour."

Preacher studied Tanya as he listened to her complaints about her sons. She really didn't have strong maternal instincts. All she cared about was her personal entertainment. "Well, I'm here now, so you don't have to worry about the boys," he said. "I'll take care of them and make sure they enjoy the rest of their vacation and you can enjoy the rest of yours."

She tossed her hair back over her shoulders. "Don't look for a merit badge, Preacher. You're their father, so it's the least you can do." She unzipped her purse, pulled out her compact, and checked her makeup. No doubt she had a late date. He didn't care enough to question her about it.

"What's it going to be, Preacher," she asked, running her tongue across her lower lip, "me and your boys or one of the women from your church?"

"There's nothing going on between me and any woman at church. How many times do I have to tell you?"

She snapped her compact closed. "You'll never convince me nothing was going on, so don't even try. If you can convince me that it won't continue, maybe we can work something out for our future."

He stared at her, wide-eyed. "You can't be serious, Tanya. What kind of future can we have after you've practically stolen my boys from me? How can I ever trust you again?"

"Look, Preacher, I'm willing to try to trust you again after you've betrayed me, so I figure you can return the favor. Besides, I didn't steal the kids from you. I took them on vacation so you'd have time to clear your mind."

Preacher knew this was a purposeless conversation. He couldn't penetrate the fantasyland in which Tanya lived. He didn't even want to try. "It's not going to work with us. You have to know that."

"So you're choosing your women over me and the boys?"

Preacher resisted the urge to reach out and try to shake some sense into her. "No, I'll always choose my boys, Tanya. It's you and me that can't make it."

She toyed with her diamond bracelet. "What if I say you can't have them without me?"

Fear rolled up Preacher's spine. "Why would you say that? You don't want me, Tanya. I don't think you've ever wanted me. Maybe what I could provide for you, but never just me. And I know for a fact that you don't want the man I've become."

"You changed, Preacher," she said. "Not me."

"I'll accept that," he said. "I'm letting you go but I'm not letting my boys go."

She leaned toward him, the diamonds around her neck sparkling. "You're not taking my boys. I won't have people saying I'm a bad mother who couldn't keep her kids."

Even now, Tanya's concern was for herself, not the boys. He doubted she cared about them at all. "Let's be honest, Tanya. You have other things you'd rather do with your life. You don't need those boys tying you down. Me, on the other hand, I want to be tied down."

"You're not taking my kids." She spat the words at him. "They can stay with my momma when I need to get away."

Preacher knew that would be most, if not all, of the time. "They can stay with me."

"Where are you going to be living, Preacher?" she asked, settling back in her chair. "Surely, you don't think you can continue to live in the apartment above the garage. No way is that going to work."

"You're putting me out?" he asked, incredulous.

She tossed her hair over her shoulder again. "The house is in my name," she said. "And I know my rights, Preacher. We don't need that big house if we're not going to be a family. I figure I'll sell it and buy me a condo in Buckhead or somewhere nice."

"What about the boys?" he asked.

"They'll be with my mother. Let's face it, Preacher, that's more their home than that house anyway. They lived with Momma most of the time before you went to prison and they lived with her while you were in prison. It's only after this change of life you've had that you've wanted them with us. I'm not the only bad parent here."

Preacher wanted to explain that he'd changed but what was the point? "Okay," he said, "we'll play this your way, for now. The boys can stay with Maylene during the week but they stay with me on the weekend, and I get to visit them every day."

"Sounds okay to me," Tanya said, "but you'll have to talk to Momma. She's also going to need some money for taking care of them. I'm going to need some money, too," she added.

"Come off it, Tanya," Preacher said. "You've got the house, you've got the money I left, and don't try to tell me you've spent it all, because I no longer believe you. I'll make sure Maylene gets money for the boys, but I won't be giving you another penny."

Her lips turned down in a pout. "You don't have to be so stingy, Preacher."

He stood, effectively ending her performance before she got any more revved up. "I think we've said all that needs to be said. I'm taking the boys to the Magic Kingdom Park in the morning. I've already cleared it with Maylene." Preacher knew the only reason the older woman had agreed so readily to his plans was that she didn't want to be out in the hot sun running after the boys all day.

"I guess that's it, too," Tanya said, standing as well. "I'm sorry it had to end this way, Preacher, but you're right. You never could have made me happy and I deserve to be happy."

Preacher leaned forward and pressed a kiss on her forehead. "I hope you find what makes you happy, Tanya." He pulled back and brushed his finger down her cheek. "Good-bye," he said. Then he turned and walked away.

Four days later, Preacher returned to Atlanta with Maylene and the boys. Tanya had decided to continue her vacation by joining some friends of hers in Jamaica. It had become obvious to both him and Maylene that Tanya's presence in the boys' lives going forward would be negligible. Since Preacher wanted the best for his boys, Tanya's blatant lack of interest in them hurt. The boys needed their mother. Since they didn't have her, Preacher found himself grateful for Maylene's presence. He told her so after they had settled the boys in their room at her house.

"The boys need you, Maylene," he said.

"I know they do," she said. "And I'll always be there for them."

"They need me, too," he said. "I know you don't want to believe that."

"I'm not a stupid woman, Wilford," she said. "I know those boys need a mother and a father. I was just convinced that you and Tanya weren't up for the jobs. Tanya has proven that she isn't, but you're beginning to make me believe you're serious about wanting to care for them."

"I love them, Maylene. Why is that so hard for you to understand?"

"It's becoming easier," she said, unwilling to give more. "Your not making a big fuss about them staying with me is a good sign. I want what's best for them."

"Then we're in agreement," he said, accepting her and Tanya's terms for now. He would not be content, however, until he and the boys were living under the same roof. He prayed that when that time came, Maylene would understand. "I'll say good night now and I'll see you tomorrow."

Maylene nodded as she closed the door behind him.

Since Preacher had needed permission from the probation office to take the trip to Florida, he had to report in with Wayne the next morning to show he'd returned. Shocked didn't adequately describe his reaction when he saw Loretta sitting in Wayne's office. He blinked twice. "Loretta?"

His sister smiled. "You're not seeing things, Brother. It's me."

Wayne cleared his throat. "I'll leave you two alone. I need to take care of a couple of things down the hall."

Preacher came fully into the room and sat in the chair next to his sister's. "What are you doing here, 'Retta? What's going on?"

"You worry too much, Preacher," she said. "Isn't there something in the Bible about not worrying?"

He leaned over and pressed a kiss against her cheek. "It's the big brother in me. I pray for God to take care of you, and I try not to worry, but I'm not always successful. Despite what I said when we last talked, Loretta, I do love you."

"But you meant what you said?"

He nodded.

"Your words hurt me," she said. "More than I've been hurt in a long time, probably since Big Momma died. You've been the only person in my life I could count on and you turned on me."

"I didn't turn on you, 'Retta. I'm still here for you."

"If I leave the drugs alone."

He shook his head. "Either way, I'm here for you. I can't help you if you choose a path of destruction, but I'm here for you whenever you want help."

She nodded. "Like I thought," she said. "Your words did get me to thinking, though."

Preacher's heartbeat increased. Was God about to answer his prayer? Was Loretta leaving the business? "What did you think about?"

"I don't want to be a harm to you or the boys, Preacher. I've never wanted that." She shrugged, and then looked away from him. "The drugs never really meant that much to me, except as a business where we connected. We were each other's best friend because we knew we couldn't trust anybody else. You know, I never had that after Big Momma died. Nobody should have to go through foster care," she said. "Everybody should have someone who loves them, and who sees them as more than a monthly check. Why couldn't I be like some of those kids who ended up in loving families?"

Preacher's heart ached for his sister. He reached out and took her hand in his, rubbing it softly. "I don't know, 'Retta. What I do know is that you have a loving family now if you want it. Me and the boys are waiting for you. And if you're interested in the mortuary business, I certainly could use a partner."

She lifted damp eyes to him, her smile weak. "You mean that, don't you?"

He wiped her tears with his forefinger. "Of course, I do."

"Me in a funeral home? I don't know." She took a long sigh. "But maybe I did the right thing, for once."

"What did you do?" he asked. "Why are you here?"

"I talked to that lawyer you sent my way." She gave him a wry smile. "Cute guy."

"What happened?" Preacher asked, battling impatience. "Tell me."

"Come to find out our little Andre had his hands in a lot of candy jars. When your lawyer friend told me how I could help myself and hurt Andre at the same time, I knew it was a deal I couldn't pass up." She chuckled. "Ironic, huh? An attorney making a criminal an offer she can't refuse."

Preacher couldn't laugh. "What's going to happen to you?"

"I'll do a little time," she said. "The lawyer's cute, but he's not a miracle worker. I expected it. Besides, it's worth it if Andre pays."

Even now, his sister was exacting revenge. "You did this as payback?"

"I won't lie and say that wasn't part of it. To be honest, the deal just made sense. I told you the business was only good for me when it was about us. Without you, it wasn't the same. When you were away, I cared for that business the same way I cared for Tanya and those boys. I was keeping them safe for your return. Now that I'm convinced you don't want it, what's in it for me?"

Loretta's words pierced Preacher's heart. How empty Loretta's life must be if a drug business was her substitute for family. He began to pray silently, but earnestly, that she would find true fulfillment behind bars the way he had. "How much time are you looking at?"

"Not clear yet," she said. "Maybe as little as a year and a day."

He squeezed her hand tighter.

"There you go worrying again," she said. "I'll be fine. My cutie-pie lawyer is getting me tucked away in one of those resort prisons, whatever that is. I'm getting a sweet deal, so be happy for me. I'll do the time, and then I'll come back and hook up with you and the boys."

Preacher wanted that more than anything. "Are you going to be safe?" he asked, knowing that there was sometimes greater danger getting out of the business than staying in it.

"I've giving enough information to confirm what they already know, which will make Andre angry, but shouldn't cause much more damage beyond that. Apparently, Andre has more connections than I do. They get enough information from me to convince him to give information on others. It's all about what you have to give the government. Talk about a racket." She lifted her shoulders in a shrug. "That Andre surprised me," she said. "I never would have guessed he had it in him."

"What about his partner and the dealership?"

"Everybody has a lawyer but that's all I know."

"So when do you have to report to the prison?"

She bit her lips together. "Today. As soon as we finish talking."

Preacher shook his head. "Not today," he said. He needed more time with his sister.

She patted his hand. "It's all right, Preacher. They want me under lock and key to make sure I don't skip town on them, and I want to get started serving my time now. The sooner I start, the sooner I get out."

"I don't know what to say," he said.

"Say you'll call, visit, and write."

"You know I will, 'Retta."

She nodded.

"I'm proud of you, Sis," Preacher said. "It takes a lot of courage to do what you're doing."

She smiled back. "Don't get carried away, Preacher. I'm getting the better end of this deal, so there's not a lot of courage involved."

Having no more words to say, Preacher pulled his sister into his arms and rocked her back and forth. God had answered his prayer, not in the way he had wanted, but He'd gotten Loretta out of the business. Preacher believed it was only time before this blood sister he loved became his sister in the faith as well. He pressed a kiss against her forehead and continued holding her close.

CHAPTER 25

Sean had gone from the Boss's star pupil to a wanted man in no time flat. The enemy had swooped in and snatched Preacher and his friends from their grasp so quickly that Sean hadn't had time to mount a counterattack.

Despite his failure to regain Preacher or acquire any collateral damage, Sean didn't want to be sent to Third Hades. He'd been hiding from the Boss since Preacher had been reunited with his kids. He knew his time was short, though, because he had no support. Jessie, his only real friend, had disappeared on him until her unexpected call this morning. She said she'd been in hiding, too. Apparently, the Boss held her partly responsible for Sean's failure and planned to send her to Third Hades along with him. Sean feared for both of them.

He arrived at the address Jessie had given him about half an hour after receiving her call. His heart raced as he knocked on her door. When she opened it, a bright smile on her face, he closed his eyes and breathed a relieved sigh. When he opened his eyes, he moved to pull Jessie into his arms but she stepped back and another set of arms engulfed her. Sean's eyes followed the arms to the face—the Boss!

His knees grew weak as the door slammed closed behind him. Two big burly men grabbed his arms, ending whatever ideas of escape he may have had.

Jessie's smile did not falter.

"What's going on?" he asked her.

She turned to the Boss, pressing a kiss against his cheek. "You're right," she said to the Boss. "He is an idiot."

The Boss kissed her deeply. "Have I ever lied?"

Both of them broke up into hysterical laughter at the question. Sean's legs buckled under him as understanding dawned. He would have fallen to the floor without the support of the two goons.

Jessie turned back to him. "Have you figured it out yet?"

Sean nodded. "You're working with the Boss. You've been working with him all this time."

The Boss snorted. "Leave it to you, Jones, to state the obvious. I don't think I've met a denser executive. Not only am I sending you to Third Hades, I'm also sending the idiot who brought you into 3Sixes."

Sean considered a last-minute plea, but he knew it was no use. He'd been given chance after chance and he'd still failed. Preacher and his friends had ruined it for him. He hated Preacher and longed to see his soul in Third Hades one day soon.

"Don't beat yourself up, Sean," Jessie said, as though she'd read his mind. "You were going to Third Hades, regardless of what happened with Preacher."

Sean raised questioning eyes to the Boss. "What?"

The Boss snapped his fingers and a guy in a black suit placed a glass of wine in his hand. He took a sip. "You heard her, Jones. I knew you were a lost cause from our first meeting, but I gave you a chance anyway."

"You lied to me," Sean exclaimed. "All this time you've been lying to me."

The Boss and Jessie laughed again. When they sobered, the Boss said, "You really don't get it, do you, Jones? That's why you'll never make it here." The Boss thumped his chest with his forefinger. "I'm a liar. Lying is what I do. Why did you ever think I was telling you the truth?"

Preacher had no response. Of course, he knew the Boss was a liar. He was a liar himself, but he thought they only lied to the enemy and souls they wanted to win, not to each other. What was the purpose of lying to each other? They all had the same goals, or he thought they did. He said as much to the Boss. Then he added, "Why not just ship me straight to Third Hades instead of sending me through all these hoops?"

The Boss shrugged. "It was fun," he said. "And it gave Jessie here a chance to prove her worth to me." He kissed Jessie's cheek and patted her bottom. "She did a fine job, too. When she goes after prey, she gets him."

"Guess who my prey was, Sean?" she asked, her eyes sparkling with delight.

Sean couldn't answer, didn't want to answer. Jessie was liar, too. He knew without asking that she'd never cared for him. Everything between them was a lie to gain his trust. It had worked.

"Come on," she said. "I know you've figured it out."

"Me," Sean muttered. "I was your prey."

"Ding, ding, ding," the Boss chimed. "Give that man a one-way ticket to Third Hades."

"It was either me or you, Sean," Jessie said. "Nothing personal."

Nothing personal. Sean closed his eyes as he absorbed the pain of her words. She'd treated him as callously as he treated the souls he tried to win. He wondered if they felt the way he felt now. When he finally opened his eyes, Jessie and the Boss were gone.

"It's time," the goon on his left said.

Sean tried to shake off their arms, but they held on tight. "I'm not going to run," he said.

The goon on the right laughed. "But you're going to try. They all do. Nobody goes to Third Hades willingly and you're not going to be the first."

The sounds Sean had first heard on the Boss's iPod rang in his mind, growing louder with each passing moment. Sean had reached his destiny, a dark, dreary place filled with screams and wailings. As the goons pushed him forward, the sounds grew louder, so loud Sean thought they were in his head. Then he realized the sounds were coming from him.

EPILOGUE

Three months later

Preacher strolled down the hallway of Faith Community Church. He'd finished his consultation with the pastor about the funeral being held at Faith Community tomorrow, and thought he'd peek in on Barnard. Though he prayed for his dear brother and Serena every day, he hadn't spoken to either of them in three months. In fact, it had been three months since he'd stepped inside Faith Community.

Barnard's closed door signaled that he wasn't in, but Preacher knocked anyway.

"He's not here."

The soft familiar voice made him smile and he turned in its direction. Natalie stood before him, the welcoming smile that he recalled from their first meeting shone prominently on her face. It told him she was as happy to see him as he was to see her. "Natalie," he said. "It's good to see you."

She came closer and pressed a kiss against his cheek. "It's been too long, Preacher," she said. "Much too long."

He shrugged, unsure what else to say. Her warmth humbled him. "I've been keeping busy," he said, not wanting to bring up the past events that forced his absence when it might make her uncomfortable.

"With boys as active as Jake and Mack, I can imagine," she said. "We miss them around here. How are they?"

"They've settled in well at our new church and they love the day care there. You know kids, they're pretty resilient."

She nodded. "I'm happy you worked things out with Tanya."

"Me, too," he said. "The boys are still staying with her mother during the week, but as soon as I finish school, they'll be moving in with me."

"School? I didn't know you were in school. Good for you."

"Yeah," he said. "I have to complete some course work to get licensed to run the funeral home."

"I'm impressed," she said, her eyes full of pride for him. "I don't know if I could go back to school."

"It's amazing what you can do when you put your heart and mind to it," he said. "It took me a while to get in the rhythm of going to class, studying, working, and spending time with the boys, but it's turned out well. I'm enjoying it."

"Sounds like you are," she said. "I still remember the day you told me you believed the Lord had given you a sign about the funeral home. Look where moving in faith gets you."

Preacher shook his head in amazement. "It's been a trip, Natalie. When I was released from prison, I knew exactly what God had in store for me." He chuckled. "My life is nothing like that today."

"You have your boys," Natalie said.

"Yeah, I do, and I thank God for them every day, but you know what I mean. Tanya's seeing some high-profile attorney, Loretta's in prison, and my boys are living with their grandmother. My godly family didn't quite materialize the way I thought it would."

"God had something better in store for you."

He nodded. "Right now, I just know it's different. Don't get me wrong, though. I'm happy with my life. I just wonder sometimes about the cost others paid in order for me to have it."

Natalie pressed her hand against his arm. "Don't think like that, Preacher. I'm sorry about Loretta and even about Tanya, but God knows what He's doing. He always does."

"I know you're right," he said. "It's you that has me talking like this. It's always been easy for me to talk to you, since the first day we met."

"Same for me," she said. "I think about you often. I miss our budding friendship."

"Me, too," he said. Then when the past could no longer be avoided, he asked, "How are Barnard and Serena?"

"Getting better," she said. "They're on vacation now. A sort of second honeymoon. Barnard surprised her last week with a two-week trip to Bermuda. They should be back next week."

Preacher laughed. "Barnard, the romantic, who would have thought it? That's my boy."

Natalie laughed with him. "Serena was pretty psyched." She sobered. "She really is getting better, Preacher. I know you don't believe this, but what happened has strengthened their marriage and their faith. Don't be surprised if you get a call from her one day soon."

"That's my deepest prayer. I never meant to hurt her or Barnard or you. If I could change everything, I would."

Natalie shook her head. "I wouldn't," she said. "The Bible tells us that all things, not some things, work together for good for those who love the Lord and are called according to His purpose. I thank God every day that you came into our lives."

"I can't believe that," he said in all earnestness.

"Believe it," she said. "If you hadn't come into our lives, I could be married to Dante and then where would I be? Serena would still be hiding from the shame of her past and her marriage to Barnard may have been crushed under the weight of her guilt. The pain we've suffered has been like the fiery fire of trials that God puts us through to build our faith. I thank God for you. I really do."

Preacher didn't know what to say, so he said nothing. Joy welled up in him and threatened to spill out in unmanly tears. Here he was, a reformed drug dealer, a man who'd made a living wreaking havoc in people's lives and profiting from their despair, being told that God had used his life to strengthen and make a difference in the lives of others. It was beyond his comprehension.

"See, there you go. You old softie." She pulled him into her embrace. "I love you, Preacher," she said. "And I thank God for you."

With tears spilling down his cheeks, Preacher wrapped his arms around Natalie and returned her embrace.

ACKNOWLEDGMENTS

Up Pops the Devil made its way into print due to the hard work of a lot of people. I want to thank each and every person in the process for their contribution. Though it is impossible for me to name them all here, I'd like to single out a few.

Natasha Kern, my dear agent, thanks for finding a great home for me and my baby. Your tireless efforts on my behalf did not go unnoticed or unappreciated.

Carol Craig, my personal GPS, thanks for keeping *Up Pops the Devil* on the right track. I don't know what I would have done without your fresh eyes.

Likisha Renfroe, my "insider" contact, thanks for sharing your knowledge of the Georgia penal system. Everything I got right in this book is because of you; everything I got wrong is because of me. Thanks so much for your help.

Carolyn Marino and Wendy Lee, editors extraordinaire, thanks so much for the care that you took with my story. I trust your instincts and appreciate your guidance. I look forward to working with you on the next book.

I offer a special thanks to the other members of the Avon/HarperCollins team who worked to get *Up Pops the Devil* into print and into bookstores. Without a doubt, I have the best cover in book publishing history along with the best back cover copy. Thanks so much for your excellent work!

Angela Benson

Photo by Glamour Shots

ANGELA BENSON is a graduate of Spelman College and the author of numerous novels, including the Christy Award-nominated *Awakening Mercy* and the *Essence* bestseller *The Amen Sisters*. She is currently an associate professor at the University of Alabama and lives in Tuscaloosa.

www.angelabenson.com